*Christmas 1980*

FROM THE BOOKS OF

*Lita E. Lanegran*

# SONS OF ADAM

# BOOKS BY FREDERICK MANFRED

THE GOLDEN BOWL   1944

BOY ALMIGHTY   1945

THIS IS THE YEAR   1947

THE CHOKECHERRY TREE   1948

THE PRIMITIVE   1949

THE BROTHER   1950

THE GIANT *   1951

LORD GRIZZLY   1954

MORNING RED   1956

RIDERS OF JUDGMENT   1957

CONQUERING HORSE   1959

ARROW OF LOVE *(stories)*   1961

WANDERLUST *(trilogy)* **   1962

SCARLET PLUME   1964

THE MAN WHO LOOKED LIKE THE PRINCE OF WALES †   1965

WINTER COUNT *(poems)*   1966

KING OF SPADES   1966

APPLES OF PARADISE *(stories)*   1968

EDEN PRAIRIE   1968

CONVERSATIONS ‡   1974

MILK OF WOLVES   1976

THE MANLY-HEARTED WOMAN   1976

GREEN EARTH   1977

THE WIND BLOWS FREE *(reminiscence)*   1979

SONS OF ADAM   1980

* Mr. Manfred wrote under the name Feike Feikema from 1944 through 1951.
** A new revised version of three novels, *The Primitive, The Brother, The Giant,*
and published in one volume.
† Reprinted in paperback as *The Secret Place.*
‡ Moderated by John R. Milton.

# SONS
# OF
# ADAM

A *Novel by*

# FREDERICK
# MANFRED

A HERBERT MICHELMAN BOOK
CROWN PUBLISHERS, INC.
NEW YORK

Library of Congress Cataloging in Publication Data

Manfred, Frederick Feikema, 1912–

Sons of Adam.

"A Herbert Michelman book."

I. Title.

PZ3.M313705So    1980    [PS3525.A52233]    813'.54    80-12648

ISBN: 0-517-541866

Design by Camilla Filancia

10 9 8 7 6 5 4 3 2 1

First edition

*To*

WARING JONES

*To the National Endowment for the Arts
go my sincere thanks for a grant given
in 1976 to help me write this novel.*

*Also in remembrance of*

CHARLES MONTAGU DOUGHTY

# SONS OF ADAM

# Chapter 1

# ALAN

Alan Ross hadn't known he was a twin until he was in high school. His father, Rollo Ross, farmed a half section of flatland near Holabird, South Dakota. Because of the size of the farm, Alan's father wouldn't let him go out for football and basketball. Alan was needed to do the yard chores while Pa worked the fields. Pa did say though that Alan could go out for track part-time.

Alan turned out to be a fine distance runner, both cross-country and the mile. When the weather was fair, Alan always ran to and from school. In Alan's senior year Pa let him go out for track full-time, and Alan won several medals in the district meet.

It was after Alan lost out in the state meets in two events that a conversation took place at a Sunday dinner which changed Alan's life. It came as a profound shock.

. . . . Pa helped himself to another plate of boiled white potatoes, a slice of beef, and some gravy. Pa had fine manners. He always sat bolt upright, surprising for so old a man, and he cut and ate his meat English-style with fork in his left hand and knife in his right hand. Pa had young pink skin, a high forehead, and a soft wise smile on rather full lips. Today he was dressed in his black suit and blue tie that he'd just worn to church. Pa cut himself a small bite of meat and then, about to lift it to his mouth, paused to say, "Wonder what the other one would have done at the state meet?"

Ma looked up warningly from her end of the table. Ma was as skinny as Pa and like him had the high forehead with the reddish-brown hair. She freckled easily in the sun. Pa had really robbed the cradle when, at fifty-five, he'd married Ma at nineteen. There been a lot of talk in Holabird the day of the wedding about what a downright shame it was that that old codger, Rollo Ross, who had been living alone in his drab homestead, had all of a sudden married pretty Ada Tull, the new country schoolteacher across the road. However, as the years went by, talk died down, and a stranger coming to town would have probably thought of them as of about equal age. Both had bags under the eyes, with Ma's being the worst.

Ma did all the letter writing and kept in touch with the various branches of the family, including Pa's, while Pa kept a daily journal. Every spring cleaning Ma wanted to throw out the green ledgers Pa had stored on a shelf in the living room and every spring Pa would declare that if she burned them he'd pack up and head farther west. Actually Ma and Pa got along very well, they were a loving couple, but she had nothing but contempt for those journals. It was mostly because one day, while Pa was in town, she looked up the date of their marriage in the green ledgers and discovered that all he had written down for the day was: "Got married today. No wind to speak of. Rained in the evening." When she read on to see what he might have written for the next morning, she was even more upset to discover an equally laconic entry: "Sowed oats today. Weather bone dry. Strong wind from the north."

Pa didn't catch Ma's warning glance. "Alan might have been an even better runner if he'd had competition from his twin brother."

Alan almost fell out of his chair. Twin brother? Alan slowly put down his fork and knife. "Run that past me again, Pa. Did you say I had a twin brother?"

Pa looked across the table mildly. "Yes, you did." Then with a look at Ma, Pa said, "Ma, I always did intend to tell the boy someday. He deserves to know. And today is as good a time as any."

Alan stared. "What happened to my twin brother?"

Then it all came out, in bits and pieces, first Pa telling a little, and then Ma a little.

Ma was due early in January, but already in December it became quite apparent she was going to have twins. She was so very slender that any kind of swelling would've looked big on her, but her pregnant belly was positively huge. Even Pa, who took the various birthings on the farm in stride, became concerned. He brought Ma to see Dr. Athens. Dr. Athens took one look and suggested that Ma stay in town for the rest of her term. Pa didn't like the idea.

On the eighth of January, Ma felt a struggle in her belly. Pa promptly got out horse and cutter and fetched Dr. Athens. Four days earlier there'd been a tremendous snowstorm and there were vast snowbanks everywhere. The horse plunged and snorted and lunged through the deep snow, but they made it home safely. By that time the struggle in Ma's belly had calmed down. Dr. Athens, however, decided he'd better stay over for the night.

On the morning of the ninth, Ma began to have birthing pains about an hour apart. They weren't very pronounced. Doc didn't like it. He gave her some castor oil. Nothing happened.

Again at around nine that night Dr. Athens gave her a stronger dose of castor oil. "That should precipitate something," he muttered to himself.

It did. Shortly before midnight Ma gave birth to a bouncing baby boy. Reddish hair. Fine limbs. Perfect. Doc gave the boy a quick slap on the butt to make him breathe and then put him to one side in a basket on Ma's hope chest. The baby coughed once, and it looked as though he'd made it.

Meanwhile Ma was having her troubles. For some reason the second baby just wouldn't come. Doc soon discovered the second baby wanted to be born breech first. Ma finally passed out. Then Doc went in. He turned the baby around. It was touch and go there for a while. When Ma came to, the first thing Doc told her was to "push like hell!" and Doc's swearing at her so scared Ma that that's exactly what she did, pushed like the dickens, and out came another boy. The second boy wasn't quite as husky as the first one, or as healthy-looking, but he too had reddish fuzz for hair. He had one mark on him. It was where Dr. Athens had used the forceps on his head to turn him around. The mark was across his eyes.

When both mother and second boy were safe, Doc turned to the first boy to see how he was doing. It was then they discovered that in all the commotion, Dr. Athens had not made sure that the first boy had begun to breathe properly. Doc thought that first cough meant the boy was breathing regularly. But the boy hadn't kept on breathing. Somehow, just as he came out, in taking his very first breath, the boy had sucked in some birthing fluid, and the lungs had instinctively quit breathing. Dead.

Ma took it the hardest. While Pa . . . well, Pa had a way of hiding his griefs.

Alan's hands lay flat on the table. He stared through the kitchen window. Outside a circular cloud hovered over the Ree Heights to the east. The sun shone on an endless wheat field. Dark-green waves moved across the field.

He'd had a brother. Man. So. He could have had a playmate all these years. There could have been wrestling and laughter and horse-backing together. With the two of them to help Pa with the chores, maybe both could have gone out for football and basketball. They could've maybe have been stars on the gridiron and the court.

Instead there was now suddenly a great big hole in his life. Alan wished they hadn't told him. What you don't know won't hurt you. Now all his life he would be burdened with a vast regret.

"Pa," Alan asked, swinging his eyes from the window to his father, "you say he was a bouncing baby boy. With reddish hair. Perfect. Would he have grown up bigger and stronger than me?"

"Might have."

Ma interposed with her soft voice. "You really shouldn't say such things, Rollo. Only the Lord knows such things."

Pa smiled his philosophic smile. "I've seen a lot of red calves born and a lot of red calves growed up."

Ma said, "What about that colt you thought wouldn't live? Because it couldn't stand up and we had to feed it until it could. It became the best trotter you ever had. You said."

"Well, that's true."

Alan asked, "What would you have named the other boy?"

Pa said, "I never gave that any thought. Because we didn't have to think about it."

Ma fingered the edge of the green-and-yellow tablecloth. "I did, though."

Alan swallowed so hard his throat clicked. "You did, Ma?"

"Yes."

"What would you have named him?"

Ma threw a look at Pa. "We would have named him Alan, like we did you, and then we would have named you John, after my wonderful grandfather, Grampa Great John. Grampa was my mother Alberta's father, and she used to tell some great stories about him."

Alan swallowed hard again. He tried to imagine what it might have felt like for the other boy to have been called Alan all those years. Alan's heart began to beat faster and harder. He could feel his eyes begin to flick back and forth. "And his eyes, did he have eyes like mine?"

"Well," Pa said, "they were blue like yours."

Alan's eyes were a very light blue. Sometimes, when he'd been out in the sun too long, his eyes would begin to flick back and forth as if they couldn't center on a point. Dr. Athens had remarked once, when he was giving Alan a complete physical examination, that Alan was a near-albino and as a result sometimes had what was called "the searching eye." "Nothing to worry about, though," Dr. Athens had said. "When you feel it coming on, stay in a darkened room for a few hours." When Alan had given him a bewildered look, the doctor went on to say, "Look, a lot of people have eyes that flicker a little." When Alan was a little boy, full of strong likes and dislikes, his eyes would sometimes be milk-blue in love and ice-blue in hate. His father only smiled quietly about it all and said the boy had a mild case of the walleye. In horses it was sometimes called sockeye.

Ma interposed again. "You're just naturally light-complected, son, and it can't be helped. Besides, it's not good to wonder about such things. A person can go crazy doing that. Best to leave it alone now. Which we should have done in the first place." Ma shot Pa a glittering look.

Alan pushed back his half-eaten plate of food. More things began to fall into place. There was that business where Ma would ask Pa to skip the Esau-Jacob chapter in the Bible at family worship. Sure. He, Alan Ross, was the Jacob to a dead Esau. It was too painful for Ma to think on all that again.

Alan could just see the two of them, the twin boys. The other Alan would have won all the foot races, and run all the game-winning touchdowns, and led the basketball team in scoring, while he, the second boy, John, would've had to play second fiddle. At the same time, though, all those years, eighteen of them, he had missed having a brother chum. They would have slept together, milked cows together, had a sandbox together.

Ma broke in on his thoughts. "Finish your plate, Alan."

"I'm not hungry, Ma."

"But you must always try to finish your plate, Alan. Especially when we remember the poor in faraway places who'd give anything to have even so much as a morsel from our rich bounty."

"All right, Ma." Dutifully Alan pulled up his plate again and began working on the rest of the beef.

Ma smiled at him. The smile moved over her face like a wrinkled mask. "Leave a little room for the dessert, son. Today we're having your favorite dish."

That would be canned apricots. He loved tangy fruit. Sometimes he could hardly stand the tanginess of apricots at the same time that he had to have them.

Pa was very quiet in his highback swivel chair at the head of the table. He sat looking out of the south window, far into the distance.

His blue eyes were high. Pa had left them again, busy with his own thoughts, never shared with anyone. . . .

It was sometime after the initial shock, when Alan went to bed one night, that a clear mental picture of the other twin popped into his head. Alan was on the edge of sleep when he saw him. The other twin was an inch taller than Alan. Hair a little darker red. Wider shoulders. Skin not quite so light-complected. Eyes a deeper and steadier blue. And on his lips a confident smile. It wasn't a big smile, just an impish one. Alan could just see the other twin breaking in a bronc, or connecting for a home run, with always that little smile on his full lips. Where most athletes grimaced at the moment of their supreme effort, even making a horrible face, his twin brother had that superior smile of the champ.

It was also about the same time that Alan decided since he himself had the name of Alan legally, he'd think of the other twin as John. Otherwise Alan felt he'd go nuts. Alan pretty much liked who he was, liked being called Alan, so the imaginary twin had to be John.

After that, in his mind's eye, Alan often saw John on horseback bucking snowstorms on the wild prairie. He saw John joshing waitresses in restaurants.

By the time Alan went to Macalester College in St. Paul, he had begun to commune at length with John. Where some people talked to themselves when they were alone, Alan talked to John. He made a confidant of John. Alan took up track in college, too, but not until he'd talked it over with John. He also majored in English and journalism, but again not without some discussion with John.

Alan next took to sizing up young men he met to see if they measured up to his imaginary John. Upon seeing a fine male physical specimen on the campus his first thought always was "Could John have looked like him?" When Alan went to a basketball game he'd check out the players of a certain height and color of hair; and he'd especially check them out to see if they had the quirked smile of the champ. Something in Alan had to flesh out the haunt twin.

Alan graduated with honors from Macalester. It was the time of the Great Depression, the Dirty Thirties, and jobs were hard to find. Alan worked as a busboy for a while in St. Paul, then as a bellboy in a Minneapolis hotel, then as a taxicab driver in both cities. His bosses liked him, though they thought him a bit absentminded.

Several times it happened, as he walked down Hennepin in Minneapolis, that he was sure he saw someone who looked exactly like John. Once he even ran after a fellow to get a better look at his face.

Then one day in March he got a job on the Minneapolis *Chronicle.* Alan heard of the opening from a customer he was taking to the airport in his taxi. Burt Cowens, columnist and head of the *Chronicle* sports department, appeared to like Alan at first glance and said he'd try him out. After Alan had covered track for a couple of weeks, Burt Cowens hired him.

Alan moved from his dank hole in a cockroach hotel in downtown Minneapolis to a two-room apartment at 1128 Sixth Street SE, Minneapolis.

The bunch in the sports department were pretty good guys. All had played some sports in their youth, though none had been a star. It was while listening to Burt talk about an athlete's "killer instinct" that it occurred to Alan that none of the sportswriters had that little curling smile of the champ. Burt was too rational, too intellectual, to kill off a rival. Quinsey Quinn, who covered baseball, came the closest to having it, but he was so full of humor and whimsy that while he'd have given the fans a lot of laughs, he'd never quite have won for them. Hank Williams, the bowling expert, liked to knock things down, but he too really was too kind to break into a rage. Mark Josephson, copy editor, who relished cutting out flights of fancy, was too much of an asslicker to be mean in a big way.

Alan knew he himself wasn't mean enough either to be a champ. He'd once let off a guy he'd caught picking his pocket in the *Chronicle* elevator. He just didn't know how to bite in when the enemy's neck was exposed.

But there was a mean side to his haunt brother John. It wasn't evil. It was just simply kingly. It made John just mean enough to make him interesting.

# Chapter 2

# ALAN

Alan had been at the paper a couple of months when Irene Crist wandered into the sports department with several metal cuts of athletes. Mark Josephson had ordered them earlier in the morning from the library. Irene placed the blue metal plates on the edge of Mark's wide desk, and then, as she turned to go, she let her dress brush past Alan's knee.

Irene was an odd-looking one. The outlines of a second face strained to break through to the surface of her given face. The result was a curious mixture: a fine chiseled nose vs. a heavy jaw; a woman's brow vs. mannish chin; a blue left eye vs. a brown right eye, and both astigmatic so that she had to wear thick glasses. The same sort of mixture was at work in her body: long slim feet vs. large hands; lovely small breasts vs. high thick hips. Two different bloodlines had failed to make a good mix.

Yet Irene had her points. She exuded the quiet knowing air of the confident woman. She read well and could talk intelligently about books. And she walked in a slow slinging manner, one silk stocking lightly rustling past the other.

As the whistling stockings vanished down the hallway toward the library, Quinsey looked up from his typewriter and remarked, a well-chewed cigar butt caught in the corner of his curving red lips, "Now I wonder what those whispering things were trying to tell us."

Mark folded up a story he'd just finished editing, thrust it into a round brass capsule, shoved the capsule into a pneumatic tube. With a sucking click the story shot upstairs to the composing room. Mark creaked around in his swivel chair, "If you're in any doubt, Quinse, maybe you should cover girl's tennis."

Quinsey reared up. "I've already got too many women in my life, what with my wife Doozie and my daughter Putzy and my mother Tatsie." Quinsey placed his still-lighted stub of a cigar on the edge of his desk. There were a dozen black scars along the edge where other cigar stubs had been left to smolder. "No, Mark, my boy, my motto has always been: never dip your pen in the company ink."

"Damn," Burt Cowens said from his far corner where he was writing the day's installment of his column, "Cowens' Corner."

Mark cast a wary eye in Burt's direction.

Burt shook his head. "All this talk about whispering lady's things . . . I wonder what Bernie Bierman's going to think when he reads tomorrow that he could use a pair of fast-whispering underpants in his backfield. Because that's what I just typed here."

There was a fine roar from Quinsey. "Holy cow, Burt, you bothered by such talk?"

"Well, I was here."

Quinsey tolled his head. "Reminds me of the announcer describing the colors of the Michigan uniform at the Michigan-Minnesota football game. 'Here they come out on the field, folks, wearing maize shirts, maize socks, maize pants . . . wonder what Mae thinks about that.' Ho ho ho."

Burt groaned from his corner.

Alan thought Quinsey's motto pretty good. Never dip your pen in the company ink.

The next Saturday night, as Alan was sending up some late basketball scores from the West Coast, he heard those whistling stockings again. They were coming down the hallway. In a moment Irene Crist appeared in the doorway. Her thick glasses blinked in the sharp overhead light. "Here is that Hornsby cut Mark ordered."

Alan smiled. "A little late in the day for that, ain't it? There's only one more run at midnight."

"It's for next week's bullpup edition. You know how Mark is. He hates to get caught short of copy."

"I know. Put it on his desk."

Irene passed by Alan's desk with her slow-lifting legs. She put the cut down and came back past him.

Alan could feel her looking down at him with her strange double smile. He looked at his watch. Ten-thirty. "You're working late."

"Yes. Roberta and I are still revamping the whole library, and we have a lot of catching up to do." Roberta was Irene's boss. Roberta was a slim muscular woman the boys took to calling Viggles after her last name of Vig. "I had nothing else to do tonight, so I thought I'd just put in some extra time free."

"The Newspaper Guild isn't going to like that."

"But they still haven't signed a contract with the newspapers. Sufficient unto the day." Irene gave Alan a thickened smile. "Besides, what about you with all those hours you put in on Saturday, first for the afternoon paper, and then the dogwatch for the Sunday edition?"

"You got me."

She lingered by his desk. A musky perfume emanated from her green dress. The odor reminded him of crushed tiger lilies.

Alan wanted to make a move, yet was afraid. He had kissed several girls but had not yet gone to bed with a woman. He was green around women.

Irene asked, "How long are you on duty tonight?"

"About twelve-thirty. Just in time to catch the owl streetcar down by the Andrews Hotel."

"I might work that late too. Mother's got the house full of boring company."

"What streetcar do you take?"

"I catch the owl car down on Fifth."

Alan could feel his heart thumping. Maybe this Irene Crist would be his first one. He looked at her, pulse jumping under his tongue. "I live near the U."

"Yes, unfortunately. I live the other way."

Something was going to happen. For once he wasn't going to need his haunt brother John's example. "Tell you what. I'll just walk across town back to my place afterwards. Nothing to do but sleep Sunday morning."

"Until twelve-thirty then?"

Alan had to swallow to get his throat to work. "Yes."

"I'll meet you downstairs in the lobby."

Alan nodded. Meeting him in the lobby, usually empty at night, she was making sure there'd be no office gossip about them.

When he took the elevator down at twelve-thirty, he found her standing in the shadow of the entryway.

She greeted him with a twisting smile. "All set?"

"Set."

They walked down Fourth Street to the corner, then down Marquette to Fifth. They'd stood talking but a minute when her owl car came along. Alan fished up two tokens and they boarded, taking a seat in back. There were only four other passengers on the streetcar.

Alan, sitting on the aisle, put his knee up on the back of the reed-covered seat ahead. In the weak light inside the streetcar Irene kept looking out of the dark window. After a few blocks Alan became aware that she was watching his reflection in the mirroring window. The streetcar soon angled onto Hiawatha, shooting blue electric sparks overhead when the wheels crackled over an interchange of tracks. Twice the headlights of oncoming cars bathed Irene's face with an eerie blue.

Irene pulled the bell cord at Thirty-first and they got off at Thirty-second and Hiawatha. She led them a short distance down one side of a triangular block and then with a light touch on his elbow guided them toward a neighborhood grocery store. She got out a ring of keys. "We live in back of this," she said. "We can visit in the store."

"I was wondering how you were going to arrange it when you said the house was full of company."

"They won't notice us in the store."

She finally managed to find the right key and unlocked the door. They entered quietly, in the dark.

Alan could smell ripe bananas in the store somewhere. There was also the sweet biting odor of oranges. Over it all hung the yeasty scent of Wisconsin cheese.

Irene whispered, "I don't dare to put the light on." She led him down a wide aisle. The floor was wooden and gave off a freshly oiled smell. "This way. There's a big swivel chair in back here, by Ma's desk where she keeps her accounts."

Alan found himself tiptoeing behind her. Her fingers leading his hand turned warm and moist.

She bumped into a chair. "Here we are."

Alan felt around until he found the back of the chair. He turned it around and settled himself in it. "This way?" he asked, drawing her down on his lap.

She sat stiff for a moment. She craned her head around to the sound of women talking beyond the connecting door between the store and the house.

"Think they heard us?"

"No. I was just trying to make out how long that party of Ma's is going to last."

"Oh." Alan wasn't sure what to do next. His arm was around her middle to hold her firmly on his lap. His fingers felt like fat sausages. She slowly stirred on his lap. After a moment Alan caught on that she was turning on his lap to face him better. His eyes slowly adjusted to the dark, and he began to pick out things, the vague light from the streetlamps spreading through the window in the front door, rank on rank of canned goods on the far wall, a stand full of brooms, and packages of cereals. He also made out her face above him. Her thick glasses caught the vague light from the door and lit up like a pair of very pale moons.

The chair creaked under their weight. Relaxing, he toward her and she settling against him, their hair touching, they began to warm toward each other.

Alan touched his lips on hers, dry, the surfaces catching with a very light wisping sound. It struck him she was way ahead of him. She was following his lead with modest mien, but there was an air about her that she was waiting for the tiger in him to break loose, that she wouldn't resist him. It made him feel disappointed in her at the same time that it excited him. He pressed another kiss on her lips, firmly, until he felt her teeth a little. She always waited until he pressed first, then pressed back. He nuzzled past her ear and kissed her neck. She made a little mewing sound.

"Where's your dad?" Alan whispered.

"My father died two years ago. That's why Mother's had to take on this store to make ends meet."

"What did your father do?"

"He was a carpenter."

"Does your mother make out pretty good?"

"She'll never get rich in a neighborhood grocery."

His right leg began to hurt where the hard edge of the chair caught it. He shifted her about a little.

"Am I hurting you?" she whispered.

"No. It's all right. Better now." He could feel her trying to ride lightly on him. "You all right?"

"Oh, yes."

He drew her face around. Her eyes blinked behind her thick glasses. He traced the edges of her lips with his finger. Then he slowly narrowed the gap between their lips and let them touch. She seemed to think he was ready for a bigger push, and she let her lips open and for a quick fleeting second the tip of her tongue touched into his mouth and then as quickly withdrew. He could feel her wondering if she'd gone too far.

She sat couched on him and waiting.

He whispered, "Can we stretch out on the floor?"

"The floor is oily."

He kept wondering how he could get her body turned over and facing him while still on that uncertain swivel chair. In holding her up on his lap his arm got tired, and he shifted himself about a little and reset her. His left hand happened to land just under her breast. He could feel its underside welling over his thumb. After a moment he held her breast. It was surprisingly firm. He cupped it gently. She sighed and let go against him and waited.

The chair cracked under them. Somewhere in the store a big clock tocked off the seconds.

The musk smell of her became thick in his nose, and after a while he dropped his hand on her thigh. She was wearing a girdle. A fold of flesh lapped over the top of it. She was going to be fat someday. He slid his hand past the girdle down to her knee, gathered up her dress, and then slid his hand under it. His fingers moved to where her stocking was rolled up with an elastic band, then moved onto her bare skin. She didn't have any pants on; just a girdle open at the bottom. Her skin was slick. She didn't resist him; only began to breathe hard.

He thought of what Ma would say could she see him at that moment. The sin of concupiscence. But he'd waited so long for that first time with a woman.

Irene stirred on his lap.

At last he dared to push his fingers up where she was wonderfully wet. She gasped above him; controlled herself; waited. At that moment he knew she'd go all the way. He lifted her and set her on his right hip and turned her toward him. He stiffened himself out on the swivel chair, catching his neck and his seat on it, and pulled her over on him. For the first time she resisted him a little. He was sure it was only momentary. He undid himself, having a little trouble untangling himself through his shorts. At last he was clear. He drew at her again, pulling her over and spreading her over him. He reached a hand under her and began guiding himself into her. She gasped again; tightened; relaxed, tightened; then of a sudden gave a little involuntary thrust. He exploded; quick drew away.

"I don't want to give you a baby," he whispered.

"No," she whispered back.

About then they heard talking ouside the store. "Shh," she whispered. "Mother's company is going home."

"Yes."

The voices died away; a door closed. Then inside another door clicked. Silence.

He wanted to suggest they go inside the house and visit on her davenport. Then he checked himself. No, it was time to go home. Another day, maybe.

"She's probably asleep by now," Irene whispered.

"Maybe I should go home too." He liked Irene, but he knew she'd never be the permanent one. He could never fall in love with her. He'd have to go on looking.

His right leg began to hurt him again, stinging all the way into his hip. He shifted, then lifted her. She let him stand her up.

They said goodnight at the door. "See you soon," he said.

"See you Monday at the paper," she said.

He began walking home. As a sockeye he could see well at night. An old moon hung low over a sea of leafless elms. He was glad it was over. He felt relaxed and at ease. He regretted it hadn't happened with a permanent one, but Irene was a good kid, so it was all right.

She probably wasn't a virgin, he thought as he walked along Hiawatha. She's probably had a lover before. It went so easy.

He gave a little leap of joy. How wonderful. Too bad it had all happened so fast. The next time, now that he knew what it was all about, he'd linger along the way and enjoy the sights. Wow. Haunt John would have been proud of him.

The snow had melted, and a good smell came from the awakening lawns. All of that section of Minneapolis appeared to be asleep. With each step he took he watched the thin moon bounce on the spriggy treetops. Once the moon moved behind a very tall treetop, giving the moon the look as if it might have black veins.

By the next Wednesday, Alan began to wonder how Irene was doing. He was working on a story about the local preliminary tryouts for the next Olympiad and needed some kind of cut for it. Instead of calling the copy boy to get the cut, Alan went down to the library himself. He took the inside stairs, very tight with sharp turns, down to a narrow hallway. Four steps and he entered the library.

The library had changed under Roberta Vig's revamping. New lighting, newly painted light-green walls, new chairs, new filing cabinets. Several trays still stood on chairs.

Roberta looked up pert and bouncy from her desk. She had sparkling black eyes. "Well well, look who's our new copy boy."

Alan laughed. "I need a cut for the next Olympiad. But I decided to see for myself which one I really wanted." He spotted Irene working behind stacked-up trays. "Hi."

Irene had a knowing smile for him. It made her jaw seem even heavier.

Roberta got up and bent down beside a filing cabinet. "I think the O's are in here. Yes." She pulled out a tray and set it on a table. "Help yourself."

Alan found the one he wanted right away, but he was hoping there'd be some way he could talk to Irene a moment without Roberta overhearing them.

Roberta sensed what was going on. She pushed up her dark hair in back. "I'll be back in a jiff." She vanished into the dark hallway.

Irene smiled behind her glasses. "We have to be careful here at work."

Alan nodded. "I know. But now that I'm here, how about a movie tomorrow night? Thursday's my day off, you know."

"It's my day off too."

"Well, then we'd both be rested up. How about it?"

Irene sat doubled up about something for a moment. "All right. What movie do you want to see? Can I meet you there?"

He picked up a newspaper from Irene's desk and checked the movie houses in her neighborhood. "*It Happened One Night* is showing at the Avalon on Lake Street. That's a good one, I hear. Meet you there at seven?"

She smiled. "Seven."

He was there five minutes early. So was Irene. They had to laugh about it. Consulting his pocketbook he found he had just enough for the movie and each a candy bar to munch on. Irene turned down the candy; she was dieting, she said.

They took seats about halfway down. The place was almost full. There was a smell of melted butter and of antiseptic around. People were popping popcorn into their mouths on all sides. He felt so thick about what was going to happen later on that he had trouble following the movie. Twice he let his hand trail into her lap, and after a moment, eyes troubled behind her glasses, Irene lifted his hand and set it back in his own lap.

They walked back to her house, past the dim gravestones in Layman's Cemetery, past the red Twin City Streetcar barns.

Irene guided him to a side door in back. It took her a moment to find the right key in the dark. They entered. There appeared to be a light on upstairs somewhere. He helped her out of her spring coat and then shed his own. The Crists had had fried sausage with cabbage that night. Irene took his hand and led them across what he took to be the parlor. The refracted light from upstairs touched the end of a davenport.

They settled down together on the davenport, stiffly. In a moment they were kissing. She became quite passionate, and clung to him until they both fell over side by side. She divided for him a little, and it wasn't long before he discovered that again she wasn't wearing pants.

"My, you're a fast worker," she whispered hoarsely.

"It's all right, though, isn't it?"

She kissed him with her tongue in answer.

There was a sound above them of heavy feet hitting the floor and then some steps to the head of the stairs. "Irene?" The voice was flat, sourish.

Irene broke free of Alan. "Yes, Mother?"

"You got home all right?"

"Yes, Mother."

"Can't you find the light? You oughta really have a light on."

Irene sighed. "I was just going to, Mother."

"That's good. 'Night."

Irene sighed again and then wrestled herself up off the davenport and put on a light in the stairwell. It lit up one side of the parlor. She came back and settled beside him. Her ardor had dampened.

"Shucks," Alan said.

Irene smiled. "We can always close our eyes."

Soon they were warm together again, and he found her warm slippery place.

"Do I have to worry?" he asked.

"No," she said.

A big question shot up in his head. Why not? Had she taken precautions? After a moment the question vanished when she opened for him.

He kept reaching deep into her until the sweet release.

After a while, in their breathing silence, he asked, "Did you?"

"No."

"Oh, but I want that for you too."

She kissed him warmly. "It's all right."

"You know what I mean?"

"Yes." She snuggled warmly up under him. "Maybe in a little while we can try again."

Alan rested upon her. My God, what that woman didn't seem to know. Now he knew for sure she'd had a lover before, and for some time too.

Presently the heavy steps sounded above again. There was a pause. Her mother had seen the stairwell light on. "What are you doing down there, Irene?"

"I have company, Mother."

"Oh. Excuse me." The heavy steps went back to bed.

Irene whispered, "You better not stay too long."

"What's with your mother that you can't date? You're twenty-one, aren't you? Twenty-three?"

"Twenty-four."

"Well?"

Presently they were at it again. Alan clutched her to him. She certainly had a heavy seat for so slim a pair of legs. "I want you to have fun too," he whispered.

"It's all right if I do?"

"Of course." What sort of lover had she had before?

She began thrusting rapidly at him and soon swooned with a low repressed groan.

It pleased him to hear her groan and then he too coursed out through a pair of gates.

Alan saw her three more times. It was right after he'd bought himself a secondhand blue Dodge. He took her to the last hockey game of the year. Then he took her riverbanking below the University of Minnesota campus, the waters of the Mississippi lapping a lullaby just outside the car windows. And finally he took her home from work yet again late one Saturday night.

That second late Saturday night Alan discovered the Crists had rearranged the furniture. The long brown plush davenport had been moved into a small side room off the parlor. Alan decided it was Irene's idea. Irene also saw to it that they entered the side room without having to meet her mother. Her mother had company again and they were having a jolly time playing whist in the next room.

For a while Alan and Irene sat on the davenport in its new location hardly saying anything. The clink of coffee spoons and cake forks and the garrulous talk in the next room hardly made for cozy kissing.

Irene turned on a radio.

They listened to Guy Lombardo awhile.

Alan slipped an arm around her.

She said, "Let's wait until the company's gone."

"But I can hardly stand it. I'm going wild waiting."

Irene sat like a hunched-up mouse.

"Please."

"Well, quick then."

"But I want you to enjoy it too."

"No. Later on for me. Just quick. Oh, I'm so scared they'll catch us."

Alan hardly touched her and was gone.

"Feel better?"

"Much."

Irene turned up the radio. A commentator came on discussing some of Hitler's atrocities.

Presently there was a knock on the door from the parlor. "You in there, Irene?"

"Yes, Mother. We're learning all about Hitler."

"Just wanted to make sure you got home safe."

Within a half hour her mother's company left. Her mother with heavy steps cleaned up the cups and plates and cutlery and washed them. At last she trudged upstairs to her bedroom.

The moment her mother's door closed upstairs Irene woke up. That marvelous musk smell rose from her again. She led him. Alan began to understand the painting *The Temptation of St. Anthony.*

Alan went home refreshed. Twice. Man, man.

The next week Irene turned him down.

"Your mother?"

"Well, that, yes. But . . ."

"I don't understand."

Irene blinked back tears.

"Well, okay, have it your way."

In a way he was relieved. He wasn't sure he liked it that the moment they were alone they right away had to make love.

Owning his first car made up for a lot. He explored all the lovely blue lakes of Minneapolis: Nokomis, Lake of the Isles, Hiawatha. He watched the swollen Minnehaha Creek thrash over the Minnehaha Falls. He cruised out beyond the city limits, exploring the mucky valley of the Minnesota River, the bubbling springs west of Savage, the confluence of the Minnesota and the Mississippi rivers below Fort Snelling. In Sioux Falls the city fathers had allowed commerce to ruin the magnificent cataracts and falls of the Big Sioux River. It delighted him that the city fathers of Minneapolis had gone out of their way to keep Minnehaha Creek and all the lakes from being destroyed by realtors. Every day that went by, Alan fell more and more in love with his new city.

After several weeks Alan began to think good thoughts about Irene again. She really was a swell gal, a decent woman. He noted she didn't flirt with any of the other men at the *Chronicle.* Everyone seemed to think well of her. A piece of him hungered for her like a calf after beastings.

Finally he couldn't stand it any longer, and on his next Thursday off, around four o'clock, he drove down to her home. He parked his blue Dodge on a side street and came walking up to her back door.

Irene was alone in the house part. She had on a housecoat and was holding a novel to her bosom, a finger in it for a bookmark. Without makeup on she looked better than she did when all dressed up for work at the paper. "Alan! I thought we'd agreed not to see each other again."

"We see each other at the paper every day."

"I mean, date."

"Irene, I just couldn't stand it any longer. You know."

She thickened. "I know." A tear began to sparkle in her eyes where the late-afternoon sun caught it. "But this time of the day?"

"Quick, get your duds on and I'll take you out for dinner."

"But what about Mother? She's in the store there, you know."

"Leave a note for her." He looked at her beseechingly. "I can't hardly stand it."

She shivered. Then her heavy chin set out a little. "All right. Where've you got your car?"

He pointed.

"Wait for me there. I'll be with you in a jiff."

Alan took her to the Covered Wagon in St. Paul. They had a drink, Alan a glass of orange juice and Irene a smoky Forester on the rocks. They ordered Lake Superior pink trout and baked potatoes. The drink loosened Irene's tongue, and for once she began to talk about books. The book she'd been reading was Hemingway's *To Have and Have Not,* and Alan was disappointed to see how little she got out of it. With a blush she said she thought the best part was where Helene kept saying, "Please don't stop."

It was dark when they left for home. Irene of a sudden had nothing to say. She sat as far apart from him as possible on the car seat.

He brought her to her side door. She stood in the doorway in such a way it meant she wasn't going to invite him in. Alan reached up and drew her face down and kissed her thin lips. He kissed her hard, and after a moment she relented and slowly opened the door and let him inside.

Irene turned on a lamp. She sat down on the davenport.

Alan watched her eyes. "There's something the matter, isn't there?"

"Yes. Sit down a moment. But not close to me."

He settled down on one end of the davenport. Had he knocked her up, for godsakes? Maybe she hadn't taken precautions after all.

"Alan, it isn't going to be easy to tell you this."

"Where's your mother?"

"She's gone to church. This is her night out. Some kind of church bazaar."

Alan's eyes began to flick back and forth.

Irene swallowed and swallowed; at last hardened up to it. "I'm not what you think I am."

"Wait," he said. "I don't want to hear about any other love affair you may have had. I don't believe in telling everything about one's past when it comes to love. Once a fellow knows about the other fellow, he can never get it out of his head. It haunts him for the rest of his life."

Iren sat doubled up in herself.

Alan slid along the davenport and slipped his arm around her. He reached in for a kiss.

Irene liked the kiss; wanted to go on; stopped. "Listen, I've got to tell you this. It's not what you're thinking. Alan, I'm not a single woman."

"Oh?"

"Alan, I'm a married woman."

Alan drew away from her a little. "Then where's your husband?"

"He's in England. I married an Englishman."

So that was it.

"Yes. We had an argument. And since he already didn't like America much, he went back."

"Do you still hear from him?"

She pinched it out. "Sometimes."

"Do you think you two still might get together someday?"

"We might. And that's why, until he either comes back, or we get a divorce, we shouldn't date anymore."

So that was why there was this strained air with her mother.

"You aren't angry with me?" she asked.

"No."

"You don't think me cheap? Easy?"

"Oh, Irene, you've been wonderful to me. You don't know."

Irene smiled at him. She knew. "I was your first one, wasn't I?"

"Yes."

They looked at each other. Then an understanding passed between them. They would make love one more final last exultant time. Then they'd never mention it again or ever date again.

Never dip your pen in the company ink.

# Chapter 3

# ALAN

One afternoon Bill O'Brian came wandering into the sports department. Bill worked on the city desk.

Bill threw a glossy print on Alan's desk. "How do you like them pair of gams?"

It was a picture of a girl sitting in a canoe on the Lake of the Isles. She had blond hair, a partly surprised arch look, full calves.

"Good-looker, ain't she?"

"Another one of your conquests?"

"No. She won a prize. The *Atlantic Monthly* short-story contest." Bill had a cheeky Irish face. "She's just out of high school. Boss sent me out to write a story about her."

Alan looked at the glossy print again.

Bill went on, "Gonna be one of those damned intellectuals. Always got her nose in a book. More your type."

"I'll have to meet her sometime."

"Well, you're in luck. She's dropping by this afternoon. Her mother wants a couple extra copies of the pix."

"When are you running the story?"

"Next Sunday." Bill bent him a knowing look. "Shall I bring her around?"

"If you want to."

Bill ushered her into the sports department at three. Alan was alone at the time. "Alan, I'd like for you to meet Jael Hemlickson, famous Minneapolis writer. Jael, this is the Alan Ross I told you about."

Alan pushed back from his typewriter. "Hi."

Jael was a good-looker all right. White-gold hair, almost as pale as his own. Her eyes were also light, of a blue seen on distant trees on a misty day. She didn't have much of a bosom, but her waist was a marvel, slim as a running hound's. The best was that little wise smile on an innocent face. "Hi," she said. Her voice was moist, milky. She was wearing blue.

Alan got to his feet. "I hear you made the *Atlantic Monthly.*"

Her blue eyes measured him. "Oh, it isn't as much as it sounds. It's just their yearly high school contest, and they printed it in the back pages."

"I must get a copy."

They stood smiling at each other. She looked him in the eye, but she was also picking up the rest of him. She liked it that he was six foot three. It went well with her slim height. He noted her broad high forehead, and liked it. It was the way Sappho might have looked.

Bill looked at Alan's hips and then at Jael's hips.

Alan asked her about her English teacher, did she plan to go on to college and where, and what did her folks think about her talent. Jael said that if it hadn't been for her spinster teacher Abigail she'd never have written a line, and yes she planned to go to the University of Minnesota the next fall, and well her folks were a little cool about her becoming a writer.

"What would you really like to become?"

"Abigail thinks I should try to write a novel. Something she never got around to."

Alan steadied his eyes on her. "But what do you want to become?"

"Well . . ."

"When you're alone in your bed at night, you know, in the dark, what is it that you dream about that you'd really like to do? Your secret dream of life?"

"That'd be telling."

"Don't ever be ashamed of talent, if that's what you've got. There's only one person inside that envelope of skin you have, and that's you. When your body dies, no one outside it can enter that envelope and help keep you alive. So you're always on your own. So dare to be what you are."

Bill broke in. "What about conception?"

Jael colored prettily. She'd thought of it too.

Alan changed the subject. "Your people live in town?"

"Yes, Portland and Thirty-sixth."

"What does your father do?"

"He's an insurance salesman. Part-time these days."

Alan nodded. It was 1937 and times were hard.

The phone rang on Alan's desk. Alan picked it up. "Sports."

"Is Bill O'Brian there?"

"Just a second." Alan placed a hand over the mouthpiece and handed the phone over to Bill. "Your friend Minus wants you." Minus was their nickname for Manus McNab, the managing editor.

"Yeh?" Bill listened for a second. "Okay, I'll tell her." He put down the phone. "Jael, your father's been asking for you."

"Hooo," Jael whispered. "That mother of mine. She's always getting Father to check up on me." Jael opened her white leather purse and with slender oddly fumbling fingers picked out a streetcar token. She gave Alan a warm smile. "I better be going. Nice to have met you." Then she turned to Bill. "Do you think those pictures will be dry now?"

"Sure thing." Bill led the way out.

A couple of nights later Alan looked up Jael's number in the telephone book. There was a Tor Hemlickson living near Portland and Thirty-sixth. Colfax 3590. That had to be her father. Alan dialed the number, and Jael answered. Jael seemed pleased that he'd called. They talked for about a half hour. About books they liked. About plays. As Alan listened, he cocked a critical eye at the ceiling. Jael had brains all right. She sure was different from Irene Crist.

Again one afternoon alone in the sports department, he looked up to see her standing in the doorway. She was wearing the same light-blue blouse and powder-blue skirt he'd seen her in the first time. She was bare-legged and had on blue socks and white tennis shoes.

"Hi," she said with an opening smile. "I've only got but a minute. Mother's shopping around the corner at Powers' and I thought I'd slip away a few seconds and surprise you." When Alan started to get to his feet, she quickly said, "Don't get up." She moved toward him with a leggy stride. "I'll just sit here on the corner of your desk a second." She settled with easy grace right in front of him. "How are you?"

"Fine." He broke out in a big smile. "I've been wondering when I'd see you again. Just talking on the phone isn't enough."

"I know. But for now that'll have to do."

Alan had to work to get his breath. "Can't you at least come down for lunch once in a while?

"I'll see what I can arrange."

"What are your folks so worried about?"

"Wait'll I'm eighteen and going to the U. Then I'll just put my foot down and go out with whom I wish."

"Good. But do try to see me when you can." He placed a hand on her hand, and then after a moment slid it up over her wrist and held her forearm warmly.

She looked down at his hand. "You've got freckles over the back of your hand." Her fingertips trailed up along his forearm. "And lovely soft gold fuzz. I like that."

Alan looked at her hand lying on his and thought of it as a kind of plighting of troth. The odor of an opening peony came from her clothes. A little white glow ignited far back in his head. He looked at her long flowing sun-white hair and thought of the Holy Grail. It was the first time he'd ever felt quite that way about a girl. Compared to her, Irene Crist wasn't in it at all. Alan gave her arm a little shake. "You know, I don't like it that you have to sneak up here to see me."

"I don't either."

"Then I've got a suggestion to make. This coming Thursday on my day off I'm gonna drive over and walk into your house and ask your parents face to face if I can see you."

Jael sucked in a quick breath. "Oh God, don't do that!"

"You afraid of them?"

After a second she pushed his hand aside and jumped to her feet. "I guess I better go."

He got up and slid an arm around her waist. It was the first time. His long hand cupped her hipbone. "Wait. Not so fast." He drew her against him, gave her a loving shake. "I mean to keep seeing you, Jael. I've come to like you."

She turned her face into his shoulder. She said into his shirt, muffled, "I like you too, I guess."

Guess? "And I mean to get to like your folks. What else? I think after they get to know me they'll like me too."

"Oh God, I'm scared. You don't know."

He took her face in both of his hands. "I'll see you Thursday. Now, run along to your mother at Powers'."

She left in a hurry.

Getting up his gumption, thinking that this was the way his haunt brother John would do it, Alan on his next Thursday off drove over to the Hemlickson house on Portland Avenue. He rang the doorbell, and got himself invited inside. It happened that Tor Hemlickson was home between insurance calls. Very stiffly both Tor and Gretta Hemlickson settled themselves on a light-green davenport, and, quite nervous, Alan settled in a light-green chair facing them. Even sitting down Gretta Hemlickson was taller than her husband. She had a handsome matronly face with a pained look around her nose. He was as bald as an eggplant and had a slightly apoplectic complexion. There was a pinched banker's expression around his thin lips. Jael meanwhile was in the back of the house somewhere.

Alan said now that they had met him, would it be all right if he dated their daughter Jael occasionally. He realized his coming to see them like this was the old-fashioned way of doing things, but that was the way he'd been raised.

Gretta Hemlickson shook her head. Their Jael was only seventeen. And how old was he?

"Well, twenty-five."

"Finished with college?"

"Yes. Macalester."

"And you're a . . . sports reporter?" Gretta Hemlickson made it sound as if he slopped pigs for a living.

"Yes." Alan added, with a toss of his head, "That's where all the best writing is done on a newspaper."

The Hemlicksons completely missed the sally. It was like wasting a popover on a pair of police dogs. "No," Gretta Hemlickson said, shaking her head. "No, there's too much age difference."

"Well, as for that," Alan said, "it just happens I'm the child of an October-April marriage myself. My dad, Rollo Ross, was fifty-five when he married Mother, Ada Tull, nineteen. And Dad and Ma have made a fine couple. Wonderful parents."

A stiff silence followed.

Finally Tor Hemlickson turned a little and called into the back of the house. "Jael?"

Jael came out, quite subdued. She'd been listening and was as pale as an egg. She sat down in the other light-green chair. She crossed her full calves.

Finally Tor Hemlickson said, "All right, Jael. Your friend Alan Ross here can see you once in a while. But no dates at night. Because that's when the Devil works his wiles."

"But," Gretta Hemlickson began, "I thought—"

"Never mind, wife," Tor Hemlickson said firmly. "It's going to be the way I say. Okay?"

Alan lit up inside. "Hey, that's very nice of you." Alan gave them his best smile. "How about next Sunday then, if the weather's nice? I'll take Jael out for a ride in the country and have her back in the house here at least an hour before dark."

# Chapter 4

# ALAN

Alan Ross sat up in bed. The sun was shining across his feet. It was Sunday morning. Later on he was going to take Jael out for a ride in the country.

His eye caught movement in the open window. The white lace curtains billowed toward him like the prancing rumps of ghost horses. A soft breeze was pushing into his two-room apartment. It was refreshing; felt deliciously cool on his bare chest. In August the nights in Minneapolis could sometimes be perfect for sleeping.

He swung himself up out of his Hollywood bed, caught his toes in a pair of slippers, snaked his arms into his blue bathrobe. He picked up his shaving kit and towel and headed for the bathroom down the hall. None of the other roomers were up. He'd have the bathroom to himself.

Alan shaved himself with the quiet leisure of a gentleman. The whiskers over his upper lip and around his chin were heavy. His beard was light-red with some gold in it, while the hair on his head was light-gold with touches of red in it. Every Thursday and every Sunday the past summer, on his days off, he'd tried to pick up a tan in the sun, but the best he'd been able to do was to turn a pinkish gold. Alan checked the one spot, right in the middle of his left cheek, where a whitehead occasionally formed. It was beginning again but wasn't quite ready to be pinched. He had to be very careful about pinching his tender skin or it would leave a red partly hemorrhaged spot for a couple of days.

Alan checked the hint of bags under his eyes. Ma said her mother's people all had bags under the eyes; it was a family trait.

He showered, careful not to use too much soap. Afterward he let himself dry naturally. If he toweled himself down too briskly his skin itched for hours. The boarders in the other rooms, graduate students at the University of Minnesota, often looked askance at him as he sailed naked down the hallway.

Back in his two rooms, Alan put coffee on the hotplate, set out a bowl of cornflakes with raisins and milk, and halved himself a grapefruit. He smiled to himself when he thought ahead to the day when Jael would discover he liked to eat breakfast naked. That would be, of course, after they were properly married.

Finished with breakfast, Alan slipped into a pair of shorts. He made the bed, putting on fresh sheets, making sure the red daisies in the gold bedspread lined up evenly at the corners. He washed the dishes. He got out broom and dustpan and cleaned the place, even moving his low bed to get the dust rolls out from under it. Next he got a bottle of furniture polish and dusted all the woodwork. He made the place shine. Ma couldn't have done it better. Someday Jael would be visiting him in his two rooms, and he wanted her to see how neat he was. And if her folks should ever happen to come along, well, they'd see what a helpful husband he could be for their precious Jael.

Slipping into an old pair of jeans, he went down and washed his 1934 blue Dodge with a hose. He also waxed the car and then buffed it until it shone like a bluebird. Except for a tricky clutch, the old Dodge was a good car. The engine had only 43,000 miles on it and it still didn't eat much oil.

Back upstairs again, he settled down in his Morris chair and picked up the *Sunday Chronicle* that he'd taken home with him the night before.

Alan liked working late Saturday nights after the others had gone. From ten P.M. on there was little chance there'd be a major crisis in the world of sports. Occasionally a late bulletin came in to announce that Dizzy Dean had pulled off another crazy stunt on the diamond, but never much more than that.

Alan checked the stories and rewrites he'd handled. Satisfied there were no typos, he then checked Hank Williams' column on bowling. Next he had a good laugh over Quinsey Quinn's humorous account of the Minneapolis Millers baseball team's antics the afternoon before. He wound up reading "Cowens' Corner." Burt Cowens wrote the best sports column in the Upper Midlands, precise, laconic, crystal clear. It was said that Bernie Bierman, football coach of the Minnesota Gophers, paid more attention to Cowens' column than he did to his assistant coaches' scouting reports.

Alan tossed the sports pages onto his bed. He began to think about Jael and his coming date with her. Too bad he couldn't have met Jael before he'd had that affair with Irene. Then the two of them could have discovered the wonder of that first time together.

He looked at the clock. Going on twelve. Time to start dinner. He boiled himself a potato and a small Polish sausage, halved a green pepper and filled it with cottage cheese, and brewed himself a pot of tea.

He was well into the potato when one of the grad students, Martin Vann, poked his head in.

"Do I smell Polish sausage?" Martin asked. There was always a sound of doubt in Martin's voice. He spoke in an Upstate New York dialect, somewhat cultivated with the hint of a throaty lisp. He was slender, had dark haunted brown eyes with shadows reaching down into his cheeks. Martin was writing a dissertation for his doctorate at Harvard University while at the same time teaching summer classes at the University of Minnesota, in the English department, as a teaching assistant. He was temporarily living apart from his wife and one child, a little girl. His wife, Willi, had elected to stay with her folks in Chapel Hill, North Carolina. "Where do you get those Polish sausages?"

"At Welch's in Dinkytown. Would you like a piece?"

"No, thanks. Later maybe." Martin stepped farther into the room, dressed only in a red dressing gown. His dark hairy legs were almost all bone. "What I came in to ask was, are you using your car today? My Ford broke down yesterday and I still haven't found us a house."

"Sorry, but I've got a heavy date this afternoon."

"Hmm. Too bad. Well, then I'll have to walk it."

John Charles, the other graduate student, next poked his head in the doorway. "Did I hear someone make an offer of Polish sausage?" John Charles was also skinny, and almost as tall as Martin Vann. John Charles was balding, had a heavy grayish beard, thin brutal lips, and a considerable underbite. He had offish eyes, mackerel in cast, and he never quite looked one in the eye. He was wearing a blue bathrobe from beneath which his shanks protruded like crane legs. He was unmarried, never had anything good to say about women, and hated his horsy father. John Charles had his master's degree and was also a teaching assistant in English at the University. He liked to talk about the noble Greek marathon runners and their great love for the human male body. John Charles spent much of his spare time watching high school track stars perform. "I lo-ove Polish sausage," John Charles went on to say, wetting his lips, "and have ever since I started batching."

"Help yourself." Alan pushed the meat platter toward him.

John Charles looked down at the half sausage still left. "You sure you don't want it?"

"No. I'm not really hungry. Too nervous."

John Charles picked up the red half sausage, and then with a coarse gesture slipped the entire half sausage into his mouth and wolfed it down.

Martin Vann smiled at Alan. "Nervous? That heavy date must be something special."

"Wait'll you meet her. She's a jewel."

John Charles scowled at Alan. "How can you speak of women being jewels when once a month they're about as foul as a creature can be?"

Alan countered, "Well, you were born to a jewel of a woman once, weren't you?"

"Rrach!" John Charles snapped his slender fingers so sharply that a couple drops of sausage juice still left on them flipped up and hit him in the face. "Ugg." Getting out a handkerchief from his bathrobe pocket, he wiped his face with a decorous gesture.

Alan smiled at Martin Vann. "You guys must've been out late."

"Yes. John Charles and I went down to see a mellerdramer on the *Mark Twain*. You know, on the old riverboat docked below Washington Avenue bridge there."

"How was it?"

"Not very good." Martin always pronounced the word "good" with the sound of the letter U in it, prolonging it as if to give it elegance. "Too much Wild West in it for me."

John Charles agreed. "Fare for boors. Too much hogges tord in it, as Chaucer was wont to say."

Alan had to laugh. "Well, in that case I should go see it." Alan had a running argument with both men about American literature, especially Western American literature. Alan argued that the American novelists of the last quarter century had it all over their English counterparts. When Martin and John Charles told him he wouldn't say such things if he'd "read any English literachure at alll," Alan would then start lauding the work of Charles Montagu Doughty and Robert Smith Surtees, about whom they knew little or nothing. It always upset Martin and John Charles that Alan could run better with their ball than they could.

Martin and John Charles soon retreated to their rooms.

As Alan cleared off the table and washed the dishes and put them away, he thought about that strange pair down the hallway. Martin was all right, and Alan liked him. There was something more than just fine airs about Martin; he had a good warm heart. But that John Charles . . . well, John Charles had the look of a person who would someday come to a sad end.

Glancing at his wristwatch, Alan noted it was just one o'clock. Still two hours to go before he could pick up Jael. A yawn welled up in him, and after a moment he decided to have himself a snooze.

Alan slept until the white lace curtains began to snap in the open windows and woke him.

He looked at the time. Good God. Two-thirty. He'd slept a hole in the day. In a half hour he was to pick up Jael. He bounded out of bed, ran down the hall to freshen up and comb his hair, then came back and dressed in his new blue suit and white shirt and red tie and gray suede oxfords.

He drove rapidly across town, taking the Tenth Avenue bridge over the Mississippi River, at Seven Corners swinging down Cedar Avenue to Thirty-sixth Street, tooling west sixteen blocks until he took a left on Portland Avenue.

The sun shone beautiful on the leaves of the trees. On both sides of Portland the shadows under the elms resembled diaphanous purple tepees.

Jael lived in the second house from the corner, 3609 Portland, on the east side of the street. Alan pulled up across from it along the curb. He was about to shut off the motor when his eye caught movement in the doorway of her house. It was Jael. She was hurrying out, letting the screen door slam behind her. She ran toward him in an easy lifting jog, bare calf muscles swelling becomingly, a glad smile on her face. A yellow pleated skirt billowed and folded over her legs. She had on a green sweater over a white blouse. The sweater was unbuttoned, and it lifted up behind her as she ran. Her long blond hair, combed back, flowed out from her slender shoulders. Before Alan could jump out and open the door for her, she was around the car and tugging at the door handle. Alan quickly reached across and opened the door from the inside.

Jael slid in. "I saw you coming so I thought I'd just run out and save you coming to the door."

"That was nice of you." Alan would have preferred to see her folks a moment if only to let them know he meant to do right by her.

She gave a little jump in the seat. "Let's go."

Alan smiled. "You looked like some Greek goddess come running down from her father's mansion on a hill. To meet her Theseus by the sea."

Jael's cheeks dimpled in an arch smile. "Yes, and if this pirate

Theseus doesn't soon pull up anchor my father's minions will soon catch up with him."

It struck Alan he'd taken to Jael in part because her smile reminded him of his haunt brother John's champ smile. She was a superior one too. "Your folks are all right then?"

"Oh, sure."

Alan mulled over her remark, then turned in his seat and waved to the big picture window in Jael's house. Sure enough, between the blinds, there stood both Tor and Gretta Hemlickson watching them. After a second they waved back, stiff, correct.

Jael lowered her blue eyes. "That was very thoughtful of you."

Alan was pleased to notice that around Jael he didn't feel in the least self-conscious. He decided it was because he was some eight years older than she.

Jael asked, "Where are you going?"

"I thought maybe we'd explore south of town."

"Goody. I love adventure."

Alan drove south down Portland Avenue, past Diamond Lake, past an old-time truck garden at Sixty-second Street, and past still another at Seventy-sixth Street. At Seventy-eighth he took a right to Lyndale, and on Lyndale took a left.

"Now I know where we're going," Jael cried. "Dad's told me about the Old Shakopee Road. It's the old fur traders' trail, where they used to drive oxcarts. And the pioneers used it to go to town in their box wagons." She pronounced the name Shakopee as Shock-o-pee, giving it the old Dakota pronunciation.

"Right. Originally it probably was an old Indian trail. And before that a buffalo or animal trail."

Going west they had to pull down the sunvisors over the windshield. More truck gardens showed up on both sides of the road. In the sleepy village of Bloomington, the road dipped down into a little wooded dale where Ninemile Creek trickled slowly away into blue shadows. They angled southwest through open country. Cabbages and muskmelons in the fields gave off a ripening smell. Twice they passed roadside fruit stands manned by children. Watermelons stood piled up like huge green potato bugs. Ripe tomatoes gave the air a reddish tinge. But the best were the apples, red crabs, red Wealthies, yellow Harvesters, green pie-apples.

"Would you like an apple?" Alan asked.

"I'd love one."

Alan pulled up beside a roadside stand and bought them some Wealthy apples. He placed them in Jael's lap.

Jael peeked into the bag. "So tasty-looking and juicy." She counted them. "Seven. Seven red apples hanging from a red-brown bough."

"That's a good line."

Jael selected one and rubbed it up and down her thigh until it shone like varnished red mahogany. "This is for you."

Alan took it. Out of the corner of his eye he watched her select one for herself, polish it, and take a small decorous bite. He noted she had fine teeth. A little spray of juice squirted out of the apple, landing on her knee. Jael got out a handkerchief from a pocket and quickly brushed off the drops. "Mmm, it's good."

Alan snapped off a bite. In his case the juice spurted up against the roof of his mouth. The taste was one for the gods. No wonder Adam was tempted to eat of the apple. Delicious. The sound of the apple being crunched echoed in his skull.

Alan started up the blue Dodge again and they continued to roll southwest down the Old Shakopee Road. Presently tar paving petered out into a gravel road.

Sandy fields with eroded yellowhead hills rolled by on either side. The gravel road dipped, curved, and then dropped into a miniature jungle of great oaks and elms and hard maples. They rode through a green world. It opened a moment, revealing a wooden bridge over winking Purgatory Creek. The planks of the bridge lay irregularly and screeched when the four wheels of the car flattened them out. Then the gravel road rose steeply up through more trees, curved around to the right sharply and suddenly leveled out onto a very high field.

Soon they were riding along the very edge of a line of high bluffs. Below lay the Minnesota River Valley, curving off to the west, long and slow. A placid river doubled and redoubled down the valley. Several shallow lakes lay on either side of the river. The valley was lush. Deep grasses and cattails and bending willows gave off a green so vivid the valley appeared to be lacquered.

The old road took a sharp left and pinched down through a cleft in the bluffs. Dust puffed up all around the car.

Jael's eyes turned a high green as they went down under towering cottonwoods and then, veering right, as they tunneled through a grove of huge ash trees. "Can't you go a little slower to keep down the dust?"

"I'll just let the car coast here."

The road leveled. It began to veer around the humps of the bluffs coming down into the bottomland. As the car slowed the dust no longer billowed up around them.

They passed through a farmyard, the house and the privy on the right set up against the bluff, the barn and the cattle sheds on the left built on a flat of land just barely out of the swamp. A half dozen kids played baseball in the yard below. They were using the barn as a backstop. All were barefoot, all wore overalls, and all were as blond as bleached hemp rope.

Alan smiled. "Jael, how would you like to grow up on a farm like that?"

"My Aunt Sophie married a farmer near Grandy. Horace Green. I stay out there a month or so every summer. She's my mother's sister."

"Farms that far north? What do they raise there?"

"Grain. Hay. Cattle."

Alan was pleased to learn she had a background similar to his. There was no way of explaining to a stranger what it meant to be raised on a farm. Diurnal rhythms were set deeper in farm children than in city kids.

The road curved around more humps coming down from the bluffs on the right. The grass on the steep slopes of the bluffs ran like the manes of frolicking mustangs. Several black-and-white cows grazed halfway up the steep slopes.

The Old Shakopee Road rose to join Highway 169. Several light planes were banking around in the sky, circling Flying Cloud Field off to the north.

Alan pulled up at a stop sign. Black cars rushed by both ways in front of them on 169, some going up the long sloping road toward Minneapolis, some going down to Shakopee.

Alan looked for a break in the traffic. "What's everybody doing out on the road today?"

"Sunday is when everybody goes for a spin down the beautiful Minnesota River Valley."

Alan watched the cars flash past in front of them.

"If you think this is busy, you should see it in early October when the colors come out. It once took Dad and Mother and me three hours to come back from Mankato."

Alan spotted oncoming breaks in both lanes of traffic. The breaks would meet in front of them like two slots lining up to receive a cotter. At the exact right moment Alan shifted into low and shot across into the right lane going down. "There. Made it."

The sudden surge of the blue Dodge and then the turn to the left made Jael roll against the door. She had to laugh. "Whew. Where did you learn to drive like that?"

"You should see me sometimes when I'm rushing back to the *Chronicle* with a hot story, hoping to beat the opposition into print."

"It must be exciting to be a reporter."

There was a thick line of cars behind them as well as up ahead of them. Those behind them honked for Alan to get going; he wasn't keeping up with the cars ahead. Alan didn't like all the honking, nor the smell of burned oil and exhaust gas. Ahead he noticed a dirt road leading off to the left down into the swamps below. He spotted a small opening in the oncoming traffic in the other lane, and suddenly whipping the wheel over and stepping hard on the footfeed, making the Dodge engine snort, he aimed for the dirt road. There were screeching brakes on either side of them. Horns snarled. Men cursed. But Alan made it. And in a moment, in a swirl of fine yellow dust, they were plunging down a very narrow winding lane.

"For goodness sakes," Jael cried, rubbing her head where she'd rolled against the door again.

The dirt trail led down between two little lakes. Grass on both sides of the lane rustled against the car. In a moment they rode into blue shadows under tall arching elms.

Alan smiled. "I wonder where this road goes."

"You've never been on it before?"

"Nope."

"This is fun!" She liked their doing something wild in a new and secret place. Her light-blue eyes once again took on the green of the jungle.

The dirt road ran south about half a mile, then turned sharply west. A natural vaulted hall opened under the enormous arching limbs. A few feet farther the edge of a riverbank appeared, abrupt and black, and beyond, in the sun, floated a boat with a single fisherman in it.

"Man, the Minnesota River is wide and deep here," Alan whispered.

"Yes, it is," Jael whispered.

The dirt trail followed along the edge of the steep bank. Long drooping elm twigs brushed the car. Once both Alan and Jael ducked involuntarily when a hanging branch brushed the roof of the car.

A little way farther on sunlight bloomed over the trail, and in a moment the trail opened onto a hayfield. Two sleek haystacks appeared in front of them. A hayloader stood nearby. One of the stacks was newly made.

Alan stepped on the brakes, stopped, and half turning in his seat backed the car into the shadows again. Alan let the car murmur underfoot a second, then with a shy glance at Jael, turned off the key. "Let's just sit and look at it awhile."

Jael turned modest in turn. She looked down at her knees. She brushed her skirt out over her knees. One of the yellow pleats wouldn't fold under, and she pressed it down several times.

The birds were silent in the jungle green behind them. Insects ticked against the windshield. The fisherman behind them cast and recast his fly, the line lifting out of the water with a sibilant liquid sound and resplashing farther along with a gurgling fall.

Alan dared it. He reached across and picked up her hand. He was surprised again to notice how very slender her fingers were. It struck him that if she were to put pressure on them, holding a pencil, they'd buckle.

Jael responded. With her outer hand she stroked the back of his hand. "I just love the gold fuzz on the back of your hand." She trailed a fingertip along a blue vein running up the center of his longfinger. Then she threw back her falling white-gold hair, revealing a lovely girlish impish smile. "And I just love this place."

"Except for the fisherman, we're alone in paradise."

Jael looked past Alan. "The river is slowly carrying him downstream. We don't have to worry about him."

The word "worry" caught Alan, and he had to work for breath. He could feel his eyes begin to shimmer, flick back and forth. He reached his arm around her and slid her toward him and drew her close. The sweet odor of a delicate soap was in her hair, and when she pushed her head against his cheek her hair made a just-washed crinching sound. He nuzzled in her hair and then with his chin edged her face around. She let him. Their noses touched. He reached in for a little kiss. Their first. Their lips barely flattened and after a moment lightly stuck together. She smiled under his nose and her eyes opened directly into his. He could see, mirrored in her eyes, the trees outside the car. It was strange to see the green of the trees bluing down into the deeps of her eyes.

"I love the electricity of your eyes," she whispered.

It startled him. Should he tell her he couldn't help it if his eyes misbehaved when he got excited?

"Alan the searcher, endlessly looking for the ends of truth."

He decided to tell her later. With his nose he nudged up her face again and kissed her lightly. She kissed back. They kissed chastely. Dry. He remembered suddenly that almost right after he'd kissed

Irene Crist he'd moved in. Well, with this Jael it was going to be different. Already he loved Jael so much he could hardly imagine them having sex. Tenderly, delicately, he held her floating lightly in a dream. He wished it hadn't happened with Irene Crist. His haunt brother John probably would've disagreed with him. Haunt John would've plunged in with Jael. But there he would've been wrong.

Jael broke out of it first. She looked past Alan. "The fisherman's out of sight now."

Alan's heart troubled around in his chest.

She slimmed up against him, fitting her limbs into his.

He remembered her father and mother. He also remembered that at age seventeen she was jailbait. But mostly it was her folks he thought about.

She kept pressing against him. After a moment she twisted her bosom against his and then lifted her breast into where his hand rested on her. He could feel himself become aroused under her. Spots before his eyes became whirling planets. She felt him and then she stilled.

"We better be careful," he said. "Your folks."

"Yes, them. But what about you? It isn't good for you to get all worked up and then have nothing happen."

"I don't know about that," he said. "But at least your folks. I owe them something."

Her hair spilled across his face, and he looked through it. The whole world was golden. He wondered, because of his sensitive eyes, if he saw the world with a lighter tinting than she did. Was the gold he saw a deep yellow to her? He wondered if there was some kind of standard they could use to determine if they were both seeing the same color. He lifted his head. "Jael, see that pale leaf hanging there at the very end of that bough? That elm?"

Startled, Jael looked around for the leaf. "Yes?"

"Tell me, exactly, what color do you see there?"

"What's this all about?"

"What color do you see?"

"Well, a leaf yellowing at the edge with still a little green in the center."

"What kind of yellow? Like what other yellow?"

Jael laughed. "Well, like a ripe banana."

He nodded to himself. He saw in the leaf the color of a banana that still wasn't ripe. He was seeing a lighter hue in the colors around them than she was.

"What are you trying to prove?"

"Nothing." He nuzzled his head down into her hair again.

Once again she slimmed her length along his and pressed herself onto him. Then she lay very quietly as though content to dream for a while.

He couldn't help it. He'd gone down that road with Irene Crist. He slid his hand under Jael's dress. Her leg was bare and soft and supple all the way to the elastic in her panties. She appeared to be a little startled at first, and he could feel a tremor on the inside of her thigh. Gradually she relaxed and again slimmed and pressed herself against him. He took a full hold of her thigh in his long hand and gave it loving warm pinches. She liked that.

They rested and breathed in dream.

She turned on his thigh and opened herself to him. In a moment his hand was inside her panties. Out of the corner of his eye he could see her panties were a light blue. Then he found her and shivered and held her.

They rested and breathed in dream some more.

There appeared before his mind's eye, like a sharply defined black-and-white print in an old album, the picture of Tor and Gretta Hemlickson standing in front of their picture window watching their Jael get in the car with him just a couple of hours before, of them waving back at him, stiffly, a little curt. He groaned. Well, for the life of him he couldn't betray their trust. He withdrew his hand.

Jael sighed.

In the opening ahead the sun slowly went down across the meadow. Green shadows moved out of the underbrush in waves of spilling ink. Little wisps of fog misted up off the silently moving river. A thrush awoke and called several short evening songs.

"What time is it?" she whispered.

He lifted his left wrist and looked past her light-gold head. "It's getting on, all right."

"What time?"

"Sixish."

"I'm hungry."

He loved it that she spoke like a child. "Shall we see where this road ends up and then go have ourselves a hamburger and an ice-cream cone?"

"Let's."

They disentangled, she more reluctantly than he.

They followed the dirt road along the edge of the meadow, curving along with the meanders of the Minnesota River, and presently to their surprise they arrived at the foot of a long cement bridge just outside Shakopee.

They found a refreshment stand and both ordered a hamburger and an ice-cream cone. Napkins in their laps, they sat eating in the car. Each time she licked at her cone the tip of her tongue appeared to smile at it.

Again Alan wondered what his haunt brother John would have done that afternoon. Probably have no compunctions at all about Tor and Gretta Hemlickson. Haunt John, had he wanted to, could have probably stolen Jael from him. The son of a bitch.

Alan took Jael home. It was seven when he pulled up at her door. And there in the picture window stood Tor and Gretta Hemlickson, bent forward a little. They looked as if they hadn't moved since he and Jael had left at three. Alan wanted to kiss Jael once again but knew he shouldn't.

Jael gave him a quick smile, and then got out of the car before he could open the door for her. She skipped up the walk and vanished into the house.

Alan waved at the picture window, but by that time her father and mother had turned to greet Jael. Alan watched them talking together. Jael appeared to be explaining what they'd done that afternoon, and her parents appeared to be satisfied with what they heard. Then all three headed for the back of the house.

Alan drove home. As he crossed the Tenth Street bridge over the Mississippi, Alan hit his steering wheel with his fist. "I've got to remember that the next time we don't go that far again. Huu! that was wrong." Then he shook his head to himself. "As those cynical nuts up at the paper would say, I've got to remember she's Jael-bait."

# Chapter 5

# JAEL

Jael went to her room and kicked off her tennies. She considered a moment and then went to the bathroom. She sat erect.

"Jael," her mother called into the bathroom, "close the door." Mother spoke in a pained polite voice. "You're not a little girl anymore that you have to leave the door open so that we may know you've tinkled."

"Yes, Mother." Jael spoke as a child might, a mischievous smile on her lips.

"Well then, close it! There are men around, you know."

"Yes, Mother." But she finished anyway without closing the door. Her father would studiously close his ears to the sound of anything his women might be doing, as he always did on Sunday. It was on Sunday that Mother leveled her attacks on him for not providing them with a better (what she really meant was richer) life. As for her little brother Dickie, he was playing with his blocks and never bothered about who had to go to the bathroom. Dickie was sometimes so lost in play they had trouble getting him to go wheeter before he stained his pants. Jael flushed the toilet.

Back in her room Jael undressed. Standing naked in front of her mirror, she examined her body, from the light-gold hair on her head to the eggshell nails on her toes. She was pleased with her hair, the way it fell in a slow natural wave to her shoulders. Shampoo always gave it a fluffy ambience. Alan's hair was almost exactly like hers. Her shoulders were slender, as a woman's should be. But her breasts were too small. She'd been working on them, massaging them around and around and kneeding them gently with her knuckles. The only change that she could detect was that her nipples were bigger and a darker brown. She liked her waist and her hips. She liked her legs, especially her calves. Her calves were full and well shaped, narrowing down to slender ankles. Her eye moved up her body to the wispy gold hairs over her mount of love. She couldn't quite make out the groove, and to see it the better she arched herself up. She stared at it. "So that's what Mother says all men want so bad."

Then there was her mouth. What a fuss her father had made over her mouth being so small when she was five-six years old. He'd so worried about it he finally one day took to slipping his gold watch in and out of her mouth to try to make it larger. He told her to wet her lips with her tongue and then he'd slide it in and out. Whether the watch helped or not she didn't know. When she turned ten, her mouth gradually enlarged to what it was at the moment.

She also remembered the time when she'd overheard her father talking angrily with her mother in their bedroom. "Trouble with you is, Gretta, you're too damned tight. Stiff and unbending. And right along with that you're too tight with sex too."

Wasn't it curious that while he'd once tried to make her mouth larger, widen a tight mouth, her father now joined her mother in trying to make her tight and stiff around boys?

She stared some more. If it was so wonderful for boys, why wasn't it wonderful for girls? What was there in it for the boys that made them so excited? When one played with it, well, it was sort of pleasurable, but it never seemed to get anywhere.

She remembered the time up at Grandy, at Uncle Horace's farm. She'd left the door to the outdoor privy open, and the sun was shining in on her, making her limbs and belly warm. She was twelve and had looked to see if her fuzz was changing to hair. Her friend Jerre Thornton had hair. It was a very private moment, nobody was supposed to be around. Jael examined herself closely, her hair falling around her face and obscuring everything except what she was looking at. She bent so far over her stomach wrinkled up like the belly of a crayfish. Then, at that very moment, when she thought she was most alone, she heard a sound outside the privy. She swung her hair up and back with a lashing motion; and there on the path stood Uncle Horace. Uncle Horace had stopped in midstride, was leaning forward a little, lively brown eyes quirked as if he couldn't quite believe what he was seeing, full mouth twisted up in a wise smile. Jael snapped erect. Her thighs slapped together. She hadn't known what to do with her fingers so quick, and she was for the moment so terror-stricken she set them flat out on the wooden seat on either side of her and pressed down so hard that after a second she lifted herself off the hole. That appeared to startle Uncle Horace. Then she came to. She reached out a hand and slammed the privy door shut, hard, so that a spider up in the quarter-moon slit flipped out and unreeled down like a yoyo slowly losing momentum.

Still later that day, Aunt Sophie sent her out to fetch the eggs. Jael liked that. She got a big kick out of the way the hens tried to hide their eggs, and she enjoyed searching out their hiding places. And the last place she always looked for eggs was up in the haymow.

She'd just stepped onto the soft sweet-smelling hay when she spotted Uncle Horace in the far dusky corner, up on a higher mound of alfalfa, playing with himself, eyelids closed tight with the pupils of his eyes rolling around under them like mice playing under a blanket. His full lips were drawn back in an elegant yearning expression. Her eyes opened in great surprise to see how large he was.

Steathily she backed down. She thought of making a noise of some kind to let him know she'd caught him. Like he'd caught her. But she decided against it.

Mother was probably right. Maybe there was something unholy about the way she left the door open when she went to the bathroom. Maybe she had a fixation of some kind. Like she might be inviting somebody, Uncle Horace, to come looking at her sitting on the seat. And catching her in an intimate moment.

Jael slipped into some lounging clothes, a blouse and a pair of slacks. She brushed her hair in front of the mirror until the hair ends jumped out like split cotton. She tried various postures to see which looked best; posed herself sideways to see what her silhouette was like; then, with a sigh, picked up the novel *Gone With the Wind* and lay down on her bed to read.

She had trouble concentrating on the story. She kept going back over the afternoon and all the things she and Alan had done. She loved the silky gold hairs on his arms. And the way those light-blue eyes of his looked at one, back and forth, it was as if he meant to pry into her very soul. She'd never met anyone so intense. She liked the gentle way he'd handled her. And as far as they'd gone it was lovely. She wondered if there was more. Of course when he'd reach into her someday that'd be new. There had to be something wonderful. And she wanted that. She'd help him hurry on to that time. She was ripe for it. She could still feel where she'd felt wet when they were kissing by the river. It had surprised her. She'd never felt that spreading soft feeling down there before. Like she was melting. She'd once heard her other aunt, Aunt Pauline, the one who'd married James Cameron, a broker, talk about how her knees always turned to butter when she looked at Clark Gable in a movie. It was a little like melting butter, all right. That thought reminded Jael of something. She got up off her bed and washed her blue panties in the bathroom. Mother was always complaining about her spotting and all the rest connected with her periods.

In fact, Mother often sounded like she preferred boys to girls. She'd told a friend of hers, Theodosia von Leer, that boys were a whole lot cleaner and easier to raise than girls.

Theodosia von Leer agreed with her. Theodosia had her own story about children. Theodosia had never wanted children, but her husband, John von Leer, felt it was his duty to carry on the von Leer line. So she'd submitted. The first one was a girl. Of course, a girl couldn't carry on the line. So after a lot of spitting and fighting over it, Theodosia'd submitted again. Postponing her own career. Well, their second child was also a girl.

Theodosia declared that was the end. No more. John von Leer was a warm and reasonable man, and he left her alone for a time. But when the second child was six years old, he began to lament he had no son to whom he might pass on his name and his business. He'd become a very wealthy corporation lawyer. If he'd had his druthers, he'd much rather had been named a justice to the state supreme court. When some politician would sidle up to John von Leer to feel him out about running on the Republican ticket, Theodosia would be right there to squelch it. "Heavens, don't encourage him to want to be judge. There's nothing he'd like better. When I need the money."

Theodosia lost out on both fronts. She caved in and allowed herself to become pregnant a third time. A month before the baby arrived, the governor suddenly announced the appointment of John von Leer to the state supreme court to fill a vacancy. And when the baby arrived, Theodosia shrieked when she learned she'd given birth to a third daughter.

Everybody in their set got ready for the next act in the Judge von Leer family drama. Would Theodosia submit once again to the judge's importunings in the hope their fourth child would be that longed-for heir and son? Well, they finally did try for the fourth child. But she never conceived. Nor did she ever embark on her own career. Poor Theodosia.

The von Leer story always made Jael smile.

And then there was Jael's own mother with her notion that she and her sisters had royal blood in their veins.

It'd taken Jael a while to work it out. Her mother, Gretta, and her two aunts, Sophie and Pauline, never talked out in the open about it, only whispered about it. One of their ancestors had been involved in something unholy, and they were afraid that if the truth ever got out, they'd be the scandal of the state of Minnesota. It involved royal blood, somehow. Some kind of bar-sinister line of descent.

One afternoon it finally popped out. Uncle Horace Green was one of those no-nonsense farmers, and when the three sisters at a family reunion rejected the idea that they have wine with the dinner, he exploded. "What the hell are you goddam dames so afraid of? That you won't be able to control yourself around men? Because your father was the bastard result of a wild moment by William the Third? If there is any of William the Third's blood left in you gals after two generations, it's pretty well watered down by now. If not dried up the way you three deny yourself fun of any kind. Good Christ. When the truth is, a royal line is more apt to improve, be built up, if a horny gardener sleeps with the queen, instead of a croupy king."

Back in 1877, William the Third of the Netherlands, Willem Paul Alexander Frederik Lodewijk, lost his wife, Sophia, and his two sons by her. Full of grief, William the Third began to drink, and in one of his drunken moments, seduced a Frisian girl named Gretta Hoffman from the island of Fosite. A bastard son was born to the Frisian girl. She named the boy William after the father. As fate would have it, the Frisian girl, Gretta Hoffman, died a year later. The bastard boy was spirited away to Denmark, to the island of Sylt, where he was raised a Dane with some foster parents named Paulsen. When he was ten years old he came to America with his foster parents. When he was twenty-one he married a Danish girl from Tyler, Minnesota, and with her he had three children, all girls—Gretta, Sophia, and Pauline Paulsen. William the Third, meanwhile, married Adelheid Emma Wilhelmina Theresia, second daughter of Prince George Victor of Waldeck-Pyrmont, and with her he had a daughter, who later on became the great Queen Wilhelmina of the Netherlands.

Jael didn't quite know what to think about all that royalty stuff. Her mother and her aunts were sometimes wrong about things. For example, they all three thought Uncle Horace was a good man, even Christlike the way he never bothered Aunt Sophie in bed anymore. They thought that despite his occasional outbursts of anger.

The fact was Uncle Horace, sweet as he might be, and Jael loved him, was a lecher. Jael knew. Uncle Horace had caught her in yet another intimate moment.

Jael was taking a bath in Uncle Horace's kitchen one Saturday night, using an old washtub, when, on looking up from soaping her limbs, she saw Uncle Horace standing in the doorway. She'd forgotten to close the door, thinking that everybody was outside on the lawn having a cool glass of lemonade. Uncle Horace, though balding, was a handsome man, brown lively eyes, full-lipped mouth, a good strong nose, wide square shoulders, and big muscles in his neck and over his back suggesting great power. Jael loved strength and she loved seeing it in Uncle Horace. She loved watching him pull off stunts on the yard, throwing a colt to the ground and hog-tying it so that he could castrate it, lifting the rear wheel of their Chevy onto a block of wood instead of jacking it up. He had big hands but he could be very tender with them.

Standing in the doorway, he quirked his eyes at her, finally said, "Jael, you're getting to be so grown up, pretty soon I'm going to have to open you up." Then he smiled at her in an uncly way and disappeared. Jael had never dared to tell anyone about that. Besides, she loved him. But she knew about him.

What griped her most was that her father, Tor Hemlickson, who had no particular claim to royal descent, should agree with Mother that Alan Ross wasn't good enough for their daughter Jael. Who was Father to point the finger, when he was making so little money they were slowly going deeper and deeper into debt?

Jael knew times were tough. The Hemlicksons were lucky to have a roof over their heads. Uncle Horace himself was just barely hanging on, mostly because his farm was clear of debt. Only Uncle James Cameron had it good; he and Pauline still had their Park Avenue apartment in New York. As a broker Uncle James had somehow managed to pick up several dozen farms for a song just before the great Bank Holiday, and the farms were now paying off handsomely.

Father was a dreamer, really. Anyone selling life insurance in hard times had to be a dreamer. People considered life insurance a luxury. And it seemed the less insurance Father sold, the more he dreamed of the day when they'd buy a home near the Edina Country Club as well as buy a membership in the club. "A couple of breaks," Father promised Mother, "and the whole thing just might turn around for us."

Lying on her bed in her own room, Jael thought again about the afternoon she'd had with Alan, and how they'd dreamed in each other's arms as they sat by the placid green Minnesota River, and how Alan had wanted to but out of deference to her parents had held back.

Finally Jael flipped herself off her bed and sat down at her little green study table and wrote Alan a letter. She used her best-scented stationery.

*Dear Alan,*

*I'm still up in the clouds after our tryst in our secret place, our private paradise. I'm writing this to let you know that all that happened this afternoon was wonderful. Doors are opening ahead for us. Remember how we sat just at the edge of a grove with a meadow opening out before us? That's how it will be for us in life. We are just emerging from youth and ignorance and are about to sally forth onto the wide meadows of life. Oh, Alan, how I love the electricity of you. How I love those strange wonderful eyes of yours. I sense power in you. And I must have power.*

*I'll try to surprise you again at the paper next week.*

*Yours,*
*Jael*

*P.S. Seven red apples hanging from a red-brown bough!*

Jael looked at the letter, pleased at the way she'd centered it all on the page. Jael then read the letter as Alan might read it, then read it critically as her teacher Abigail might read it. With a little self-smile she addressed the creamy envelope, licked the flap, and sealed it.

She searched through her little desk for a stamp; couldn't find any. "Darn. And I don't dare ask Mother for one." Jael sat scheming a few moments, and then hit on it.

She changed into a blue dress and blouse, white socks and blue tennies, and slipped the letter to Alan inside her blouse. Then casually she strolled out into the parlor where Mother and Father were sitting listening to the radio, and said, "I'm going down to Jerre Thornton's a minute."

Father was instantly alert. "What for?"

"I'm going to try once again to persuade her to come to the U with me this fall."

"Oh."

"That'll be all right, won't it?"

"Yes, I guess so."

Mother all the while sat looking sad and petulant.

Smiling, Jael passed on through the door and down the steps. A half block down the street, she broke into an easy run. Jerre lived three blocks down Portland.

Jael walked into the Thornton home without knocking, calling ahead, cheer in her voice, "Hello? Hello?"

"I'm in the bathroom," Jerre called out. "Be with you in a jiff."

Jael sat down in a blue armchair in the parlor. The Thorntons liked warm blue floral designs, in the wallpaper, in the slipcovers on the armchairs and davenport.

Presently Jerre came out. She was as tall as Jael but not put together as well. She walked a trifle awkward and had large kneecaps. Her hair was not quite as gold. She had, though, a fuller bosom than Jael. She was one of those who, when they reached the age of thirty, would suddenly be considered a beautiful woman. She'd grow into her beauty. Jerre had a quiet warm smile for Jael. "This is a nice surprise." She settled in a blue armchair across from Jael.

"I need a three-cent stamp." Jael removed the letter to Alan from her blouse. "I ran out."

"Just a sec." Jerre got up and rustled through a writing desk in a corner. "Ah, still got some left." She handed Jael the stamp.

Jael licked the stamp, placed it on the envelope, and then put the letter back in her blouse.

"That must be a special letter."

"It is. To Alan." Jael had been careful not to tell Jerre too much about Alan for fear of hurting her feelings. Jerre never had dates. The boys liked to talk to Jerre but never dated her.

"Then you didn't see him today like you planned."

"We went for a ride down along the Minnesota River. It was so enchanting. The river flowing silently outside our car."

Jerre sat a little more erect in her armchair. "Then did you park somewhere?"

Jael thought it over, then decided that for once she could tell somebody something intimate. She couldn't help it if Jerre often had that left-out feeling. "Yes, we went riverbanking."

"You mean . . . ?"

"Not all the way, if that's what you're wondering." Jael smiled to herself. "But we had a wonderful time."

Jerre sat even straighter. Her mouth remained warm in its smile, but her eyes opened in startled light-blue wonder. "If he ever asks you to do it, will you?"

Jael thought it over. She parried, "Would you?"

Jerre settled back in her chair, eyes half closing in reverie. "If it ever got to that, and I loved him . . . yes! I can't wait to begin life."

Jael was startled in turn. "Jerre!"

A lovely flush suffused Jerre's face, making her look very pretty. "Dad and Mother are always having so much fun together I just can't wait to start my own life. I just know they do it every night."

Jael envied Jerre her parents.

"You don't know how lucky you are," Jerre continued. "I'm so anxious to meet Alan."

Jael smiled a half-smile. She wasn't going to let Jerre see Alan until she herself had him securely in hand. "Well, maybe even he isn't going to be the right one." Jael was remembering an athlete at Central High who was madly in love with her.

"You don't think he'll be the permanent one then?"

"I'll tell you more after we see each other some more."

"Well, I wish you a lot of happiness."

"Thank you." Jael looked at the clock on the mantel. "Heavens, I've got to go. They collect the mail on the corner at eight. And I want Alan to get this at work tomorrow." She jumped to her feet.

Jerre took her to the door. "I haven't met your Alan yet, but he sounds exciting. Give him my best."

"I will. I will."

Jael hurried down the street in the dark. The wind had turned north, and it blew a few early fall leaves toward her down the sidewalk. She was just about to drop the letter in the green mailbox on the corner under the streetlight when a brown mail truck drove up. She handed the letter to the gray-clad driver.

On the last few steps home she dragged her feet. One thing she was going to make sure of. Jerre was not going to meet Alan until she herself had him safely in hand. Jerre was probably better for Alan than she was. Like Alan, Jerre was serious and true-telling. Like him, Jerre would also be faithful to the end of her days. He probably came from stock a lot like Jerre's with no bar-sinister problem involved.

As she climbed the steps into her house, Jael once again made up her mind that, come fall when college started, she'd visit Alan Ross in his apartment near the university and really get to know him.

Seven red apples hanging from a red-brown bough.

# Chapter 6

# ALAN

---

Alan could hear Quinsey Quinn come laughing and ho-hoing down the hall of the *Chronicle*. In a moment Quinsey waddled into the sports department, face red. His cigar, burned to within an inch of his lips, waggled loosely. "Gents, I just now heard the best yet. Heh, those blokes who rim the horseshoe upstairs, holy cow."

Everyone looked up, Alan, Burt Cowens, Mark Josephson, Hank Williams.

Quinsey settled in his chair, carefully removed the short cigar from his lips and set it precisely on the edge of his desk with the burning ash sticking out, then hauled his chair around. "You know our Harvard aesthete on the rim, Sir Waite Taylor? Well, I just heard about him getting his comeuppance." Quinsey swelled up like a bellows and laughed some more. His fingers began to flex spasmodically as though cramps were setting in, two of them bending back at an awkward angle.

Burt Cowens smiled quietly from his corner. "Well, Quinse, you better get it out before you choke to death."

Quinsey pinched his brown eyes shut several times. "I guess it is improper for a man to laugh about a joke before he's told it. Well. So. Our Sir Waite has been giving the Yale boys on the rim a rough time of it lately, about a story that came over the teletype. You know, those stories the teletypists send each other when there's a lull in the news? A son of one of our own downtown babbitts, Donald Day, was involved in a scandal at Yale. One of the lads in a Yale dormitory picked up a girl some thirteen years old, mature for her age but dumb, and began passing her around among themselves, first on the main floor of the dormitory, and then on to the second floor and so on, until our dear Donald also had a chance to dip his pen in the common inkwell. Well sir, the upshot of it all was, one of the boys got compunctions of conscience and spilled the beans. The dean of men got hold of it, and now it seems dear Donald is going to be hauled into court for contributing to the delinquency of a minor. A gang shag in the upper crust. Hee-hee-hee." Quinsey exploded into another laughing fit. "Lightning can strike anywhere, can't it?"

"Quinse," Burt broke in, "I'm sure what you're about to tell us is going to be one helluva story, but I've got to get this column finished by eleven."

"Oh. Good point. Well sir, Sir Waite, our Harvard aesthete, has been riding our Yale men about this until not even hell would have it. Finally Ned Perkins, our vet from Yale, had enough. He quietly went over and asked the teletype man if he couldn't get one of his friends up the line to make up a story about a Harvard sex scandal." Quinsey shook his grizzled head. "The one he got back over the wire was a honey. Hee-hee-hee."

Alan himself was in a hurry to finish a story before eleven. Yet he couldn't resist leaning back in his chair and waiting.

"Well sir, once again this morning Sir Waite just simply had to ask if there'd been any more bulletins about the Yale-bluebloods-screwing-that-young-girl situation. After a proper pause, Ned Perkins says, 'No, nothing new on that Yale affair. But we did get a hot flash about a Harvard scandal.' 'Harvard? What happened there?' 'Oh, some fellows in one of the dorms got caught playing with a little boy of twelve.' Perkins picks up a fresh teletype and tosses it over to Sir Waite. 'Here, see for yourself.' Sir Waite stares at the teletype. Perkins says Sir Waite's mouth dropped open like a tailgate to a truck. Then Perkins asks, 'What do you think, Waite, shall we make that a box story on the front page? I know just the head for it too. "Cornholing in the Halls of Ivy at Ol' Harvard." ' "

There was a hearty laugh all around.

Soon they were all back at their typewriters, irregularly clattering away. The noisiest typewriter was Quinsey's. Quinsey was a remarkably fast hunt-and-peck typist. He used only one finger, all the while leaning on his left arm.

Later in the morning, right after the first edition had been put to bed, Alan was surprised to see Waite Taylor come shambling in through their door.

Quinsey took one look, allowed himself a rippling shudder of the right shoulder, and then turned his head and neck against Waite and set to typing furiously on a feature story for next Sunday's paper. His one finger pecked so fast and hard it resembled the bill of a red-shafted flicker. Burt, who could watch the Gophers score a winning touchdown in the last second of a football game without skipping a heartbeat, looked up in mild interest. "Well, Waite, what brings you in here?"

Waite glanced around the room, giving each man a fatuous smile, then finally advanced on Quinsey.

Quinsey set his head even farther against Waite.

Burt barely smiled. "You aren't bringing us any bad news now, are you, Waite?"

Alan and Mark and Hank leaned back in their chairs, waiting. In a moment Quinsey was going to explode if someone didn't get Waite out of there.

Waite was one of the most unlikely men to have ever graduated from fastidious Harvard. He was hump-shouldered, balding over the back of his head with the strangest brush of short brown hair shooting off the forehead, gap-toothed, Adam's-appled, no buttocks whatever, with the front of his pants almost obscenely thrust forward.

Waite put his foot up on the edge of Quinsey's desk, right next to where Quinsey's still-burning stub of a cigar was smoking away. "What was all the merriment about I heard down here this morning, hey? Sounded like it was some kind of comedian." When Waite talked he had a curious way of wobbling his lips.

"Merriment?" Burt interceded. "This morning? No, in fact things have been rather placid around here."

Waite leered across the room at Burt. "C'mon now, I heard someone down here braying away like Sancho Panza's old gray donkey." Waite threw a knowing look down at Quinsey's bowed head. "Everybody upstairs heard it."

"Must have come from the darkroom behind us then," Burt said. "You know how those photographers like to tell off-color jokes."

"No no, I heard it from here. Some silly fellow was braying away here to a fare-thee-well."

Alan could understand how Quinsey felt about Waite. Sometimes their editor-in-chief, Harley Smathers, or Old Smithereens as the boys liked to call him, made a visit to the sports department and invariably stopped at Alan's desk, the first desk by the doorway, and, lifting his trouserleg and then his leg, planked his elegant shiny black oxford right on top of Alan's desk, often right on top of Alan's notes. Alan often had to sit a good quarter of an hour staring out of the corner of his eye at Harley Smathers' blue silk Argyle sock, all the while listening to Smathers' theories as to why the Gophers were losing or the Millers were splitting doubleheaders.

Waite rattled on, lips wobbling away. "I thought maybe you were laughing at the way our paper handled the latest pheasant story."

"What was that?" Burt asked.

"Oh, hadn't you heard? No? Well, it seems Judge Jack Connell got caught with twenty-five pheasants in the back of his car by a local game warden out near Canby. Way over the legal limit. But what did our paper do about it? We stuck the story in the back part of the paper, in the financial section. Besides that, we dropped the judge's title, changed his first name to John, and so didn't in effect really report who he was."

"Hmm."

Hank Williams loved Quinsey and decided to put in a thrust for him. "Say, Waite, how are you and your buddy Ned Perkins getting along these days?"

There was a choked cough from Quinsey.

Waite sneered. "Ned? That asslicker?"

Burt said, "C'mon, Ned is one of our very best men."

"Burt, I don't know if you knew this or not, but Ned is truly a first-class asskisser. Why, years ago, when he started on the rim, he was so nervous he'd sweat so hard he'd stink by four o'clock. Fact."

"Maybe we all were nervous when we first got started."

"Yeh, but the trouble with Ned is, he stayed nervous. Why, Harley Smathers' ass hasn't had time to get chapped yet."

"Strange language for a Harvard man to be using."

"And while we're talking about asslickers, we mustn't forget old Minus McNab, our managing editor. Why, Minus is a plain down-and-out son of a bitch. I discovered that the night I helped him get out the last edition of the Sunday paper two weeks ago. I found him falling-down drunk in the foyer downstairs. I helped him upstairs here, filled him full of coffee, wrote his heads for him, did all his work . . . and what did he do? When it came time to cover up for me once, he chopped me up. The son of a bitch."

No one had much to say to that. Minus wasn't liked by anybody on the paper.

Waite hauled up his crotch where it hung over Quinsey's head. " 'Course, the owners of the *Chronicle* here ain't much better. Strange crew, that lot." Waite tolled his head lugubriously. "The Jeffry boys. Four of them. There's Lloyd, he's the magician. There's Jack, he hunts and fishes. There's Philip, he's one step from the loony bin. And then there's Bose; he sits and picks his nose . . . and eats it."

Everybody looked at Quinsey. Quinsey was often seen at the Jeffry social doings up on Mt. Curve Avenue.

"But now you take their old man, old Thomas Jeffry, why, there was a real newspaperman. When he ran this show here at the *Chronicle,* we had a tight-run paper. Were he alive today, the first one he'd boot out of here, besides Ned Perkins, would be that hoity-toity Glenda Underland. God, the mistakes she makes. And the hell of it is, we aren't supposed to touch her copy. Orders from Old Smithereens himself. She comes from Smathers' social set and that makes her his equal."

Alan sort of liked Glenda Underland. Glenda had deep-set haunting brown eyes. She'd written one novel, *Myself,* which had gotten good reviews in New York. She wrote a high-class gossip column for the *Chronicle.* And she was the editor of the society section. Alan had several times stopped by her desk upstairs to talk about books, and once went to a cocktail party at her house on Lake Calhoun. She was by no means merely a social butterfly. She worked. She loved to probe inner thoughts and feelings, her own as well as those of others.

Waite prattled on, "Glenda is a soul-sucker. She's always asking you about your innermost innard feelings. Christ! Well, I fixed her the other week."

Quinsey ducked down even farther.

"Technically, her copy is supposed to go over my desk. But hell, I just go through the motions. Because if I do touch it, she bitches to high heaven, and then old Minus McNab eats out my ass because Old Smithereens next eats out his. Well, she not only writes her own copy, she writes her own heads. So this one day she turns in a story about Mrs. Pillsbury. The Minneapolis Women's Club'd held a business meeting at which the various officers gave their reports. Mrs. Pillsbury, the treasurer, gave the financial report. Glenda decided to feature her social buddy Mrs. Pillsbury in the lead paragraph. Then she wrote the banner headline. MRS. PILLSBURY TO GIVE ASSETS. The minute I spotted that headline I knew there was something wrong with it. Too long. So I counted it, and sure enough it was three letters too long. There was no way it was going to fit across the top of that page."

Alan got the picture instantly, and laughed.

"So I decided to let it go as typed. I took it up to the composing room and got them to agree, along with the pressroom boys, to run off one copy of her banner head with as much of it as they could set, then to stop the presses and put in a corrected headline for the city run. I myself saw to it that that one copy landed on her desk. Well, boys, you should have been there when she came back from lunch around two o'clock. She comes in tinkling compliments right and left and settles down at her desk. Right away she opens on the society section. She reads the banner headline once. MRS. PILLSBURY TO GIVE ASS. She reads it a second time; shrieks; faints. Both Minus and Old Smithereens come rushing out wanting to know what the hell all the fuss is about. When it's explained to them, they cuss a little, but then I'll be damned if they still don't leave orders that Glenda Underland's copy is still to be set up as is. The witch."

Quinsey hadn't been able to resist listening to the last part of Waite's account and let out a short blast of laughter to join the other boys, took a suck of his cigar butt, and went back to typing.

Waite finally ran out of talk. He looked at his wristwatch. "Well, gents, I guess I better get back to the salt mines." He removed his foot from the edge of Quinsey's desk.

Quinsey threw a long-suffering look up at Waite and fixed his eyes on Waite's lips. "Well, holy cow, Waite, I'm sure glad you finally thought of something to do. You were talking so much your mouth was beginning to look like a duck's ass wobbling away."

Everybody had been waiting for a Quinsey squelcher of some kind. There were roars of laughter. Burt, the calm one, laughed the hardest. He slowly slid down in his swivel chair.

Waite turned beet red. Then, abashed, he slunk out of the sports department.

Around four o'clock, only Alan and Burt were left in the office.

Burt finally finished the piece he was writing, pulled it out of his typewriter, and proofread it himself. When he finished, and had spiked it on the spindle at the head of his desk, he threw Alan a look. "Working late today, I see."

"Yeh, I ran into a pretty good story over at the Northeast Neighborhood House. Thought it might make a good Sunday feature."

"What's that?" Burt had a smile for him. After the first rough month Burt had decided Alan was all right. Burt had asked him to do a little sleuthing for him in the University of Minnesota locker rooms to help him write even more penetrating think columns.

"Well, I ran into a fellow who's probably responsible for all those basketball stars coming from that part of town." Northeast Minneapolis, or Nordeast as the natives called it, was truly the melting pot of the Twin Cities. Immigrants usually first landed in Nordeast: Danes, Swedes, Norskies, Poles, Russkies, Slovaks, Jews. It was also the district with the highest crime rate: rapes, robberies, muggings, and runaways. "Marty Koler. Used to be a guard for St. John's.

Wanted to be a priest, instead took up social work. And in his spare time he goes over to the neighborhood house and teaches the little kids how to shoot baskets one-handed."

Burt's thin brown brows came up. His light-blue eyes widened. "One-handed? So that's where they got it."

Alan said, "I think he's right, too. Coaches up to now have been teaching kids to shoot two-handed. But Koler says your two hands never moved in perfect tandem. One arm is usually stronger and more fluid than the other. If you're right-handed, your right hand will move stronger and smoother than your left. When you shoot with one hand there is only one motion. If the motion is true, the ball will go in. When you shoot with both hands, one hand is apt not to move as true as the other."

"I'll be damned." Burt looked out of the window, musing to himself. "It just might revolutionize all of basketball."

"And you should see how Koler teaches the kid how to hold the basketball. In one hand, like a waiter carrying a bowl of soup through a crowded cafe. Up over the head and out of reach of the guard. Then he shows him how to flip it, easy and smooth. With just the right rifling, so it won't drift off course. Float off."

"You got that all in your story?"

"Yes."

"Good." Burt's eyes narrowed. "Give it to me before you hand it over to Mark. I want to see it before he marks it up."

"Okay."

Alan concentrated on the last paragraph. If he could end it with just the right kind of flourish, it would be the best story he'd written so far for the *Chronicle*.

Burt got up from his swivel chair and slipped into his gray suit jacket. "You know, Alan, I've been thinking." Burt moved stiffly past his typing stand. He groaned and rubbed his right side. "How would you like to help me cover boxing some?"

"Well, I don't know much about it, but I sure as heck can learn."

Burt nodded. "My hip's been kicking up a lot lately, and it's slowed me down. There are a half dozen spots in town I should drop in on now and then. Kott's Gymnasium for one. The back room behind Al's Bar. But I find I just can't cover them all anymore."

"They box a little at the Northeast Neighborhood House too."

"There you go." Burt rubbed his side some more. "What do you say?"

"What shall I cut out, then?"

"Well, not track. Tell you what, skip doing half as much nosing around the locker rooms at the U, and spend the other half of that poking around Kott's Gym and so on."

"If you say so, boss."

"Good." Burt stepped over to a mirror in a corner and combed back his few gray hairs. He wriggled his wrinkles at himself. Then, turning stiffly, he left for the day.

Alan sat awhile in thought. He turned to look out of the window. Across the street pigeons were clappering over the roof of Rothchild's Clothing Store. The sun struck sideways across the various heights of the downtown black-tar rooftops. Purple shadows had begun to mist up from the paved streets. The sidewalks were thick with throngs of women shoppers and secretaries leaving for home. Minneapolis really had beautiful women: tall and sun-blond and long-legged, all of them smiling as if they were just then ready to fall in love. Far off in the distance Alan could just make out the pink church spire of the Russian Greek Orthodox Church near the Northeast Neighborhood House. The far window near Quinsey's desk was open, and through it came the roar of the late-afternoon traffic, horns snarling, streetcars dingling their bells a block away, trucks snorting, newsboys hawking their papers.

At last, with a sigh, Alan turned back to his typewriter, scratched up his scattered thoughts into some order again, and finished the story on the Nordeasters. He read it for sense and typos, then spiked it on Burt's spindle.

As he took the cage elevator down, he noticed the hot air drifting up from the pressroom. The smell of ink had become for him in the short while he'd worked for the paper as pleasant a thing as the aroma of alfalfa hay in Pa's barn. Alan thought it thrilling to be a newspaperman. If society could be thought of as a flowing river, then he was sitting in the middle of one of its cataracts.


The following Friday, desk clear of work, Alan headed for Kott's Gym on Hennepin and Sixth. He turned into the Hennepin Arcade and descended some steps into the basement. Kott's Gym took up the entire basement. There were support pillars everywhere, yet despite them Stanley Kott had managed to install four separate boxing rings, along with an exercise room, a shower room, and a locker room.

Stanley Kott was a health addict, a tough bantam athlete who hadn't aged much over the years. He had dedicated himself to the cause of keeping the American male healthy through exercise and proper eating habits. He loved boxing especially, and was always on the lookout for a promising new find. Several of his boys had gone on to become challengers in the various weight divisions.

Alan wrinkled his nose at the smell of sweaty socks and jockstraps. There was also the smell of liniment and red Mercurochrome. Two big exhaust fans in the basement windows just couldn't keep up with the rank odors.

In the exercising area there was the slap-slap of a boxer skipping rope. Still another novice was working in front of a mirror. A flabby fellow was banging out a rhythm on a light punching bag while a skinny fellow was thudding his fists into a heavy bag suspended from the ceiling.

All four rings were busy. The one nearest the door had a couple of bantamweights going at it, grunting with every heavy punch, their boxing gloves smacking wetly as they hit flesh, with seconds cheering them on and a referee peeking into their clinches to make sure everything was above the belt. There was a continual squeak of boxing shoes twisting on canvas. In the second ring a coach was showing a crude young fellow how to bring in a right cross. In the third ring an old pug was showing a youngster how important footwork was, in ducking shots as well as in delivering them.

Stanley Kott himself was watching a pair of boxers in the fourth ring. Stanley kept rising on his toes and leaning his body left to right and back again in unconscious imitation of the action above him. Stanley was about five foot six, with small hands and feet, yet because of a good-sized chest and large biceps appeared to be a big man. He was some sixty years old and had the bouncy look of a man of twenty-five. The skin over his lean freckled cheek was pink. He wore his hair cut short and there wasn't a touch of gray in it. The only place his age showed was in the corners of his blue eyes.

After Alan introduced himself, Kott asked, "Where's Burt?"

"He's got it bad in the hip. He asked me to check your joint."

"Well, he's missing something then. I've told him a couple times to drop around and watch this new guy I got working out here. He's something."

"In the ring there now?"

"Yep, the guy in the red trunks. With his back to us."

The guy in the red trunks at the moment didn't look particularly impressive. He was slow, almost to the point of being clumsy, though he did have a powerful body, good legs, round compact narrow hips, wide-spreading shoulders, and a thick neck. Just before he made his moves he had an odd way of shaking or trembling.

"Pigsticker named Red from South St. Paul," Kott went on. "Moonlighting as a boxer."

"What's he doing here on a workday?"

"Slack part of the week for him. If not too many hogs come in, they only kill in the early part of the week."

The pair up in the ring slowly veered around, and Alan at last had a good look at the fellow's face inside his headgear. Alan said. "My God."

Kott looked at Alan. "You see it too?"

"Yeh."

"Power to burn there."

"Yeh."

"If I could only find some way to ignite it."

Alan wasn't seeing what Kott was seeing. "There he is at last," he whispered to himself. "My lost brother John."

"Hey," Kott said, "you mean Red's your brother? And his real name ain't John Engleking?"

"Is that his name?"

"Yeh, John Engleking." Kott gave Alan a high wondering look. "What do you mean, Red's your brother?"

Alan quick covered up. "What I mean is . . . this Red reminds me of someone." Alan stared up at John Engleking. Besides having the same first name, Red had many other characteristics of his haunt twin brother: ruddy face, live gold hair with a touch of red in it, deep-blue eyes. The only thing Red lacked was that confident little smile of the champ.

The other boxer, an older man known as Blackie Kavold, landed a low blow. It caught Red in the testicles. Red doubled over in pain, stumbled against the ropes to recover. Blackie, a squat alley fighter, with black hairy arms, seeing his advantage, jumped in for the kill.

Kott arched himself up on his toes. "Oh, dear." Kott was never known to swear. "Watch out, Red!"

It was too late. Before even the referee could jump in between them, hairy squat Blackie caught Red on the side of his face, snapping his head around, dropping him to one knee.

"C'mon, Red, fall into a clinch if you have to."

Red rested on his one knee, trying to get his breath, while the referee shooed Blackie to a neutral corner.

"Red! You knew Blackie fights dirty. Even in sparring practice."

Red slowly got on top of the pain in his crotch. His ruddy face turned a deeper red, and a cunning little smile curled back his lips.

Then Red erupted, whirling up off the canvas and around so quickly that he caught Blackie with his hands down and his mouth open. Red slid forward and made just two short moves. His left hand shot out as quick as a cat's paw, a lightning jab which landed with crackling force; his right hand followed with a short right cross, a real jolter socking home. It was done in almost one continuous move, bing-bing. Blackie fell in a heap, knocked out.

"See what I mean?" Kott cried. Kott was beside himself with excitement. He leaped up and down, did the one-two punching motion, then leaped up once more. "That was a wonderful maneuver. That means quick reactions, sound legs, good balance."

"Holy suffering Peter," Alan whispered.

"The thing is, Red doesn't do that often enough. And I don't know just how I can get him to do it oftener, either. I can't very well ask the other fighter to hit him in the family jewels every time."

Alan sat down on a folding chair. Not only was Red up there in the ring a dead ringer for the haunt twin brother Alan had whomped up for himself over the years, but for a moment he even had Haunt John's little cunning smile of the champ. What a strange and wonderful coincidence. Alan stared so hard at Red that his eyes began to hurt in the sharp light coning down over the boxing ring.

Kott noticed Alan's staring. Again he misread it. "Ain't he something? Wow!" Kott shook his head. "The trouble is, that's only the second time I've seen him do that, and he's been working out here for a couple of months. Buster, that ain't often enough to get by as a pro."

"Has he had any bouts yet?"

"Three. He won the first one by a knockout when the other boxer called him a pig humper. I guess that's the one thing you don't call a farm boy. But then Red lost the next two on points."

Red stood over Blackie ready for more. But Blackie was done for the day. He came to very slowly. He lay blinking his black eyes up at the cone of light. Finally he snorted and shook his head several times and raised himself up on his elbows.

When Red saw that Blackie wasn't interested in fighting anymore that day, he relaxed. "Sorry about that."

Blackie stared up at him. "You kiddin'? Hell, I had it coming to me." Blackie shook his head once more. "Christ almighty, I feel like I've been hit by a wrecking ball."

"No swearing, please," Kott warned.

"You'd swear too, Stanley old boy, if you got hit like that." Blackie reached up a hand and Red helped him to his feet in a single powerful pull. "Kid, I'd heard you had a killer punch. But when I crawled in the ring with you a little while ago, you didn't look like any great shakes to me. And after rubbing mitts with you for a couple of rounds, I figured it was just a lot of ringside bullshit."

Red's big gloved hands tried to find a pocket to hide in. A curious tremble moved through him.

"Take it from me, kid. If you could just once, in any given fight you're in, turn that tiger loose in you for ten seconds, you could be the champ of the world."

"That's what I say," Kott cried. "But how do you get him to turn it loose?"

Red looked down at the floor of the ring. "Funny thing is, I hate myself when I get that way."

"You don't mean it."

"I sure do."

Blackie cuffed himself over the forehead with his boxing glove. "And when I get mad I can't see a damn thing and completely lose my head. While you, why . . ."

Red shook his head. "It ain't Christian. I was only hoping I could take up boxing to pick up a little extra change."

Blackie next clapped Red on the back with the side of his boxing glove. "Red, you're some case, you are. Come on, let's call it a day and have us a shower."

"All right. I guess I've had enough too."

Both boxers climbed through the ropes and together ambled off toward the shower room.

Kott gave Alan a beatific smile. "Ain't he something? A nice good-natured kid from the country and he's got a concealed weapon in him."

Alan got out paper and pencil and began making a few notes. "You say he's a pigsticker?"

"Yeh. Steele Packinghouse in South St. Paul."

"How come he trains here in your gym?"

"Guess he heard I run a Christian place."

"Is he married? Got kids?"

"Married, yes. Kids, no. I guess his wife is sick a lot and can't have any."

"Maybe that accounts for it."

"You'll tell Burt what you saw?"

"I'll tell him."

The next morning Alan talked to Burt.

Burt listened with a quizzical smile for a few minutes, then broke in. "Well, Alan, I haven't seen him, you have. If you think this Red is worth a story, write it."

"But I thought . . . well, if he turns out to be the real McCoy, don't you want him? You usually cover the main fighters around here."

"No, you found him, you cover him." Burt smiled indulgently. "After reading your Nordeast story I know you can handle it."

Alan began to glow inside. "Thanks." Burt could have dropped him when he first started at the *Chronicle* because of all the mistakes he'd made, misspelled names, typos, wordiness. Each day after the paper came out Burt always made it a practice to circle a misspelling or a typo with a big red-leaded pencil and then to tear out the sheet and tack it up on the bulletin board for all to see. The first two weeks Alan made nine such mistakes, and all of them with Burt's noisy red marks had wound up on the bulletin board.

Burt added, "Dig into his background a little. What kind of family life he has. So on."

Alan was going to say, "The who what when and where of him, eh?" but then remembered that Burt had once said there were only two things a reporter should remember when he bellied up to his typewriter to write a story: "What did you see and how did you see it."

Alan found nothing but broken toothpicks in his head that morning. He kept making one typing error after another.

The truth was Alan hadn't had much sleep. Running into a boxer named Red had been a scary thing to him. It was almost as if, far back, some kind of prescience had been at work in him, getting him ready to meet a certain John Engleking. It was as if the fates had first arranged for him to learn he'd had a twin brother, then had helped him whomp up a haunt brother, and then had presented him with a live flesh-and-blood one.

Alan envied Red his ruddy coloring. Alan had often wished there might be a pill he could take which would give him more pigment, a redding agent that would work like bluing. Then he could have had brown eyebrows and brown lashes instead of faint white brows and thick white sandy lashes.

Alan wandered off to the men's room. He found Quinsey relieving himself at one of the urinals.

Quinsey gave him a smiling nod. "It comes to all men sooner or later. Even the President."

"I guess so." Alan first spit in the urinal and then let his stream fly.

"Holy cow," Quinsey said, "then it's true!"

"What is?"

"That when a man starts to take a leak he always first spits in the urinal."

"Did I spit first?"

"You sure did." Quinsey laughed. "I caught on to that when I went to interview Ox Ecklund after he'd hit an opposite-field home run. I spotted him doing it."

"Like a dog having to circle around a couple of times first before he finds the right spot to lie down in."

"Right, right." Quinsey finished and buttoned up.

"It's probably something that goes back to when we were monkeys up in the trees, and we first spit to make sure there were no enemies below, and then let fly."

"Hey there, boy, now you're getting deep on me."

Alan finished up too and joined Quinsey at the washbowls. He soaped his hands. "I wonder what the girls do before they take a leak."

Quinsey's brown eyes rolled, and he let go with a good hearty laugh. "Maybe they were the ones who did it in the first place, to make sure there were no snakes in the grass, and then turned around and squatted over the spot. And then we men aped them."

"Or they were making sure there were no mice lurking in the grass."

Quinsey laughed some more. "Or a wild asparagus about to pop out of the ground."

At eleven-thirty, desk cleared and the makeup of the first afternoon edition finished, Alan got out the St. Paul telephone directory and looked up John Engleking's address. There was only one John Engleking and he lived on 324 First Avenue South in South St. Paul.

Alan got his car from the parking lot and in very bright sunshine headed east down Washington Avenue. Crossing the Mississippi on the Lake Street bridge, he was soon tooling easy through the shadows of the arching elms along Summit Avenue. In downtown St. Paul he again crossed the Mississippi on a high arching bridge. Soon he found Concord Street and followed it all the way out to the stockyards.

By the time he got to Steele Avenue, where it led down to the gates of the Steele Packinghouse, he found himself hungry. He drove into a parking lot alongside Nick's Cafe. Nick's was a one-story structure fitted in between the street and a high steep cliff. Looking up, Alan could see that houses had been built out to the very edge of the precipice.

Alan entered Nick's. It was dim inside. A bar ran along the right wall. Some dozen tables with four chairs each stood in neat even rows down the middle of the cafe. Booths lined the left wall.

Alan spotted an empty table in the corner near the front window. He took the fartherest chair so he could sit with his back to the wall. He had a good view of both the activity inside the cafe and the movement of animals in the stockyards below.

A good dozen men stood at the bar drinking beer. The barkeep was a wide-smiling man with straight-back black hair. When he wasn't setting up a beer, he was busy polishing the shiny mahogany bar. Two women cooks, middle-aged, heavy-set, slaved over a long black hot stove in back, whacking down hamburger patties, flipping steaks, heating biscuits. Four waitresses scurried out among the tables taking orders, cleaning up tables.

At a nearby table five yard workers in dung-spattered jeans were playing a quick game of pinochle while waiting for their orders. All wore red rubber boots, freshly hosed off. Every now and then one of them would get up and refull his cup from one of the coffee pots behind the counter. They were at home in the place. Two tables farther down sat a young family, father and mother and two little girls. From their clothes Alan guessed them to be from the farm. The whole family had come along with the old man to deliver a load of hogs. The missus was pin-neat and kept picking at the girls to sit straight. The mister kept smiling to himself. It was obvious he'd got a good price for his animals. Sitting alone one table over was a great fat fellow. He sat with his legs apart, belly almost resting on his knees. He wore expensive clothes, a shiny blue suit, white shirt, expensive red silk tie with a gleaming ruby-crested stickpin. Even his chin ballooned down.

Two men at the bar fell into a good-natured wrangle. One was very tall with a high potbelly which he kept hefting up with the inside of his elbows. The other man had an artificial right arm which he was at pains to show wasn't a handicap. He kept picking up his glass of beer with his metal hand and taking a quick swig. The metal fingers made a strange crinkling sound on the glass.

Tall potbelly said, "Trouble with you is, you don't read enough out-state papers. Then you'd know if the farmers out there was going to market their hogs during a certain week or not."

Iron hand said, "I listen to the market reports over WCCO. And if they don't know, then nobody knows."

Tall potbelly said, "How do you think I got where I did?" He gave his pot a hard whack. "By reading what the editors at Holdingford and Sleepy Eye say."

Iron hand said, "I ain't done so bad."

A fat blond smiling waitress finally spotted Alan. She came over with a glass of water and the menu.

Alan pushed the menu to one side. "I just want a malted milk and a hamburger with."

"Chocolate? Pineapple?"

"Chocolate."

"Comin' up." She gave him a wink, and ambled off. Her heavy legs were well shaped. Her green smock fit tight on her, buttons straining in the eyeholes.

Alan sipped his water. It tasted of minerals.

Two farmers in overalls came in and settled at the next table. Their faces, freshly shaved that morning, shone like lacquered apples. They'd barely got their order in for a hot beef sandwich when high potbelly lolled over.

High potbelly said, "Well, Si, how's she going down your way?"

"Kinda dry."

"You farmers all say that. Always complaining. If it rains, it's too wet for the corn to mature, and if the sun shines, it's too dry and you get nothing but nubbins."

"We take what the Lord provides, Harvey."

Clanging noises continued to come out of the kitchen. A marvelous smell of frying prime hamburger wisped through the place. Someone stuck a nickel in the jukebox, and after the sharp sound of a record being whapped into place, an old tune, "When It's June in January," began wailing through the cafe.

A tall handsome man with sunny blond hair and swinging a cane entered the cafe with an easy limber stride. He wore the clothes of a buyer for a commission firm, tan tweed pants, white shirt, a pair of high leather boots.

Harvey spotted him and grabbed him by the arm. They whispered together a moment. Harvey wanted the latest dope.

The plump waitress came out with a malted and a hamburger and placed it in front of Alan. She placed the bill at Alan's elbow. Then she rolled over to where the blond man stood. She placed her hand on his elbow and with a wink asked, "Well, Elmer, and how's Mr. Handsome today?"

Elmer gave her a fleeting smile.

Harvey was jealous. "How come Nell never touches me?"

Nell smiled. "It's that tumor in your belly, Harvey."

Harvey rubbed his high pot in a circular motion. "But this ain't fat, Nell. It's all muscle. Just feel once."

Nell said, "I'd believe you if I saw some of it on your arms."

Harvey gave Elmer a jab in the ribs. "Tell me, Elmer Rice, what makes women think you're so damn good-looking?"

Elmer tilted his shining head. "My father and mother were both good-looking."

"So?"

"I have to be good-looking, don't I, because I look so much alike?"

There were guffaws all up and down the bar. Nell gave Elmer a loving stroke on his arm, winked again, and went back to waiting on tables.

Alan bit into his hamburger. His smeller had been right. The cook was using prime meat. The hamburger with onion and sliced pickle was almost sweet it was so delicious. And his malted milk turned out to be so thick some of the lumps clogged the straw momentarily. He could feel nourishment going to all parts of his body.

Alan sucked up the last stiff drops of his malted milk and then, with a little smile, called Nell over. "Excuse me, but could you tell me where 324 First Avenue South might be?"

Nell said, "I think it's right above us here. On top of the cliff."

"You mean right here up behind Nick's?"

"Yes."

"Thanks."

Alan got up and paid for his lunch at the far end of the bar. Then with a little nod at Nell, he stepped outside. Getting into his blue Dodge, Alan tooled back up Concord and at City Hall took a sharp left and climbed a steep hill. Taking yet another left, he emerged on top of the cliff onto First Avenue South. The houses on both sides of the street were mostly one-story and clapboard, the lawns cluttered with children's playthings.

Alan watched the house numbers until he finally spotted the number he wanted: 324. He pulled up across the street. He sat a moment inspecting the house. It was a story-and-a-half with a tar-shingled roof. Four huge oaks, one at each corner of the lot, spread their branches high over the ridgepole of the house. The house was painted white with green window trim. Standing in the shade, it had the look of a cool comfortable place to live in. The lawn was neatly mowed, clean of children's debris. Some roses grew under the bay window.

Alan got out and went up the walk and knocked on the door. He thought he heard some kind of noise inside, as though someone had carefully stepped to the bay window, had peered out past the blind, and then seeing who it was, had quickly stepped back. Alan knocked again, sharply. Maybe the person inside, Red or his wife, thought he was a bill collector.

There was the sound of strong springy steps behind Alan. Turning, Alan saw Red. Alan brightened.

Red gave Alan a look as if he couldn't place him.

Alan held out his hand. "I'm Alan Ross from the *Chronicle*. I saw you boxing down at Kott's Gym the other day."

"Oh, yeh." For a powerful man Red had a limp handshake. "The wife didn't come to the door, did she?"

"No. I knocked but nobody answered."

Red's full lips shaped themselves into an amused side smile. "Yeh, Jen is a little nervous about meeting people. She thinks the woods is full of wolves."

"But this is the city."

"That makes it all the worse in her mind. When I'm gone she's got the door locked and won't answer the door. You came to see me?"

"Yes. I thought maybe I could work up a story about you moonlighting as a boxer."

"Oh, there ain't much to say about that."

"I'd like to ask you about your job at Steele."

"Oh, what I do at Steele won't make anybody clap their hands. I'm just a pigsticker."

"How did you happen to land that job?"

"I shouldna been so honest when I first came here. When I applied for the job, they asked me what my father did, and I told them farming and that he sometimes butchered for the neighbors. Well, then they right away stuck me in the kill. When I would much rather have worked outdoors in the yards."

Alan smiled. Outdoors in the stockyards was still a pretty smelly place.

Red trembled a second, finally said, "Well, I suppose I should invite you in. Though, shucks, I don't see what all the fuss is about." He stepped past Alan and, taking a key from his pocket, opened the front door. He called inside. "Jen? It's only me. Everything's okay."

Someone, a woman, sucked a breath, and having gotten it, let go with a deep sigh.

"Come on, Jen. It's only me. You're safe now."

Red peered around the corner, past a blue curtain hanging between the parlor and the sitting room. "You see?" He leaned in and there was the sound of a warm kiss.

"Where's . . . where's that man?"

"The one at the door? I know him. He's a reporter."

"A reporter? What's he want from us?"

"Oh, he just wants to write a story about my boxing."

"Do we want that?"

"It'll maybe mean more money. Publicity always helps in sports. Come." Red drew his wife from behind the blue curtain. "Jen, I'd like you to meet . . . what's your name again?"

"Alan Ross. Glad to meet you, Mrs. Engleking."

Jen Engleking stared at Alan with wide deep-set brown eyes. The whites of her eyes sharpened the scared look of her. She was wearing a very bright yellow dress. She was quite slender and almost as tall as Red. She had long flowing wavy brown hair falling to her shoulders, a good full bosom, and curiously long, even gangling, legs. She stared especially at Alan's very light hair. She blurted out, "I don't know if I'm gonna like you."

Red shook her lovingly. "Come on now, Jen. He's all right."

Jen continued to stare at Alan critically. "What's the matter, you need glasses?"

Alan had become aware that the last few seconds his eyes had begun to flick. "No, I can see all right." Alan gave her a warm smile. "No, it's just that my eyes flicker a little when I get excited. Or when there's sharp light around."

"Tain't very bright in here."

Alan let himself laugh heartily. He did it so she could hear the true inner sound of him. "No, it's not. Actually I've got good eyes in the dark."

Red roughed up Jen's hip in a loving manner. "Do you think you could wrastle us up some coffee?"

At that Jen relaxed and gave Alan a part apologetic smile. "Living near the stockyards ain't exactly paradise, you know. Almost every day we hear about someone getting raped or beat up or something."

"Oh, now, Jen, that's cutting the baloney pretty thick."

Jen stepped out of Red's arm. "What about that big fight down at Nick's? Where one of the men got stabbed?"

"That was just a union fight." Red dropped a shoulder in apology to Alan. "We're pretty much CIO down here and when the Teamsters sent some organizers, we had to let them know they was stickin' their nose in where they wasn't wanted."

Alan asked, "What happened?"

"Oh, we busted a few noses. And some of our guys threw a couple of their goons back over in the hills."

"That wasn't in the paper, was it?"

"Nope." Red pointed to an easy chair. "Take a load off your feet. And Jen, to, get us some coffee."

Jen gave her husband a warm secretive smile. "Be out in a jiff."

Alan took a seat in a purple mohair armchair nearby and Red sat down across the coffee table from him. A radio stood in the far corner and beside it a black leather easy chair. A purple davenport just fit under the bay window. On the piano were various family portraits. The walls were papered a light purple. There was only one picture, an overly gaudy painting of an evergreen beside a lake, and it hurt the eye.

Red said, "Well, what do you need to know?"

Alan got out some folded gray scratch paper and a heavy-leaded black pencil.

"Where you from originally?"

"Bonnie. That's down in Siouxland. About forty miles from Sioux Falls."

"Farmers?"

"Yeh, Dad had a quarter section."

"How come you landed here in South St. Paul?"

"Couldn't find a job in the Sioux Falls stockyards."

"But why the stockyards?"

"All I knew was animals."

Alan began to make a few notes. "How come you didn't take up farming like your father?"

"I was kinda feelin' my oats."

"I see."

Red smiled down at his big hands. "And then pretty soon I got lonesome here in South St. Paul, and the next thing you know I got married."

"But why take up boxing?"

"I needed the extra money."

"I mean, how did that idea ever come to you?"

"Well . . ." Red shoved one hand in his pocket. "There was a fight in Nick's one night. Not the one Jen just mentioned, but another one. A guy called me a name I didn't like and I hauled off and hit him." Red appeared to be embarrassed about it. It was apparent Red had grown up in a family where bragging was frowned upon. He wiggled his hand in his pocket. "Well, one of the guys who saw it told me I should take up boxing. He said I could make a killing at it. Because I could hit."

"What was your church?"

"You probably never heard of it." Red played some more pocket pool. "We called it the Little Church."

"Lutheran?"

"No, Calvinist."

"Your wife that too?"

"Her family's Presbyterian. Heh, that is, when they go to church."

All the while they talked, Alan found himself comparing his vision of his haunt brother John with the ruddy John sitting across from him. Alan began to like Red.

Alan said, "I'm a little puzzled about something. How come you're a union man when your father is a farmer? Most farmers have no time at all for strikes."

"I was kinda buckin' my dad."

"I see."

"And then there was my brother Bert." Red let go with a short laugh. "Bert's the local socialist in Bonnie. He even had a dog named Debs once."

Alan thought: "Hey, there's an interesting ferment going on in those Englekings."

"Then o' course there was Jen's Pa, George Haron. He's an aginer too. In fact, he wasn't gonna let me date Jen until he learned that my brother had a dog named Debs." Red shook his head. "You should meet him sometime. Gassed in the last war. Captain. Made pontoon bridges across rivers ahead of the infantry. So the mortality rate in his company was awfully high."

"But nobody in your family ever was a boxer?"

"Nope. We wrastled a little. And we played baseball."

"Were the men in your family big people? Strong?"

"My father and Uncle Sherm and Uncle Paul are."

Jen came in with a tray, carrying coffee and cups and cake and cream and sugar. She set it on the coffee table between the two men. She'd been listening to their talk in the kitchen. "Tell him that story about your dad and Case Tollhouse, John," she said with a laugh, sitting down.

"Oh, that." Red coughed a short laugh. "It's sort of personal."

Alan waited. It was interesting that Jen called her husband John and not Red.

"You asked if there was any big people in my family . . . well, my dad and ma are really awfully big people. Stanley Kott thinks I can hit. Shucks, he should see my dad. Dad once knocked down a mule with one punch. Why, he could lift a barrel of salt off the ground alone and set it onto a wagon. I don't think there's ever lived a stronger man. And is he fat. About three hundred pounds. We're all heavy meat eaters."

Alan nodded.

"And Ma, she's fat too. Well, this one Sunday morning Dad drove us all to church in our old Dort, Dad and Ma up front and all us kids in back. It happened that we arrived on the churchyard the same time Case Tollhouse did. Case himself is a skinny runt. But, man, does he have a fat wife. She's so fat she can't slip in between the benches in church. She has to sit on the front bench under the pulpit. And you really can't tell when she's sitting down or standing up, her dress hangs out so wide around." A laugh escaped Red. "Well, actually there was one way you can tell. She doesn't look quite as tall when she's sitting down."

Alan found himself smiling.

"Well, Case pulls up in his old Ford right beside our old Dort, Case up front with all his kids, while his fat old lady takes up the whole back seat alone. Both Case and Dad shut off their engines about the same time. Case looks at us fat Englekings in our old Dort and he gets a kind of a look on his old grizzly face showing he's getting set to say something clever. Finally he says, 'You know, Fat, it's always been a kind of a mystery to me that your old Dort hain't collapsed yet with all those fat people in it.' Well, Dad, he don't crack a smile, but he throws a look at Case's great fat wife sitting alone there on the back seat of the old Ford all bulged out, and he says, 'Well, Case, I tell you, and I've been kind of surprised that after you and your kids step out of your old Ford, it ain't tipped over backwards yet."

Jen had heard the story many times before but she still broke out with a hearty laugh.

Alan had a good laugh too.

All three sipped coffee and helped themselves to the cake. The cake was raisin-chocolate with maple frosting.

Alan asked, "Ever think of getting yourself a fight manager?"

Red shook his head. "I ain't good enough for that yet."

"Would you like some more coffee, Mr. Ross?" Jen asked with a warm smile.

Alan placed his spoon across the top of his cup. "No, thanks. Too much coffee makes me high."

"Coffee nerves, you mean."

"Yes."

"John?"

Red nodded.

She cut a second slice of cake for both of them.

Alan said, "I notice you don't call your husband Red."

Jen prickled up. "I don't like that name."

Alan asked Red, "What would you rather be called?"

"Don't make no difference to me. John. Red. Just so it ain't Fat."

Alan said, "I take it you really don't care much for your job, then?"

Red said, "No, I don't."

"Why don't you ask for another job there?"

"The pay in the kill is good."

Alan studied the coffee dregs in his cup. He stirred them around a little with his spoon. "I know it's something I couldn't do. Sticking pigs." Alan shuddered. "I'd have nightmares."

Red fell silent.

Jen couldn't resist letting one cat out of the bag. "Well, John has nightmares. Some real bad ones. Where he scares the wits out of me the way he yells."

Red took his hand out of his pocket and reached across to touch her wrist. "They ain't all that bad."

"Some of those you had last month . . . hooo. The one where you was dreaming you was drinking a glass of milk? And it all of a sudden turned to blood on you?"

"I knew I shouldna told you about that one."

Jen rolled her dark-brown eyes in memory.

Red stood up. "Well, it's time for me to skip rope." He looked down at Alan. "You got what you wanted?"

Alan looked at his scribbled notes. There was much more he wanted to know. "You don't have children, do you?"

Red didn't quite look at Jen. "Not yet."

Jen began to have that upset look again.

Red said, "We're still working on it."

Jen slowly crossed her arms over her stomach.

"Do you own this house?"

"Me and the bank. It's mortgaged. That's why we're in such a bind."

"If you had your druthers, where would you rather live, out in the country, or in the city?"

Red said nothing.

Jen said, "I haven't been out in the country much. So I don't know how I'd feel about living on a farm."

Alan decided he'd learned enough for now and placed his notes on the coffee table. "How do you feel about your husband boxing?"

Jen's lower lip came out a little. "I hate it."

Red said, "Really, you know, I gotta get going."

Alan got to his feet. "And I should get along too. I can talk to you some more at Kott's Gym sometime."

Alan went out to his car. Motor started, he had one last look around. The great oak trees were wonderful to look at. It surprised him that the rich hadn't glommed onto the plateau above the cliff and built themselves beautiful mansions overlooking the Mississippi Valley. Probably the packinghouse and the stockyards were there first and the rich didn't want to live near the stink. In the old days St. Paul probably hadn't grown out that far and the stockyards' stink was safely outside the city limits.

Alan threw one more look at the Engleking home with its neatly mowed lawn and swept walk and uncluttered front porch. Red and Jen were different all right. Both had maggots eating away in their brains.

Alan decided to have a closer look at the Steele Packinghouse Company. He drove down to Nick's Cafe again and parked across the street from it. He got out and started walking down Steele Avenue. Ahead loomed the high brick Steele plant. Two steam engines were working in the switching yards on the right, chuffing along, pushing cars from one track to another. Loading docks and wood-walled pens stretched off on the left. Most of the hogs and cattle and sheep had been disposed of for the day. The smell of old dung was heavy on the air. Looking down an alley he could see all the way across to the high brick walls of a commission building. Several yard workers wearing red rubber boots were hosing out a hog pen. The smell of it was acrid, wetly rotten. A lively wind whisked bits of old straw across the road.

There were two brick shelters on either side of the main gate to the plant, with the United States flag furling and unfurling over the left shelter. Two security guards dressed in blue blocked the entrance, one on each side.

After watching Alan approach for a half block, the two guards began to talk about him. Both guards had a left thumb missing.

Alan put on his best face, an easy Dakota smile, and asked the guard on the left, "Who do I see for a conducted tour of the place?" Alan nodded toward the main building.

The other guard stepped over. He was the bigger man and had the more glowering look. "What do you want to see?"

"Nothing in particular, really. I've never been through a packing plant before and thought it might be interesting."

"You got a permit?"

"No."

"Sorry, we can't let you in."

"When do you have guided tours?"

"That you'll have to ask the head office."

"How do I get to the head office?"

"Telephone."

Alan smiled. He was going to have some trouble seeing that kill.

The first guard said, "Besides, there ain't nothing much going on right now. Most of the guys have gone home."

Alan nodded. "You don't mind if I walk along outside the plant here though?"

"Go ahead. So long's you don't try to climb the fence."

"Thanks."

Alan strolled down a straw-littered lane beside a chain-link steel fence. The high and long dark brick packinghouse with its tall dusty windows towered on his right. The building was ominous in its silence. About halfway down, an enclosed chute rose out of the stockyards on the left, arched high over the lane, and connected with the top floor of the plant. Alan remembered having heard somewhere that the gravity system was used in the packinghouse, with the kill on the top floor. After the animal was stuck, it was slowly dismembered as its own weight caused it to descend down through the bowels of the huge plant.

The thought made Alan sick to his stomach. He'd often seen poor hogs packed tight in a truck, some of them with their snouts sticking out through the rack, the snouts wriggling as they smelled strange air. Every day of their short lives they'd lived in luxury. They'd been fed rich yellow corn and had been allowed to run in sweet green alfalfa fields and had been slopped with the richest mixtures of ground meal and leftover milk and bran and at night had slept in deep warm straw. Grunting and oinking in sloth, they'd slowly become great fat carcasses. And then, abruptly, they were whisked off and herded together in a foul-smelling stockyards and shouted at and whipped over the back, and then one by one they were sent up a chute where a knife awaited them.

North of the packinghouse, where the chain-link fence ended, Alan noticed a high wall of stones beyond a railroad track. That had to be a retaining wall of some kind. Alan clambered up over the railroad track and then climbed the stones. When he got to the top, he found himself looking down at the Mississippi River. On the far side an island rode in the water, and beyond that several hills formed an undulating horizon. He watched a tugboat push two barges full of coal up the big river. The sound of the pounding engine seemed to come toward him through the water rather than over it. He looked north. The river swept in a long graceful curve toward St. Paul. Over the trees he could just make out the golden horse atop the state capitol.

He sat down on one of the top stones.

A strange gray-black spider began racing over a rock near his right shoe. It raced a couple of inches and then hid itself in a crack. It ran in fear; it hid in fear. Presently the enemy appeared, a patrol of big red ants. They too moved over the rock, but not nearly as fast. They moved scouring every tiny seam of the rock. Presently the patrol of ants took the wrong route and ran off the stone. Safe, the little gray-black spider shot forward another couple of inches and hid in the next crack.

If all life was one, as the Sioux Indians believed, just how was his own life, and Red's and Jen's life, tied in with the little gray-black spider and the large red ants moving over the rock near his right shoe?

The next morning Burt asked Alan what he'd learned about his fighter, Red Engleking.

"Not too much, really."

"Got enough for a story?"

"Not yet. But I'll get one out of it before long."

# Chapter 7

# RED

Red couldn't find sleep. He lay on his right side awhile, then carefully, so as not to awaken wife Jen, rolled over on his left side. Jen could sleep anywhere anytime, and she'd drifted off the moment her head had hit the pillow. Jen had learned to sleep deep to block out hearing her father and mother fight every night.

Listening to one's parents fighting was a bad thing, of course, but it was nothing compared to what he himself had to live with all his life.

Because I have to watch my tongue day and night, Red thought, or it'll slip out.

. . . . It all went back to that time in Bonnie, Siouxland, when he was visiting Monte Goring after school. Monte was his best friend.

He and Monte had fed all the cows together, and then in that free time left before milking, while Mr. Goring had a cup of coffee in the kitchen, they'd gone to the hog barn to see if the new boar might be topping a sow.

They found the boar asleep and the sows busy rooting through the feeding troughs.

Disappointed, Monte wanted to know if Red had ever played with his pud. Monte had a black forelock like the bill of a cap and he had narrowed brown slits for eyes.

Red said, no, he hadn't yet. It was a lie.

"You hain't? Man, it's fun. Specially when you faint." Then Monte asked, "Did you ever ride a sow?"

"What? Cripes, no."

They were sitting on a high pile of straw, and the smell around them was of freshly crushed oats. Nobody was watching and soon they both began to feel hot.

Monte asked, "Have you ever with a heifer calf?" Some spit was hanging out of the crack of his lower lip.

Red shook his head.

"What they got is pretty much what little girls got."

Red knew he should get out of there. Monte had a way of getting him to do things he didn't want to do.

"See that sow over there with white mostly over its back? That's Peggie. She was about dead when she was born. Pa gave up on her but I begged Pa to let me raise her in our kitchen. I fixed a little pen for her by the warm stove. Fed her with a baby's bottle. Sometimes I even took her to bed with me on cold nights. Man, was she cute. Everybody thought Peggie the perfect name for her." Then Monte unbuttoned himself. "I think I'm gonna have me a ride with Peggie. It's been a while." Monte climbed over the board partition and went after Peggie. "Come, pee-eg. Come, Peg. Come, pee-gie. Come, Peggie."

Red didn't cry out to say it was wrong, that the Bible was against it. Watching Monte he was as guilty as if he'd done it himself.

A strange swamp stink rose from the bristles of all the sows. . . .

Lying in bed beside Jen, reliving it all again, Red's legs suddenly kicked out. Remembering it was like touching an old sore with a live wire.

Jen turned over. "Mrp?"

Red lay very still.

In a moment Jen drifted off again. Jen was lucky. Except for her fear of strangers, Jen really had nothing on her conscience like what he had.

For many years Red hadn't thought about that time with Monte Goring. It had sunk to the bottom of him, beyond even the reach of his dreaming.

But then one day, when he was twenty-three, in bitter cold January, it came back to him.

Dad had decided they should butcher a hog. They were out of meat again. They were such heavy meat eaters they had to butcher almost every other week.

. . . . As they got up from the breakfast table, Dad said, "Red, you're helpin' me butcher today."

"But I was gonna—"

"But me no buts." Dad clapped on his blue woolen cap. "In fact, you're gonna stick the pig today."

"But, Dad—"

"Yeh, I've noticed it already, that when it's time to butcher you always find some kind of excuse. It's always Albert that has to help me. Well, this time you're gonna do the sticking or my name ain't Fat John Engleking."

Red began to shake.

"You'll be getting married pretty soon and then you'll have to do your own butchering." Dad pulled open a cabinet drawer and got out his sticking knife and his flensing knife. "C'mon, let's agitate them rear legs of yours."

Dad led the way across the yard, waddling along with his great belly swinging on each step. They put up a pulley in the corncrib alley and then went out to the feedlot.

Dad called up the barrows. "Suu-boy! Suu-boy!" When the barrows didn't right away come running, Dad called again. "Pee-eg! Pee-eg!"

When all the barrows had piled into the feedlot, hairy ears and round rubbery snouts raised up, Dad pointed out the one he wanted, the very fattest barrow, a red one.

Red thought: "What a dirty trick. Calling up the pigs for food when he really means to kill one of them."

Dad climbed over the wooden fence, rope in hand. He pretended to be just walking through. When Dad got close to the barrow he wanted, he nimbly flipped a slipknot around its right rear leg and shagged it out through the gate and then pulled it toward the corncrib.

Red closed the feedlot gate behind them.

The red barrow squealed and ran on three legs as far as the rope would allow to the right, and squealed and ran on three legs as far as it could to the left.

Dad's big teeth were set tight together. "Go get the sticking knife. I put it there over on the wheelbarrow."

The newly honed edge of the knife glittered in the morning sun. Red picked it up by its wooden handle. He was so clumsy at it he almost let it slip out of his hand.

"Get over here now."

Red came over.

"Reach around under the pig and jerk his opposite leg out from under him. C'mon."

"Dad, I can't."

"What?"

"I can't do it. I just can't kill animals."

"Well, by God, then you are a sissy after all. Like I was suspecting all along. A momma's boy."

Tears began to film Red's eyes. The knife shimmered. It almost fell out of his hand again.

"Lord God in heaven, you're about as much use to me as a fifth tit on a cow."

"But Dad, you know I can't even kill a chicken."

"For catsake. Here I was hoping I'd raised me a man."

Red quivered. He loved his father and he had hoped that by working hard he could help his father pay off the mortgage on the farm. He'd even been a little slow about dating girls, thinking that so long as he didn't get married he could stay home and work.

"Your younger brother Bert is twice the man you are. He don't flinch when it comes to sticking or cutting a pig."

"Bert and me are two different people."

"Grab that pig by the leg and tip'm over on his back!"

"I can't."

All of a sudden Dad dropped the rope and dove for the barrow. Dad's wide right hand shot under the barrow, grabbed the off leg, and quickly as if it were only a bundle of oats flipped the barrow over on its back. Dad held the barrow's front feet apart. Between set teeth, Dad growled, "Stick him!"

"Dad."

"Gott dammit, stick him!"

Red stared down at the underside of the barrow's chin. It was the only white spot on him. The barrow squealed so loud its tongue vibrated like a garter snake's. Red couldn't bear its utterly helpless look.

Dad grabbed the hand in which Red held the knife. "You're gonna stick that pig even if I have to take your hand and make you do it!" Dad's grip was powerful on Red's fingers over the knife. Dad's great bulk was so balled up with anger Dad almost rode up off the ground. "Now!" Dad guided Red's hand and knife for the white spot below the barrow's jaw. "Stick him just ahead of where the breast bone joins. Where it looks like he's talking. Stick it in. Deep!" The curved point of the flashing knife went down. It made a crisping noise as it cut through the white bristles. Then it sank in easy. Still between set teeth Dad snarled, "Now twist the knife up and around a little to catch the aorta . . . ah! There."

Blood geysered up out of the barrow's slit throat. It gushed over Dad's hand and Red's hand.

Dad let go of Red's hand. "All right. That's it. Now let him up so he can bleed out while up on his feet."

With a twisting roll the red barrow struggled to its feet. It ran a few steps; stopped. Blood spilled over its forefeet. It screamed wetly; lolled its head; finally had to stand all straddled out on four feet to keep from falling. Blood spilled in pulses from the rent in its throat. As the stream of blood slowly thinned the pig's head lowered. It fought to keep from fainting. It coughed. Coughed. And collapsed.

Red went to wipe his nose with the back of his hand and then stopped. He smelled the strange swamp stink of stiff bristles on his bloody hand. In a flash he saw again that day in the hog barn with Monte Goring. "Come, pee-eg. Come, Peg. Come, pee-gie. Come, Peggie." The knife dropped from Red's hand and clattered to the frozen ground.

Red hated Dad.

Dad let his big shoulders down. "Well. So. You've finally stuck your first pig."

Red vomited his breakfast on the ground.

"Good. The next time it'll be easier for you."

Red wiped his mouth with the back of his clean left hand. "I hope you're satisfied. That I'm a man now."

"Not quite. We still have to scald it in a barrel. And then scrape the hair off."

Two weeks later, after they'd butchered again with Red doing the sticking and all the cutting, Red looked up from his cup of coffee at breakfast. "Dad, I've decided something. I'm getting to be too old to stay at home."

Dad held his cup halfway to his thick red lips. Dad's little pinky was lifted like it was too good for the other fingers. Dad had on his little straw hat, something Ma had never been able to get him to remove in the house until he went to bed. "So?"

Red said, "So I thought I'd go get me a job somewhere and help you pay off the mortgage on the farm."

Dad lowered his cup and set it in its saucer. Slowly he raised his blue eyes. "Well now, that might not be such a bad idea. You're the oldest and'll probably inherit the place."

Red felt a funny gush of love for his father. If he could earn a couple of thousand dollars, and if Dad could have one good crop, together they could pay off the debt on the quarter section. Then he'd have Dad won over at last. "You and Bert can handle the farm, can't you?"

Ma's blue eyes were full of soft warmth. "Albert wants to buy that butcher shop in town." Ma glanced at Bert sitting beside her. Ma favored Bert too. "Ha, Albert?"

Bert had very white hair, already thinning at twenty-one, and he had a nose like the plucked tail of a chicken, a regular pope's nose. His white brows moved up his forehead. "Well, not right away, Ma. I can wait a year or two for that. It would be nice for you and Pa to own this place for a while without anything against it."

Dad threw Red a look. "Where will you go?"

Red tried to act like he knew exactly what he was doing. "I thought maybe I'd try the cities. They pay a dollar an hour in some places. There ain't a farmer around who can match that."

Dad's eyes opened wide and blue. "Where'd you ever get such a crazy idea, for catsake?"

"Been reading about it in the Sioux Falls paper."

Dad had himself a sip of coffee. The sun had just popped over the horizon, and it filled the wide kitchen with a sleepy pink glow. "Well, I guess you can easy catch a ride with some trucker to Sioux Falls."

Ma's eyes began to tear over. "My oldest boy John to leave the nest for the city."

Red said, "I'll be the same no matter where I live, Ma."

Dad nodded. "Working hard in some factory might just be the finishing off you need."

Bert smiled at his cup of coffee. "Wait'll some city floozie gets hold of you. That'll really finish you off." Bert had always been hot for girls.

Red gave Bert a look. "Dad's mortgage comes first. If it ain't paid off for him in the next couple of years, it'll never get done."

Dad set his cup down. "That's right. That's why we had you kids in the first place."

Ma said, "Fat, I wish you wouldn't wear your straw lid at the table. It always makes you look so comical I have trouble eating I have to laugh so."

A month later Dad decided to ship some hogs to Sioux Falls, and Red, suitcase packed, went along with the trucker, Hod Walling.

Red tried the Nonnamaker Packing Plant employment office. The personnel man, who had a face like the Indian on a nickel, said, no, they were full up.

Disheartened, Red went back to Hod Walling. Hod was waiting for him in the cafe under the commission house. Hod was sitting at the short-order counter. Red slid onto a stool beside him.

"Any luck?" Hod always kept his trucker cap on to hide a bald spot.

"No."

"Well, maybe you can try there again tomorrow. Beggars and old maids can't be choosy."

The cold hard city made Red sick to his stomach. He sat crimped forward on his stool. The darned trembles took over his fingers again.

"Gosh, kid, your eyes look like a pair of pissholes in an old snowbank. Don't be so down on yourself."

Red stared down at the counter.

"Get yourself a cup of coffee. C'mon, I'll cough up for it. Waitress? And give him an apple turnover."

Red had never really liked Hod Walling. Hod liked to break wind on the least excuse. Did it in front of company even. All the way to Sioux Falls the truck cab had stunk like the dickens. Yet because of Hod's friendly cheer and because of the coffee and the turnover, Red felt close to him for the moment.

Hod finished his snack and lit up a cigarette. "Well, time to get highballing. You riding back with me?"

Red shivered. He couldn't go back home the same day he left. "No, I think I'll try somewhere else."

"Why don't you try one of them big implement companies in Sioux Falls?"

"You mean, do piecework at a machine?"

"They pay well."

Red shook his head. "I want to be near something that's more connected with the farm."

"Well, hell, then try the South St. Paul yards up in the Cities."

"I suppose they're bigger."

"They sure are. About three times as big."

"You've been up there?"

"Hell, yes. A dozen times. Sometimes a farmer gets a wild-hair idea that he can get the top market up there instead of in Sioux Falls."

"Maybe I'll try them then. I want to be near animals even in the city."

Hod slipped off his stool. "Look. I know a suicide jockey who has a run between here and the Cities. Clem Houghtaling. He usually hangs out over at the Pheasant. C'mon, I'll take you over there."

In a few minutes Hod Walling pulled up across the street from the Pheasant, a dinky one-story joint standing in the shadow of the towering pinkstone Minnehaha Courthouse.

They found Clem Houghtaling having a grape pop with some beer-drinking buddies around a table in a semicircular booth in back. Hod introduced Red.

Clem looked Red over, finally said, "Sit down and take a load off your feet." Clem was humpbacked and his chin just barely made it to the edge of the table. He looked like a horse jockey bent forward riding for glory.

Red slid in beside Clem.

Hod asked, "You all set then, kid?"

Red nodded. It was going to happen. "But don't say anything to Dad about where I'm going. I'll write him when I get settled."

"Will do." And Hod, with a final cracking salute, waved and was off.

"So you want to go to South St. Paul, do you?" Clem played with his grape pop, savoring each drop. "Well, you're in luck. I'm leaving this afternoon with a hot load for some blasters north of the Twins. I can drop you off anywhere you say." Clem had a considerable nose. On the very point of it lay a strange pink blister that made it seem all the larger. His eyes were close-set. He had the air of a tame white rat.

The two other fellows in the booth were big fellows, each with a beer belly. Like Hod and Clem they wore trucker caps covered with chauffeur license badges They had an easy smile for Clem and slowly sipped at their beers.

The phone rang in the bar. It was for Clem.

Clem got to his feet. Standing up hardly made him any taller. Clem just missed being a dwarf. "They probably got it loaded. I'm never within a mile of that tag-along while they're loading it with nitroglycerine."

Soon Clem came back. "Ready, kid? They got the rig loaded all right."

A few minutes later Red found himself heading east on Highway 16 sitting beside Clem Houghtaling in a red semitrailer. It was two o'clock and shadows had just begun to show on the east side of buildings.

Red wondered about that cargo bouncing along behind them. "Hod called you a suicide driver. That stuff back there really that dangerous?"

"We hit a deep chuckhole and you'll have your first glimpse of old St. Peter himself."

"Why do you haul the stuff?"

"The nitro people pay, bo. Three times the usual."

"But what good does it do you to get blown up?"

"I have nothing to live for. No woman will take me. And my folks are all gone."

Red watched the dead cornfields go by. It tore at him that he was leaving his own home country.

They rolled through Whitebone. It was a pretty town of neat green lawns and big white houses and a lot of tall trees. Beyond to the north, in the haze of a humid afternoon, the Blue Mounds reared up like a miniature mountain range.

Ten miles farther along, up on a low rise, Clem pulled over onto the shoulder of the road. He shut off the motor. "Like a good drink of water, Red? That's a natural spring there and it tastes wonderful."

Across the road, an iron pipe poked out of the north slope of the ditch. Clear sparkling water spilled from it and splashed on a pile of red rocks. The grass around the rocks was tall and shone a velvet green.

Clem hunched out of the cab and hobbled across the road.

Red followed him.

"What's always puzzled me," Clem said, "is where this water comes from." His head swiveled around on his humped neck. "So far as I can make out this rise is the highest point around here." Clem got down on his short knees and with his two hands cupped up several drinks of water.

Red was reminded of the story in the Bible where the Lord God told Gideon he had too many fighters in his army with which to smite the Midianites, that he should lead his men to a brook where he should watch and see which of them lapped up water with their tongue, putting their hand to their mouth, and which bowed down on their knees to drink. "I see you ain't among the Lord's chosen."

Clem got to his feet and wiped his hands on the sides of his trousers. "Come again?"

Red told him about Gideon smiting the Midianites.

Clem pursed up his lips. "I've often thought about that too, about why the good Lord should want those who drank as a dog lappeth to fight His wars for Him. Probably figured they were more animal-like and so would fight like savages. Where the others were too citified."

Red got down on his knees, and then with a little smile at Clem cupped up water in his hand and then lapped it up like a dog.

Clem laughed, and ambled back to the truck.

On they rolled. Blue Wing, Windom, Madelia. It was mostly flat land, frozen plowed fields black, cornfields and pastures white with snow.

At Mankato they pulled into a filling station. Clem kicked rubber all around. He checked the load, making sure the cartons were still riding on foam rubber and were tied down securely. He called to Red, still in the cab, "Want a Coke?"

"I better keep that nickel for later."

"Get down and have a Coke with me. I'm paying."

They walked across the street to a hamburger joint and slid onto a couple of stools at the end of the counter. Clem ordered a grape pop and Red a strawberry pop. Clem asked, "Care for a roll?"

Red shook his head.

Clem gave him a wise look and then ordered two pecan rolls anyway.

When they finished, Red said, "You don't drink beer."

"Never cared for it."

Red licked some pecan syrup off his fingers. "I dunno, if I was to haul that nitro stuff regularly, I might be tempted to take a swig now and then."

Clem swallowed the last of his roll and finished his pop. "That's what your friend Hod says too. But I tell you, I respect that stuff behind me and I mean to be cold sober every inch of the way."

"Has a load of that stuff ever blown up?"

Clem cleaned his teeth with a sucking tongue, making a little whistling sound. He swallowed, and the motion of it was exactly like a chicken trying to down a big grasshopper. "One fellow did get careless down in Illinois a couple of years back. All they ever found of his truck was bits of tin and glass. And as for the driver, all they found of him was one fingernail and one shirt button. One. And the buildings for blocks around were leveled to the ground. It was like the Lord God had found himself another Sodom and Gomorrah to destroy."

"You go to church too, I see."

"You bet. I'm Catholic. Only church that don't bother you if you ain't married."

Red thought that a prejudiced remark and showed it in the way he looked at Clem.

"Fact. Out in your and my country, the Catholic Church has more time for the off man."

They walked out to the truck and got in. In a few moments they were rolling up the main drag of Mankato, up a slope on the north end of town, then around a huge hill. The motor was powerful and in high made it easily onto a wide height of land.

Clem felt like talking. "So you didn't go to school after the eighth grade."

"No, my dad don't hold much for schooling."

Clem nodded. "Me, I was born with wheels in my head. Education would have been of about as much use to me as a prick on a pope."

Red burst out laughing.

"Fact. You don't have to go to high school to know how to make an engine run. And you sure as hell don't have to go to college to know how to spin a steering wheel."

"That's true."

"I knew a guy who couldn't read or write who could shift gears like he was stirring up a pail of syrup with a spoon, it was so smooth. Never a rough catch."

St. Peter came up. They slowed down to twenty-five miles an hour through downtown. They made all the green lights. Dusk began to fall.

"Which reminds me," Clem said with a humped smirk. "What do you do for it?"

Red didn't know what Clem meant.

"You know? Play the femmes."

Red blushed.

"Hey, don't tell me you haven't had yourself a left-handed love affair yet?"

Red said stiffly, "I thought I'd wait until I got married."

Clem snorted. "Marriage is for the birds. Besides, no woman would have me for long. For a week, yeh. For an eternity, no."

Red could see where that might be true in Clem's case.

"But, at the same time, I'm gonna have me some fun. Even if I have to pay for it through the nose."

At Shakopee, Clem took 101 toward Savage. A full moon lit up everything as though in half-sunlight.

Red wondered what kind of people might be living in the homes high up on bluffs on either side of them.

Clem drove the tag-along carefully across the Mendota bridge over the Minnesota River, then across the Fort Snelling bridge over the Mississippi River. He drove always with one eye on the traffic coming and going to make sure no one came close to his suicide cargo. Clem eased up on dimly lighted Seventh Street. Clem said, "The city always makes me feel like a squirrel with his tail chopped off, cars sometimes come so close."

The city was dirty with melted mounds of soot-pocked snow. Water glinted in the streetcar tracks. Traffic became heavy. Several other trucks were caught in the traffic up ahead. Horns sounded anguished demands.

Clem glanced at his wristwatch. "Kid, I'm not going to be able to take you to South St. Paul after all. I've got to get to my warehouse by eight and it's already seven-thirty. Tell you what. I'll let you off on a corner where you can't help but catch the right streetcar. Okay?"

Red began to tremble. Riding through the city in the dark, with lights flashing at him from all sides, and horns blaring, and gears crashing, made it all seem a hard place.

"Okay, kid?"

"Okay."

Clem pulled up at a corner in the busiest part of St. Paul. "Your streetcar pulls up by that lamp post over there. It'll be marked Concord. That'll take you all the way to the stockyards. Got that clear?"

"Yes."

"Hate to dump you off like this, kid, but I gotta. Now that I got this far with this nitro stuff, I want to make sure I get it in safe the rest of the way."

Red picked up his suitcase and swung out and closed the cab door behind him. He stood on the curb bewildered. People hurrying somewhere cast odd looks at him. Numb, legs stiff from the long ride, he stepped off the curb, and promptly was almost run over. An angry car horn blasted at him. "Watch where you're going!" Red jumped forward, suitcase lifting after him. Dodging, darting, he made it to the streetlight on the opposite corner. It was when he was catching his breath, and his wits, that he noticed Clem's truck still standing where he'd jumped out of it. Clem had waited to make sure he'd made it. Red waved, and Clem, shaking his head, smiling a twisted smile, waved back. Then Clem, shifting gears, started up his tag-along and was gone.

The full moon shone on the tops of towering buildings with a soft amber light.

The Concord streetcar appeared within minutes. Red got aboard, dug out a dime for the fare, and took a seat right behind the motorman.

The yellow streetcar dinged its way down several blocks, finally took a run for it, and crossed on an arching bridge over the Mississippi River.

Red said, "Let me know when we get to the stockyards, will you?"

The motorman nodded, not looking back.

The streetcar turned slightly and soon began to head southeast. Houses and an occasional corner grocery went by. The streetcar stopped every few blocks to let somebody off. The steel wheels trundled at the intersections, and the trolley overhead crackled vivid sparks of electricity.

Presently the streetcar careened between two high buildings, a bank on the right and a commission house on the left. Despite the closed windows the old familiar farm smells of animal dung and rotted straw wafted through the streetcar. Red watched the wooden partitions of a yards go by. There'd be the place to get a job.

The streetcar ground to a stop. The motorman looked back at Red, hand on the brake. "Here you are."

"Thanks." Red picked up his suitcase and, stepping carefully, let himself down to the ground.

The streetcar ironed off, gathering momentum.

Off to the east loomed a high building with a lighted sign above it: THE STEELE PACKINGHOUSE.

Hungry, Red headed for a lighted place, Nick's Cafe. He found the bar jammed with merry patrons. The smell of hot hamburgers was sweet in the nose. He selected a corner table.

A slender waitress emerged from a door in back and came slowly toward him. She had gangling legs and a full bosom and long brown curly hair. Her eyes were brown with large whites in the corners. There was a scared look about her. She held her pad and pencil awkwardly. "What would you like?" She spoke so softly Red could hardly hear her over the rowdy noise at the bar.

Red studied the chalked entrees on a little blackboard above the bar. "Hamburger. Big one. Got any pie?"

"We have apple, custard, mince."

"A piece of apple pie then, with ice cream on it."

"Coffee?"

"Yep. But before you bring me any of that, get me a beer first. Hamm's."

A look of disapproval appeared in her brown eyes.

"I can have a beer, can't I?"

Her face became expressionless, and she turned away and got the beer for him.

The Hamm's beer hit the spot. Red guessed the beer tipplers at the bar were mostly packinghouse workers. They were big, rough, red-lipped men.

Red had just had the last of his beer when the slender waitress brought his order. She set it all neatly in front of him. "Will that be all then?"

Red spotted her name sewn on the front of her green-and-white smock. Jen. He liked the name. She was pretty. She had the clear cream skin of girls he knew back home. "May I ask you a question, Jen?"

"Yes."

"You from the farm? Or South St. Paul?"

"That's two questions."

Red perked up. She might look scared, but she could be pretty spunky too. "I was just wondering."

"I come from a small town called Brokenhoe."

"Hey, I had you pegged right. A country girl."

Jen didn't know whether she liked that or not. "I just started working here. Dad was laid off at Honeywell and I'm trying to help Dad and Mom out a little."

"Hey, I'm looking for work, too, to help out the folks."

Her brown eyes deepened and warmed. She stood a little less awkward. "Where you from?"

Red told her. "And tomorrow I try my luck down at Steele there."

She frowned. "Steele ain't hiring much these days."

Red shrugged. "Just my luck."

Jen idled some more at his table. "You got a place to stay tonight?"

"No, I haven't."

"Nick's got a place upstairs here for floaters."

"Thanks. I'll ask him when I finish."

Jen smiled and trailed off to the kitchen in back.

Red ate hungrily.

The beer and the food, plus the long ride that day, made him sleepy, and when he got up to pay his bill he was ready for bed.

Nick had a bunk for him, just as Jen had said, in a dingy room upstairs that ran the length of the building. Luckily he was the only one up there and the place was quiet. He took the cot near the windows facing the street. He was so sleepy he just barely noted that the cot stank of the sweat of strangers.

The next morning, after a breakfast of pancakes and little pigs downstairs, Red went down to the Steele Packinghouse. He'd put on new overalls and a new denim jacket and felt peppy. He walked briskly along Steele Avenue. Trucks of all sizes, from pickups to tagalongs, and filled with bellowing cattle and squealing pigs, nosed after each other down the avenue, each seeking an unloading dock in the yards. There was a brisk northwest wind out and bits of manure flew about along the ground. Overhead the sky was clear blue.

Two guards at the main gate spotted Red. They saw he didn't have an identification card pinned on his jacket and stopped him. Red explained where he was from and that he was job hunting. They pointed out the right door for him.

Inside the huge packinghouse the power of the big city got Red down again. The dark wood halls were gloomy, windows smoky, the lights overhead weak. The air smelled of open flesh and half-digested corn.

Red stood in line for the employment window for a long time. The men ahead of him looked like able workers with families to feed.

Finally it was his turn at the window.

A pale man leaning on a ledge gave him a waiting look. "Yes?"

"I'd like a job out in the yards, please. I come from the farm and would like to work outdoors if I could."

The pale man shook his head.

Red's glance fell on a strange whorl in the wooden ledge, reminding him of a tornado he'd once seen. "Well, uh, I'll take anything then, for the present. Just so later on I can work out in the yards."

"What did you do on the farm?"

"You know, plow, pick corn." Then like a fool, Red blurted, "Sometimes I even butchered."

"We have an opening in the hog-kill department. Just a moment." The cold man riffled through several sheets of paper. "Yes. They need another shackler down there." The cold man pushed an application blank at Red. "Fill this out. At that table over there."

Very reluctantly Red filled out the application: name, date of birth, names of parents, work experience to date. Red wet the point of the lead pencil to make his writing clear. Then he brought it back to the cold man.

The cold man examined it; nodded. He wrote something on a small slip of paper. "Take this up to Sylvester Simes. He's the foreman up there. You go through that door over there on the right. Follow the hallway all the way to the end until you run into a guard. The guard will take you up the rest of the way."

"Thank you."

"Next? Yes?"

Red numbly walked down the long hallway. He wondered what shackling meant, hoping it didn't mean tying an animal to a singletree and then dousing it in boiling water.

The guard was a good-looking fellow with a slight pot. He took Red's slip of paper and held it up to the light to read it. The thumb and first two fingers of his left hand were missing. He gave Red a look. "Follow me."

They turned up a cement stairwell and climbed three stories. The smell of cut bowels became sharper with every step.

The guard pushed through a steel door. Instantly a welter of noise burst around them: men cursing, pigs squealing, overhead trolley wheels clanging.

Red was surprised to see animals that high up in the building.

The guard noticed Red's look. "We drive the hogs up that enclosed chute outside there. Then, once we get him inside up here and get him hooked onto that moving chain, gravity takes care of the rest, his own weight, until he's been turned into bacon and hot dogs."

Red looked over to the right. What he saw stunned him. A series of little trolleys came around a curving overhead rail and then began moving toward a slowly dropping slope inside the building. Squealing hogs were being hooked onto the trolleys with chains, then jerked up off the floor, and, head down, began rolling down the line, where various swift-moving men attacked them.

"Come," the guard said. He led Red toward a partitioned pen where two men were trying to catch skittering barrows. "Simes!"

The heavier of two men turned. He wore a pair of leather gloves and a leather apron. Part of his left thumb was missing. He wore a tight leather cap. He had a wide nose and dished eyeholes and bristly hair over his neck. He leaned against a partition a moment to catch his breath. "Yeh?"

"Here's that extra man you wanted." The guard gave Foreman Simes the slip of paper, and then with a wave of the hand at Red left.

Simes glanced at the paper, stuffed it in a pocket under his apron. He looked Red up and down. "John, is it? Is that what they usually call you?"

"Most people just call me Red."

"All right, Red, better take off that new jacket and put on a leather apron. That's your locker over there and you'll find everything you need in it. And hurry. We haven't been able to keep up with the trolleys as they come around."

Red changed his jacket for the short hard leather apron. He had to tie the apron on in two places, around his waist and below his seat. He found a pair of gloves that fit. He hurried back to Foreman Simes.

"All right, Red, hop in here with me and let's see how good you are at catching a porker."

Red climbed over the partition slowly, remembering how Dad had caught that barrow for him to kill.

"Here's your rope. When you've snagged one, drag it over to Pete there. Under that revolving wheel. He'll do the rest. Either rear leg will do."

The barrows not yet caught were all pressed tight in a bunch against the far partition. The other shackler in the pen, crouched over, snuck up on the one pig's rear end sticking out on his side. With a deft flip of his rope he caught a rear leg and with a strong jerk pulled the pig free of the melee and started to drag it toward Pete.

Red spotted a single pig on his side with a rear leg sticking out. The leg kept jerking as the porker tried to get it under itself again. Red snuck up behind the pig. The leather apron hindered the movements of his legs. Red flipped his rope and it looped itself around the leg. Red jerked the slipknot tight and had his first pig. He jerked the pig out of the milling crowd and started to pull it over to Pete. The barrow fought him all the way, jerking, scooting, lunging.

Pete was a powerful blocky man. His eyes glittered silverish. He too had part of his left thumb missing. Pete's right hand darted and in a flash he snapped one of the chains dangling from the revolving wheel around the pig's rear leg. "Unhook your rope, kid."

Red undid the slipknot and jerked his rope free.

The chain dangling from the revolving wheel tightened; easily lifted the barrow off the cement floor by its hind leg; hoisted the barrow toward the rail, where, with a click, it was hooked onto a trolley and the moving chain carried it off toward the butchers. The barrow made a strangled sound as it pawed the air with its forefeet.

"C'mon, c'mon," Simes growled behind Red, "next pig, next pig."

"Why do we have to wear these?" Red tugged at his stiff leather apron. "It only gets in the way."

"Take it off if you wanna get kicked in the balls. C'mon, c'mon, let's get a wiggle on."

Red began to sweat. Dust got into his eyes. Pigs in their terror crapped on the least sound. Wet dung lay splashed everywhere. Red's fingers sweat, began to feel greasy inside his gloves. His ears rang with all the raucous noise.

For a while Red didn't dare look at what happened to the barrows when they reached the butchers. He could tell by the gargling sounds not too far away that the barrows were being stuck.

When Red and the other shackler had caught all but the last few barrows, a partition was lifted and drovers choused in another batch of forty pigs, and the whole thing started over again.

Red began to see individual barrows after a while. Each one had its own way of trying to hide. Red thought: "They know what's coming."

The first day Red was too busy learning his job to have many compunctions about what he was doing. Luckily the run was short and nothing unusual happened.

At three o'clock he was walking back up Steele Avenue toward

Nick's. He had himself a hamburger and a beer and then went out to look for a room. After an hour's search he found one with an old lady named Mrs. Evenson living at 320 First Avenue South. It was up on the cliff almost directly above Nick's Cafe.

After a week of shackling Red's eyes began to clear. The other hog catcher was Chuck Cheny. Chuck liked to talk about the pretty baby chicks he was raising at home in his basement. The chicks reminded him of yellow angels, he said. Red liked Chuck.

Sometimes there was a breakdown in the moving chain and then the men had time to catch their breath, get themselves a good drink of water. Occasionally they had time to tell a story or two.

Most of the stories had a cruel edge. Simes told one that topped them all. "There was this farmer who had to have the best pigs around. One day he heard about a Poland China sow that's won the grand prize at the county fair. One look and he had to have her. He paid five hundred dollars for her and then had her bred by the best Poland China boar in the county. Well, pretty soon it was time for her to pig. It happened that at about the same time the local church board was going to hold a meeting about whether or not they should build a new church. The farmer was on the church board and he was against a new church. He didn't know what to do. Should he sit with the sow and help her through the pigging or should he go to the board meeting and vote against the new church building? Finally he asked his neighbor Nels, a retired carpenter, to sit by his pet sow. He told Nels that the minute he saw something going wrong he had to right away get him from the church board meeting. 'Mind now, Nels, that you make sure nothing goes wrong or I'll never forgive you.' Well, our farmer went to his meeting. There was a lot of wrangling. Pretty soon the reverend decided they should recess for a while to cool off the hotheads. The farmer thought, 'Good!' and he quick hurried home to see how his sow was doing. He went into the hog house quietly. There he saw his friend Nels looking closely at something going on in the sow's pen. The farmer looked over Nels' shoulder. And there, by golly, just then a little pig slipped out. It lay on the straw whimpering a little. Then the little pig got up and headed for titty. Now a little pig can take two routes to titty. It can go between the sow's hind legs and get right to it, or it can take the long way around behind the sow's back, past the sow's mouth, then through the sow's front legs. Well, this little pig took the long route. And just as it was passing the sow's mouth, the sow woke up and in one quick snap of its jaws, sllupp! gobbled up the little pig. 'Holy smokes, Nels!'

the farmer cried. 'I thought I told you to make sure nothing went wrong? Letting her . . . my God, man, what's wrong with you?' Nels held up a hand. 'Don't worry. That little peewee is doing all right. That's the seventh time he's made that same trip.' "

Pete and Simes laughed until they were dark in the face. But Red and Chuck only looked at each other.

Simes had a booger in his nose and tried to wipe it away with the back of his left hand.

Red had a question. "I notice a lot of you fellows in the plant here got a finger or a thumb missing. On your left hand."

Simes' dish eyes deepened. He said nothing.

Chuck humphed to himself. "What can you expect in a place where a fellow makes as many as a thousand passes at meat a day with a knife that's razor-sharp? He's bound to make a mistake some-time, not get his left hand out of the way quick enough. You just need to slip a little on the bloody floor and, sknish, there flies one of your fingers."

Simes quick looked around to make sure they weren't being over-heard. "That's enough of that now."

"Fact. I once found a human fingernail in a weenie." Chuck man-aged a little laugh.

Pete finally chipped in. "Well, yah, that might happen down in Pork Cut, where you can snip off a fingertip. But the worst is"—Pete nodded toward the butchers—"being a pigsticker. Some of them pigs are still fightin' yuh hanging head down. I seen already where one of them pigs snapped at Jack Prouty's left hand as he was about to hold the pig steady. Having a head-down hog snap at you is unsettlin', to say the least. And you make a mistake with a sticking knife, and brother, there goes your left hand."

"Let's get to work," Simes growled.

"But, boss, the chain's still stopped."

"Well, let's clean up on the crud around here. We got to keep looking busy." Simes went to get some brooms.

Chuck said, "I'll bet a guy lost his arm down the line somewhere and now they can't find it."

Pete's nose looked wise. "Aw, I bet I know what it is. Swifty Snyder down in Sliced Bacon accidentally chopped off his cock and Amanda Bauch in Table-Ready Meats passed out when she saw it coming by."

Other laughter could be heard down the line, out of sight around the turn, where workers passed the time with droll stories. The plant was marvelously quiet and voices could be heard with startling clarity.

Simes continued to be scared stiff about the brutally frank way his men were talking. He thrust a broom into each man's hand. "C'mon, get at it."

Simes and his men had just finished sweeping up the hog-kill department when there were shouts down the line and a moment later, jerking, creaking, the chain began to move again.

About two o'clock one afternoon, after seven hours of hard work, Red happened to put his rope on a particularly strong barrow. It fought him all the way across the dusty pen. Red had to pull it toward Pete with a series of hard jerks. Then, just when Red had it handy for Pete, it'd squirt off again.

Red became angry and took it personal, giving a final hard jerk. It was too much and something snapped in the fattener's legs. The fattener stopped fighting him. Red shagged it easily over to Pete.

Red said, "Something's the matter with its leg."

Pete looked with his glittering hard eyes. " 'Pears to be okay to me." And Pete proceeded to snap the revolving wheel chain around the leg.

Red unhooked his rope and stepped back.

The revolving wheel started lifting, when suddenly there was another snap, and before either Pete or Red could do anything, the leg was pulled off, blood squirting everywhere. It was like pulling a leg off a grasshopper. The barrow fell to the floor, stunned.

Red almost collapsed.

"Hold everything!" Pete yelled. "Simes?"

Simes had been overseeing the work of his pigstickers, Jack Prouty and Bud Netter. He bounded over on heavy muscular legs. "Hell! Hook onto its other leg then." When Pete hesitated, Simes with a curse grabbed the next shackling chain coming along and hooked it onto the barrow's other rear leg. An instant later the revolving wheel hoisted up the barrow. Head down, the barrow's sad eyes slowly closed over. Simes unhooked the bleeding severed leg from the chain ahead and with twine tied it to one of the forefeet of the barrow.

Red said, "But that leg fell on the dirty floor."

"Never mind," Simes barked. "It'll go down through the scalding vat in a minute."

The moving chain carried the barrow into the sticking area, and swiftly one of the two pigstickers, holding the barrow's neck with his left hand, jabbed his knife upward into the exposed throat, gave the knife a quick neat twist, and withdrew it. Blood spurted down. It looked as if a hose full of red ink had suddenly been turned on. The blood splashed into a trough below and began running down to the blutwurst department.

"C'mon, c'mon, get to work," Simes ordered. "That ain't the first time that's happened."

When the run finished at three, Red quietly changed clothes and then went down to the personnel department.

He was ushered into a big dark-wood room. The desks and chairs were polished, but the tall windows were dirty with soot. He found himself staring at a kind-faced older man. A nameplate on the desk read, *Norval Packenham.*

"Well, and what can I do for you?" Packenham asked.

Red turned his cap around on his dirty knee several times. "Ain't there some kind of opening for me out there in the yards? I told your other fellow, the one at the window, that I really wanted to work outdoors in the yards."

Packenham put on a sympathetic smile. "We have a long list of men wanting to get in there."

"Oh."

"What's wrong with where you are?" A glint of steely interest entered Packenham's light-blue eyes.

"I don't care much for the killing end of it."

"But you're only catching them, not killing them."

"Where I catch pigs is right next to where they kill them, and I don't have much stomach for a machine that tears the legs off pigs before they're dead."

Packenham stiffened slightly. His gray suit rustled. "There's always accidents, you know. Even out on the street you can get run over by a car."

"I take it then you won't give me a job in the yards."

"No, I'm sorry." Packenham's eyes became harder. "Of course, if you're not happy where you are, you can always quit. There are dozens of men with families to feed who'd be more than happy to take your place."

Red got to his feet. "Thanks." He was afraid he was going to break down and cry. He could already feel the trembles coming on. Quickly he turned and left the big dark-wood room.

That night he had a bad dream. He was trying to cross a swamp. He kept calling for Monte Goring, but Monte only laughed at him. Monte had put a saddle on his pet pig Peggie and had taken to riding her horseback-style across the mud and sluck. The dream was so real Red woke himself with his own cry. He could smell the swampy stink smell of Peggie the pig.

Having watched his friend sin with Peggie and not telling him it was an awful thing to do made him equally guilty. He might as well have done it himself. Cold and wet from the bad dream, Red turned over to find more sleep.

Then one forenoon Red learned that a shipment of fatteners had just come in from a farmer living near Bonnie. It wasn't long before the Siouxland pigs were choused into the shackling pen and Red and Chuck had to start catching them.

Right away it seemed to Red that the batch from Bonnie, a mixture of barrows and gilts, had a familiar look. Soon he saw a dead ringer for the barrow he'd killed for Dad. It was red all over with a white throat.

Red caught it by its hind leg with his rope and dragged it over to Pete. The red barrow fought him all the way. Once it tried to scoot between his legs and he had to catch it in his arms and turn it the other way. It even had that funny swamp stink.

Minutes later Red spotted a black gilt with white mostly over its back. It resembled Monte Goring's pet Peggie exactly. Red stood very still. Catching her would be kind of like murder. Chuck could catch her and drag her off to the revolving wheel.

Then Red heard, in his head, his plump mother reciting a nursery verse:

> "This little pig went to the market,
> This little pig stayed home,
> This little pig had roast beef,
> This little pig had none,
> And this little pig cried wee-wee
>     all the way home."

Red looked around. He was almost afraid someone else might have heard it. But Chuck was grimly going after the next fattener, Pete was hooking a hog onto the wheel, and Simes had gone over to check his stickers.

Red broke out of his stance. He made it a point to take the pig furtherest away from Peggie's double.

He passed over Peggie's double until there were only four fatteners left. For some reason Chuck hadn't grabbed her either. The four left were as wild as pheasants, sailing from one side of the pen to the other. A couple of times Red had a chance to snatch the rear leg of Peggie's double, but he let her get away.

Simes meanwhile had come up behind Red and Chuck, wondering why there were no pigs coming down the moving chain. Simes was aghast. "Hyar! Red! What the hell, you playing favorites now? By God, catch that gilt the next time she comes by or I'm gonna fire you."

Red still hesitated.

Simes cursed, and all of a sudden stepped forward and gave Red a tremendous kick in the butt.

Red was shocked. Not even Dad had ever done that to him. For a second Red thought of jumping Simes, catching him around the neck with his rope and choking him. Instead, crazy mixed up, he went after Peggie's double. She had climbed on top of the other fatteners in a corner. They all squirmed together in a mass of pawing feet and whirling curlicue tails.

"Catch her!" Simes roared.

Red tried to snare one of her legs with his rope, but she kept jerking it under her.

"Goddammit, catch that goddam whore from hell!"

Exasperated, shaking so that he could hardly see, Red grabbed her whirling tail and jerked her out of the squealing melee, got the jump on her, and on the run dragged her to Pete. The voice in his head awoke again: "This little pig went to market." With a vindictive side look at Simes, Red cried, "Here, Pete, here's your whore from hell."

With a flip of his wrist Pete shackled one of her rear legs with his chain, and the revolving wheel drew her up off the floor. The moment she was airborne, head down, she quit squealing and closed her eyes. She knew.

Red watched her go. Jack Prouty with his left hand took hold of her gently behind the ears and then with his right hand stuck her precisely in the white of her neck, giving the knife a deft twist up into her jugular. A gush of blood followed the knife out. Only her flat knob of a nose twitched.

The mechanical ducker took her over next. There was a click and down she plunged into scalding hot water. It was then, as her tender white rubbery nose hit the steaming water, that her soft brown eyes quirked open and she let out a great squeal. She didn't want to die even as blood was pouring from the ragged fatty slit in her throat. She hunched up and away from the boiling water an inch. But the dunking machine continued its revolution and her soft brown eyes, still open, vanished underwater, and then her whole body followed, including even the leg held by the shackling chain. In a moment she emerged, water sluicing off her, steam rising from her crimped tail and butt, and moved on to the dehairing machine. Again she screamed when the steel-rough brushes of the dehairer touched her.

Red turned and puked.

Simes made an awful face. "Son of a bitch."

Red got out a red handkerchief and wiped his mouth. "Sorry." He headed for the lockers.

"Where you going?"

"Get something to clean that up with."

"No you don't. Get back to catching pigs. And no more favorites or as sure as hell—"

"Okay!" Red flipped his rope against his leg, once, and went after the next fattener.

Another bunch of fatteners were choused into the catching pen.

Every once in a while Red's legs on their own gave a little jump.

Luckily no more gilts came by.

But Simes, smoldering, appeared to get madder and madder. His fur was up. He kept watching Red for the least sign of weakness in catching pigs.

They worked right through lunch. There was a heavy run of hogs that day, and the moving chain rattled on and on. Each man had to gobble his sandwiches on the run and catch himself a drink between times.

Around three o'clock Red came upon an unusually large and frisky porker. The porker was almost pure white with a thin black stripe down its back. It was powerful and was one of those who would have made a good boar had it not been cut. Red flipped out the loop in his rope, and surprisingly the barrow stepped into the loop. Red gave the rope a jerk and he had the barrow by the hind leg.

When Red began to pull it across toward Pete, the barrow somehow got the jump on Red and started to run, and by sheer power pulled Red with it until it managed to duck under other milling pigs in a far corner. The rising dust made it hard to see.

Red gave the rope several hard tugs and couldn't budge the barrow.

Suddenly Simes was behind him again. "You must have a muff for a brain."

"Pigs are stubborn sometimes. That's what we mean when we say somebody is being pigheaded."

"Are you calling me pigheaded now?"

Red could feel the trembles coming on. "No."

Then Simes gave Red another kick in the butt. "Pull that goddam pig out of there!"

Outraged, Red gave the rope a tremendous yank, so hard it snapped apart where it had become frayed at the edge of the loop. Red lost his balance and fell on his seat.

"Well of all the goddam dumb things!" Simes' dish eyes glowed like two little moons with halos around them.

It was strange, but Red could feel a little smile creeping along the edges of his lips.

The little smile enraged Simes all the more. "That cuts it. Get up!"

Red got to his feet.

"Give me the end of that rope." Simes jerked what was left of the rope out of Red's hand. "Now come with me. I'm switching you around with Bud Netter. He can catch pigs and you can stick. I'm gonna make or break you here in the kill. A couple of weeks of sticking alongside Jack Prouty will make a real man out of you. Like the rest of us." Simes grabbed Red by the arm and getting the jump on him ran him toward Bud Netter and Jack Prouty. "Bud, put your knife down and go help Chuck Cheny."

Bud looked pleased. He rinsed off his sticking knife in a pail of pinkened water and placed it in a tray. Then he strolled over to where Chuck and Pete were watching.

Simes grabbed up the sticking knife and thrust the handle into Red's hand.

Red's hand didn't close on the handle right away and the knife clattered to the bloody cement floor.

"Well, for godsakes. Not only have you got a heart of mush, but you got butterfingers. Here." Simes stooped to retrieve the knife and once again thrust its handle into Red's hands.

Red managed to hang onto it.

Simes pointed. "All right, Jack, you step back and let Red take the next pig. Now, come on, step up and stab it. Stab it. Goddammit, stab it."

The pig coming up was almost all red. Red heard his father again. *"Now. Stick him just ahead of where the breast bone joins. Where it looks like he's talking. Deep."* Red moved on the red barrow. In anguish, he stuck upward, the knife going in easy, making a crisping noise as it cut through bristles. *"Now twist the knife up and around a little to catch the aorta. Ah. There."* The smell of raw blood, as heady as sweet beer, burst over his hand and splashed down. Blood sudsed up into a creamy froth in the blutwurst trough. . . .

Lying in bed beside his wife Jen, Red agonized over it all again. He was afraid he'd never fall asleep. That bloody memory was getting worse every night. No matter what he did to explain it away, his mind kept going over it again and again.

God should have made man an eater of grass and not an eater of meat, made him a browser instead of a killer. Stabbing a poor helpless creature in the throat, spilling its blood, was not something a child of God should be doing.

Red's legs suddenly kicked out.

Jen turned over. "Mrp?"

Red didn't move.

# Chapter 8

# JEN

Something had awakened Jen. Had John kicked out with his legs again? Jen hoped he wasn't having another one of those awful nightmares. Sometimes John groaned out a name.

Jen listened. John was breathing evenly and slowly. Good. He'd gone back to sleep.

John was lucky. It sometimes took him a while to get to sleep, but once under he was dead to the world until morning. While she was exactly the opposite. She could fall asleep right away, but then around three would wake up and she'd lie there reliving those old sad days again. It made her feel cranky all morning long.

When she was a little girl her father sometimes beat up on her mother when they first went to bed. Those times something in Jen made her fall into a deep sleep. Occasionally Jen caught a glimpse of her mother in the bathtub. Ma was covered black and blue with bruises.

John turned on his side, still sound asleep.

There was a good reason why Jen didn't call her husband Red like other people did. It went back to her Uncle Red, her father's younger brother.

. . . . Uncle Red was a favorite of the family. When Uncle Red came over for a visit, Dad would quit being mean and would get along wonderful with Ma. Ma always welcomed Uncle Red too. During supper Uncle Red would tell a lot of funny stories. Uncle Red was in real estate and had come across a lot of comical clients. Later on in her bed, Jen could hear Dad and Ma laughing in their bedroom about the stories.

But while Dad and Ma were laughing in their bed, Jen was trembling in her bed. Pretty soon, after Dad and Ma had fallen asleep, Uncle Red would come tiptoeing into her room and get into bed with her.

Jen was thirteen the first time he came into her room. She'd just had her first period and had been pretty frightened about that. Ma hadn't been of much help about the period either, except to say it came because Eve had once sinned. "And now you be neat about yourself, you hear?" So in a way Jen was kind of glad to see Uncle Red come smiling through the door in the moonlight and seat himself at the foot of her bed. She loved him because he liked to play little tricks on her when she sat on his lap by the table, like pinch her on one side and then pretend Dad had done it, or pull a single hair on her head and pretend Ma had done it. He was so jokey. She liked his green eyes. There was a look about them which seemed to say: "You and I have a secret, don't we?" She liked secrets. So that first time Uncle Red came into her room she brightened and raised up on her pillow and got ready for some fun.

"Jennie, you're getting to be such a big girl . . . just how old are you?"

"You know. You sent me a birthday card."

"You're almost too heavy to sit on my lap."

"Oh, you. I'm not either."

The moon was shining bright into her room. All he had on was his shorts. He had a hairy chest. It was almost as red as the hair on his head. It made her shiver. She looked at his green eyes instead.

"I don't think Ma would like your being here."

He picked up her hand and played with her fingers. "I bet you've got a lot of boyfriends in school, haven't you?"

"I'm not old enough. You know that."

"You're big enough. What is it the boys say? A real hot tomato."

"Now you're teasing me."

"No, I'm not." He moved up on the bed and then slipped his legs under the covers with her. "Come, put your head on Uncle Red's shoulder." When she didn't move right away, he slipped an arm around her. "There. That's better. Now we can have a real heart-to-heart talk. You and I have never had one of those, have we? And here you're a great big grown girl already."

"You shouldn't be here, Uncle Red."

"Come, let's have a kiss."

"I don't think we should, Uncle Red."

"You've kissed me before."

"Yes, but that was in front of company."

Slowly Uncle Red slid his arm farther around her. His hand moved to her breast. "Why, Jennie, you're a grown girl already."

The moonlight in the room began to bounce funny. What was happening was wrong, but she didn't dare cry out either. She didn't want her father and mother to think bad of Uncle Red. She liked Uncle Red too, and that made it all the harder.

Uncle Red began to breathe hard. His hand began to hold her breast harder. He began to kiss her hair and then her ear and then her brow.

She could feel her eyes cross.

"Jennie, Jennie," Uncle Red whispered winningly in her ear, "what a sweetheart you are. It's so nice to be holding you in my arms. I wish you were older, because then I'd marry you."

"But we're related," she said out loud.

"Shh, not so loud. You don't want your dad and ma to find us like this, do you?"

She'd let her nightgown slide up and her belly was exposed.

Uncle Red's hand moved down. He began to rub her belly up and down. He began to breathe hard again.

Something was going to happen.

Uncle Red parted her legs with his hand and held her in that place where she'd never let anybody touch her before. He really began to breathe hard. "You're big enough." Then Uncle Red pushed down his shorts and got on top of her and that place began to sting something awful. Her eyes hurt in the corners. Pretty soon he was done. He lay beside her awhile and slowly his breathing went back to normal.

It really stung her inside. It hurt like that time when she had her tonsils removed.

Pretty soon Uncle Red sighed, and he patted her shoulder, and said, "You're a good girl, Jennie," and pulling up his shorts got out of bed and went on tiptoe to his room.

She lay a long time feeling the stinging in her belly and the tickle of his hairy chest on her breasts.

Uncle Red came quite often after that, about a dozen times. Both Dad and Ma were surprised, and pleased, that he suddenly wanted to visit them so much.

Jen always smiled at Uncle Red at the table, a little, guardedly. But she was in terror that her father and mother would discover them some night. Worse yet, it was a bad sin.

She didn't know what to do. She thought of killing herself. The worst was that she was afraid she was going to like what he was doing to her. She also thought of getting a scissors and stabbing Uncle Red.

She began to wonder if the way Uncle Red treated her wasn't the reason why Dad and Ma fought so much when they first went to bed. Maybe Dad wanted the same thing from Ma. Men were certainly beasts.

One Saturday night Jen decided she'd had enough. She was going to fix him.

At supper table she asked him why he didn't have a date that night with some girl. "Most other guys are out with their girl on a Saturday night, ain't they?"

Uncle Red winked at her, on her side of his face so Dad and Ma couldn't see it. "Well, you're my girl, ain't you?"

"Uncles don't marry nieces."

"Well, I wasn't thinking of marrying you." Again he winked sidelong at her.

"Oh, so you were going to throw me aside like some old dishrag, were you?"

Uncle Red warned her with another look to be careful around her father and mother. "Honey, Jennie, I was only joking. You know that."

Dad asked, "Why, Jennie, what's got into you?"

"I know what he wants. And no, I don't love him anymore." It was like a balky cat had got into her throat and it wasn't going to behave.

Uncle Red was scared. He began to squirm in his chair.

Ma woke up at her end of the table. "Whatever has happened between the two of you? Jennie?"

"Well, Uncle Red can just quit coming into my room at night when he thinks you people are asleep."

"What!" Dad jumped straight up out of his chair. He upset his cup of steaming coffee.

Ma almost fell off her chair. "Jennie," she whispered.

Uncle Red put down his fork and knife very carefully.

Now that it was out, Jen decided to ease things a little. At least Uncle Red wouldn't be visiting her room anymore. "Well, I just don't like it that he wakes me up to talk to me. I like my sleep just like anybody else."

Dad sat down very slowly. He ran a jumpy hand through his curly brown hair. His eyes glowed as though they were burners on an electric stove. He drilled a look into Jen for a moment and then like a slow-turning spotlight on a police car looked at Uncle Red. "Is what she just said true, Red?"

Uncle Red picked up his fork and knife again. He cut his meat in his usual fancy city way and with his fork still in his left hand lifted the meat into his mouth. Between chews he said, "I heard her coughing one night and I went to see what was the matter. If she had a cold."

Dad turned his spotlight eyes on Jen. "Is that true, Jen?"

Ma broke in. She was afraid of what Jen was going to say. "You're not going to call your brother a liar, are you now, George Haron?"

Dad said, "Well, no, I guess not."

After that Uncle Red didn't come very often.

Jen often wondered if her life would have been different if her baby sister Veloura hadn't died. Jen was four and Veloura was two when they both got the croup. They were very sick. But finally Jen pulled through and Veloura didn't.

Jen was glad Veloura was gone. Jen had hated to share her playthings with Veloura, she hated to share Dad and Ma with her.

Had Veloura lived, though, and had Veloura slept in the same room with her, Uncle Red wouldn't have dared to come into her room.

When Jen was a little girl Dad wasn't home much. They lived in the town of Brokenhoe and Dad was a drummer for a nail and wire company out of Minneapolis. He sold nails, staples, barbwire, and woven-wire fencing all over Minnesota and the Dakotas. When he'd come home once a month, he and Ma would right away get into one of their awful rows about a husband's rights.

The nail and wire company finally went broke. Dad next barbered in South St. Paul near the stockyards for a year. For a while he was a lot of fun again. He'd gotten over Veloura's being gone and didn't drink much.

Dad often came home with great scary stories.

Once a man had come into Dad's barbershop and collapsed whitefaced in Dad's barber chair. "Godd!" the man gasped.

"Haircut?"

"Yeh. Jesus, yeh."

Dad tied the apron string around the man's neck and then spread it over his chest. "What happened out there?"

"Just saw a nigger slice open a white man's belly. Just as they was leaving Steele's."

"A nigger really did that?"

"Yeh. 'Course the white guy had it coming. He'd been needling the nigger for weeks. So finally the nigger exploded. Got out his razor and sliced him open. Godd. Bowels boiling out."

"Did they arrest the nigger?"

"Yeh. When Chief of Police Tom Price heard the nigger had gone up to his room above Nick's, he went to get him. But the nigger had already left. While looking out of the nigger's window, Chief Tom spotted him ducking through the stockyards amongst the cattle. Well, the chief flushed him out right before my eyes, the two of them shooting it out with the nigger using one of them old long horse pistols. Chief Tom finally cut him down."

Sometimes barbering was slow, especially for the second chair. The first barber did well, but not Dad, and pretty soon Dad began to drink. Dad got to thinking about his dead Veloura again.

Ma took to visiting spiritualists. She wanted to get a message that Veloura was in heaven. Ma thought that if she could get such a message in a seance she could then take Dad down some night and have Veloura tell him. If Dad could just hear Veloura once, talking to him from the other side, it might cure his drinking.

The medium never convinced Ma that she'd heard Veloura from the other side, and so Dad continued to mourn the loss of Veloura. Jen hated Veloura.

Jen went to the Brokenhoe High School. She was a scared kid all the way through. She was too shy to recite well in class. She always had the feeling that, behind her somewhere, a cloud was following her around. She refused all dates, wouldn't go to the junior-senior prom, didn't join any clubs.

The first year out of high school she moped around home, helping Ma with the housework, sometimes helping Dad clean out the cellar and the garage. She learned to start the mower and pushed that around in the summertime.

No matter how much Dad and Ma urged her to go to church socials and mingle with people, Jen wouldn't go. Jen said she was cured of men. Uncle Red never came anymore, and that was the end of that. She heard he'd gotten married and had two little girls. She often wondered what Uncle Red's thoughts were when he looked at his girls.

Several times Jen thought of becoming a nun. Once she went so far as to take secret instructions from the local priest. But the priest queered that when he told her that he'd blessed Brokenhoe first and Robbinsdale second and that was why that great wheel of clouds with five tornadoes in it had all of a sudden headed north toward Robbinsdale instead of east toward Brokenhoe. Their Presbyterian preacher would never have tolerated such nonsense. God didn't play favorites with towns.

A couple of times Jen visited Dad while he barbered. She'd ride along with him in the morning and first go visit with a high school friend in South St. Paul for lunch and then around two would wait in back of the barbershop, reading the magazines, sometimes cleaning Dad's sink for him. The customers got used to her and after a while talked as if she weren't there. It always amazed her the way Dad could pick up a conversation with a customer where they'd left off from the last haircut. "Now this Irene you was mentioning . . ." It was like Dad was knitting a hundred stocking caps at the same time, one each with a different customer, and always knew what thread he'd left off with.

At last Dad got himself a good job closer to home. It was at Honeywell in South Minneapolis. Dad knew metal, and they put him to work as a spot welder. Dad had always been good at soldering Ma's pots and pans. Dad didn't have to rush on the job and he was making something with his hands that would be around for a while. Gradually Dad quit his drinking. And Dad and Ma didn't fight as much anymore either.

Jen was twenty-three when it hit her that she was about to become an old maid. It wasn't that men weren't interested in her. There'd been two men who'd tried to date her. But both had been married. She wondered what there was about her that attracted older men instead of younger men.

Two more years went by. And then Dad came home one evening to say that Honeywell had temporarily laid him off. Dad looked very sad. The Harons still owed some money on their house.

It was then that Jen decided to get out of the nest and get a job somewhere to help her parents pay for the house. She studied the want ads in both the Minneapolis and St. Paul papers. None looked very promising. She couldn't sell. She couldn't type or take dictation. She couldn't teach. There just wasn't much she could do except housework.

Finally one day she saw an ad in the *Pioneer-Press* that caught her eye. Nick's Cafe in South St. Paul needed a waitress. It was down the street from where Dad had once barbered. She'd had a chocolate sundae there several times. The customers were mostly farmers and stockyards workers, the simple people Dad liked.

Jen rode the streetcar over. Nick took one look at her and hired her on the spot. She was exactly the kind of girl he wanted. Farmers liked to josh waitresses, but they liked to think it was virgins they were joshing and not whores. Nick found a room for her up on the cliff at 220 First Avenue South.

She hadn't been at work more than a month at Nick's when one night a strong-looking young man with a red face and golden red hair and lost blue eyes wandered in. The young man took a corner table. She saw him sit down from where she stood in the kitchen in back. It was her section to take care of, and after a moment she brought out a glass of water. He looked out of place. He ordered a beer, which made her frown, remembering her father and his drinking.

She got the fellow a hamburger and a piece of apple pie à la mode. He spotted her name sewn on her smock and started to talk to her. He was very bashful, yet he kept talking. It turned out he too was looking for a job to help his folks. She liked him right away and was reluctant to leave his table. She told him that Nick had beds upstairs for floaters. She was sorry she'd used the word "floaters" because she didn't mean he was one. He had a wonderful healthy country look about him. He was exactly the kind of young man she should have.

She didn't see the young man again for a couple of months. At least he didn't drink at Nick's. But she was sure that in the meantime he'd forgotten her. She began to feel sad.

She'd just started working her shift one afternoon at four when there he was, sitting at the corner table again. She brightened immediately and went over to the mirror behind the door to make sure her brown hair was all right, the waves in place and smooth, and then, filling a glass with water, went out to get his order. She had a little smile for him. "The usual?"

He looked up. "What?" It took him a moment to remember her. It helped when he saw her name sewn on her tan-and-white smock. "Oh. That's right." He was crying. "What was it that I ordered again that time?"

"A beer first," she said. "And then a hamburger and an apple pie à la mode."

"Now I remember. That first night I was in town."

"So it'll be the usual then?"

"No," he said. "No, I didn't come here to eat. I don't know what I came here for." A sob shook him.

"What's the matter?" She looked around. Nobody was looking their way. "Did you get hurt?"

He cried down at the table. "Oh, I didn't lose a finger or a hand or anything like that. But what I am missing is a backbone."

"Here, why don't you take a sip of water."

He took a sip. One of his tears, yellow, fell into the bubbly city water. A tiny pinched wail escaped him despite gritted teeth. "I'm a goldang failure. My dad will never forgive me." He shook his head. "If only I had a friend."

Jen held her bosom. So he felt what she felt. Well. She made up her mind. "Just a minute," she said. "You stay here. I'll be right back."

She went over to Nick behind the bar. "Nick, could you call Ella to see if she can take my shift tonight? Something's come up."

Nick frowned. He'd been watching Jen talk with the red-faced fellow. "Is he relation?"

"Tell Ella I'll take her shift any day she wants to take off."

Nick ran a hand through his straight black hair. "All right. But don't do this to me too often. A lot of my customers depend on seeing you here on this shift."

"I know. Thanks, Nick."

She got her coat and hurried back to the young fellow's table. "You really weren't going to order anything, were you?"

"No. Except maybe a beer."

"Why don't we go take a walk instead?"

"You can take off just like that?"

"Nick's a good boss. Shall we go?"

He got to his feet and buttoned up his jacket.

They stepped outside. Sunlight lay warm over the stockyards. The red coats of the cattle shone as if rubbed down with hair oil.

"Let's go to my rooms first," Jen said, "so I can get out of this smock."

"All right by me."

While she changed he waited downstairs in the hallway. She put on her best dress, a green suit with white blouse, and green velvet shoes. Here was her man at last. And right now that man needed comfort. She hurried down the steps.

He looked up. "Say, you got all dressed up."

"Well, I don't often get a chance to wear it."

"Don't you have a boyfriend?"

"Not really." She didn't want him to think nobody wanted her. "Don't you have a girlfriend?"

"I've never had a date in my life. Been too busy scrambling to help Dad save his farm."

"If that ain't the cat's pajamas."

He looked down at his clothes, blue denim jacket and overalls. "Maybe I should change mine too."

"You look all right to me." She took his arm. "Come, let's take a walk over to the city park. It's on the other side of City Hall."

They didn't have much to say. The children were in school and only a few housewives were out getting groceries. The trees had put out their first spring buds. Instead of the usual acrid powdered-manure smell coming up off the stockyards there was the sweet water smell drifting in from the Mississippi.

They found a stone seat near some bridal wreath bushes. It was out of the wind, and the late-afternoon sun caught them both on their cheeks.

After another silence, Jen finally asked, "What was it that got you so all worked up?"

John picked up a twig from the dead grass and broke it into tiny pieces. His tears had dried, but the corners of his eyes were still red.

"Did someone you know die?"

He threw the pieces of the twig away.

She waited.

Again that tiny pinched wail escaped him. "I'm just not man enough to be in the hog kill. I guess."

"Ask for a job in some other department then."

"I have. And if I quit, where would I go?"

"What's so bad about the hog kill?"

"I can't kill things."

"But don't we have to eat?"

"I guess we do. But why couldn't we all have been like sheep and eat grass?"

Jen had to laugh. "Just grass? Couldn't we eat a little lettuce too?"

"The Bible speaks of Jesus as being our shepherd and that all we like sheep should follow Him."

Jen gave his arm a pinch. "You funny fellow you. I suppose you think Jesus didn't eat meat?"

He sighed. "Yeh, I suppose he did."

"What does the minister say when we celebrate the Lord's Supper? When he breaks bread and gives us a piece of it, doesn't he say, 'Take, eat, this is my body'? And when he fills a cup with wine and passes it on to us, doesn't he say, 'Drink ye all of it for this is my blood'? Jesus wouldn't have talked that way if He wasn't a meat eater." Jen allowed herself a little laugh and a shrug of the shoulders. "The funny thing is, I think plants have feelings too. I feel just as bad when a tree is cut down as when a dog is run over by a car."

"But a tree can't talk."

"But if you cut a tree it bleeds, doesn't it? What's blood for one is sap for the other."

The red in the corners of his eyes slowly faded. "Are you trying to tell me it's just as bad to eat grass as it is to eat meat?"

"Yes. All are live creatures of God."

"You funny woman you." Then he laughed.

"There's nothing I like more than to plant little trees in the spring. Or tomato sets. When they're tender and bendy, they're all like little babies to me."

"Boy, what a tomato you turned out to be."

At that Jen ruffed up. "Don't call me a tomato."

He held up a hand. "All right, all right. I'm sorry."

Jen collected herself. "So. There. It isn't all that bad that we kill hogs. We have to eat. It's a necessary thing. As long as we don't kill hogs for the fun of it, but only because it has to be done, then it's all right."

"You make it sound pretty nice."

She gave his arm a shake. "You stubborn nut you." Then she said, "Here I am talking to you like I've known you for years and I still don't know your name."

"I'm John Engleking."

"That what they call you? John?"

"They mostly call me Red."

She almost jumped up. Red? My God. Well, she wasn't going to call him Red.

"Don't you like that name?" he asked.

She ignored his question. "Really, John, butchering can be a good thing."

"Some of those pigs coming in look almost human. You can see in their eyes they know what's coming. It tears me all up when I see that look just as I'm about to stick 'em." John shuddered.

Jen fell silent. He felt like she did when she had to thin out the little evergreen trees because she'd planted them too thick when they were seedlings. She felt sorry for those she had to throw away.

He shuddered again. "Uhr."

She gave his arm another shake. Around this man she wasn't shy. "Let's talk about something else. So gloomy."

"Okay, what shall we talk about?"

She couldn't help but giggle. "Is it really true you've never had a date?"

"No, I never have."

"Don't you want to?"

"I guess so."

"Don't you know?"

"I guess so." Then he had to laugh. "Sure I do."

"Well then. Why don't you get busy?"

His fingers began to twitch. It was with an effort that he finally faced her. "Would you go out with me?"

For a fleeting second she thought of being a tease, but then she remembered she'd seen him crying back at Nick's. "Sure."

"You will?"

"Why not? Is there something the matter with you?" Then she bit her tongue, remembering what Uncle Red had done to her.

"Not that I know of. Just that I hate killing."

"If that's all that's the matter"—she overcame a little catch in her voice—"with you, why, you're practically perfect."

John laughed. "My dad ought to hear you say that."

"Maybe it was the Lord's wish that we both waited."

"Yes. Well, when shall it be? What nights are you off?"

"Sunday night. I work the other six nights."

"I suppose you go to church Sunday night?"

"Not always."

"Would you go to a movie with me?"

"Sure. If you wanted that."

"I've never seen one. And it's about time I did."

"Neither have I."

"No? Say, this is going to be a lot of fun."

They looked at each other, and then both blushed.

It took four dates before John got up enough gumption to put his arm around her. Even then he twitched so much she really didn't enjoy it. He made her timorous too.

On their sixth date he made his move. She'd invited him up to her two rooms to show him her family pictures. She was sitting on the bed and he on the chair, and they were looking at the wedding picture of Dad and Ma, when he got up and plumped himself down beside her and put his arms around her and gave her a tremendous smack. With a startled laugh she kissed him back. Encouraged, he pushed her back into her pillows and got on top of her. Scared at last, she shoved him off. At that his hands fell slack. Slowly turning red, like he'd been stained through and through with a dye, he apologized. He looked exactly like a penitent little boy. It was then she knew he truly was innocent, that he knew nothing about lovemaking.

They continued to date, but it was understood that they'd wait until they got married.

She took John home with her one Sunday to announce they were engaged. Ma looked relieved. And Pa was somewhat shocked.

Recovering after a while, Pa gave John the third degree. John was a man about it all; he didn't once tremble. Then Dad began to question her close. How could they keep on sending money home if they got married? Two could not live as cheap as one; in fact, soon there'd be babies and then instead they'd be coming for help.

But John had to have her. And she was anxious to have a man of her own at last.

The first night she decided she was going to pretend she was a virgin, and she resisted him and each time he was about to start told him it hurt awful. Pretty soon he couldn't. They let go of each other and slept as far apart from each other as the bed would allow. Sometime during the night he awoke with a little yelp and made some grabbing motions. Then he sighed. The next morning she found a stain in the sheets on his side of the bed.

A week later they fumbled each other awake and were surprised to discover that they'd almost become man and wife in sleep, and it made them both laugh and then they did. It appeared to be wonderful for him but not so very wonderful for her.

At first they lived in her two rooms. Then she heard down at Nick's there was a house for rent at 324 First Avenue South. It overlooked the stockyards and the wide Mississippi and was painted white with green windows like Dad and Ma's bungalow and it had four oaks on the lawn, one on each corner.

She grew to love him. She learned to indulge him in bed, though it always remained painful, dry, for her. For a time he got over his nervousness and rarely talked about his work in the kill.

She became pregnant at about the same time Dad got his job back at Honeywell. She no longer needed to worry about sending home part of her paycheck.

The third month into her pregnancy she got the trembles. It was as if she'd caught them from John. The least sound outside at night made her jump. She would sometimes shiver in bed for hours. Occasionally John had to hold her in his arms all night to quiet her down.

She lost their first baby at the end of the fourth month. It happened while she was ironing. She felt an awful cramp and rushed to the bathroom. She just barely made it. There was an awful mess in a pail.

She was bleeding badly. She stood awhile in the bathroom swabbing herself. Finally she decided to drive their old car to the doctor's office near City Hall. The doctor got the bleeding stopped and sent her home and told her to go to bed. Before she did, she took the mess in the pail and buried it in the backyard at the edge of their garden.

When John found her in bed late that afternoon, she told him about losing the baby. But she didn't tell him that she'd buried it behind the house.

Recovered, she went down to a nursery along the Mississippi and bought a small evergreen seedling, a balsam fir, and then with eyes screwed up into narrow gimlets planted it on top of the fetus. Within a year the balsam fir's roots would reach down to where the fetus lay and would begin to take nourishment from it.

The dead child under the balsam fir made her think of her dead sister Veloura. She still didn't regret that Veloura was gone. She began to wonder too if maybe it wasn't a good thing after all that the baby was out of the way.

She continued to work at Nick's. She and John decided to buy the house they were living in with the money she no longer had to send home. They got a good mortgage with a low interest rate.

Several months later, when she became pregnant again, she decided to go see a doctor. She told him she was spotting. The doctor gave her a grave look and informed her bluntly that if she didn't quit work she'd lose the second one too. So she quit her job. The thought came to her that while her first baby might be like the lost Veloura, the new baby in her belly was like herself, and it would live.

John thought it was all right she quit her job. He had never really liked it that she worked down at the cafe with all those rough characters joshing her. It was about that time John hit that fellow in the cafe because the fellow had called him a dirty name. Soon after John took up boxing in his spare time. He said it would take up the slack of her not working.

She lost the second baby. Eyes screwed up even tighter, as if she weren't going to allow either God or man to have even as much as a peek into her, she buried the second fetus next to the first one at the edge of the garden. She planted a balsam fir seedling over that one too.

She never told John where she'd put the dead babies. He accepted what she might have done with them like he accepted what she did with her sanitary pads.

One morning she noticed that one of the little balsam firs appeared to have the wilt. It was the one on top of her first baby. She went out to look; couldn't see anything wrong. She got her clippers and cut off the dead-looking needles. She touched it with love. She hoped it would be all right.

A week later the other little balsam fir began to turn yellow. Again she pruned it and touched it with affection and hoped it would be all right.

Both balsams died. It was when she dug them up to replant them with new seedlings that she discovered what had happened. She could smell it in the dirt. Before going to bed John liked to urinate outside in the grass. John had killed the two little balsam firs with his piss.

She went into a rage. She burned his potatoes that night. She told him off. "You're no better than a dog lifting his leg at a tree."

"Oh, c'mon, Jen, the way I do it nothing dies. I keep backing up, so no one spot gets too much. Burns out."

"You're crazy."

"Fact. Where the grass grows greenest is where the cow keeps walking along as she pees. It turns out to be the deepest grass in the pasture. But where she stands still, there it burns out. If you ever look at a pasture you can just see them little green islands and them little burnt-out deserts."

Jen threw a potholder at him. "Don't you dare to come within ten feet of those new seedlings I'm going to replant out there with your dingus or some night when you're asleep I'll cut it off with my scissors." She looked at him with her eyes just slits. She dared him to look into them.

She was never going to tell him what she'd buried under those seedlings. It was her secret, along with her other secret about Uncle Red. Besides, if John learned about where his seedlings had gone, it might bring on his nightmares again. . . .

Jen listened to her husband sleeping on his side. Then she sighed and turned away from him. She tried to make out the clock on the bedside table. It was six o'clock. She'd been awake at least two hours. In a few moments she'd have to get up and make John's breakfast. The kill started at seven.

# Chapter 9

.

# ALAN

A few days later, at the paper, Alan couldn't find his sheaf of notes. He looked everywhere, in his jacket pockets, out in his car. Mentally he went back over the day. He'd talked with Burt Cowens about the new white boxing hope from the stockyards, taken a leak with Quinsey in the men's room, finished his work on the desk, got into his car and drove to South St. Paul, found Red Engleking's home, had trouble getting someone to answer the door until Red happened along, and then the interview . . . oh, yes. He'd placed his sheaf of notes on the Engleking coffee table just before he left their house. The notes should still be there.

He telephoned the Englekings.

Jen answered. "Hello." She spoke so prutish he almost didn't recognize her voice.

"Mrs. Engleking? This is Alan Ross. You know, the man who was over at your place the other day to talk with your husband?"

"Yes?"

"I think I left my notes on your coffee table. Would you please go look to see if they're still there?"

"They are here all right. I found them."

"Oh, good. Would you put them to one side for me? I won't be able to pick them up today anymore. But I'll be along in a couple of days to get them."

Jen said, "I'll put them on the dining table." Her voice became softer. "Next to that bowl of wax flowers there."

"Good. I'll be seeing you."

It was three days before Alan got around to driving out to South St. Paul. He'd finally needed his sheaf of notes because Red Engleking was going to fight a ranking heavyweight contender and Burt had decided they should run a feature on Red in the Sunday paper.

Alan knocked on the Engleking door. When there was no answer, like the other time, he knocked again.

Nothing happened. Nor was there any movement in the curtains. Nor was there the sound of stealthy footsteps on the other side of the door.

Darn. He had to have those notes. He didn't dare trust his memory. He'd only recently got to the point where his stories were printed pretty much as he wrote them.

Alan walked around the house and rapped on the back door, hoping that if Jen was at that end she might hear him knock there.

Again no answer.

He decided she'd gone shopping. God only knew when she'd be back. And Red of course was at work.

Darn. He had to have those notes. He tried both front and back doors. Locked.

He next tried the south windows. Hooked.

Coming around the north side of the house, he noticed that a bedroom window was partly open. If a fellow could somehow unlatch the hook on the inside of the screen, he could then open the screen, shove up the window, and get in.

It wouldn't be any fun if somebody caught him, of course. He could be nailed for breaking and entering.

He didn't feel like coming all the way back out to South St. Paul later again in the day. Too bad he hadn't called ahead. He thought: "Well, I'm sure Red would understand. It's not like I'm out to steal anything. I'm only getting what's mine and about which I've already talked to Jen."

But suppose Jen were inside and scared stiff like the other time? What a fine how-do-you-do that would be. He could just see Burt holding his head sideways at him and asking, "Were those notes really all that important?"

Most people hid an extra key near the front door in case they lost their key ring. Wouldn't hurt to try that first. He went around to the front of the house and began looking, under the welcome mat, in the tin mailbox, in the flowerpots on the edge of the porch, and on the ledge over the door. Nothing. Dammit.

He had to have those notes if he was still going to work on that story yet that day. There were just no two ways about it.

If he could only find a piece of stiff wire. He kicked through the gravel near the Engleking garage in back, then checked the garbage cans along the alley, at last poked his nose into the garage. He was a little startled to see their car inside. That meant Jen had gone shopping on foot.

Walking around the garage yet again, he spotted a wire tacked up on one side of the big door. Red apparently used it to tie back the door on windy days. Alan unhooked it and straightened it out. It was just right, stiff and springy both.

He went back to the window that was partway open and got down on his knees and peered in through the rusty screen to see what he had to contend with. It was a simple hook-and-eye device. The hook didn't appear to be very tight in the eye screw, either.

Just to make sure no one was in that part of the house he tried to peer into the room itself. But the tan blind had been drawn down too far to make anything out.

He bent the stiff wire into a curve with a looped hook at the end, then pried a tiny opening into the screen, began working the looped hook over and down past the frame. Twice his looped hook caught at the screen's hook and moved it slightly. But the screen's hook didn't move quite enough to slip out of the eye. He pulled his wire pry out and reshaped it, putting a sharper angle into it.

He tried again. Carefully he caught his looped hook on the screen's hook and carefully wedged his wire pry around. And, click, out it was. He removed his wire pry from the screen, lifted the screen open, and thrust his head and shoulders inside, brushing under the blind.

There was an anguished sound of someone sucking in a great breath. And a woman, Jen, managed to gasp, on a bed not a foot away, "I know what you want!"

It was Alan's turn to gasp. "Jen! You're home after all!" His eyes began to flicker. He reached in a hand and placed it firmly on her hip to let her know he was a friend. "Jen. Jen. It's me. Alan Ross. You know, I called you about those notes? I came to get them."

"You scared me half to death, you crazy fool!"

"Oh, Jen." He gave her hip a comforting shake. "I knocked and knocked. And tried all the doors first. But nobody answered." Lord, what must her thoughts not have been as she listened to him trying to get in. "And I really needed those notes this very afternoon, and I thought it wouldn't hurt any if I got 'em this way. I figured we were friends enough for me to do that."

"But people just don't push into other people's homes without getting permission first."

"I know."

"I could have you arrested."

"Yes. And I'm sorry."

"If I hadn't been so scared I'd have got up out of bed and called the cops."

"I wish you had got out of bed. Because then if you would have just looked you'd have seen who it was."

"Oh, you scared me!" She raised herself up on her elbows. Her brown eyes glittered blackly at him in the darkened room.

"I should have just waited until your husband came home." Alan shook his head at himself. "But that's the way I am sometimes. I get a bee in my bonnet and then there's nothing for it but what I've got to do something about it right then and there. Like I'm obsessed."

"Crazy, you mean."

"Yes, I guess a little crazy too." He was thinking of the haunt he'd made out of his dead brother John. Even worse he'd lately linked up his haunt John with this woman's husband.

She swung out of bed and brushed down her blue dress.

With his butt still sticking out of the window, he knew he must look a sight to anyone outside. "Why don't I just back out of here and go around to the front door and knock all proper and nice."

"Do that," she said. A hint of a smile edged into her voice. "And I'll hook the screen here again."

He backed out, brushed himself off, and went around in front and rapped on the door.

Jen opened up. Her voice was firm. "Well, now that I know who you are, besides getting your notes you might as well have a cup of coffee."

He stepped inside. "That I'd love. And you're a sweetheart to let me in after what happened."

She allowed herself a light snort. She showed him to the same chair he'd sat in before, and poured him a cup of coffee. Then she got him his notes.

Just as he was about to pocket the notes, he noted they didn't seem to be in as tight a pack as before. With a smile, he asked, "You didn't by any chance take a peek?"

She pinkened slightly. "No." Then she said with a little laugh, "But I'm not hysterical."

He laughed too. "I couldn't think of the right word at the time, so I used that one. Later on, when I was to write it up from these notes, I'd have picked a more friendly one."

"But why must you write us up at all? We're just ordinary people."

"When your husband took up boxing he was suddenly in the public eye."

She picked at a thread in the hem of her blue dress.

"Don't worry. I intend to be friendly in my story. Fair but friendly."

They talked awhile. Soon she was at ease with him. Several times she laughed merrily at his tries at wit.

Alan couldn't resist asking, "Have you always been like this when home alone?"

She got red and looked down at her lap. "Well, not always."

"You must've got good and scared once."

"Maybe I was."

"Hasn't your husband tried to help you get over it?"

"John? What can he do? It's the way I am."

Alan thought: "If I were married to her I'd spend a lot of time being tender with her. Understanding."

"Once you burn yourself on a stove you're always careful again around that stove."

He got to his feet. "Jen, I've got to go. And I'm real sorry for what happened. I guess I was a little nuts thinking I had to have these notes today. I could have waited."

"Forget it," she said, at last giving him a wide white smile. "We've got a secret we can laugh about now."

Later, on the way back to the office, Alan murmured to himself, "Funny she's so scared in her own home that she can't even turn her head a little to see who might be at the window. Going into a freeze like that, somebody must have really wracked her up once. Her bursting out with that 'I know what you want!'—it almost sounds like somebody tried to rape her once."

# Chapter 10

# ALAN

Burt Cowens went along with Alan to cover the Moroney-Engleking fight at the Armory. Only a small crowd was on hand. Alan's sympathetic story about Red hadn't drummed up much business.

Alan and Burt had ringside seats. Other Twin City reporters were there with their typewriters. Photographers kneeled around the ring's edge, waiting for Moroney and Engleking to come in. Peppery Stanley Kott also had a ringside seat and was chewing gum a mile a minute. There was a scattering of dignitaries in the audience: the mayor, Mt. Curve socialites, flashy gamblers, a pair of rabid ladies who in private life were scrubwomen, ex-pugilists, fathers and sons.

The boar smell of the passionate fan was in the air. The small crowd was noisy and lusted for action. Except for the brilliant white light coning down on the ring, there was only dim lighting in the Armory.

Red Engleking, the challenger, came in first, followed by his manager and a second. Red quickly climbed through the ropes and stalked over to his stool.

"Say," Alan said, "that's not the Red I know."

Burt wriggled his straight nose. "How so?"

"He's usually shy. Almost apologetic. But look at him. He's all riled up. Something's going on."

Burt's gray eyes narrowed in icy speculation. He glanced at Red's manager. "Maybe Ernie Fliegel's stuck him in the butt with a prod pole."

Alan studied Red some more. "No, it's something else."

"Hmm."

"Maybe something's happened down at the kill where he works."

Burt grunted. "Sounds kind of funny to say a shy guy works in the hog kill."

Alan studied Red some more. "I dunno."

Figleaf Moroney came trooping in next with his manager and seconds. Moroney had such huge thighs his tight boxing shorts looked like a figleaf on him. It hadn't taken long for boxing fans to give him the appropriate nickname. Figleaf climbed into the ring to a rising roar from the crowd. He was a favorite. He raised his gloves and shook them as if he already was the victor.

Figleaf's florid face was all chewed up by cuts and bruises from boxing, and deeply pitted by acne, and very puffy around the eyes. The eyes were those of a ferocious mink, black, quickly darting, savage. His hairy shoulders sloped off into biceps as large as picnic hams. His arms were short but very thick. He had a considerable belly, which in turn sloped down into surprisingly narrow hips.

Referee Johnny Dunn slipped between the ropes into the ring next. He was a slim dapper fellow. High forehead, slicked-back brown hair, slender-waisted, a former lightweight Golden Gloves champion from Duluth. A moment later fight promoter Jack Burns climbed into the ring with a bullhorn. Jack had a belly that looked exactly like a just-risen mound of bread dough. It swung about loosely, pretty much controlling what direction Jack would take next. Jack Burns first waddled over to check Red's boxing gloves for foreign objects, then waddled over to check Figleaf's gloves. Satisfied, he raised the bullhorn to his lips.

"Ladies and gentlemen. As your promoter, it is my pleasure to bring you, as the main feature of this fight cahd, in that corner on my left, in red trunks, weighing in at one hundred and eighty-two pounds, known as the killer from the stockyards in South St. Paul, none other than Red Engleking."

There were boos and catcalls.

Jack Burns lifted his bullhorn again. His long cheeks had the color of stretched dough. "And in this corner on my right, in black trunks, weighing in at two hundred and thirty-seven pounds, known as the ladies' cherce at the Stockholm Cafe in Minneapolis, the one and only, Figleaf Moroney."

There were cheers and huzzahs. One woman shrilled, "Go after him, Fig old boy, you're the greatest!"

Burt said, "So that's what Jack's doing. Preying on an old rivalry between Minneapolis and St. Paul."

Alan said, "Like in the old days when champions fought instead of armies."

"Right. David and Goliath."

Alan thought that an apt comparison.

Promoter Jack Burns retired through the ropes, one banty leg at a time, his doughy blob of a belly giving him a pendulumlike motion, his pasty face flushing over for a moment.

Referee Dunn waved for the two fighters to come to the center of the ring. Both shed their robes. Heads bowed, both listened to the referee's last-minute instructions. Figleaf through it all kept up a series of sniffs and snorts, arms constantly pistoning back and forth. He couldn't wait to eat Red alive. Meanwhile Red stood stiffly, eyes staring at the canvas floor. The referee's words could just be made out over the din. "Now I want a fair fight and I want a clean fight."

The fighters returned to their corners, Figleaf windmilling his arms, Red moving on the balls of his feet.

"What do you think?" Alan asked Burt.

"This will be a good test for your friend."

"You've seen Figleaf fight?"

"Twice."

"What's he like?"

"Street-brawler type. Keeps flailing away. Best punch is a left hook. And that, oddly enough, is smoothly oiled."

Both fighters sat waiting on their stools with their fight managers talking fast.

Alan asked, "Can Figleaf take it in the stomach?"

Burt said, "If he's vulnerable anywhere, that's it. He's been souping up the beer."

Figleaf had originally signed up to fight Blackie Kavold. But Blackie had come down with a burst appendix. Promoter Burns had then substituted Red Engleking. That had put Figleaf in a rage. "Who's ever heard of this Englefart fellow?" Figleaf wanted to know. "I haven't." But Promoter Burns wouldn't let Figleaf back out of his contract. Thereupon Figleaf announced to all and sundry that he was gonna get the bout over with in the very first round by a knockout. He was going to get that pigsticker Red Englequeen from South St. Paul before he got a chance to get roused up and use that wrecking-ball punch of his.

The bell rang; the crowd roared in anticipation.

Figleaf charged out of his corner on a leaning run, snorting, arms windmilling, legs driving.

Red advanced a few steps, and then stopped. He waited until Figleaf was almost upon him, then deftly skipped to one side and jabbed Figleaf a glancing blow on the side of his head. Figleaf was shoved off his course and bounced against the ropes.

Figleaf set sail for Red again, arms windmilling. The soles of his leather shoes catching on the canvas floor squeaked like crickets.

Red jumped forward to meet Figleaf head on. Red's face and jaw were set hard. Just as Figleaf's famed looped left came around, Red slid forward a half step, leaned his head to the right a little to slip Figleaf's left, let go with his own left hook. He beat Figleaf to the punch by a split second, a crackling shot that halted Figleaf in his tracks. It was as though someone had grabbed Figleaf by his collar and had jerked him back a foot.

Burt raised an eyebrow.

Alan had trouble sitting still. His stomach shrank to the size of a peanut.

The crowd fell silent. People had trouble believing what they were seeing. Photographers leaped into action, lightbulbs flashing. Referee Dunn leaned in from the hips from his spot, watching the boxers, face impassive.

Figleaf pawed around until he found Red and then fell into a clinch with him. Figleaf clearly was hurt. His knees were rubbery.

Referee Dunn skipped over and separated them.

Red waited, fists up.

Burt frowned. "He's not a killer. He should have jumped in there before Figleaf could fall into a clinch."

"Wait," Alan said.

Figleaf slowly fixed his black mink eyes on Red and charged him again. Once more Red jumped toward him to meet him head on. Both moved like two unforgiving bulls. Red flicked out a left jab. It fell short. Red immediately slid forward with a second jab which landed with a hard snap. Then he shot a short hard right. Something had to give, and it was Figleaf's head. It bobbed back even as his great chest and belly rolled forward. It almost upended him. Again, instinctively, boxing habits taking over, Figleaf fell into a clinch. He clung to Red.

Referee Dunn parted them.

"Now!" Alan cried up at Red. "Go after him."

Burt looked askance at Alan. "I thought I took an objective reporter along with me."

The crowd had fallen very silent. Though the shrill woman still believed. "C'mon, Fig old boy, you're still the greatest. Kill him." The odor of sweat-soaked leather became sharp.

Yet once more Figleaf went to the well. Head cleared, he bulled into Red, arms flailing, hoping to catch Red with a lucky punch. Red met him with a short crushing right cross. Figleaf crumpled to the floor.

Alan jumped up. "Atta boy. You got 'im."

Referee Dunn had to chase Red to the opposite corner. Red went reluctantly. Then Referee Dunn started counting.

On the count of eight Figleaf stumbled to his feet. His black hair hung tumbled over his brow. His left eye was almost shut. His swollen lips resembled the lobes of a liver.

Burt said, "I see now. Your man was measuring him. Figleaf is too big to be knocked out with one punch."

"Yeh," Alan said. "Like trying to knock out a horse with one punch."

Figleaf had one more charge left in him. He tried to butt Red down with his head. Red jumped back two steps, then as Figleaf hauled up short, Red let him have it, two lefts and a right. The two lefts landed as loud thuds and the right exploded like a sledgehammer cracking a two-by-four. Figleaf fell backward, bounced on his seat.

"See!" Alan cried.

Burt nodded. "So that's what Blackie Kavold meant when he said he'd been hit by a wrecking ball."

Alan was jubilant. "He sure can hit, can't he?"

"That he can."

The crowd was disappointed. When Referee Dunn held up Red's arm as the victor, they hardly cheered. Even Figleaf's shrill woman fan was silenced. But there were no boos. They admired the surprise power.

Alan and Burt went down to the dressing rooms to interview the fighters.

Figleaf's face looked as if a catcher's mask had been fitted in under the skin. "I was right not to want to fight this guy." Figleaf's voice was mushy. "Blackie I knew and I coulda taken him."

Red sat like one who had lost, eyes on his hands, contemplating some inner thing. He was unmarked. No amount of prodding by the sports reporters milling around him could get him to say anything.

"Funny bird," Burt commented as they left the Armory.

"Something's going on there," Alan said. "That's not the Red I know."

# Chapter 11

# ALAN

It was Thursday, Alan's day off. He tried to sleep late but that restless period around six-thirty, his usual getting-up time, made him toss in his sheets for a while. Finally he went to the bathroom and relieved himself and then tried to find sleep again. That helped.

He awakened slowly around one o'clock.

It was the first week in October, cool and clear, a white-wine day. The sun shone into his south windows, filling his room with shafts of golden light. Slow motes rode around like dreaming white moths. One window was open a crack, and every now and then little pushes of chilled air touched Alan's face. That cool air coming in smelled as sweet as an apple just bitten into.

Someone was coming up the steps. It was a woman. Irene Crist? Martin Vann's wife come to see Martin at last?

At the head of the stairs the steps came toward Alan's rooms; hesitated. Then the door opened. Someone, a girl, took in a breath, and cried: "Alan! I found you home!" Then the steps gathered in a rush and she fell into bed with him.

Still sweetly stiff with sleep, Alan rolled over on his side. Jael Hemlickson. He threw back the blanket and sheet and drew her close. He kissed her neck, and with eyes closed searched out her lips and found them and kissed her softly and sweetly and then hard and hungrily.

"My, it's a long way over here from the campus," she whispered. "At least eight blocks."

He shook her a little. "You modern spoiled kids."

"Well, anyway, it was good for my legs." With her toes to her heels she pushed off her slippers. She released herself from his arms and shouldered off her yellow sweater. Then she slipped back into his arms. "Why," she exclaimed then, "you're naked in bed!"

He laughed softly. "I always sleep naked in bed. I can't stand the way pajama bottoms bind me down there."

She stroked his back. "You have smooth skin. Blond and so clean. That's neat."

"How's school going?"

"Fine. Though I'm already two themes behind in Miss von Emden's English class. Lord, is she strict!"

Alan held her close.

"Von Emden is going to ruin me as a writer, with all her emphases on balanced structure and participial phrases and restrictive clauses. My being published in the *Atlantic* didn't help me any with her."

"Well, every now and then you run into a teacher who's wrong for you."

"I'm going to be in her class for three quarters."

"Why don't you turn everything she says into humor in your own mind? Besides, a tough adversary as a teacher will be good for you."

"Ho! and in the meantime watch my poor hesitant shoot of a talent wither away under a pair of baleful eyes?"

With his toes Alan could make out she had on short bobby socks. Her full limber legs were bare all the way up to her panties. With his fingertips he could also make out she was wearing a slip under her yellow dress but no bra. He ran his hands under her slip and then up and down her slim bare back, giving each of the tiny firm knobs of her vertebrae a little circling rub. "You have smooth white skin too."

Hair settling around his face, she kissed him on his neck. It was as though they were kissing under tall slough grass. "I'm so glad I found you home."

"Are you through with classes today then?"

"No. I'm skipping Contemporary Political Issues."

"Won't your prof miss you in class?"

"Professor Jorgenson miss me? Never. You'd never believe how many he has in his class. Two hundred and forty-three. It's the most popular class on the campus. There's no classroom on the campus big enough, so we meet in Northrup Auditorium. We never get to see him except from a thousand feet off."

"Poor Aristotle and his little peripatetic school."

She looked at him puzzled. "What was that again?"

"Aristotle had no classroom in which to teach. He taught while walking up and down in the open air."

She looked at him in admiration and ran her hand through his tousled hair. "How I love the electricity of your eyes. Alan the Searcher, endlessly looking for truth."

"Cut out the guff now."

An impish smile drew back the corners of her lips. Her yellow dress had worked up over her bare belly. "Is there anybody at home?"

He knew what she meant. "When must you be home?"

"Dad is picking me up in front of Perine's Book Store about twenty minutes after Professor Jorgenson's class lets out."

"Do they still watch you that close?"

"They're afraid I'll go over and visit you."

"How do they know where I live?"

"Dad was once an investigator in insurance."

He brushed her light-gold hair away from her high brow. "Suppose some young fellow on the campus wants to date you?"

A tiny flicker moved in the corner of her right eye.

"Have you met anybody yet you'd like to date?"

"No. Not really." She looked past him up at the ceiling. "Though there is a Shelby Hines I talk to once in a while. He sits next to me. You know, alphabetical seating? But he's so shy. So completely unlike you."

Alan laughed. "Your folks better not hear you say that too often."

She laughed with him. "But Shelby is shy. I know he's been working himself up to ask me."

Alan could feel himself become jealous. "What's he like?"

Jael turned reflective. "He's rich. Clothes. Manner. Slender and dapper. Dark hair and dark eyes. Terribly bright. But he just drifts through school, and smiles a little in a shy way, and buys himself another beer."

"Hey, you know a lot about him already."

"I can smell the beer on him in class."

Alan pursed his lips. "Well, at that it's hardly fair of me not to let you date some of those college fellows you meet. I've already had my college friendships."

She laughed. "You went riverbanking then in college?"

He looked at her, serious. "Not in college."

"But after?"

"Once." He sighed. "I'm sorry, but I'm no golden cock."

"What's that?"

"A boy virgin."

She let her eyes close slowly. "Oh."

He nodded to himself. "It's wrong of me to rob you of the experience of dating college kids your age."

"But I don't care for anybody else but you, Alan." She rubbed her belly against him. "You know that. I just want you." Her eyes became dreamy with desire. "Oh, I can feel you. May I touch you?"

Alan thought he could keep himself under control even going that far. "If you want to."

They'd become warm together under the sheet and blanket. Her long fumbly fingers slid across his belly. She explored. He could sense her going over in her mind how it was. She was like a child finding the key to the pantry and not knowing what to have first, figs or dates.

Alan's eyes volved under their lids. The corners of his eyes began to flicker a little.

With a breathy laugh she slipped off her panties and then with an upward sweeping motion of both arms took off both her slip and dress at the same time, her gold hair emerging and flying up and then falling back into place. She laughed breathy again as she took his hand and guided it. "If I can play with Sir Gawain you surely can play with Lady Genevieve."

He loved the touching. He thought her sweeter by far than Irene Crist. Making the comparison wasn't fair, though. "We have to be careful," he whispered.

"Yes," she said huskily.

"I want to be able to look your father in the eye when I see him."

They breathed and dreamed together.

"I believe Lady Genevieve would like a romp in the forest with Sir Gawain," she said.

"I know. But I'm not going to give them permission."

"You're as bad as Miss von Emden. Against everything that comes naturally."

Waves of desire washed away all thoughts of her folks, Tor and Gretta Hemlickson. "Will I hurt you?"

"I won't know until we try it."

He thought: "If we try it just a little, then we'd know that later on, when we'd feel free to, it would be perfect."

She opened her limbs around him.

"Gently now," he said. "I don't want to hurt you."

"You won't. Let me be the judge of that." They were very warm together. They breathed as if they'd already run miles. She said, "Oh, what the heck. Let's." Her slim golden arms suddenly became very strong and she clasped him around the waist, hard, yielding herself to him. "I want your seed." She winced once and then it was done.

He remembered Chaucer: "They kisse and clippe togider, she smarte but a little."

Gradually their breath leveled.

He asked, "Did you?"

"No. But that's all right. That'll come later."

"I hope so. I want you to have as much fun as me."

"Oh, I did, I did."

They held each other silently for a long time.

She said, "We're a perfect fit."

"Yes."

She said, "There's going to be a big party at Hoyt Jorgenson's house Saturday night."

He shook his head to clear it. "What?"

"There's to be a big party at the Jorgensons'."

"Oh. Would you like to go?"

"My folks won't let me go with you at night."

"Where'd you hear about this party?"

"Shelby told me." She withdrew a little the better to talk. "You know, while the rest of us can't get within a thousand feet of Professor Jorgenson, Shelby sees him regularly in his office. It seems his father and Jorgenson are friends."

"What kind of people are going to be at this party?"

"Shelby says it's the leading edge of the local cultural ferment."

"Your friend Shelby likes to mix his metaphors."

"He says it with a little smirk."

"Who are these bubbles in this cultural ferment?"

"Shelby says it's the more avant-garde at the university."

"I've never been to one of those parties."

Her eyes opened blue upon him. "Would you like to go?"

"Yes."

She closed her eyes. A sly look came over her face. "Tell you what let's do. I'll have Shelby invite you. Jorgenson told him to bring over a few of his friends. That's you. Then I'll accept a date from Shelby—"

"Hey! Then he's asked you?"

"Yes. And then—"

"Then he's not so shy after all?"

"Well . . . he still really is. Wait'll you meet him."

Alan was stunned. He and Jael has just made love, their first time, and here she was already scheming to go to a party with another man.

"Then after Shelby brings me to the party, I'll ditch him and be your girl and go home with you."

"After he invites me I'm to run off with his date? Besides pulling off some skulduggery on your folks?"

Her blue eyes turned steely. "What do you think this was, what we just did?"

"Something that just happened naturally."

She cocked her head sideways at him. The look of an older woman came over her face. "What a wonderful man you are."

"Don't you agree?"

"I guess so," she said.

"Tell you what. You go with Shelby to this party. You should have an occasional date with fellows your age in college anyway. Meanwhile, there's two guys in this house here who consider themselves part of the avant-garde at the U, and I'll just bet they've been invited. I'll go with them."

"Oh ho," she said. "You're a pretty good schemer too."

They looked at each other a moment, and then began to laugh.

When she got up to put on her clothes, she announced with a satisfied look, "So. One drop of blood. In the old country you could no longer call me a golden hen."

They laughed some more. Then she hurried away to meet her father in front of Perine's Book Store.

# Chapter 12

# ALAN

─────────────────── •◆• ───────────────────

When Alan arrived with Martin Vann and John Charles, the old mansion of Dr. and Mrs. Jorgenson was jumping. Some of the party-goers had even spilled out onto the front porch. The long living room and the sunroom were both jammed, standing room only. Both stair-ways were packed with seated couples. Most carried a bottle of beer, the old-time Depression drink, and a few jiggled martinis.

The Jorgensons had bought the old mansion in Southeast Min-neapolis from the estate of a mail-order tycoon, and had restored it as nearly as possible to its onetime ornate beauty. They'd painted the outside a vivid gray with white shutters and white windows and doors. They'd dressed off the roof with shakes, even the two corner towers. The living room had two bay windows, with thick plate glass below and colored glass above. The fanlight over the front door also had colored glass, primitive greens and blues and reds. The house towered as high as the old elms outside, three stories high, with nine gables. Everybody thought the Jorgensons had a steal at the price.

Alan followed Martin Vann and John Charles around at first. Soon Martin found the head of his English department, Dr. Jason Larchwood, holding forth with critic and novelist Percy White in the alcove part of the west tower. Martin suggested they listen in. Alan nodded and settled on the floor with his two housemates.

Percy White finally made an emphatic statement. *"Moby-Dick* is *the* greatest American novel."* Percy was a slim handsome man with graying hair and gray eyes. He looked as though he might have been raised an aristocrat in England. He had very thin fingers, so pale the bones almost shone through the skin. *"Moby-Dick* is written in a great high style, at the same time that it manages to give us much concrete detail about whaling. The figures of speech are all vivid, every one of them precise and telling. And it is a complex novel which at the same time is easy to read."*

Larchwood held his noble head slightly to one side. "So say you.

But why is it then that my brightest students have trouble with it?" Larchwood took a genteel puff of his cigarette and then held the cigarette to one side of his face. A thin plume of smoke trailed up past his ear. His wavy gray hair had thinned enough for a gleaming skull to show through.

"Perhaps they are not as bright as you think."

"Well now, they have no trouble with *Daisy Miller.*"

Percy took a puff of his cigarette with pursed lips. He too held his cigarette to one side of his face. "Well, Jason, James is your man and I hear you teach him with enthusiasm. Whereas Melville gets short shrift at your hands."

"Possibly."

"Personally, I liked James' *The Portrait of a Lady* best. More concrete than his other work. The trouble with James is, he is so busy delineating his characters with all that delicate psychological probing of his that you never *see* his characters but only know of them through the minds of other characters—who in turn are never clear."

Larchwood smiled. "But I like to argue that that constitutes James' great virtue, this delicate probing you mention. For those who love true refinement he is the perfect novelist."

"Oh shit, Jason," Percy said, "I want some mud and guts in my novels." From the very way Percy pronounced the four-letter word it could be seen he had to work at being crude. The word was clumsy to his tongue. "Nobody in James' novels ever has to go to the bathroom."

"Take a shit, you mean." Larchwood had the faintest hint of a mean little smile in his manner. He pronounced the four-letter word elegantly.

"Yes," Percy said, and then smiled.

A murmur of precious excitement stirred through the listeners sitting at the feet of the two men.

Just then a boor by the name of Foster Cocksford blundered into the group. Cocksford wrote advertising. He'd once taken a writing course from Larchwood and considered himself as having an in with the old gentleman. "Great to see you, prof." He held out a big blond hand.

Larchwood examined the hand as though it were a badly written paper which probably might be better handled by one of his assistants. Finally he shifted his cigarette from his right hand to his left hand and shook Cocksford's hand. Cocksford gave Larchwood's hand a hard squeeze, and Larchwood winced like an English lord.

Cocksford nested himself down at the feet of Larchwood, unaware of hostile eyes. Cocksford carried a little dish of cocktail nibbles, tiny sausages, small pickles. "Well, prof, how you doin' these days, got any bright boys coming up?"

Larchwood smiled, said nothing.

Cocksford was wearing a gaudy outfit, light-purple jacket, cream-colored trousers, pink shirt with open collar, striped red-and-white socks, and tan-and-white two-tone shoes. He was a great success in his field.

Percy felt a little sorry for Cocksford. Percy remarked that the business world in the Twin Cities seemed to be recovering from the early Thirties.

Cocksford, encouraged, painted a glorious future for the grand republic.

Martin Vann and John Charles glared at Cocksford.

Percy couldn't resist asking, "What with that writing talent you had to begin with, Foster, don't you think you're wasting your time in advertising?"

"Not at all. I help sell goods. Make the wheels of industry go around. I call people's attention to things they really should have."

"But it's so artificial to pretend you're wild about some product when, in actual fact, deep down, you probably despise it."

"No, I believe in what I'm doing. Like anybody else."

"Isn't it a little like the clothes you wear?" Percy's eye fell on Cocksford's pink shirt with the open collar. "Mostly front?"

Cocksford reddened. "Don't clothes make the man?"

"Ah, *Sartor Resartus.*"

Cocksford finished his dish of nibbles and set it to one side. He licked his fingertips. He pulled out a cigarette and lit it with a flourish, waving his glittering silver lighter about. "But clothes do. I know it may sound funny, but when I wear a business suit I feel all business, and when I wear sport clothes I feel like having fun, and when I wear a dress suit I feel like going out."

Larchwood allowed himself a mobile smile. "And I suppose when you take a bath your mind is a blank?"

A titter swept through the listeners.

John Charles, who loathed all salesmen and most all American business practices, let fly with a derisive cackle. "And I suppose when you're given an enema you've completely vanished from the scene."

Cocksford hated academicians with an equal fury. "You know, John Charles, when I look at you, I'm reminded of that time when I went to the Mardi Gras in New Orleans. I was staying at the Roosevelt Hotel. I had to go to the men's room and there, by God, standing right next to me, was what looked like a woman lifting up her dress and unfolding the biggest dong I ever saw."

John Charles quivered he was so outraged.

Cocksford wasn't finished shaking the doll. "Yeh, I know you guys. There's a fellow living three or four doors down the block from me who has a very nice garden, neat and beautifully arranged. But he's planted poison ivy around the perimeter of it so nobody else can go in and enjoy it. And he weeds his garden without any trousers on, wearing great long elastic garters, from his shorts all the way down to his anklet socks. Funniest sight you ever saw."

"Up yours."

Martin Vann shook John Charles sadly by the elbow. "Come now," he said, "don't be such a passionate ass. Cocksford is hardly worth it."

Alan had had enough and rose to his feet and began wandering through the milling party-goers looking for Jael.

Alan heard two old university doctors in a doorway laughing about the time they'd made a wrong on-the-spot diagnosis. They were returning from lunch across the Washington Avenue bridge. They'd been following a man walking ahead of them toward the university and had wondered what could possibly be wrong with the fellow. The man had a most peculiar gait, stiffish, weirdly agitated. The one doctor diagnosed the man as having arthritis while the other doctor was sure the fellow was suffering from a very bad case of general paresis. Finally, to satisfy their scientific curiosity, they ran after the man and catching up with him asked him what was the matter. "What?" the man said. "Why, you crazy nuts you. There's nothing the matter with me except I got a bad case of the trots and I'm hurrying to find a can somewhere."

In an alcove inside the east tower, Glenda, the wife of Foster Cocksford, was talking earnestly with Roxanna Larchwood, Professor Jason Larchwood's wife. Glenda was trying to reassure Roxanna that Foster was doing all right. Roxanna was a short slender woman with a square box of a face. While still a student of Jason's, Roxanna had written a novel, *Old Missouri,* which was critically acclaimed. Later, when she married Jason, she quit all writing, went to cooking and housekeeping for her learned husband. To make sure that little would ever be said about her novel, Roxanna went about methodically buying up all copies of it still for sale in the area, even taking out all copies of it at the local libraries and then declaring she'd lost them. It cost her. But she loved Jason and wanted him to be the center of attention in their household. Listening to Cocksford's wife, who'd graduated with honors from a beautician's college, Roxanna was being her usual considerate self.

"Yes," Glenda said, "Foster didn't know where he stood with the agency, until one night the president, Mr. Gaylord, who'd flown in all the way from New York, asked us to a cocktail party in his suite in the Nicollet Hotel. We sure talked to a lot of important people that night."

Roxanna held her head to one side sympathetically, at the same time that she stole a glance over to where her husband Jason was holding forth.

"Well, then a wonderful thing happened, and it made up for everything. As you know, Foster never was sure he should have gone into advertising. He'd shown so much talent when he wrote stories for your husband, he once thought he should have just chucked everything and gone for broke to write a novel. But then just as we left Mr. Gaylord's hotel suite, Mr. Gaylord took me by the arm and said, 'Glenda, we like your husband Foster. We think he's a nice boy. He has a chance to make it big with our firm.'" Glenda beamed a big smile, and a happy wriggle possessed her, starting at her full calves and ending up in her well-groomed burst of gold hair. "And you know, we thought that pretty wonderful. After all, you know, they're practically millionaires."

"Yes," Roxanna murmured, "yes. Perhaps Foster made the right choice after all."

Alan made his way into the big kitchen. Several students were tending the bar, uncapping bottles of Jordan beer. The Jordan brew, made of specially grown hops and sweet spring water from Jordan, Minnesota, was one of the smoothest beers around.

There was some commotion in the roomy pantry and some laughter, and in a moment the host, Dr. Hoyt Jorgenson, emerged carrying a huge glass punch bowl filled to the brim with a mix and studded with ice cubes and floating cherries. There was a cheer from some of the older faculty members. Hoyt Jorgenson wore the clothes of the popular man: cream-colored suit with black bow tie and pink shirt, white socks with black oxfords. He had quick gestures and quick black eyes and a sharp long nose.

Jorgenson set the punch bowl down on a table in the dining area. Several pretty girl students carried in trays of small glass cups and a ladle.

"There you are," Jorgenson said with a wide knowing smile, "a special punch for those of you who think beer is beneath you."

"I thought this was going to be a beer party for liberals," a familiar voice said behind Alan.

Jorgenson flashed an even wider smile. "This party was starting to die on the vine, so I thought I'd liven it up a bit."

Alan turned. The familiar voice belonged to Bill O'Brian from the paper. "Hey."

"Hey yourself." Bill's cheeky Irish face was redder than usual. "What are you doing here with all these super brains?"

"I was going to ask you the same thing."

"You here with a gal?"

"No. But I am looking for Jael."

"Oh, she's upstairs sitting in Jorgenson's study with a bunch of other lightning brains. Between the smoke from their brains and smoke from their pipes, I started to cough and I had to get out of there." Bill pointed at the punch bowl. "Take it easy when you imbibe any of that." Bill waved his bottle of Jordan's about. "Me, I'm strictly a suds man."

"Why, what's in that punch?"

"Oh, Hoyt is famous for his punch. Faculty members tend to be pretty formal at parties. It wouldn't go over very good with our conservative state legislature if it got around that faculty members drank. So Hoyt invented something he calls his artillery punch. To loosen up the profs. Calling it punch, you see, makes it okay. He pours various bottles of hard liquor all into one batch: bourbon, scotch, rum, gin. The punch of one cancels out the punch of the other and the result tastes bland. Innocent. But oh boy, not so far as effect goes."

Alan started to leave.

"Where are you going?"

"Look for Jael."

"I've been wondering how you've been making out with her."

"We're getting along fine. A Shelby fellow is bringing her over here but I'm taking her home."

"Got a ride home?"

"Well, my car is only a couple of blocks over from here. Where I live."

"Oho, you were going to leave the party early and have another party at your apartment, eh?"

"Not really."

Bill's canny eye spotted something. "You having some kind of trouble there with her? Her folks maybe?"

"Her folks don't like me."

"I get it. You've got to sneak around to see her. Do they know your car?"

"I guess they do."

"Look, I'll take the two of you home. My gal is here somewhere and after this bust is over we'll go out riding for a while. And then we'll drive Jael home for you. They won't know my car."

"I'll ask Jael."

"Do that."

Alan headed for the back stairs and climbed past couples seated on some of the steps. The four bedrooms upstairs were packed with people drinking beer. Alan found the study at the end of the hall and peered in. Bill was right. The place was thick with veils of tobacco smoke. Some professor, standing stiff on heron legs, was holding forth on the absolute cleavage between hoi polloi and the high-polite. A half dozen hands were waving at him to get his attention. Alan looked closely in all that smoke but couldn't find Jael. Bill was mistaken.

Alan hunted up a bathroom. A woman was just leaving it, a smile of accomplishment on her face. Alan went in and locked the door behind him. As he relieved himself, he casually noted the fresh towels in several racks, the shelf of shaving things for the mister, the shelf of beauty aids for the missus, the spotless mirror over the sink, the pink cover over the toilet seat.

There was a light knock on the door.

"Just a moment," Alan called out.

Washing up, Alan opened the door.

Before him stood a gnome of a man. Alan recognized him right away as Judge Vincent Knight. Alan had seen his picture many times in the paper. Judge Knight could be hardly more than five feet four, with toddly legs and short arms. He had the head of a wise old owl. It had been said of him and the now dead governor, for whom he'd worked as private secretary, that the two of them had more savvy and political tricks up their sleeve than the President and his entire cabinet.

Judge Knight ambled over to the toilet seat and unbuttoned his fly. "Well, it looks like we all have to come to it sooner or later, great and small, rich and poor, don't we? Pay our dues at a urinal of some sort."

Alan laughed. "Yes, even the women finally have to take a seat."

"Hah. Yeh." The judge curled a finger around his nose. "Don't say that too loud. I've got a wife who's been threatening to put a urinal in our bathroom at home just to show me she can stand up to one too."

"One of those old-time bloomer girls."

"Shh. She already wears the pants in my house."

Alan laughed some more, and left.

Out in the hallway, the artillery punch was beginning to take effect. Several of the older faculty members were fairly doing a dance as they gossiped. There were several shrieks of wonderful laughter from the women.

Standing at the top of the stairs, watching it all, Alan suddenly thought of Red and Jen Engleking. How different those two were, really, from the people at this merry highbrow party. For a fleeting second he saw Jen's sad dark eyes, the utterly stark scared look in them when he'd climbed into her house by way of her bedroom window. Alan saw too the strange new hardness in Red's eyes after his fight with Figleaf. Alan wondered what those two, Red and Jen, were doing right that minute. Alan decided he should look them up again, soon, have some coffee and cake with them.

Alan worked his way down through sprawled couples on the stairs.

Jorgenson took up a banty-legged stand in the center of the living room below. He looked brightly around at everybody sitting on the floor. He called out several times to get everybody's attention. Gradually the house stilled.

"Ladies. Gentlemen. Friends." Jorgenson's strong lecturer's voice boomed through the house. "I have a little surprise for you. I've managed to talk Maura Shoemaker into giving us a reading of one of her new poems."

One grayhead from the university faculty muttered, "Who wants to listen to that Communist? Let word get around about this and that's all State Senator Chessick'll need to cut back on our funding."

Jorgenson held up his hand. "Wait. There's more. Lucille Heathcote, our noted local dancer, will interpret Maura's lines as they are being read."

A murmur of approval stirred the crowd.

"Also, Maura's daughter Fawn will play the guitar."

"Yeah." Soon everybody crowded around a clearing in the center of the living room.

Maura Shoemaker and daughter Fawn and Lucille Heathcote emerged from the library. Maura and Fawn sat down in chairs provided for them, and Lucille Heathcote stood to one side. Both Maura and Fawn were as dark as gypsies. Maura had an earth woman's bearing and Fawn a sprite's mischievous manner. Lucille had the green eyes of a falcon.

Maura had had several novels published, well written, but spoiled by proletarian endings. The worker in her novels always triumphed over the fat-cat boss. Bill O'Brian had once called on Maura to get her opinion on the recent developments in Spain where the Loyalist army had suffered setbacks at the hands of Franco's forces. Fawn had opened the front door and let Bill in and asked him what he wanted. He told her. Whereupon Fawn called upstairs to where her mother was writing, "Mother, there's a reporter here from the capitalist press." Both mother and daughter had glittering black eyes.

Alan managed to find a place to stand against the wall near the foot of the back staircase. He stood at ease, left hand in his pants pocket.

Maura glanced around at the crowd, slowly, wavy dark hair catching the light. She wore sandals, was barelegged to her calves, had on a long flowing gray-purple dress with a purple mantilla caught over the back of her head and shoulders. She wore a string of red corn kernels for beads.

Maura fixed Jorgenson with a look. They were friends, but it was obvious she didn't think much of his lukewarm liberal ways. "I belong to the left, which is the side of the heart, and not the right, which is the side of the gallbladder."

No one dared snicker in the presence of such a grave earth mother. Her voice was a soft alto, remarkably clear, warm and loving, though what she said stung.

"Because I am of the left, and of the heart, I have time for the people. I try to be one of them, let them speak through me, to make poetry out of their griefs and joys. It is a sad thing that so far there haven't been any big victories for them I might write about."

Her black dolorous eyes singled out various people in the crowd and dared them to look at her. She was a marked woman and was quietly arrogant about it.

Foster Cocksford listened with a darkening face. "Cut out the propaganda and get on with the poetry, for chrissakes," he growled.

Stiff silence followed. Everybody watched to see what Maura would make of that.

Maura spoke a single word, softly. "Huckster."

Lucille motioned to Maura that they should get on with the reading. She'd been arching on her toes, waiting to leap into her interpretative act.

Fawn became restless too. "Oh, Mother, don't worry about such Fascist remarks. We know."

"Go ahead, Maura," Roxanna Larchwood murmured from where she sat, all attention at the feet of her husband Jason. "We're all anxious to hear you read."

At last Maura raised her voice, reciting from memory:

> *"My grandmother was a prairie woman.*
> *When she spoke*
> *the sound of gods was in her voice.*
> *My grandfather was a fine man*
> *but he wasn't half the rock Grandmother was.*
> *When the terrible dust storms came*
> *and tumbleweeds bounced across the land,*
> *when the corn withered*
> *and calves sucked their mothers in vain,*
> *when the price of corn fell so low*
> *it became cheaper to burn it than sell it,*
> *it was Grandmother who was the first*
> *to swing out of bed in the morning*
> *and get her family ready for yet another day."*

It took Lucille but a few lines to get a sense of Maura's rhythm. She did several whirls on her toes, arms first outflung and then crossed over her lean belly. Pausing, she began the interpretation, turning Maura's words and images into symbolic gestures, becoming a tumbling weed rolling before the wind one moment, a gaunt mother giving suck the next, then an ear of corn burning. All the while Fawn plucked softly on her guitar, accenting the more fleshy words and the furtherest limits of the dance gestures.

> *"I learned all about love and sex*
> *at my grandmother's quilting bees around the table.*
> *While each neighbor lady worked on her section*
> *I crawled under the table*
> *and sat on the lion's paws,*
> *listening.*
> *I heard how some men were continual pests,*
> *other men only mildly interested,*
> *some as brutal as boars,*

*some as tender as sisters,*
*how it was best to keep walking*
*until the waters broke."*

Fawn's plucking deepened. She executed several sweeping chords, gestures liquid and quick. Lucille became even more active, eyes closed, body opened.

Maura's alto voice became Delphic:

*"When Grandmother spoke after the Bible was read,*
*or questioned the minister during house visitation,*
*or poured peroxide over our scratches,*
*or let us down into the storm cellar*
*while clouds crackled and blasted overhead,*
*we knew we were safe.*
*The Devil feared her.*
*When at bedtime she knelt with us and prayed,*
*we knew They had to be listening.*
*Gramma was a god."*

Quickly everybody gathered up the courage of their alcohol and the applause became enthusiastic. Students whooped and stomped. Jason Larchwood and Percy White exchanged significant glances. Roxanna, sitting crosslegged, slowly nodded her head in approval.

Someone called, "Alan?"

Alan turned. It was Jael, coming toward him, carefully stepping across legs in the way, blue eyes alight. She was wearing a long billowing pleated green dress. She took him fiercely by the arm.

Alan smiled down at her. The way she was pinching his arm meant she had no regrets about what had happened in his apartment. He remembered how pliantly, how eagerly, she had impaled herself on him.

She stood on her toes and whispered in his ear, "You're the handsomest man here, do you know that? My golden cock." She leaned against him. "And I just love you in that gray suit with the red tie."

He was aware that some eyes had turned to watch them. "Where's Shelby?"

"He went home."

He looked at her. "Really?"

"I picked a fight with him and he left in a pet."

Alan could feel more eyes frowning at them. "Shh, we better listen. Maura Shoemaker is an important person."

"Yes," she said, pinching his arm again.

Fawn's accompaniment on the guitar became stronger. Lucille flung herself into a series of frenzied leaps and pirouettes, one moment a grasshopper, the next a butterfly.

Maura continued to recite from memory:

> *"When hungry Sioux mothers*
> *tapped on Grandmother's screen door,*
> *apologetically,*
> *asking for bread,*
> *their babies suckling empty breasts,*
> *their eyes dull chestnuts,*
> *bellies distended with brown wind,*
> *Grandmother would invite them in,*
> *feed them beloved cornbread*
> *smothered with butter and syrup,*
> *poured them pitchers of fresh warm milk."*

Fawn's plucking softened. Bass notes. Lucille slowed her movements. Slow languorous steps.

> *"Wobblies, grain hands, bindlestiffs*
> *knocked on her screen door.*
> *Again Grandmother dropped all work*
> *and fed tham all a square meal.*
> *She was a soft touch*
> *for the hungry toiler.*
> *But for the rich crook*
> *she had a hard heart. . . ."*

Jael whispered, "Alan, that newspaper reporter, what's his name again? He's trying to catch your eye."

Bill stood in the doorway to the kitchen. He motioned with his head that it was time to go. A dainty woman was hanging onto his arm.

Alan very much wanted to hear Maura finish her piece, but the thought of holding Jael in his arms won out. "Oh, yes, that's Bill O'Brian. He says he'll take us out riding. Then later he'll take you home."

"Ah, that way the folks won't see your car."

Alan pushed through the seated listeners, Jael following him, having to lift her dress a little. They left by way of the front door.

Bill and his girl emerged from the gloom around the side of the house and joined them on the walk.

Bill said, "Alan, Jael, I'd like you to meet Polly Borg. Polly, this is Alan Ross and Jael Hemlickson."

Polly Borg had a pointed chin, with the hint of a wrinkle already leading away from it. Her yellow hair was frizzed up as though each hair had been individually given an electric shock. Twice she wetted her eyebrows with her fingertips. For the life of him, Alan couldn't imagine what Bill saw in her. Bill had a little wobbly potbelly but aside from that was a handsome man and deserved better.

Bill led them to his blue Buick around the corner. Every available parking space for blocks around was taken. Bill helped Polly into the front seat and Alan helped Jael into the back seat. Alan sat directly behind Bill.

Bill cruised north out of town. "There's no rush to go home yet, is there, Jael?"

"No."

"Good. There's a nice place to park out near Lake Johanna. Nobody'll bother us there."

Jael snuggled up to Alan and nibbled his ear. She whispered, "Tonight when I saw you standing there against the wall listening to Maura Shoemaker, a hand in your pocket, not drinking or smoking, just taking it easy, you looked so romantic."

He held her close.

Bill said over his shoulder, driving slowly, "Hey, Alan, did you hear the latest about our society editor Glenda Underland's daughter Babba?"

"No." Alan had trouble making his voice sound casual. Jael had begun to explore him.

"Because of what she did on the president's table?"

"You mean our President in Washington, D.C.?"

"No, I mean the president of the university here."

"What happened?"

"Well, the president's assistant, Jay Grobstein, had the hots for her, and she for him. But what with both being married they had trouble figuring out where they could meet in secret. Finally one day Grobstein called her to say that the president and his wife were going to be out of town for a couple of days, so why not meet in the president's office. Grobstein ran the office and could lock up as he wanted to."

"You mean, on the campus? In the administration building?" Jael wondered.

"No, I mean in the president's office at home." Bill looked down at his date, Polly. "What's the matter with you?"

"Nothing." Polly sat very stiff.

"This isn't going to be a dirty story. This is just a plain fact story."

Polly said, "Your plain fact stories are always dirty."

Driving with one hand, Bill slipped his other arm around Polly. "Ah, c'mon now, don't be such a damp rag."

"I don't care," Polly snapped.

Bill shook his head, then went on anyway. "Well, during her lunch break Babba quick took a taxi and met Grobstein in the president's office. There was no couch in there, Babba didn't want to be laid on the floor, she said she wasn't no common trollop, so Grobstein pushed the mail off the president's desk onto the floor and laid her on that."

Alan had been more than a little puzzled that Glenda should have such a mental lightweight for a daughter. There were stories around town that Babba was the result of an affair Glenda had had with a famous Minnesota author. "How come you know so much about it, Bill?"

"Grobstein's wife had the wild hair herself that noon and she too went over to the president's house for a little visit with Grobstein. They say the fur really flew in that office for a while. Broke a lamp. Busted an old heirloom armchair."

"Mrp," Alan said. Jael had found him, and all of a sudden to Alan's surprise she sat herself on him. Jael wasn't wearing pants. The way she placed herself on him it became an agony. The little bumps in the road were okay; just so the car didn't hit a chuckhole. Alan spotted Bill observing them in the rearview mirror.

Jael caught on too that Bill was watching them. She sat quite erect, almost primly. She asked, "Is anybody getting a divorce because of what happened on the president's desk?"

"No," Bill said. "Though Babba's husband got mad. He was wild when he heard about it. And the first night he and Babba had dinner together, as he was carving the meat, he all of a sudden laid her back on their dining table and held her there at knife point. I wouldn't know about this, but he bragged about it later uptown in a bar, how he'd cleaned the lint out of his wife's belly button with the point of their carving knife."

Alan laughed, more because of what Jael was doing to him than because of what Bill said.

Polly began to act as though she'd caught on to what was going on in the back seat.

Yet to all appearances Jael was sitting perfectly proper on a man's lap.

Luckily about then Bill found the quiet spot beside Lake Johanna. He pulled up on a gravelly stretch of beach. Water lapped on one side of the car and a cornfield rustled on the other.

Bill sat looking straight ahead. "Anybody here care to go for an Adam and Eve dip?"

"Did you say dare?" Jael asked.

"No, care."

Polly said, "Well, not me!"

Jael whispered in Alan's ear, "Let's take a walk or something."

Alan nodded. "Bill, four's a crowd when it comes to riverbanking. We're going for a walk."

"Okay." Bill slid his arm around Polly to draw her closer. Polly dodged him and sat away from him as far as she could against the door.

Alan lifted Jael up. At the same time she slipped her dress down as though she'd all along been sitting modestly on his lap. Alan opened the back door and they stepped out.

"Don't be gone too long now," Bill said. "I've got to get Polly home in time. Besides Jael."

"We won't."

Jael led Alan back up the lane. Corn pollen hung thick in the air, giving it a creamy taste. It was almost like smelling ice cream. "Let's go in the cornfield a ways."

"All right."

They took turns leading each other down a corn row. A dim gray light from a quarter moon gave the gold tassels a strange silver sheen.

"Isn't this far enough?" she said.

Alan looked back. Bill's car was out of sight. "Yeh." He scuffed at the dirt underfoot. "And it's dry enough. Though your dress will get dusty."

"I'll brush off my dress when I get home."

"Wait." He took off his gray jacket and spread it on the ground. There was some pigeon grass underfoot and it made for a fine bed. He helped her down; she giving way pliantly. He slimmed himself alongside her.

"Oh darling, when you touch me I just fall apart."

"Then what we did the other day was all right?"

She suckled up a kiss at him. "It was time I lost it, and you were the right man."

Alan wondered.

"You really don't drink, do you, Alan?"

"Oh, a beer now and then in the summer. Otherwise not."

"I'm glad. Because, Alan, if you drink I won't have you. I've seen enough of that with my father's insurance friends."

Alan slid his hands up along her creamy body.

She kissed him. "And I'm glad too you don't smoke. Boys who smoke stink so."

Alan studied her pale oval face. The dim moonlight filtering down through the tassels and leaves gave her flesh the look of a page in a sacred book. Some of her was in a foreign language.

Soft moon dust opened up time. Just existing was a drifting dream. There was no rush to make happen what would happen in its own time.

Presently they made love.

"Home at last," Alan murmured.

"Prometheus bringing fire to my body."

When they emerged from the cornfield, the quarter moon lay nestled in the leaves of an oak. The lapping water in Lake Johanna had turned black. The blue Buick almost looked gray beside it. They climbed into the car.

Bill and Polly were having words. Bill said, "The whole damned evening shot."

Polly snapped, "I have a right to my feelings."

Bill snorted. "That reminds me of a story."

"Not another of your dirty stories now."

Bill went on anyway. "There was this homesick traveling man, see. And, man, was he lonesome for his wife. Well, he tells the bellhop to dig up the best call girl in town. When the girl comes into his room, the traveling man tells her, after she's all naked in bed with him, 'Listen, this is what I want you to do. When I touch you, I want you to cross your legs and say, "Don't, John. Please. I'm too tired to-night." ' "

Nobody laughed. Alan thought it a cruel story.

Bill said, "Polly, your dad had the gall to tell me you were a brilliant girl and would make a fine wife. What he forgot to say was that a brilliant daughter makes a brittle wife."

Alan interposed, "Bill, I think the Hemlicksons would like to see their daughter safe home in bed."

"Yeh, okay." Bill started up the car, and crashing the gears, first in reverse, then forward, roared out of their hideaway and back to town. "Hell," Bill growled.

# Chapter 13

# ALAN

———————— •◦•◦• ————————

Four days later the phone rang on Alan's desk.

"Sports. Ross speaking."

"Alan Ross?" It was a man. Sounded familiar.

"Yes?"

"This is Tor Hemlickson. Would you be busy for lunch this noon?"

No wonder the voice sounded familiar. "Not this noon."

"How about meeting me at Frenchy's?"

"All right. What time?"

"Oh, make it twelve-fifteen."

"I'll be there."

Alan hung up. What in the world? Had Jael let something slip after all that she'd been out with him despite Bill's bringing her home?

Frenchy's was a block over from the *Chronicle* and across the street from the white towers of Richman's. Alan entered the wide black doors promptly at twelve-fifteen. The restaurant was dimly lighted. The maître d' in a black suit and white tie greeted him. "How many in your party?"

"Two. Could we have one way in the back? This is going to be confidential. Very."

"I have just the table for you."

Alan was shown the very last table in a dusky corner. He took the far chair in the corner to have the whole place in view in one glance.

The place was about half filled, a few clerks from Richman's, several matrons out on a shopping tour, and four young girls. Two old-fashioned long-bladed fans revolved slowly from the ceiling, making some of the white tablecloths waver off the edges of the tables.

Hemlickson came in through the door alone.

Alan stood up and waved.

Hemlickson saw him, removed his trim gray hat, and came stepping toward him briskly. He was wearing a gray business suit with red tie, and snapping black shoes. Hemlickson spoke first. "Sorry to be late. But at the last minute the phone rang and I had to check out a policy for a customer."

"That's all right."

Both sat down. Hemlickson placed his hat on the extra chair. With his hat off his bald head shone.

A waiter in black with a white napkin over his left arm came along. "Would you gentlemen like to order?"

"Yes. Mr. Hemlickson, you first."

Hemlickson studied the menu briefly. "I'll have the sole. With coffee."

Alan thought he'd compliment Hemlickson by ordering the same plate. "The sole. And coffee."

The waiter picked up the menus, nodded over the napkin, and departed.

Alan and Hemlickson eyed each other across the table.

Hemlickson broke first. "I suppose you know why I'm here."

"Not really."

"Well! it's about Jael, of course."

"Yes. That I knew."

"As her father, you know, what with her being only seventeen, I'm concerned about her."

"Of course. You should be." Alan sprinkled a little salt in the palm of his hand and, wetting a fingertip, licked up some of it. The salt was good. "And so am I."

"I wish I might believe that."

"Why shouldn't you believe that?"

"There's such a big difference in your ages."

Alan's heart beat thickly in his neck. "Not really that much. And the older Jael and I get the less it's going to mean between us."

Hemlickson's blue eyes slowly turned stone gray. "Then you mean to keep on seeing her even though she's only seventeen?"

"If she wants to see me, yes. I'm in love with her."

"She's too young to be in love. When she's through college, maybe then."

Alan dipped some more salt with a wetted fingertip. "I've thought of that. That we really shouldn't get serious until she has college behind her."

"I don't believe that."

"No, really. I've told her to accept other dates."

Hemlickson shook his head slowly. "Then you really don't love her. Because when you're in love with a woman you don't want other men hanging around."

"I was only trying to be fair."

The soles came and they both began eating. Both had trouble swallowing.

Alan asked after a while, "Did you have in mind she shouldn't date at all?"

Hemlickson pushed aside his plate. He couldn't eat any more. His knuckles were white on the dark oak table. He drew an envelope from a pocket inside his gray jacket. He held it up so Alan could see the address on it. It was a *Chronicle* envelope. "You wrote this?"

Alan recognized it instantly. He'd written Jael a note on *Chronicle* stationery to ease her mind about that first time. Lord, was he in a pickle now. Darn that Jael for being careless with her mail.

"You wrote this?"

"I did."

Hemlickson took out the note and studied it a moment. "What did you mean by 'crossing the Rubicon'?"

For once, the gods be praised, Alan's eyes didn't flicker on him. All he had to do was just shut up and stare the man down. It was the way Haunt John would have handled it.

"Did you . . . screw . . . my daughter?"

Alan's stomach constricted. Such a crude word. It made Alan angry. "Don't talk that way about your daughter. Not in my presence anyway."

"Are you saying you didn't then?"

"Mr. Hemlickson, what Jael and I do together is really our business. Just as what you and Mrs. Hemlickson do together is your business."

"I can have you arrested for molesting a minor, you know."

"Is kissing molesting?"

"No, but getting your hand in her pants is."

"That's pretty rough language, Mr. Hemlickson."

"And I can put you in the penitentiary for raping a minor."

Alan could feel himself blanch over his belly under his clothes. "Don't say something you may regret later on."

"How so?"

"Suppose Jael and I get married after she's through college? You and I will have trouble forgetting rough talk." A surge of love for Jael lifted him. He just had to like her people. "Look, Mr. Hemlickson. I love Jael. I mean nothing but good for her. I shall make her happy. And I want to like her father and mother. Love them and treat them with proper respect."

Hemlickson slowly sat back. His eyes widened a little but they remained stone gray.

The waiter came along. "That will be all?"

Both Alan and Hemlickson nodded.

The waiter deftly placed a little tray with two checks on it on the corner of the table.

Alan grabbed up both checks. "It'll be my treat today, Mr. Hemlickson." Alan dug out some loose change for the tip. "And I won't say anything to Jael about our lunch today." Then Alan got to his feet and paid up at the counter out front.

As Alan left the restaurant he looked back. Mr. Hemlickson was still sitting by himself. After a moment Alan saw him pick up his cup of coffee and begin to sip it.

# Chapter 14

# JAEL

The phone rang. Jael got up from her bed where she was studying physiology and went into the living room to answer it. "Hello."

"Jael?"

"Yes. Oh, hi, Uncle Horace."

"Hi. Say, I'm in town today. On business. How'd you like to come have lunch with me here at the Radisson?"

Jael's eyes turned inward. It was Saturday. Weren't most businesses closed on Saturday? "I'd like that, Uncle Horace."

"I'll meet you down in the lobby at twelve sharp."

"Okay."

As Jael hung up, she was glad neither her father nor her mother were around. She wasn't sure she wanted her father and mother to know she was meeting Uncle Horace downtown.

She put on her yellow dress and yellow sweater. She dug out her white anklet socks and slipped on her yellow shoes. She combed her hair until the light-gold ends over her shoulders began to spring up.

She had lunch with Uncle Horace in the Flame Room. Uncle Horace ordered lobster tail for her.

"Isn't that a bit expensive, Uncle Horace?"

"Tain't often I have a chance to treat my favorite niece."

She saw people glancing around at them with a smile. She thought they made an interesting couple. Uncle Horace was handsome in his best suit, a brown that went well with his lively brown eyes. When he smiled with his full-lipped mouth he looked like a young man, powerful, with big wide shoulders and muscular neck. He told her several good stories about what had happened to him since he'd last seen her. She didn't mention Alan Ross.

When they got up from the table, Uncle Horace suggested she

come upstairs with him for a minute. He had something he wanted to show her.

As they rode up the elevator, Jael began to feel funny. They got out on the sixth floor. He took her by the arm, gently, and guided her to his room, 611. There was a musty smell of old carpeting in the dark hall. Uncle Horace got out his key and opened up and ushered her inside.

"Sit down," Uncle Horace said, pointing to a neatly made-up bed. "Take a load off your feet."

Jael sat down, looking up at him with waiting eyes.

Uncle Horace went over to a sideboard and poured himself a shot glass of bourbon. He turned and took a sip. "You don't drink, do you, Jael?"

"No."

"Mind if I have a shot?"

"Not you, Uncle Horace."

He smiled at her. "How old are you, Jael?"

"You know. Seventeen. I'll be eighteen in November."

His luminous brown eyes looked her up and down, from her calves to her lips. "Well, if I'm any judge, you are more than ripe enough."

Her heart began to beat faster. She didn't dare to think of what was coming next. He was her uncle and she loved him and respected him. She knew that being in that hotel room alone with him she was in the wrong place. She was not being very true to Alan.

He tossed off the rest of the shot. "Jael, I think it's time you were opened up."

Jael straightened up. Jumbled thoughts wriggled around in her head. Would he catch on she'd already been opened up? Hadn't she better keep control of her emotions so he'd think she was still a virgin? She wished Alan had wide powerful shoulders like his.

"Isn't it, Jael?"

"What, Uncle Horse?"

His brown eyes opened in surprise. "Uncle Horse, is it?" Then he began to laugh, deep and hearty. "Yeh, I guess I am a horse at that." He took off his suit jacket and sat down beside her. He gave her another smile and then put his arm around her and kissed her. His wide tanned hand slid up over her small breast.

Jael liked the smell of bourbon on him. It went well with the aroma of the shaving lotion on his skin. "Uncle Horace, you shouldn't, you know." She tried to push him away.

"Why not? That's what uncles are for."

"Would that be true of aunts with nephews too?"

He gave her a widening look. "Hey, pretty sharp there, kiddo." Then a completely different expression swept over his face. He let go with a snort. "Certainly not with your aunts."

Jael tried to push him away again, gently.

After a moment he masterfully kissed her again and pressed her back onto the bed.

She need not have worried. While in part she longed to have that wide powerful body invade her, she still felt chilled enough by who he was, her uncle, not to loosen up too much. It hurt. It also hurt to think about gentle Alan. But she and Uncle Horace had liked each other long before she'd ever met Alan. And Lord, was Uncle Horace big.

The next Saturday Aunt Pauline arrived at their door in a taxi. Aunt Pauline came up the walk in a flourish, the taxi driver carrying her luggage behind her. She didn't bother to ring the doorbell, just barged right in. "Gretta, I'm here." Then Aunt Pauline spotted Jael sitting by the wide picture window. "Jael. So there you are."

Jael got to her feet. She was feeling a little lost. "Hi, Auntie."

Aunt Pauline shook her head. "Must you call me Auntie? I know you called me that when you were a little tyke. But you're a grown girl now." Aunt Pauline had on a dark-blue suit, well cut. Her bright-gold hair was done up in a modish Grecian knot in back. Several diamond rings sparkled on her fingers. It all gave her gray eyes a snappy city look. She had the firm clear pink skin of a girl. Of the three Paulsen sisters Pauline had the class. She'd married a Wall Street stockbroker. "Isn't that right?"

"I guess so, Aunt Pauline."

"Where's your mother?"

"She skipped across the alley to get some baking soda from a neighbor."

"Poor Gretta. Still trying to be the perfect cook." She turned to the taxi driver. "You can set them by the stairs there. How much?"

"Two dollars even."

Aunt Pauline dug into her patent-leather purse and fished out three dollar bills. "The extra dollar is for your family."

"Thank you, ma'am." A smile edged into the taxi driver's naturally set sour lips. With a little bow he left.

"Well!" Aunt Pauline said. "I suppose I might as well change clothes. I'm to have my guest room again, not, Jael?"

"Yes, Auntie."

"Aunt, you mean."

"I feel like a little girl today, Aunt Pauline."

Aunt Pauline studied her, head held slightly to one side. "We'll have a nice talk later."

That noon Aunt Pauline, Mother, and Jael had lunch together in the breakfast nook. Father was out looking up life-insurance prospects and Dickie was playing pickup football over in Powderhorn Park. It began smoothly enough. Aunt Pauline had just gone on a shopping tour along Fifth Avenue, where she'd bought several dresses in the latest style. She told stories well. The one about the old woman miser in New York, who died with her house so packed full of magazines and newspapers piled up for some sixty years that there no longer were any pathways into the back rooms, was the best. The city police discovered when they had the stuff carted out that the old woman miser had tucked money into almost every rolled-up paper, twenty-dollar bills, hundred-dollar bills. It took two months to go over everything carefully.

"You'll never believe how much they finally found there," Aunt Pauline said, flicking her gray eyes from Jael to Mother to make sure she had them enthralled. "It amounted to a little over three million dollars. Cash!"

Mother's blue eyes turned green. "Of all the strange things. What could have been wrong with her?"

"She had some kind of phobia or other. You know. People sometimes do get the strangest notions."

Mother poured them each some tea.

Aunt Pauline fixed her New York look on Jael. "What's this I hear about you falling in love with a newspaperman, Jael?"

Jael squirmed in her chair. "I didn't know I'd told anybody I'd fallen in love with him."

"Well, crush, then."

Jael parried some more. "That's another word I never understood. Crush. As my preceptor, Miss von Emden, would say, 'Miss Hemlickson, precisely what do you mean by the word "crush"?' If I used that word in class I'd better know exactly what it meant."

Aunt Pauline waggled her teaspoon at Jael. "Getting back to this newspaper bum of yours—"

"I looked up the word 'crush' once," Jael went on. "It means, 'to press and bruise between two hard bodies.' And I don't have a hard body yet."

Aunt Pauline turned brusque. "Don't trifle with me, Jael. I once had dreams too. Luckily, nothing came of them. And then I married sensibly."

Mother sat up haughtily. "Jael is a long way from being ready to get married. I hope."

Jael said, "What do you know about Alan Ross? Really?"

Mother said, "I didn't like him the first time I saw him."

"Is that fair, Mother?" Jael asked. "It often happens that someone you didn't at first like turns out to be someone you really like."

Aunt Pauline smiled down at Jael with the air of one who was going to be big about it all. "Tell me about him."

"Well, he's a sports reporter for—"

"Sports!"

"Wait. He's also a well-read man. He stays with some graduate students. He's handsome and—"

"He has such strange eyes," Mother broke in. "As if he can't look you in the eye."

"Mother!" Jael interrupted in turn. "That's the electricity of him. That's what makes him so exciting."

Aunt Pauline gave Jael a look. "Dear child, you are far gone on him, aren't you?"

Mother went on, "And he has such pale skin. So terribly blond. Like he's almost an albino."

Aunt Pauline rolled up her eyes. "Albino? Heaven forbid. He's the last person on earth you should marry then, Jael."

"Why?"

"Because you're already so light-complected yourself. You two will have nothing but squinty-eyed pink rabbity kids."

Jael became sick to her stomach. After what had happened with Uncle Horse she felt all torn up defending Alan. "But I love him. He's got brains. He just gleams with it when he's aroused." Jael buried her face in her arms on the table. "But it's no use telling you two about him. You'd never understand. Oh, if I only were eighteen, I'd tell you both to go to hell."

"Jael!" Mother cried.

"Yes," Aunt Pauline said, "where are your manners, girl!"

"Well, I don't care. Don't try to talk me out of the first wonderful man I've met so far."

Mother's usually fair face sagged into haggard wrinkles. "I'm afraid Reverend Whiffletree is right." She was referring to their Baptist minister. "The younger generation is literally going to the dogs."

Jael snapped, "The younger generation? Listen, we're much more true-blue and loyal to each other than some members of your generation I could name."

"Such as who?" Mother said.

"If I told you, you'd run for the sheriff to have somebody shot."

Both older women sat up. They gave each other an old and borrowed look, of a handed-down grief.

Jael fell silent. Lord. She'd almost blurted out what Uncle Horse had done to her.

Mother poured some more tea. The three sipped a little together.

Aunt Pauline said, "Your mother mentioned this Alan Ross is much older than you."

"He's only twenty-five."

"And you're just seventeen."

"I'm going on eighteen."

"That's still a seven-year difference in age."

"So what? His father is a whole generation older than his mother and he tells me they make a wonderful couple."

Aunt Pauline mused to herself, "Yes, it sometimes happens. Daughters who get hooked on their fathers often do feel more at ease with an older man."

Jael became angry. "Me a crush on Father?"

"No no. I was just thinking out loud."

Jael realized if she weren't careful they'd find out about Uncle Horace. Those Paulsen sisters, with that blot of bastardy hanging over their heads from the past, were awfully shrewd guessers.

The autumn sun struck at a sharp angle into the breakfast nook. It gave a golden tone to the blond wood shelves and made the glasses and the ware on the shelves gleam as though varnished. All three faces of the women took on a glow as if they'd been cream-fed all their lives.

Aunt Pauline placed her hand on Jael's arm. "Jael, I have a proposition to make to you."

Jael shrank from her aunt's touch.

Aunt Pauline went on, "I've had a long talk with James about it. As you know, James and I were unable to have children, and we've often thought of adopting. . . ."

Jael thought: "I'll bet you did!"

"Anyway, to come to the point, James and I have decided, since your father is having his problems financially, through no fault of his, of course, that we would offer to finance your way through college."

Jael sat up a little.

"How would you like to go to Vassar?"

Jael's eyes opened very wide. Vassar was an elite college and it would be quite an honor to be able to say one was a Vassar graduate. Jael instantly saw herself growing up to be another Pauline Cameron. People often said she resembled her Aunt Pauline more than she did either her mother or Father's mother. While there at Vassar she would probably meet some rich man's son, and marry him, and then she could live the high life of Park Avenue as Aunt Pauline did. Travel abroad. See plays.

Aunt Pauline read her face like an expert cryptanalyst. "That does sound attractive, doesn't it?"

"But I've already started here at the university."

"I'm sure we can arrange for your transfer to Vassar."

Jael recognized, of course, that Aunt Pauline's proposal was a plot to get her away from Alan Ross.

Aunt Pauline went on, "You'll be staying on the campus. But weekends you could come home and visit us and meet some of our friends. Vassar is only a short train ride away."

Jael sat with high wide eyes.

Aunt Pauline inspected Jael's clothes from collar to hemline. "And of course I'll take you to some of the better dress shops in New York." Aunt Pauline thought she was winning out and gave her a big smile.

Jael picked up her cup of tea and had herself another sip. "I'll think about it, Auntie." Coming from James and Pauline Cameron, who'd made it a strict practice never to mention money around their relatives, it was a grand offer. "And thank you, Aunt Pauline, for thinking of me. I do appreciate it, very much."

"Then you will come to New York with us?"

"I . . . I must think about it. It's a big decision, and I want to feel right about it if I do go."

Aunt Pauline let up then. "Of course. You must do everything that way. Think before you leap."


Later that afternoon, Jael walked into the living room where Mother and Aunt Pauline were sitting. She stood quite determined in the door. "Mother, I can't go up to the farm at Grandy with you today. I didn't know Aunt Pauline was coming, and I'd already made other plans for this weekend."

"But Uncle Horace and Aunt Sophie will be disappointed. They like you two children so much."

"I don't think either one regards me as a child anymore. They know I have my own life to live."

Aunt Pauline itched to say something but discreetly managed to keep still.

Mother said, "Uncle Horace will be especially—"

"I'm sorry," Jael broke in, "but I'm afraid you'll have to tell him that Jael made other plans."

"Is it that Alan Ross fellow?"

"Yes. I agreed to see the movie *Pygmalion* with him downtown at the State."

"Well, Father said we'd be leaving at four," Mother said, "so you'll have to make your own dinner then."

"Alan is taking me to the Nanking.

Aunt Pauline pursed her lips to one side. *"Pygmalion* is a fine movie. I saw it last month and thought it wonderful. As you know, I'm an admirer of Shaw, especially of his ideas on women."

Jael suppressed a smile. "Well, Alan isn't exactly an admirer of Shaw, but he'd heard down at the paper from their movie reporter that it was a first-rate film."

Aunt Pauline asked, "By the by, who are Alan's literary heroes?"

"He reads Hemingway, though he thinks him a bully. And he admires Faulkner, though he thinks him often obscure. But his real heroes are Doughty and Chaucer."

"Doughty? Never heard of him."

Jael finally let the smile come to the surface of her lips. "Alan likes to quote Shaw about Doughty. Shaw says somewhere that there are only three great writers in the English language: Shaw himself, of course, Shakespeare, and Charles Montagu Doughty."

Aunt Pauline sobered over. "I must look this Doughty up some-day."

Jael turned to leave. "Well, I'm sorry I couldn't go with you people up to Grandy. And now I better dress. I told Alan I'd meet him down at the Nanking at five."

"He's not picking you up?" Aunt Pauline said. "Pshaw, and here I was hoping I'd meet this golden knight of yours."

Jael almost laughed as she remembered Alan's remark about his no longer being a golden cock. "He can't get off until then."

Jael dressed slowly. The Fourth Avenue streetcar wouldn't be along for another half hour. She put on her best evening dress, a simple long blue with a white belt and a white collar. She polished her white leather shoes and slipped into them.

She heard Mother and Aunt Pauline talking.in the other room.

Dickie had come in with a bleeding elbow and torn pants and Mother was giving him a scolding for being a roughneck, while Aunt Pauline was trying to placate her by saying that Dickie was only being a typical healthy boy and not to be too rough on him.

Jael was checking her fingernails to see if they needed filing when Dickie pushed him impish freckled face in the doorway.

"Going somewhere, sis?"

"Yes, to a dinner and later to a movie."

"Hey, then I'll have Uncle Horace alone to play with for once."

"Think you're pretty smart, don't you?"

"Sure, why not? I can lick you any time."

Dickie had lately developed into a very strong boy. He was only ten but very quick and supple. He was going to be a good athlete. Already in sandlot baseball he was a star pitcher. He came at her in a wrestler's crouched maneuver. "I think it's about time I made you say uncle again."

"Don't. I can't stand it when you say that."

"Say what?"

"Say uncle."

Dickie held up, surprised. "You like uncles, don't you?"

Jael swallowed the wet lump in her throat. "Of course I do."

Dickie flicked a thumbs-up sign at her and then with a freckled wink left her room.

Ready to catch the streetcar, she considered skipping out the back door. She hated having to run the gauntlet yet once more. But knowing that was the way of a chicken, she sallied forth, head up.

She'd made the front door when Mother stopped her.

"Jael?"

"Yes, Mother."

Mother said, "Did you put your pants on?"

Jael stared at her mother.

Mother persisted. "Did you?"

"Mother."

"Jael, putting on your pants will give you that much more time to think it over."

"For godsakes, Mother, in that case I better put on a dozen pair of pants. So that by the time he gets down to the last pair he'll no longer be in the mood."

"Don't be disrespectful now, Jael. I was only thinking of your own good."

"Mother, I trust Alan more than I trust myself."

"Well, I don't trust him. All men are alike. They just want to use you. A man will promise you anything just to get what he wants. And after a man has satisfied his evil lusts, he'll drop you like an old dishrag."

Jael in disgust let herself drop into a chair by the door. "Alan is a wonderful man. He loves me."

"Also, I know you."

"Now what do you mean by that?" Had Mother found out about her visit to Uncle Horace's room at the Radisson?

"Never mind."

"So you think me a cheap hussy then?"

"Are you?"

Jael became angry. "Out with it. Just what do you mean?" Jael was ready to confound them by telling them what had really happened up at the Radisson.

"I was thinking about something else, Jael."

Jael felt so tight in her belly she was afraid she was going to break wind. Her mind whirled. She grasped at straws. "Oh, you mean about us being descendants of a bastard. That we all have a wild hair."

"Jael!" Her mother turned pale. Even her eyes seemed to turn pale. "I suppose that man taught you that."

"Uncle Horace is more apt to have taught me that."

Aunt Pauline ran her tongue under her upper lip in thought. "Jael, dear, why don't you run along now? I'm sure that after our discussion you'll try to be a good girl for us. And remember, it's on to Vassar for you!"

Jael met Alan at the Nanking and they had a good Chinese dinner together. Later they went to see *Pygmalion*. After the first few frames, Jael forgot about her family and about what had happened up at the Radisson.

Afterward, sitting in Alan's car in a parking lot, Jael said, "We are going to your apartment now, aren't we?"

Alan was still lost in the mood of the movie and moved as though in a dream. "Do you think we should?"

"Well, if we're not, I'm going to be terribly disappointed. I've been looking forward to it all week." She snuggled up to him, kissing his cheek, sucking his ear. "Just think, there's no one at my home to worry about how late I come in. I can stay out all night if I want to."

"We'll be the scandal of poor Martin Vann and John Charles."

"Pooh, those poor effeminate souls." Jael reached for Alan's thigh and began to fondle him. "Oh, let's hurry to our home. Your bed."

"All right, dolly. You talked me into it."

They made love twice. And twice she almost came to a head herself. She got up on a wonderful wide plateau of a seething sensation, and she wanted desperately to have more, not knowing exactly what it was she wanted to have more of, all along crying out a low keening sound.

Afterward, sliding apart, lying in each other arms, they talked.

Jael soon found herself telling him about her mother's request.

"She actually was asking you if you had your pants on?" Alan clapped a hand to his forehead. "My God, they know the worst." Alan in turn told her about the lunch he'd had with her father at Frenchy's.

Jael was astounded in turn. "Ohh, then they do know."

"Yes."

"You didn't actually tell him we did it, did you?"

"I made it a matter of honor not to say so specifically. But the worst was when he pulled out that letter I wrote you about you crossing the Rubicon for the first time."

Jael gasped. "So that's where that letter went! Father stole it! Out of my room!"

"Your father was pretty blunt about it. His words were: 'Did you screw my daughter?' "

"He didn't!"

"Yes, he did."

"What did you say to that?"

"I suggested that he shouldn't talk that way about his own daughter. Not in my presence anyway."

"Good for you, Alan, good for you." She beat her fists on Alan's chest. "Oh, I wish I could have been there. I would have scratched his eyes out."

"I also told him we might very well get married someday, which was all the more reason why he should be a little careful of what he said to me."

"Good for you. Oh, Alan, the more I see of you the more I know I have a real treasure in you. And I must learn to be worthy of you."

"Now now."

They made love again.

Just as Jael was about to get up to go home, she let slip something she shouldn't have. She only meant to tease Alan. "What a horse. Three times. You're about as bad as Uncle Horace."

"I thought your Uncle Horace's wife Aunt Sophie wasn't interested in sex."

"Well, I mean, he's all man and all that." Then Jael made a further mistake. It was like some evil genie was at work in her. "The fact is, Uncle Horace thinks I'm pretty nice, even though he is my uncle."

"Well, why shouldn't he? You're going to attract a lot of males before you're through with life."

"He even invited me up to his room in the Radisson one time."

"He did? When was this?"

"Oh, some time ago." Jael couldn't resist sticking it into Alan a little. "He said it was time I was opened up." Jael laughed a cracked laugh. "Of course he didn't know you'd already done that for me."

Alan got up out of bed and stared at her.

Jael couldn't look him in the eye. "Of course I told him that that was ridiculous." She reached for her clothes.

"He offered to do it for you? Your relative?"

Jael hedged. "I told him that the very idea of him suggesting it was awful. What would dear Aunt Sophie think?"

"Oh," Alan said. He began to put on his clothes.

Jael said, with another cracked laugh, "Oh, I managed to handle it all right. I didn't want him mad at me really either."

"Naturally not."

"Then I went downstairs and home."

Alan took her by the arm. "And now I think it's time this uncle took you home."

Jael decided to let it go at that. She hoped she'd sounded convincing about Uncle Horace.

# Chapter 15

# ALAN

Alan lay reading on his bed on his day off. He was wearing a pair of white duck trousers and a white pullover sweater. He had just come upon a fine passage in Doughty's *The Dawn in Britain:*

> *Now dies the evening red, on those cold waves,*
> *Which compass in, Isle, crowned with long white cliffs,*
> *Our foster Britain . . .*

when, after the sound of steps on the stairs, the door to his apartment opened and in walked a strange well-dressed woman.

Alan lowered his book to his chest and stared at the intruder.

The woman was about forty. Her flashing gold hair was done up in the modish fashion he'd seen recently in a rotagravure section. Her blue suit fairly gleamed. She stood a moment in the doorway, letting her cool gray eyes rove around the room. She looked at his white curtains, at his blue chair, at the gold bedspread with the red daisies Jael liked so much, at his shelves of books. That done, she swung her suave gray eyes to him. She measured him until a faint patronizing smile widened her lips. "So there you are," she said in a cultivated voice, and then she stepped toward him, blue heels clokking in slow leisurely fall. She looked down at him as though he might be some kind of stuffed animal under glass. It had all happened so smoothly Alan lay caught stiff on his bed.

It was cold out and the radiators cracked with moving steam.

Alan finally managed to say something. "Who are you?"

"So you're the young man Jael thinks she's in love with."

Alan stared at her some more. What in hell?

"What's that you're reading?" And without blinking an eye, the strange well-dressed woman reached down and picked the book off his chest. "Doughty. *The Dawn in Britain.* Jael mentioned him the other day. But I'd never heard of him. Some poor lost obscure poet, I suppose." She placed the book back on his chest as though he were a library shelf. "Well well." And she once more began to inspect his apartment. She stepped leisurely over to the table and with her white-gloved finger made a genteel swipe at the top to see how clean it was. "Yes, you are neat at that."

Alan sat up. "Who in God's name are you?"

She let her eyes play over his bed as if she were imagining what might have happened on it.

Alan remembered Haunt John and a little superior smile of his own appeared on his lips. He was going to be king in his own castle. He slowly swung his legs out of bed and stood up. For all her good breeding this elegant lady from the pleasure set was off base. "I'm Alan Ross," he said gently, inclining his head ever so little. He was barefooted and his blond hair was tousled, but for all that he managed good form. "Is there something I can do for you?"

Her manner changed. He was giving back in kind. "Why, yes," she finally said. "I'm Mrs. James Cameron. Aunt Pauline to Jael Hemlickson."

"Oh, yes."

"Jael has a chance to go to Vassar. And I wanted you to know that. So that you wouldn't stand in her way."

"Mrs. Cameron, I want Jael to have the best of everything."

"Then it will be all right with you if she leaves Minneapolis?"

"I also want to make sure that Jael has the privilege of making her own choices. At eighteen she should be allowed that right. Like any grown-up. Like yourself."

"Ah, another one of those new-generation impertinent young men who have come upon us like a curse."

"Mrs. Cameron, may I ask you a question?"

"Yes?"

"Don't you think it was a bit impertinent of you to just barge in here without knocking?"

"I came here in the interests of Jael's future."

"I can say with equal right that you are another one of those imperious dowagers of a previous generation who think they can ride roughshod over all other sensibilities around them."

The condescending expression in her eyes changed to one of grudging admiration. "Really now, Mr. Ross, you wouldn't really stand in Jael's way if we can persuade her to go to Vassar?"

That was better. "Of course not. At the same time, though, Mrs. Cameron, if Jael keeps telling me she loves me, I'm going to keep telling her I love her."

She looked down at her white glove as if hoping to find a speck of dirt on the finger she'd swiped across his table. "We shall see." Then she looked up, eying him full on. "Thank you for your courtesy, Mr. Ross. I was pleased to meet you."

Alan inclined his head ever so slightly. "Same here."

She turned slowly, and heels clokking in an easy leisurely fashion she went down the stairs and outdoors.

There was something wrong with the muffler on his old Dodge. On his next day off, even though it was a chilly wintery day, Alan slipped into some old clothes and rolled out his car onto a sunny spot in the parking lot of a fraternity next door. Crawling under the car, he slid along carefully to avoid getting dust in his eyes from the dirty undersides. Poking around he soon discovered that one of the support straps to the muffler had been ripped out of its mooring. It needed a new bolt.

He went to his landlady's garage and rummaged around in an old box of junk. By luck he found exactly the right bolt. Armed with pliers and a wrench, he skedaddled under the car again.

He was trying to get the nut started on the bolt when he heard two young students come laughing out of the fraternity. The students began to fuss over a car standing next to Alan's Dodge. Alan didn't pay much attention to their talk until one of them mentioned Jael's name. At that Alan stiffened.

First voice said, "I thought she was Shelby Hines' girl."

Second voice said, "Hell no. She dates around."

"Ain't she a bit too high-toned for that?"

"Ha. You'd be surprised. Hell, I'd barely got my car parked down by the river and her tongue was already scouring out the back of my throat."

First voice laughed. "Did you score with her?"

Second voice hawked up a gob of spit. The gob landed near where Alan's foot stuck out. "No, she was flagging, worse luck. But she told me if it hadn't been for that she would've."

"What's wrong with a red ride?"

"I don't fancy it."

"Mm, that's when they're apt to be the most lively."

"She said a very funny thing when I asked her if she was still a sweet sixteen. 'No,' she said, 'in my case you no longer can give a rose to a virgin.' "

"See, I told you. She reads."

Alan must have made some kind of sound under his car, because second voice said down to where Alan's foot stuck out, "You all right down there?"

Alan swallowed. "Just got a little dust in my eye."

Silence.

After a while Alan's eyes cleared enough for him to get the nut started on the bolt to the muffler.

Finished, he slid out from under the old blue Dodge, and without looking back at the two frat boys, headed for his landlady's garage, where he replaced the wrench and the pliers.

Then he took to bed. When hurt, and lonesome, he liked to listen to the radio in the dark, the luminous green dial vaguely lighting up the room.

# Chapter 16

# RED

There was another breakdown in the moving chain, and the fellows in the hog kill had a chance to catch their breath and help themselves to a drink of cool water. Jack Prouty and Red used the free time to sharpen their sticking knives.

Red asked, "How long you been sticking pigs, Jack?"

"This last spell it's been about two years."

Red whistled. "That long."

"While the spell before that it was about three years."

"What happened between the spells?"

"I got laid off for a year."

"How'd you pay your bills?"

"My wife worked and I went fishing."

"Why'd they lay you off?"

A rueful smile twisted Prouty's lips at the corners. "I went nuts there for a while."

"What do you mean, 'nuts'?"

"I was off my rocker. I got to seeing blood everywhere. On the floor. I kept after my wife to mop up blood that wasn't there. So my wife puts on her coat one night and drops in on our boss Simes here and tells him about it."

"What made you come back here?"

"It's the only thing I know. And I kind of like it." Prouty smiled to himself. "Oh, I'll get out of here when I feel it coming on again."

"How can you tell?"

"Some morning I won't be able to stick the pig just right. Then I'll know."

Red thought about that for a while. There'd been days when he himself didn't mind sticking pigs.

Prouty paused to stuff a pinch of snuff in under his upper lip. "Might as well stain both ends with the same color," he said with another smile.

Foreman Simes, who had been sitting on a partition, came ambling over. "Red, sounds like you're about to make a complaint."

Red looked down at the straw-littered floor.

"You may be able to knock the poop out of Figleaf Moroney boxing, but when it comes to sticking pigs you still ain't much of a man, are you?"

Red flushed. "Simes, how long did you stick pigs before they promoted you to straw boss?"

"Five years. And it never got to me."

Prouty winked at Red.

It began to soak in on Simes what Red really meant by his question. A savage expression deepened the dished look around his eyes. He reached up for the cup hanging over the water fountain and stepped spraddle-legged over to the blutwurst trough. Blood from the last several hogs was still trickling down it. With a long scooping motion he more than half filled the cup with blood. He strutted back and held the bloody cup out to Red. "Take a belt of this and then I'll know if you're a real pigsticker."

Red waved the cup away. "G'wan. All that'll prove is that I'm bloodthirsty."

"Red, you ain't man enough to drink that."

"Have the other guys here had their cup yet?"

"C'mon, here's a nice cup of fresh-spilled blood. It'll put lead in your pecker."

"You drink it."

Simes swilled the blood around in the cup a little, until it frothed up. "Got a better head on it than the draft beer up at Nick's."

Red waited.

"Red, tell you what I'll do. You drink this, and I'll put you back to shackling pigs."

"You don't mean it."

"Cross my heart and hope to die."

"You really mean that about me going back to shackling?"

"Absolutely."

Red knicked his head sideways, rolled his eyes up at the high ceiling, then took the cup. He stared down at the creamy froth riding on the livid red liquid. "All right, down the hatch." And with a shudder, willing it, he tossed down the blood. It took just four big swallows. Surprisingly, the blood had a sweet taste with an edge of salt in it.

But Simes didn't move Red back to shackling pigs.

Red let a month go by. Then one morning Red cornered Simes as they were slipping on their leather aprons. A scarlet mist already hung in the air. "I see you're not a man of your word."

Simes laughed at him. "Did you actually think I was gonna put you back to catching pigs?"

"I believed you."

"In a pig's eye I was gonna. You're the best pigsticker I got. With you and Jack handling the knife we've been breaking records every day."

"You're gonna wait until I go nuts one day."

"Sure I am." Simes sneered. "You poor horse's ass you."

"Thanks."

# Chapter 17

# ALAN

Things got a little sticky down at the *Chronicle*. Leaders of the national Newspaper Guild finally forced the *Chronicle* to hold an election to determine if its workers wanted to join the Guild. The Guild won by a big margin. Most of the members of the sports department, though, were against joining. As sportswriters they had by-lines. In their minds they were the equals of sports promoters and the owners of teams, above even the heroes they described. They could stand on their own feet and bargain for themselves.

Nobody asked Alan how he'd voted, for which he was thankful. He'd voted to join the Guild. From his point of view, as a cub reporter, it was worth it. When he'd first begun work he got $65 a month. After the Guild won the election, he suddenly got $130 a month. For $2 in dues he'd doubled his income.

Things came to a head the day the newswriters over at the WMSP radio station struck. The WMSP owners refused to recognize the Guild. They fired the ringleaders of the WMSP Guild local and then hired high school graduates off the streets at half the salary of those fired. The Guild considered that a threat to the agreements worked out with the Twin Cities press. The Guild decided not to call for an all-out strike for the whole metropolitan area, but they did call for volunteers to picket both the WMSP offices downtown as well as the WMSP transmitter out in the country north of St. Paul.

Alan found himself alone with Burt Cowens one afternoon.

After a time Burt cleared his throat. "Alan, you haven't said much about that WMSP business."

Alan let his fingers slide off his typewriter keys and slowly turned around to face Burt. "No, I haven't."

"How do you stand on it?"

"Well, Burt, the Guild doubled my salary."

Burt lifted his fine pointed nose in a sneer. "Alan, we out here in Minnesota don't want to let a bunch of New York radicals tell us what to do." Then, after a moment, Burt turned reflective. " 'Course, I keep forgetting this is a free country and every man is entitled to his own opinion without fear or favor."

Alan said, "Well, the truth is, I was thinking of driving out to the transmitter tonight to see what's up. You know, get the lay of the land. Hear what those WMSP fellows have to say."

"Harley Smathers isn't going to like it."

"He can't fire me for looking, can he?"

"He might think of it if you join the picket line."

Alan watched blue-white pigeons outside flying past the soot-streaked windows. The pigeons clappered across to the roof of the Richman building. "Guess I better tell you that Bill O'Brian asked me to report for picket duty. He's the *Chronicle*'s unit chairman. I told him I'd think about it."

"Well, I'd think carefully about it if I was you."

Alan had come to like being a newspaperman. He liked the smells of the place. By late afternoon paper lay strewn loosely on the floor, discarded proofs, various editions gutted by the scissors, stories clipped out to be rewritten for the Sunday country edition. The smells that emanated from them mingled pleasantly with the sticky sweet aroma of pastepots left open and the dark smell of raw ink. It was wonderful to be sitting in the middle of moving time. A newspaper was the hub of the world.

Alan said, "Burt, the trouble is, I have this funny notion about justice."

"Suit yourself."


Alan took University Avenue east to Snelling Avenue and then headed north. It was a lovely April evening, with the earth still warm from the day's sun, and all the trees stippled over thickly with fresh buds, and the streets washed clean by a heavy morning rain. A heady spring and a whole wonderful summer lay ahead. That people should want to fight over such a silly thing as how much money a man deserved for certain services rendered seemed completely out of place.

He found the WMSP transmitter at the corner where County Road C crossed Snelling Avenue. It stood by itself in a plot of some ten acres. Truck-garden farms lay to all sides.

Two cars stood parked along the road across from the transmitter. At the gate a half dozen men slowly strolled back and forth carrying banners. One of them was Bill O'Brian. Alan pulled up behind the last car and got out.

Bill came striding up. "Well well. So one of our capitalist sports-writers decided to get his feet wet."

"Oh, I just came out here because I'm curious. I've never seen a strike before."

"Well, if that's all you want, you better move on. Things are going to get rough around here."

"What's up?"

Bill nodded at a shack standing under the transmitter. "One of the vice-presidents of WMSP is manning the control board there. Jed Cairns. Up to now so long as we've had this picket line here, the regular engineers have just come to check it and then have rolled on. But tonight we heard the engineers have asked the 544 Teamsters Local to help them cross the picket line. The engineers didn't go out with the newswriters. They're AF of L."

The national Guild had voted to join the CIO, Congress of Industrial Organizations, and that had been another sore point with the members of the sports department. Both Burt and Quinsey believed the CIO was run by Communists. Had the national Guild voted to join the AF of L, American Federation of Labor, Burt and Quinsey might have gone along.

Bill went on. "You know what that means. 544 will send out their goon squads and then we're done."

"When's the next shift for the engineers?"

"Eight o'clock."

Alan looked at the strolling pickets. There was one other man from the *Chronicle,* copy editor Ned Strom. Ned was a slender fellow who had made it his hobby to collect newspaper booboos. He had weak blue eyes and he kept darting a look up the street as if he was afraid the 544 hordes were about to come busting in right then and there. Alan asked, "Have you talked to the Twin Cities CIO head-quarters?"

"No. The fellows thought we should fight this out on our own. After all, you know, we're professional people, not common laborers. It was a sin we even let the clerks and the newsboys in."

Alan nodded. "Well, what are you going to do?"

"Dammit, Alan, if the engineers bust through here, the negotiations downtown between the Guild and WMSP will go down the drain." Bill chuffed himself over the elbow. "And there's nothing the management would like better than that we have a squabble of some kind out here. Some violence."

"I know one guy who might put a little fear into those 544 friends of yours."

"Who's that?"

"Red Engleking."

Bill's eyes opened a little. "Say, that gives me an idea. He's probably a member of the Meatcutters Union. That's CIO, and, brother, are they tough. They threw some of the AF of L union organizers over the hills down there."

"Red told me he was a good union man."

Bill got excited. "Do you know Red well enough to give him a ring? If the meatcutters could send over some help, that would slow down the engineers."

"I'll call him."

Alan used a pay phone at a nearby filling station. Red listened a few moments, finally said he'd call his union boss. "We'll need a bunch of guys yet tonight," Alan said. "By eight o'clock."

When Alan got back to the picket line he sat on the fender of his old Dodge awhile debating whether or not to join the boys. It slowly got dark out. A saffron luminescence in the west deepened into a soft mauve dusk. Every now and then a patrol car came down to the near corner and turned east. Streetlights began to bloom in the distance. A light burned in the shack under the transmitter, and occasionally the form of Jed Cairns could be seen moving past the window. Once Jed Cairns shaded his eyes and looked out toward the picket line and then he picked up a telephone and talked into it a few minutes.

About a quarter to eight a car slowly cruised by. Both men in it looked at the picket line, then the car rolled on.

Bill called over. "That was the engineers. Funny they came a quarter of an hour early."

"When do they usually come by?" Alan asked.

"Eight on the button."

Alan watched the engineers' car circle the acreage on which the transmitter stood. When the engineers got back to County Road C they pulled up beside a half dozen other cars. The cars could just be made out in the vague light reaching out from the city. Alan could see well at night.

"Hey," Bill cried, "I never noticed that bunch of cars there before. That must be the 544 boys."

Alan watched his newspaper buddies stomping back and forth in the grass. It took a lot of guts to picket. Alan finally slid off the fender of his car and went over and asked for a banner he might carry.

Bill broke out in a big smile. "Good to see you get down off Mt. Doughty."

A patrol prowl car made the turn at the corner, slowly, both policemen critically eying the pickets.

Ned Strom got himself a mackinaw from his car. His teeth were chattering.

Suddenly at five minutes to eight a long string of headlights began to head toward them coming down County Road C from the east. They came up fast. Alan counted some twenty cars. They swung around the corner and headed for the picket line, pulling up behind the cars already there.

Red Engleking and a huge hulk of a man emerged from the first car and headed for Alan. Other big powerful men piled out of the remaining cars. Some men carried baseball bats, some picnic bottles.

Red said, "Alan, our union boss, Albert Held."

Alan and Albert shook hands. It was a little like shaking hands with a two-by-six plank.

Albert said, "Those 544 gooneys come by yet?"

Bill stepped up. "Not yet. You can just make them out on that far corner. About a dozen cars."

"If that's all they got, we'll pound them to dust," Albert said. Albert raised his voice, "All right, boys. We got here in time. Take it easy for a while."

Alan eyed all the weapons with misgivings. He could just picture someone getting a picnic bottle over the head. "Bill, what about all those clubs and bottles?"

Bill pushed back his cap. The blue of his cap matched exactly the blue of his eyes. "God, yeh. The cops have just been dying for an excuse to come in here and break this up."

Alan said, "Albert, think you can talk your men into putting those weapons back in their cars?"

Albert cupped his heavy chin in his big hand. "Hell, then we won't have them handy in case the goon squad decides to rush us with a surprise attack."

Alan said, "Tell your guys to hide their weapons in the ditch. That grass is deep enough."

Albert slapped his hands together. "Good. We'll do her."

Bill asked, "How many men you got there?"

"About eighty."

"Pick out twenty and have them join the picket line, will you? Keep the rest in the cars as a reserve."

Weapons were hidden in the grass, and twenty men, including Big Albert and Red, joined the marchers.

Alan observed Red with interest. There was a high white look in his eyes. He had the air of a man looking for an excuse to break loose.

A single car came up Snelling Avenue, rolled across County Road C, and pulled up halfway between the corner and the picket line. The car's lights dimmed out.

Bill studied the car. "Wonder who that is?"

Alan said, "Looks like there's two in it."

"Maybe it's the cops with an unmarked car."

"No, it looks more like somebody just being nosy. Jackals."

Presently a car separated from the bunch of cars where the 544 goon squad sat waiting and headed for the corner. A police car joined it from the south. With the police car leading the way, both headed for the picket line, slowly. The spotlight on the police car worked the long string of meatcutters' cars, one at a time, then the spotlight swung around on the picket line. The police car and the car following it drove slowly past the gate and then on to the next corner, turned around, and came back, slowly.

Near the gate, the police car edged over as though to push through the picket line.

Bill cried, "Hey, goddam, what the hell . . ." Bill took up a stance directly in the path of the police car. The spotlight focused directly on Bill's face. Bill had to shield his eyes with an arm.

Red and Big Albert stood near Bill like rocks.

The police car eased to within a foot of Bill's legs, spotlight still blazing into his face.

Alan stepped up beside Bill. "Don't back down. Cops have no right to run interference for unions."

The police car inched closer. Its bumper touched Alan's gray trousers. Two sets of paired eyes behind the windshield glimmered like the huge eyes of blue flies. Alan's eyes began to flicker, trying to center on one or the other of the two sets of paired eyes.

Big Albert said, "Shall I tell the boys . . ."

"No no," Bill said quickly. "Not yet. Not with the cops you don't. They're just testing us."

Red said, "Shall we go for them?"

"No! We should resist them but not fight them."

The bumper nudged into Alan's shins, pushed hard, then shoved him back a few inches, his heels gouging out loose gravel.

A car door slammed up the line and a figure, a girl's figure, emerged from the gloom. The girl cried out as she ran toward them, "Alan! Alan!"

It was Jael. She must have found out from Burt where he'd gone. She darted up and pushed her body beside Alan and the bumper. "If they're going to run over you, they're going to have to run over me too!"

The police car shoved both Alan and Jael back another inch. Jael's bare legs gleamed against the nickel bumper. Bill and Red and Big Albert, who'd been a bit startled at first by the appearance of blond wild-haired Jael, joined them and set their knees against the car bumper too.

"Kill us then!" Jael cried.

Ned Strom's teeth suddenly opened and he vomited just past the right fender of the prowl car.

Time teetered. It all hung in balance for a moment.

Then the driver of the second car tooted, and he backed up a few feet, and then shot forward past the police car down the road, gathering speed as he went.

After a moment the police car let up and backed up too and drove off.

Everybody let go with a sigh of relief.

"Thank God the engineers had the better sense," Bill said. "For a second there I thought we'd lost her. An incident here on the picket line would have wrecked the negotiations downtown."

Jael slowly turned to Alan, face tearful. "When I saw that cop bumper touch you, Alan, something hot boiled up in my belly and I had to do something."

Alan put aside bad thoughts about her. She was just a young girl and should be allowed a few mistakes. Alan said, "Who's that in the car there with you?"

"Shelby Hines."

"Oh."

"Please, Alan, when this is all over tonight, could you take me home? I must talk to you."

Alan glanced at the others listening in. "I'll think about it. I may be on this picket line until morning."

"That's all right. I'll wait."

"You better have Shelby get you out of here."

"No, I'm sticking around. I must see you." She made a motion as though to lean up and kiss him and then, with a glance at the others, passed it off as though she'd been standing on a rough stone and had to shift her feet a little.

Big Albert stomped on the dead grass on the shoulder of the road. "I wonder where our goddam governor is all this time. We CIO boys voted for him to a man."

Bill said, "He's pretty radical and he probably figures he'll hurt us more than help us if he sticks his nose into this."

Big Albert said, "Maybe you're right. He didn't do any of us any good when he ordered out the National Guard up on the Iron Range and shut everything down. He got everybody mad, the steel companies, the unions, even the housewives and the Indians."

Bill laughed, "Yeh, up on the Iron Range the governor sure stepped on his own cock that time."

Jael broke out in laughter. "What a picture."

Bill said, "I forgot there was a woman around."

"That's all right," Jael said. "I've heard worse in the Student Union."

Red moved about restlessly, flexing his fingers.

"Hey, look," Big Albert said.

The collection of 544 cars on the far side of the acreage, lights on, were moving toward them.

Bill said, "Sure enough. Here they come at last."

Alan said, "Jael, you get out of here, you hear?" He leaned down at her fiercely. "Right now! Get back into your car over there."

Jael gave him an admiring glance. "Okay, but I'm watching from there."

Bill said, "By golly, look at that line of lights. There's at least forty of them. They must have gotten reinforcements."

"All right, you guys," Big Albert yelled at his meatcutters sitting in their cars. He waved an arm for them to come join the picket line.

Men in brown and blue clothes boiled out and surged up around Big Albert. "Do we get our baseball bats now?"

Bill held up a hand. "Wait. Let the cops spot just one of us with a club and they'll get us for unlawful assembly."

Big Albert hunched his big shoulders up and down. "Five will get you one the goon squad will be wearing brass knuckles."

Red said, "Them knucks won't do them any good if they don't land."

Big Albert snorted. "Some'll be carrying knives."

Bill said, "Maybe even guns. I hear they've hired some Chicago boys as organizers. And then of course they got that big Vilm Knecht and his brother Hans. Those two are just about the biggest men around. They've beat up a lot of fellas to bring 'em into line for 544. Real barroom brawlers." Vilm Knecht's first name was legally Wilm but pronounced Vilm.

The 544 caravan turned the corner and headed toward the WMSP transmitter gate. At about the same time a half dozen police prowl cars pulled up at the intersection, spotlights working up and down the road.

The 544 caravan pulled up across from the picket line. In a moment men in brown and blue clothes piled out and came bunched and threatening toward Bill and Alan.

Red tugged at Alan's sleeve. "You know the Bible?"

"My father read it at family worship."

"Remember how when the Israelites were fighting the Philistines they were scared to death of the giant Goliath and how young David slew Goliath with a sling and a stone?"

"I remember."

"How about it if both sides was to choose a champion, instead of having everybody fight?"

"Oh, Red, that won't be necessary."

"Let 544 pick this thug Vilm Knecht as their Goliath and I'll be your man."

"Let's first see how things work out."

The 544 mob pulled up short. Only a few yards separated the two worker armies.

Jed Cairns in the transmitter had become aware of the two massed mobs. He leaned forward to peer through the window, framing his eyes with his hands to see better, then whirled and picked up the phone and talked into it, waving an arm.

One of the biggest men Alan had ever seen stumped to the front of the 544 army. His legs were so thick and muscular they filled his brown trousers as though they might have been cement poured into two sacks. A huge chest like the barrel of a bull bulged up out of his tight belt.

Big Albert whispered, "Vilm Knecht."

Vilm spoke. "Who's the boss around here?" His voice was curiously light, boyish, with an odd catch in it.

Bill stepped forward. "I suppose you might say I am."

Vilm studied Bill a moment, then a sneer moved across his thin lips. His light-blue eyes glowed like two burners turned on low. "You guys all better go home now to Momma. Because if you don't, there's gonna be some busted nuts."

Bill said, "C'mon, Vilm, aren't we all supposed to be brothers against the bosses? What are you doing here trying to bust through our picket line?"

"We don't recognize the CIO."

There were raw cheers from the men behind Vilm Knecht. They milled up close behind him. "Let's pound them into the ground."

Big Albert said, "Vilm, those big fat-cat bosses of ours are right now rubbing their hands in downtown Minneapolis. We fight here and we both lose."

"We don't recognize the CIO. Get out of the way." Vilm turned to his bunch. "Where are those goddam miserable engineers, so we can run them through and be done with it? I've got a broad to jazz yet tonight."

Somebody said, "Hans has got 'em."

"Hans!"

An even bigger man than Vilm shuffled to the front of the 544 gang. Hans Knecht was fatter and slower than Vilm and had none of Vilm's hard muscular movement. Hans also had a curiously boyish voice. "I got 'em back there all set to go through."

Red stepped up. "Wait. I want to make a suggestion."

"Make it," Vilm said short.

"Instead of everybody getting his head cracked, how about it if both sides was to choose themselves a champion and then we let the champions fight it out? If your champion wins, the engineers go through. If ours wins, they don't. Fair and square."

Vilm backed a step. "Hey! I know you. I saw you fight Figleaf."

"Do we fight?"

"Sure. I've got it all figured out how to fight you sidesteppers. No holds barred. Everything goes."

Alan said, "Why not by the Marquess of Queensberry rules?"

Vilm snorted. "What the frig do I care about any queen's rules? If I'm gonna fight for our side it's going to be plain ordinary alley fighting. Gouging, kneeing, rabbit punches. This is war, you know."

Red said, "All right. That's okay by me."

Alan became afraid for Red. In that tight little world they were suddenly in, lighted only by distant streetlights and spearing car headlights, Vilm took on the look of an evil savage. "Red, you've never played that game. He'll kill you." To himself Alan thought: "Red sure is desperate about something."

Red pointed a finger. "I don't fight nobody but what he's bare down to his belt."

Vilm protested. "Hey, what the hell, no!"

Red began to strip down to his waist. "C'mon, I got other things to do yet too tonight."

Vilm was of a mind to jump Red while Red's arms were still partly tangled in his shirt. But the exchange of talk had set up a code of sorts. "Okay, I'll be wit' you in a jiff." Vilm turned and pushed through his mob and behind a mass of bodies began to take off his upper clothes.

Bill said, "He had to undress behind those guys so we wouldn't see the knife he was carrying."

Big Albert said, "Or gun he was packing."

A police spotlight tried to pierce into the milling knot of men where Vilm was stripping down. Another spotlight flicked up and down Red's body.

Finally Vilm reappeared. Bare down to his narrow waist he looked even bigger. Built-up shoulders in a suit jacket were lost on him. His torso glistened a lively pink-tan. Vilm put up his dukes and stepped up in a surprisingly good boxer's shuffle. Here was a man who might be able to take Red.

Red smiled his rare little superior smile and squared off against Vilm.

There was a shout from the transmitter. A figure, Jed Cairns, was outlined in the streaming light of the open door. Jed yelled again. "Wait! For godsakes, wait." He came running toward them, bounding in his hurry.

"What the hell?" Vilm muttered.

Red didn't like the interruption either.

Jed pulled up stumbling between the two bare-chested men. "God! you guys really were going to fight."

Vilm's nose quivered above slit lips. "That's right."

Jed puffed. His haggard brown eyes were eloquent with tension. "It's all off, boys. The strike's over."

Silence. Vilm let down his hands. Big Albert stared. Bill's face took on a look as though he'd just been told he was the father of a brand-new baby boy. Everybody let out a big gushing sigh; then the next instant broke out into exclamations.

"What the hell happened? Did the Guild win?"

Bill asked, "What were the terms?"

Jed said, "I know you guys cussed me out for manning the transmitter. But I was an officer of the company and couldn't join your

Guild. In my heart I really was on your side, you know. Well, you won. The WMSP management decided to recognize the union and agreed to work out the fine points with an arbitration board appointed by the governor."

"Hey," Bill said, Irish eyes merry again, "maybe the governor's learned where to step after all."

Alan laughed.

Vilm grabbed Jed Cairns by his coat lapels and hauled him up close. "You ain't bullshitting us now? The strike is really settled?"

Jed finally caught his breath. Brown eyes steady, with dignity, he drew himself up stiff and tall. Firmly he freed himself from Vilm's clutching hand. "Yes, it is, Mr. Wilhelm Knecht."

"She-it," Vilm said. "And here I had my water all heated up to beat up on this pigsticker. What the sportswriters say is such a fighter." Vilm wheeled and disappeared into his crowd.

Red stood very still. "Too bad. I can't stand bullies."

There was a tug at Alan's elbow. It was Jael. "The Guild won, didn't it?"

"Yes."

"I'm so happy for you." Jael plied herself around him like a vine. "You can go now then?"

"Yeh. Sure I think so."

"Good. I'll quick go tell Shelb that I've got a ride home with you." She smiled her supple lips. "I can, can't I?"

"I guess so." Past hurts receded. "But I'd like to meet this Shelby Hines, if I may."

"Oh, sure. Come along."

"Just a minute." Alan turned back to the boys a second. "Everything's gonna be all right here now? You don't need me anymore?"

Bill waved a hand at him. "Go have your fun."

Alan turned to Red. "Give my regards to Jen."

Red nodded.

Jael hurried Alan along. She called ahead to Shelby Hines, where he was leaning out on the driver's side of his car. "The Guild won! Isn't it wonderful? And our Alan was a big hero."

Shelby got out of the car and held out a hand. It was a soft small hand. He was wearing a dark-blue jacket with light-gray trousers, white shirt with flowing red tie. His face was oval-shaped, dark sensitive eyes with rather long lashes, and a perfect nose. His dark eyes went over Alan in the cool manner of one born to wealth.

Alan could see why Jael was intrigued with Shelby Hines. Shelby was a gentleman. He would be easy to live with. At the same time she'd never change him either. He might be soft and pleasant on the outside, but on the inside would live by a core of behavior she'd never be able to touch. In a pinch he could always buy himself out of trouble, either with his manners or with his money. Far back in Alan's head, Alan's interior commentator remarked, as though it might be a throwaway line in a play, that he was someday going to lose Jael to Shelby Hines.

Jael slipped her arm through Shelby's. "I have to talk something over with Alan. Would you mind terribly if he took me home?"

"If that's what you want."

"That's awfully swell of you, Shelb."

"Thanks."

Jael withdrew her arm.

"Be seeing you around." Shelby got back in his car, sat a moment lighting himself a cigarette, then started his car and leisurely drove off.

Alan liked Shelby's cool manner. Haunt John would have handled Jael the same way. Except that Haunt John would have done it more with the hauteur of a stallion than that of a Summit Avenue playboy.

Alan led Jael to his Dodge. The car responded on the first revolution and soon the car's headlights were slicing through the dark streets of St. Paul, then Minneapolis.

Jael snuggled up close. "We're stopping at your place first, aren't we?"

Alan found himself aping the manners of a Shelby Hines. "If that's what you want."

Jael sat up. "Why Alan Ross! Of course I want to be alone with you for a while."

Alan said nothing.

"You do want me, don't you?"

For an answer, he turned off University Avenue and headed for his apartment on Southeast Sixth Street.

"That's better," she whispered. She cuddled against him again.

They went upstairs on tiptoe. Alan told her that the last time she'd been up there the landlady had been a little suspicious of the sounds she'd heard up in his apartment.

She shed her coat and threw it over a chair. Her smile was large and her eyes were full of pleading as she settled on his bed. She threw back her gold hair with a toss of her head. "Oh, Alan, I am forgiven, aren't I?"

"What is there to forgive?"

"You know. Just things generally. Shelb tonight."

Alan remembered the nights when he couldn't sleep after two o'clock thinking about her. Sorrow like a bitter alcohol had burned in his chest those times, had raced around in his head like whirlwinds of acrid smoke. Forgiven? Perhaps. Forgotten? Never. How had it been with other men with her?

"Alan?" She held out her hand to him.

Alan shed his jacket and threw it over her coat. "I'm hungry. Aren't you?"

"You're going to eat first?"·

"Why not? All that excitement out there on the picket line made me hungry."

"Come here and I'll give you something that'll make you forget your hunger. Come."

Alan studied her. That last gesture of hers was exactly the kind of gesture her mother Gretta might make. There were two routes Jael might take someday: one, become like her haughty loveless mother; two, become like her fancy loveless Aunt Pauline. Either a prude or a snob. Just possibly there might be a third route. What some called a whore.

"Alan?"

"I'm awfully tired." His eyes flickered.

The supple motions of a kitty moving through grass passed through her, from her toes up through her neck. "No one's too tired for that."

"Well," he said, "I guess I'm glad that you decided not to go to Vassar."

# Chapter 18

# ALAN

Alan decided to take his summer vacation in the woods along the North Shore of Lake Superior. He'd been lucky that a man named Morrison, formerly with the *Chronicle,* had offered him the use of a cabin up on the Stewart River above Two Harbors. Jael was going to stay with her Uncle Horace and Aunt Sophie out in the country.

The last week of July, Alan drove north out of St. Paul on Highway 61. The country was lush, green truck gardens, reed-fringed little lakes, occasional oases of white birch. The blue of the lakes made his eyes feel more blue. Ahead lay three whole weeks of pure lazy time in the dark woods. How wonderful it was going to be to go through a whole day without having to say a word to another soul on earth.

There was little Sunday traffic. The morning sun danced silk-smooth on Horseshoe Lake. Beyond Pine City he crossed the Snake River. The Snake ran through Uncle Horace Green's pasture, according to Jael. Alan threw a look off to the west wondering what sort of farm her uncle had. He'd know more about that when he dropped by to see her on the way home from his vacation.

Hinckley came up. There no longer was any evidence of the great forest fire that had wiped the town out years before.

By the time Alan passed through Friesland, Sandstone, and Willow River, the stands of hardwood trees began to thin out and the groves of evergreens began to thicken. Birches stood out like crowds of albinos.

At Sturgeon Lake he almost had a head-on collision with a fool. The fellow tried to pass another car on a hill and had nowhere to go when Alan met him at the crest. Luckily the fool froze at the wheel and stayed in the wrong lane while Alan, thinking quickly, rolled his steering wheel right and took to the shallow ditch. Alan's old blue Dodge groaned in its iron frame as it bounced around. There was one slushy reed-filled spot but the car's momentum was enough to carry it through; and then, with Alan wrenching his wheel left, it got up on the highway again. The windshield was splotched over with black mud.

Alan pulled over and with some water from the ditch cleaned off his windshield. At the next town, Moose Lake, he pulled into a filling station and hosed off the entire car. Noting there was a grocery store open, he got some groceries while the station hand filled his car with gas and oil. Alan bought bacon and eggs and bread and canned beans and butter and a sack of early Harvester apples.

He drove on to Mahtowa. Stately white pines and towering red pines formed tall walls of quivering needles on both sides of the road. He crossed the rushing St. Louis River in its little black canyon. At Nopeming he took a turn east and found himself looking down from a considerable height. Black rock, dark-green pine and fir, fell away in a steep fall of land. The city of Duluth, half hidden by trees, hung precariously on the steep rocky slopes below. Only the downtown hotels stuck out. Off to the right towered a huge elevated bridge. Still farther out stood round white cement grain elevators resembling the marble pillars of an abandoned temple. Duluth was to the Twin Cities what Edinburgh was to London.

And beyond that lay the greatest sight of all, the glorious blue curve of Lake Superior. From where Alan was riding, some 800 feet above it, he could see the curve of the earth in the lake's vast blue expanse. There was no wind out, and the lake lay like a deep-blue fantastically huge gem embedded in a black-and-green brooch.

Highway 61 zigged down, then turned onto Superior Street. Tall buildings loomed up on either side. At two in the afternoon shadows began to hang above him. Pigeons clappered from perch to perch.

Soon Superior Street turned into Congdon Boulevard and the boulevard became Highway 61 again. Forests of white pine and red pine and fir covered the little mountains on the left. Below on the right Lake Superior lapped on black rock. The green of the trees tinged the left side of the highway and the blue of the lake tinted the right side.

He crossed a bridge over French River, then Sucker River, then Knife River. Presently Two Harbors with its overhead iron ore loading docks showed up.

From a Standard Oil station he learned that the Morrison cabin lay two miles north of a golf course, then a mile east, then a mile north again.

It was easy to find. The road rose up to a height of land and ended near a farmstead. Open fields spread between squares of uncut forest.

The farmstead had a spur of woods for a windbreak, mostly fir and red pine.

Alan parked his car under a fir, then made arrangements with the farmer's wife to pick up a bottle of milk every morning. She said she'd put it in their mailbox for him to find. Then, picking up his groceries, he stepped through a steel gate and headed down an old tote road toward a ravine.

Pine and birch towered over him. The late-afternoon sun struck lavender shadows across a stony path. There was a sound of rushing water. In a moment he came upon a half-rotted log spanning a stream. He teetered across the one log, holding out his arms and his burdens to help keep his balance, and made it. The rushing water below flowed a woven silver over black bedrock.

There were flowers everywhere. Thimbleberries hung ripe and flesh-red on both sides of the path. He made a mental note to come back and help himself later on. A very narrow path, sometimes hard to make out, wriggled up a steep rise. Rocks underfoot broke loose and rattled down behind him. The rocks splashed into the stream like heavy frogs. Twice he slipped and fell to his knees, dirtying his gray trousers. He sweat. With a final effort, brushing through sumac, he made the crest.

And there it was. A one-story log cabin set in the middle of a little clearing below. A single white pine, very tall, towered over it on the west side. Beyond it tumbled a noisier stream, falling off three ledges, one of the falls a good ten feet high. The biggest fall spilled into a considerable pool. Beyond the three falls a wall of sheer granite reached up a good hundred feet. Only a few scrub pine managed to find a foothold in the cracks. It was a little Eden.

Alan stepped carefully down the path. A deer broke out of cover and leaped like a flying fantasy across the zigzagging path. Again Alan slipped, just managing to keep from falling. Then the path leveled out and headed directly for the door of the cabin.

Alan fished in his pockets for the key, found it, and opened up. He stepped in. A sweet odor of old wood and the still-lingering acrid smell of smoke from the last fire in the fireplace hung in the gloom of the cabin. There were two one-legged beds built in the two far corners covered with old comforters and quilts, a wood stove, and racks full of books along the walls. The floors were halved logs, rough and splintery, covered with a half dozen rag rugs.

He promptly stripped off his clothes and stepped outside and, barefoot, legged it down to the biggest fall. He was surprised by the considerable pool under the fall. It was at least a good twenty feet across. Where the fall hit the surface, the water had an amber color, but along the edges it was as clear as air.

Alan stretched to his full height, sucked in a deep breath, and dove in headfirst.

God was it cold! It had to be water straight from a deep spring. He shot to the surface and almost came out like a fish walking water on its tail. He swam a few feet, vigorously; then, becoming adjusted to the chilly water, dove under again. Lord!

Dripping, he climbed out on the shallow side. The rocks were sharp underfoot and he had to pick his way carefully. When he finally got back up on the ledge he actually could make out goose pimples over his arms. And here it was the last week in July.

He found himself a smooth place on the serrated black granite, a spot about as big as the iron seat on his father's gang plow at home. The low sun still lay warm over his back and on the back of his head. He let himself dry. He let his fancy track where it might, musing on one thing after another.

The moment the sun sank behind the ridge, a chill moved down out of the forest. Shivering, he got up and went to the cabin and dressed in his roughing clothes.

He made himself a supper of pork and beans, a half can of pears, several slices of bread and butter and marmalade, and two cups of coffee. The wood stove had an especially good draft and the little wood fire he built in it roared like a motor. He got some water from the falls and washed the dishes. Then, succumbing to waves of lassitude, he stripped and slipped in under a heavy quilt on one of the beds and promptly fell into a sound sleep.

A blue jay squawking outside awakened him in the morning. He squirmed deliciously under the heavy quilt. There was a faint smell of another man's personal odor in the quilt. There was also the smell of a burned-out fire in the air.

Well, if he felt like it he could go back to sleep again and nobody would be the wiser. This was one day he didn't have to worry about being late for work.

Old habits finally won out and he got up.

He stepped outdoors and stretched in the misty morning. He went back up the path over the crest and down into the ravine over the half-rotted log and then up toward his car. He found the bottle of milk in the neighbor's mailbox as promised. Breakfast wasn't right unless he had his bowl of cereal. On the way back he picked a handful of thimbleberries.

Back in the cabin he topped off his cereal with the thimbleberries.

He relished them in the cool milk. He finished his breakfast with two fried eggs and several strips of bacon.

He'd barely finished washing dishes when sleep overcame him again. He snoozed without dreams until almost noon.

Sweat running down his face woke him. When the sun beat directly down into the little Eden the air fairly darted with heat. He stripped and went down to the stream for another dip. Once more the shock of the chilly water was a thrill.

He decided not to dress for the rest of the day. He took a little sun, a half hour of it, careful not to let his overly blond skin burn, then began to explore the little glen, staying mostly under the trees. He found a patch of wild blueberries and helped himself to several handfuls, staining his fingertips and teeth. He also found a patch of wild blackberries, so dead ripe he only had to touch them and they fell into the palm of his hand.

Downstream he found a log loveseat tucked in under a cluster of birches. Someone had carried in gravel and sprinkled it under the loveseat. The yellow gravel looked out of place on the black granite outcropping.

For three days he did nothing but sleep, eat, take a dip, nap, take a little walk in the sun naked, pick some berries, take another dip, eat, and sleep. It was life in paradise. He smiled to himself. He was a pale-blond Abel living in a green glen where sparkling springwater fell into a brown bowl. The mallow smell of splashed water was very sweet.

There were four big trout in the bowl under the falls. He spotted them sometimes when he sat very still in his cupped rock seat while letting himself dry off after a dip. A fisherman would have got out his fishing pole. For himself he liked having them in the water untouched, feelers quivering when he went swimming. Sometimes their brown beauty was hard to make out against the stained brown hue of the granite bottom.

He wondered what Jael might be doing right that moment. He looked forward to his visit with her at Grandy when his vacation was over. He found himself thinking warm good things about her. The Shelby Hines business didn't seem to be too important anymore. Memory of her kisses, of her flesh, wiped that all out.

One afternoon as he was gathering up a little bowl of blueberries in the blueberry patch, eating about as many as he was collecting, standing naked in the sun, smiling to himself, he heard a noise behind him. Turning, he saw a black bear on the far side of the blueberry patch. Like himself the bear was up on two feet, gathering berries and eating them by the pawful. The bear squinted at him, cocked its head to one side as if considering a weighty thought, then turned slightly and went on eating.

Alan didn't know what to do, so he just turned aside himself and went on gathering berries.

After a while, bowl filled, Alan headed for his cabin. Just as he was about to step inside he looked back over his shoulder. It was funny but the bear too had left off picking blueberries on its end of the patch and was just then fading off into the dark-blue shadow under the firs.

Alan kept the door to the cabin locked after that.

One evening, after a good long swim, as Alan was sitting in his small smooth cupped seat on the rocks, he heard the sound of voices. The voices were loud enough to be heard over the tumbling sound of the falling water. He was still wet. The sun was just setting and dusk was about to break out from under the trees.

The voices rose, faded, then came on with a burst of excited cries. "Here it is! It's the cabin, all right." Girl voices. Then an older woman's voice said, "Yes, yes, I see it. Quiet down now, girls."

Before Alan could get to his feet and duck up the path to his cabin for some clothes, he was surrounded by some twenty Girl Scouts dressed mostly in green, bare knees, sturdy leather walking shoes. For a moment Alan's eyes wouldn't center. Meanwhile a couple dozen sets of steady eyes were going over him as though he might be an important landmark, picking out all the details of him. Quickly he pushed his genitals down between his legs and then crossed his legs to hide them. There was no leaf handy.

The older woman came up with a quiet smile. She had warm brown eyes and dark-tanned skin and good full lips. "I'm sorry. I didn't know Mr. Morrison had rented out his cabin this summer."

Alan's tongue lay like a stunned fish in the bottom of his mouth.

"If you want us to," the woman said, "we can find another place for our steak fry."

Alan could only stare at her. He was very conscious of his genitals lying pinched under him, cold against the rock.

The woman was about forty, obviously a mother, and still vigorous in her movements. Like his own mother she had patient wise blue eyes. Not once did she look down at his bare hips. She'd probably noticed when she first came on the scene that he wasn't wearing a bathing suit but had decided that the wisest thing to do with all those girls present was to act as if nothing was out of the way.

Alan thought: "I feel like a bull let loose in a pasture full of heifers. With one old cow around for old times' sake."

"As I say," the woman went on, "we can find ourselves another spot."

Finally Alan found tongue. "No, no. You can stay here. Mr. Morrison did tell me I could have this cabin for three weeks, but if your Girl Scout troop is used to coming here, why, by all means stay."

The woman bent a warm smile upon him, careful to keep it aimed on his face. "You're sure now?"

"Oh, yes."

"Good. Thank you very much." She turned. "Girls, some of you go wrestle up some wood. And the rest of you lay out the picnic goodies on that wide bare spot on the rocks over there. Okay?"

The girls quickly broke up into two groups and hurried to get the fire and the picnic started.

Unfortunately the woman picked a spot for the fire just a few feet off the path to the cabin. The path was a winding one, the only one possible where a person could walk barefooted without getting his feet all cut up by sharp rocks.

Alan thought: "What in the world am I going to do? Get up and walk boldly through that lot of fluttering chicks? Meanwhile the family jewels are getting cold down there under my legs."

Every once in a while the woman looked his way. She looked at his eyes.

Presently the fire began to crackle. The young girls, whiteheads, brownheads, a few Indian, armed their roasting sticks with gleaming pink wieners and waved them about and jostled each other at the edge of the fire Their little cries of picnic joy were sometimes in sharp contrast to the soft bruising sound of falling water.

Alan thought: "Somewhere along the line here I'm going to have to get up and reveal myself to the world. At least to these girls and their chaperon. I can't sit on the evidence forever." Then Alan laughed out loud. "Especially if they offer me a wienie."

And laughing, he relaxed. Then he got to his feet and in a leisurely, even courtly manner, strolled through their chattering midst and headed for the cabin.

They hardly noticed him. Though they wouldn't have seen much. His genitals were so shrunken from being cold they were hardly bigger than a peanut and two acorns.

He slipped into a pair of gray trousers and a white shirt. Too bad that company had forced him to put on some clothes. He liked going around naked.

He ate several hot dogs with them, a dish of warmed beans, and drank a bottle of strawberry pop.

The older woman turned out to be quite well read. She introduced herself as Mrs. Grace Threadgill, head of the local Two Harbors library board. When she learned he was a reporter for the Minneapolis *Chronicle*, she had a lot of questions about his work. When Alan began to tell stories about Quinsey Quinn and Glenda Underland, the young girls crowded around, eyes excited, lips inviting. Sometimes they touched him.

It was twelve midnight before they left. He stood awhile outside his cabin listening to their little shrieks of dismay as they stumbled up the path in the dark. Slowly the sound of their girlish laughter faded off into the black night. There was no moon out, and from where he stood in the dark gorge, surrounded by black trees, the stars shone crackling bright.

Alan wrote Jael at her country address with Uncle Horace. At first his letters were short and cryptic. But when she replied with warm letters he began to open up. "The pool beneath the falls is my tub. The falls are my showers. The leaves of the trees are my towel. The pine smell is my face lotion. I'm a regular kissingbee out to visit every pretty flower in the glen."

Jael wrote back in kind. "I'm closest to you when I'm waiting for sleep in my bed up in the bare guest room, when my body seems to be smooth and flowing with every breathing motion it makes."

The third week Alan opened up even more. "Soon there will be lost a summer's glory. Wraith, dream, vision, come back come back."

Jael wrote: "There's a dull gnawing ache at the base of my spine, with an aching ripple to the outside. It sits behind my love for you. I am afraid of it. And it isn't that Lady Genevieve has been misbehaving either. I have been uncomfortable but no more so than usual. No, it's a ghost hurt. Oh, Alan, I so long to see you. You are coming by the farm, aren't you, on your way back to the Twin Cities?"

He replied: "Of course I'm coming by to see you. Even if all the brood hens of Grandy were to stand in the way with beaks as big as tin shears, I'd come."

She wrote: "Thank God! Because if you don't come by I'm lost. You don't know. It will be wonderful to feel your smooth body curved around mine again. Oh, darling, don't disappoint me, please. You don't know."

Then, on a Sunday, Alan Ross took a final swim in his Eden pool, let himself dry sitting on the rocks in the sun, packed up his clothes and locked up the cabin, and left for Grandy.

# Chapter 19

# JAEL

---

Jael was washing dishes when she told them. Her mother Gretta and her aunt Sophie were still sitting at the table. The menfolks, her father and Uncle Horace, had gone out to check a heifer that was due.

"Alan should be along here about two o'clock tomorrow. So you don't have to feed him Sunday dinner. He'll just visit awhile and then go on to Minneapolis."

Mother got to her feet angrily. "You had the nerve to invite him out here to the farm?"

"Why not? You're all going to have to get used to having him around sometime. Because just as soon as I'm out of college I'm going to marry him."

"You are not going to marry him, that newspaper bum," Mother said in a voice of ice. "I'll never stand for it. And neither will your father, if I have anything to say about it."

Jael almost snickered. "Yes, poor father, obedient slavey, who has to give way to the memory of a bastard son of William the Third."

Aunt Sophie next reared up from her end of the table. She turned to Mother. "Are you going to let that snip of a girl get away with saying things like that?"

"No, I'm not," Mother said. Mother advanced upon Jael. "I think we better do what we threatened to do before. Send you off to the girls' reform school."

Jael put down the dish she was washing and turned to face them both, leaning against the sink. "I'm eighteen now, Mother, and legally you can't."

"Well, then we'll testify you're insane," Mother said, "and have you committed."

"Mother! On what grounds? That I fell in love?"

"On the grounds that you don't know what you're doing." Mother grabbed Jael's arms and gave her a shake. "Sitting there in the privy writing love letters. You must be crazy. No self-respecting woman would ever think of having love thoughts while sitting out there!"

"You peeked!" Jael cried, aghast.

Aunt Sophie said, "Yes, we peeked." Aunt Sophie's face was mottled over and her nose was red. It gave her the look of an enormous beet topped out with white straggly leaves. "We have your welfare at heart."

Jael scoffed. "That's a laugh."

Mother said, "I still think my idea that we take you to our family doctor to see if you are still untouched is a good one. Then we could throw him in jail."

Jael threw up both her hands. "For godsakes, Mother!"

"Him writing you that he's 'a regular kissingbee out to visit every pretty flower in the glen' . . . why! That just proves he's just using you for his own pleasure."

Jael folded her arms over her bosom. "Then you've been peeking in my mail too. Why, that's against the law. I'm of age now, where I can ask that nobody, but nobody, can look at my mail. I'll have the U. S. Post Office prosecute you!"

Whack! Mother slapped her hard over the cheek.

Jael instantly slapped her mother back.

Mother whacked her a second time. "We're only doing this for your own good."

Aunt Sophie pitched in then too. She got in several good whacks over the back of Jael's head, then after a moment doubled her fists and took to pounding Jael over the back and shoulders.

Jael couldn't believe it. She was being beaten by her own mother and her best aunt. "In God's name," she cried, "it's you two who've gone insane."

A male voice broke in on all the pounding. "What the hell is going on here?" Uncle Horace stood in the doorway, with Father standing peeking in under his arm. "You two beating up on my favorite niece? Have you damned old hens gone nuts?"

Aunt Sophie dropped to her knees. "Come, Gretta, our only hope now is to pray God to save her lost soul. Down on your knees with me."

Jael couldn't resist it. "What about Alan's poor lost soul? Shouldn't we pray for him too if we truly are Christians?"

"Him?" Mother cried. "Why should we pray for him? Who is he that we should bother with him?"

"What's this all about?" Uncle Horace demanded.

Jael said, "I merely told them that my boyfriend, Alan Ross, was dropping by tomorrow afternoon for a minute."

"For chrissakes, Sophie, what's wrong with that?"

Mother interposed, "That man is the wrong one for her. He's got those funny eyes. When you've met him you notice he can't look you in the eye."

"So?"

"We don't want any newspaper reporters nosing around in our family history."

Uncle Horace cleared his throat with a scathing sound. "You damned screwed-up Paulsen women. On the one hand too proud to know anybody common. On the other hand too damned ashamed of being a bastard's offspring." Uncle Horace strode into the kitchen and set himself between Jael and the two women. "Now you two old bags just leave her alone. I'm the head of this house, goddammit, and I say Jael can see whoever she wants. She's a grown woman now. And if I hear any more about you two women snooping through Jael's letters, I'm going to pound you both."

Good old Uncle Horace.

That night Jael went to sleep smiling to herself.

But the next morning, waking late, after the men had left the yard, Jael had a shock. Mother and Aunt Sophie had locked her in her room.

Jael was first of a mind to shriek her head off. But then a sly thought came to her. Why not let them think she'd given in? And in the meantime pull off a stunt she'd done once before—climb down out of the room by way of the rainspout. She could see the road from her window. She'd wait until she saw Alan's blue car coming and then she'd escape.

Around ten o'clock her mother rapped on the door. "Would you like some breakfast?"

"Can't I come down for breakfast?"

"I'll bring you some." Mother's firm steps receded down the hall and then down the stairs.

Jael smiled to herself. She made her bed neatly so there would be no complaint about that. She neated up the room with a dustmop, and shook it out of the window. Then she dressed, pleated yellow dress which Alan liked, white blouse, white socks, white tennies. No pants, no brassiere.

In a few minutes her mother was at the door. There was some

whispering. It meant Aunt Sophie had come with Mother to make sure there'd be no escape.

Jael laughed out loud. "Come in. I won't run away. A person can't run very far on an empty stomach."

Aunt Sophie opened the door with her key and Mother came in carrying a tray with some steaming cereal and toast.

"Well," Mother said, inspecting the room and then looking Jael up and down, "I see you've been up awhile."

"Yes. Since college I've learned to get up early."

"I see." Mother set the tray on the end of the bed. "Call us when you've finished."

"Mother? What if I have to go pee?"

Mother's face wrinkled in distaste. "Can't you use the . . . white owl?"

"I don't need to hoot, Mother. I just need to pee."

"You cat. Is that a way to talk to your mother?"

"Maybe I can just pee out the window like the boys do at Shelby Hines' frat."

Mother gave her a wild look. "Now how would you know about that?"

"Your beloved Shelby told me."

"When he was here the other day?"

"Yes. You see, that's what you get for it when you don't let me pick my own boyfriends."

Aunt Sophie listened with darkening countenance. She read escape in Jael's eyes. She pulled the door half closed and blocked the rest with her pudgy body just in case.

"Or maybe I'll just pee in a corner here somewhere. Like when I was a naughty little girl."

"Eat your breakfast." Mother turned and left the room. Aunt Sophie followed her and pulled the door shut. The key clicked with a snap in the lock.

Jael ate the breakfast with relish. In a little while she'd show Mother she really was a cat.

They brought her a sandwich at one o'clock. Jael also relished that.

About one-forty-five, Jael began to watch the road to the north.

She'd just pulled up a chair to the window to make it easy for herself when she spotted a blue car coming over the first little rise in the land. That had to be Alan. He was still a couple of miles off. There'd be just enough time to climb down.

Quickly she unhooked the screen and, backing out of the window, reached down a foot to the rainspout where it crossed below the window. With her free hand she gripped the rainspout where it also turned up past her window toward the other gable. It was easier this time. Some six years ago she'd been shorter and had trouble catching the right holds. She next stepped on the trim of the window over the hallway, and then, reaching down, caught hold of the grape-covered trellis. A couple of careful catches into the vines and she let herself drop to earth, lightly. She listened a moment. They hadn't heard her. Good. Quickly she sped across the garden behind a long row of pole beans and then out onto the road.

As she flagged down the car she saw with sinking heart that it was Uncle Horace and her father in his blue Essex. She had never learned to tell cars apart by their make. All she recognized was the different colors.

Uncle Horace pulled up and leaned out of the car window. "Jael, have those old biddies up at the house been picking at you again?"

"They locked me up. I just now climbed down out of the window."

Father turned white around the edges of his lips. "You mean, your mother locked you up in your room?"

"Yes."

"That woman. Sometimes . . ."

Uncle Horace looked at his pocket watch. "Isn't it about time for your boyfriend to be along?"

"I expect him any minute."

Uncle Horace smiled at her. "And you thought this car was your boyfriend's car."

"Yes. They're both blue."

Uncle Horace turned to Father. "Tor, don't you think it's about time that this girl of yours, who is now of age, can meet her boyfriend at the front door of her house?"

"You bet!" Father snapped.

"Jael, climb in," Uncle Horace said. Then Uncle Horace laughed. "I wonder what Sophie and Gretta are going to say when all of a sudden they see you riding up to the front door in the back seat of my car."

Jael had to laugh too. "Instead of up in my room with only an old pot to pee in."

"Now that I don't like to hear from my daughter," Tor said.

Uncle Horace shook his head. "Tearing my favorite niece all to pieces like that."

# Chapter 20

# ALAN

Jael had written that the Green farm had a white barn and a cream-colored house. "You can't miss it. Most everybody around Grandy has a red barn." Alan spotted the white barn the moment he came over the rise. He saw movement in the yard. A car had just arrived in it.

Alan was high. It seemed to him the old blue Dodge more skimmed down the road than rolled down it. The sun was out and the trees were a trembling green and the pastures a wavering blue. Birds singing on fence posts told of a wonderful time coming.

He turned into the lane. He shut off his motor and coasted up behind a blue Essex in front of the house gate. Quietly he got out of his car.

Jael stood talking with her father and another man. They were smiling about something together, lost in their own talk.

"Jael?"

She turned. She saw him. Then her face instantly filled with happy surprise, mouth opening like a broken blossom. "Alan!" She skipped over and clutched him by the arm. "You came!"

"Of course."

"Come. I want you to meet my uncle. Uncle Horace, this is my friend Alan Ross."

Uncle Horace had a powerful square grip. Uncle Horace knew what work meant. There was also the air of a gentleman about him.

"And you know Father."

Alan shook hands with Tor Hemlickson too.

Alan's eye caught something off to one side. Turning, he spotted two women looking at them out of the kitchen window. One was

Jael's mother, Gretta. The other looked like it might be Gretta's sister. That had to be Aunt Sophie. Both women had an utterly astonished look on their faces. They were looking more at Jael than at him.

Jael said brightly, "When must you be back at work, Alan?"

Alan caught on. She couldn't spend much time with him. "The moment I get back."

"But we can take a little joyride out in the country first?"

"Of course."

"Good. Let's get started then. The sooner the better." Jael turned to Uncle Horace. "Thanks." Then she smiled at her father. "Just tell Mother I won't be gone long."

Tor Hemlickson nodded stiffly.

Jael flew around to the passenger side of Alan's car before Alan could be the gentleman and open the door for her. She waved at the two women in the kitchen window. There was an air of sly glee in Jael's manner. "C'mon, Alan, time's a-wastin'."

Alan got in on his side. Things were happening in a kind of a blur.

Jael slid across the seat and pressed herself against Alan. "Please," she said, "get that thing started and let's get out of here."

"Is it that urgent?"

"Yes."

Alan started the car. He eased it into low and drove off slowly. It wouldn't have been proper to leave the yard with a roaring exhaust.

"Take a left. I know a lonely road where we can go."

The moment they were out of sight of Uncle Horace's yard, she began hugging Alan from the side, and kissing his right cheek and neck, and squeezing his leg. He had trouble keeping a steady toe on the footfeed.

They rode past small farms in cut-over country. Occasional ponds ovaled by. Cows and horses lifted their heads and stared cockeyed at them.

"Take another left here," Jael said, pointing.

Alan took the turn onto a dirt road. In a moment they topped out on a little rise of land. Ahead and below stood a small grove of aspens and a jack pine.

"There it is," she said. "I've dreamt of taking you here many times. Nobody can see us here."

Alan pulled up, parking off to one side. He noted some freshly pressed-down tracks in the grass. Another car had parked there recently. He shut off the motor. There were birds everywhere in the trees, and birdsong took over. Insects hummed and whirred. Far in the distance a cow lowed for her calf. A horse whinnied off to the right; was answered by another horse off to the left.

Jael took Alan by his ears, gently, and turned him toward her. She kissed him softly, lips barely touching. She ruffled his hair and opened his shirt. She looked into his eyes. "I just can't get over how you affect me with that strange look of yours."

Alan began to tremble beside her. He'd missed touching her.

Soon they were making love, sometimes softly, sometimes vigorously.

Later, as they disentangled themselves from under the steering wheel, Alan saw something. "Wonder what that is."

"Oh, that? That's nothing. It's just the whites."

"Some kind of female complaint?"

"Aunt Sophie told me it was nothing to worry about. All women get it."

Whatever it was it gave her the sweet odor of a beautiful deadly flower. Looking at her bare legs he also happened to notice several bruises on her inner thighs. The bruises were bluish, and one of them had a red streak stretching out from it. "What happened here?"

"It's where Mother kicked me."

"Not really!"

Jael showed some more bruises over her arms. "They had me locked in my room just before you came. I'd just escaped down the drainpipe and run to the road moments before. In fact, Uncle Horace and Father came home just before you arrived and I thought it was you."

"That accounts for the way those two ladies looked at you out of the kitchen window."

"Yes."

Alan shook his head. "That's terrible. That can't go on." He let his eyes rest on the jack pine. "Maybe for your sake I should just fade away."

She lay curled in his arms, almost purring.

"Or else . . ."

"Or else what?"

"We elope and get married."

Jael turned in his arms and came up kissing. "Shall we?"

"I'm game if you are."

"I'm game."

"You can go to school while I work at the *Chronicle*. Evenings we'll be together."

"How shall we do it? Elope."

"I know a Judge Vincent Knight. He used to be secretary to our most famous governor. The judge can quietly fix us up a marriage license. Get that five-day waiting period waived. And I from my end of it can keep it out of the papers."

Jael's eyes opened wide. "Oh, Alan, that'd solve everything."

He chucked her under the chin. "You sure you want to do this?"

She turned solemn. "I've never been more sure of anything in my life. And I'll cook us some great meals. I can really cook, Alan."

Alan mused on the jack pine some more. "I'll get in touch with Judge Knight right away."

"How do you happen to know this judge?"

"I met him at that Hoyt Jorgenson's party. I ran into him just as I was leaving the bathroom. Then later on I once had lunch with the judge downtown with Bill O'Brian."

"Do it then," Jael said.

"I'll see him tomorrow."

Jael had to laugh to herself. "So a judge goes to the bathroom too."

"You know, I've often thought about that. There they sit in their black robes, in all their majesty . . . when not ten minutes before they've been maybe sitting on a different throne, stinking just like the rest of us."

Jael was startled. "Such talk, Alan."

"I want that judge to remember, when he renders judgment, that for all the awful distance between a judge and a criminal, he and the criminal are alike when it comes to bodily needs."

"You surprise me, Alan." She beheld him with admiring eyes. "Have you any bathroom secrets?"

"A few."

"Tell me some. You know a lot of secrets about me."

Alan gave her a cryptic smile. "Not by any means all of them."

For a second a film seemed to drop over her eyes. It reminded him of the inner eyelid chickens had.

It came to him, he didn't know from where or how, that she'd spent an afternoon with Shelby Hines in the selfsame spot. Those pressed-down tracks he'd seen in the grass belonged to Shelby's car.

"Tell me some."

Alan wondered if he should tell her about his haunt brother John. It was hardly a bathroom secret. Reluctantly, slowly, he told her about Haunt John. It took a while.

Jael took it all seriously. "Alan! What an imagination. That's what I mean about your electricity."

"Think so?"

" 'Course you mustn't let that haunt thing go too far."

"For fear I might go off the deep end?"

"Well, yes."

They sat in silence for a while. The sun sank. Birdsong dropped off. Even the insects quieted down.

She took his hand and placed it on her breast. "Love me up a little there. I've got such small ones."

"Think that'll help?"

"My friend Jerre says it does."

"They'll fill out plenty fast when you have your first baby. Then you'll be glad they were small to begin with."

"I hope so."

Presently they made love again. It was all right for him. But it didn't seem to go right for her. She was still trying to reach some final moment by the time he finished. All through it she cried out like she was being denied salvation. She couldn't quite enter the kingdom.

In the distance a farmer began calling his cows home. "Ka-baas. Ka-baas."

"We better get back," Jael said.

"Yes. But before we do I better find a bush."

Jael laughed. "Me, too."

They stepped off a decent space between themselves. She was first to finish and get back into the car.

Alan smiled to himself. It had been quite an afternoon. What would Haunt John have thought of him now? And thinking of Haunt John, Alan decided to have a little fun. Quite deliberately he trudged back to the car as though he were a tired man exhausted from a day's hard work. He slumped against the door, opened it as if the door was almost too much for him, and collapsed in the front seat.

"Alan. What's the matter?"

"Oh, nothing. Just all tuckered out, is all."

"From what? You should feel refreshed."

"All day long I've had to carry this heavy piece of meat between my legs."

"You!"

Alan laughed. "Ask me how much I weigh."

"Is this going to be another one of your awful jokes?"

"Go on. Ask me."

"All right." Jael put on the air of an officious head nurse. "Mr. Ross, did you weigh yourself this morning?"

"Yes, I did."

"Well then, how much do you weigh?"

"Most times I weigh around one-seventy. But this morning when I had an erection I weighed one-seventy-five."

Jael groaned. Then she laughed. "Alan, we are going to have a lot of fun being married. Go see that judge friend of yours."

Alan called on Judge Vincent Knight the next afternoon, Sunday, at the judge's house in Edina. The judge's house had the look of being the oldest, and perhaps the first, house in that elegant section of town.

The judge invited him to come sit with him in the backyard under an old lusty apple tree. The judge's wife joined them, carrying out a fresh pitcher of lemonade and a dish of cookies. She was a plump short woman with an easy natural smile. The judge and his wife obviously enjoyed each other's company.

After a few pleasantries, Judge Knight asked, "Well, what can I do for you?"

Alan sketched out the problem he had with Jael.

Judge Knight listened as he watched a lemon peel turn slowly in his drink. "And you're twenty-six?"

"Yes."

"And she's just eighteen, you say?"

"Yes."

"You're sure about her age? That's important in this instance, you know."

"Yes, I am."

Judge Knight looked at him with a pair of glittering blue eyes. "You're sure you love each other?"

"Yes." Alan didn't think his misgivings about Jael's interest in Shelby Hines were important. After all, who was he, Alan Ross, to point the finger? He'd been intimate with Irene Crist.

Judge Knight sat thinking to himself.

Mrs. Knight leaned toward Alan with a smile. "I can see that you'll be tender with this girl. That's the whole secret, you know. After all's said and done, that you both be tender with each other."

Judge Knight flashed her a look. "All right, tomorrow I'll drop in on the marriage-license clerk and tell him that when you come in for the license he's to give it to you even though she can't be there. And then I'll issue an order to have the five-day waiting period waived."

Alan jumped up. "Wonderful! God. Jael will be so relieved. Poor gal, getting all beat up by her own mother. What an awful thing to do. Thanks so much."

"Not at all. I like making people happy."

It had been agreed between Alan and Jael that he wasn't to write her or call her house for the next weeks. To get the message through to Jael that Judge Knight had agreed to help them, Alan dropped in on Jael's friend Jerre Thornton.

The moment Jerre saw Alan, she invited him in. She got him a cup of hot chocolate and then led him out to the backyard, where they sat at a picnic table.

Alan was impressed by Jerre. She wasn't as pretty as Jael, nor as stylish in her manner, but she was receptive and quite feminine. She had a very full bosom and already had the eyes of a mother. There was an air about her suggesting she still was a virgin.

Jerre was also a listener. It wasn't long before Alan poured everything out about why he'd gone to Judge Knight to get the waiting period for their marriage waived. Several times as Alan talked the hint of a frown appeared between Jerre's clear very blue eyes.

"Will you tell Jael what the judge said?"

"I surely will." Jerre looked down at her hands where they lay on the redwood picnic table. Her hands began to twist through each other. "Oh, I hope this will make Jael happy."

The thought shot through Alan that Jerre was a little envious of Jael, that she was wishing she could have met him first. And Alan saw too that he himself might have gone for Jerre had he met her first. Jerre was a woman to grow old with. Her not-quite-gold hair would slowly lighten and be a lovely silver-gold.

"You'll need a witness, won't you, when you elope?" Jerre asked.

"I guess we will. Will you be one of them?"

"Oh yes, I'd be more than happy to."

"Good. Tell Jael I'm off as usual on Thursday. And that when school starts I'll be expecting her at the apartment after her classes. So we can agree on the date."

"I will. I'm so happy for you."

School started. On the first Thursday, from two o'clock on, Alan waited for Jael. He sat by his window hoping to catch a glimpse of her limber stride coming around the corner.

When she didn't come at the expected time, he tried willing her around the corner. Of course that didn't help much.

Finally, telling himself that she'd come when she was ready to come, he got out his favorite Doughty and began reading in his easy chair.

Five o'clock came. Still no Jael.

When she still hadn't shown up at six o'clock, he knew something had gone wrong. On an impulse, he dialed her number, Colfax 3950. He let the phone ring a dozen times. No answer.

He next wondered if maybe he'd gotten the number mixed up. Maybe it was Colfax 3590. He looked it up in the telephone book. No, he had it right in the first place. He tried it again. Still no answer.

He dialed yet once more. He counted the rings: ten, fifteen, twenty, twenty-five, thirty. No dice. The Hemlicksons, all of them, were not at home. Had they beaten it out of her that she was going to elope?

Alan began to wonder about Shelby Hines. Maybe Shelby knew something about her. He called the ATO fraternity.

It took a while for someone to answer. When someone did, the fellow's voice was full of smoochies, as Mother would say. "Shelby? Oh. Who's calling, please?"

Alan's tongue was quick. Perhaps the fellows at the fraternity knew Shelby had a rival. "This is John Roth. Shelby was supposed to take notes for me in political science last week while I was sick. Tomorrow we got a quiz coming up and I need the notes."

"Tomorrow? That's funny. Shelby said he had nothing to worry about until next Monday."

"I meant Monday, of course."

"Oh. Well, Shelby went out to the country this weekend with his gal."

Alan could feel himself turn white. "When did they leave?"

"Her folks came by for him this noon."

Her folks? Good God. Her folks were sure anxious that Shelby should be the one and not he, Alan Ross. Alan hung up.

Jael was two-timing him. She really liked Shelby a whole lot better than she'd let on. Alan recalled the time he was fixing the muffler under his old blue Dodge when he overheard two frat boys talking about Jael. "No, in my case you no longer can give a rose to a virgin." It hurt.

He felt empty. Lost. It was as if someone had disemboweled him. Even scooped out his heart and tongue.

He'd never have her kisses again. All was lost.

He thought of driving up to Grandy and catching them at it in that lonely far roadside corner near the woods.

But he couldn't get up from his chair.

The next day, Friday, he put in his time at work. The typewriter rattled under his fingers. He handed in copy. Old work habits carried him through. He did everything automatically right.

Saturday at the paper he was too busy to think about Jael. Everybody in the department had to go like hell to get out both the Saturday-afternoon paper and all the Sunday editions in one day.

By Sunday he'd become a little used to the empty feeling in his gut. He even had a little hunger and fixed himself a rib steak covered with tomatoes and peppers. He read the paper. He read a few pages in Doughty's *The Dawn in Britain*.

Around four o'clock Martin Vann burst into Alan's room, breathless. His blue eyes were gray with shock, and the usual shadows under his eyes reached down across his cheekbones. "Alan! I need your help."

Alan sat up in his easy chair. "What's up?"

"John Charles didn't come home last night."

"So? Doesn't he often stay out tomcatting somewhere?"

"He's in jail."

"Good Lord. What did he pull off now?"

Martin coughed. "Charles was caught with a young boy." Martin's fingers turned shaky.

"Here, have a chair."

Martin sat down. He clapped a hand to his head. "Lord, will this put our English Department in a bad light. Ohh. When the university already has the state legislature on its neck for harboring so-called eggheads on the campus." Martin pled with his hands. "Alan, we've got to keep this out of the newspapers."

There'd been some carping about pinkos, even reds, on the campus. If it could now be claimed that the university also harbored homosexuals, the university would really be in trouble when it presented its annual budget to the state legislature.

Alan asked, "What's he charged with?"

"I don't know. I just know they picked him up on the complaint of the parents of the boy."

"Where did all this take place?"

"In the apartment of another university prof over on Tenth."

"Did the boy resist him?"

"No. I think they've been lovers for some time."

"God."

"Yeh. And worse yet, what will my wife say? We write once in a while. And I see the child when I can. And I've been hoping we can still get back together. But when she hears this, that my roomie . . .

Alan, you must believe me when I tell you Charles never once made a pass at me. Never!"

"I believe you." Alan ran a finger over his lips. "Tell you what. I'll go call our police reporter, Marty Spiller, who's on duty weekends. My paper's out to get rid of drunk drivers by publishing their names. And weekends is when the cops catch most of 'em."

"Good."

Alan called Marty. After some talk, Alan hung up. "Well, Martin, Charles has a chance. His name still hasn't been put on the police blotter."

"Wonderful."

"Marty is kind of on your side. He thinks that if the university president can get Charles out of the state forthwith, right now, maybe the police won't press charges on the basis of the complaint. Get your university legal counsel on the job. Maybe he can smooth things over. Get the parents to withdraw the complaint if Charles will leave the state."

"You mean, we fire him?"

"Or better yet, ask your university president to find him a job in another state. Someplace where he won't be so conspicuous because of his tastes." Alan was somewhat surprised to hear himself give out that sage advice.

Martin got to his feet. "I'll call the chairman of our department right away. He'll have to carry the ball for all of us now. Thanks a lot, Alan. We owe you one."

Later that same night there was a rap on Alan's door. Martin opened the door and peered into the darkened room. "Thought maybe you'd like to know what happened."

"Sure, come in." Alan sat up and snapped on a lamp.

Martin pulled the easy chair around to face the bed. There was a relieved look on his face. He heaved a huge sigh. "Well, it all happened so fast it's hard to believe. Man, is that prex of ours a mover. The minute he heard about it, he got everybody together, even though it was Sunday—parents of the boy, the boy, Charles, attorneys, cops, everybody. He did not want the matter to ride into Monday, when all hell might break loose. He got Charles to resign, then turned around and called a college-president friend of his in western New York who gave Charles a job. Then he got the parents to drop their complaint. Since it still wasn't on the police blotter, the cops didn't have to back down and lose face."

Alan slid up on his pillow. "Wow. Now that's what I call action. And by a so-called egghead yet. An intellectual."

Martin managed to smile a little. The smile looked grotesque on his shadow-darkened face. "Though there was one fly in the whole ointment. Charles didn't want to go at first. He bucked. But we finally persuaded him it was for the good of all." Martin sighed again. "Charles was so angry. He says Minnesota is a barbaric state. A real hick place. No sophistication. It still thinks black and white."

"Well, me, I prefer sharp colors. Gray is nothing."

Martin nodded. "Thanks again. It's all been resolved, thanks to your advice in the first place."

"Think nothing of it. Glad to help out."

After Martin left, Alan had trouble finding sleep. He rolled and tossed in bed, mulling over the John Charles affair, agonizing about where Jael might be that weekend.

When he still hadn't found sleep by five, he got up and decided to read awhile. Maybe good old Doughty could put him to sleep with his good English lines. But Doughty didn't.

At seven o'clock Alan decided he'd skip work that day. He had to know something. He called in sick. Then he got dressed and walked across Dinkytown to the University of Minnesota campus. Both Jael and Shelby Hines were taking Professor Hoyt Jorgenson's advanced class in political science. It was a second-hour class, starting at nine o'clock.

Checking the registry in the hallway of the political science building, Alan discovered Jorgenson now held his class in the amphitheater of the building. Alan took up his vigil behind a bulletin board at the end of the hallway.

He waited. He watched an endless stream of students go by, girls in fluttery clusters clutching textbooks to their bosoms, boys in dragging groups slapping textbooks against their thighs.

Presently, about ten minutes to nine, some of the students began heading for the amphitheater. Alan straightened up.

The far double doors opened again and there she was. With Shelby. They were laughing together. They were teasing each other about something. Soon Jael bent over, helpless with laughter. They headed toward some lockers in the hallway. Jael opened a locker with a key and dropped some books into the bottom of it. Shelby waited until she'd locked up again. Both carried a raincoat. Their clothes were wrinkled. It was obvious they'd just come in from the country and hadn't had time to change.

For a second Alan thought of killing her.

Jael and Shelby came toward him heading for the door of the amphitheater. They didn't see him.

Shelby said, "Think you got your mind made up enough to tell Alan when you see him Thursday?"

"Oh, Shelb, you know I have."

"Well, you finked out on me once before."

"That was when I still liked him a lot."

"Yeh, and you said that before too."

"Oh, Shelby, when I'm going to have your baby?"

The two of them passed into the amphitheater and out of sight.

Alan stood rooted. His face and neck felt so drained of blood he thought he was going to faint. He had to grab hold of the side of the bulletin board to keep from falling.

The doors to the amphitheater closed. Presently Alan could hear Hoyt Jorgenson holding forth in his ringing authoritarian voice.

Alan took several deep breaths, then turned away. He let his heels drag across the white terrazzo floor.

He went home. He went to bed.

Around five o'clock he turned on his radio for the news. The first thing he heard sent a chill up and down his spine.

". . . the South St. Paul police have not yet been able to find the slaughterhouse worker. He has apparently dropped completely from sight. The police over the state have been alerted. It has been speculated that he may have caught a ride with some trucker returning to the area where he was born and raised, Bonnie, Siouxland. A description of him follows: John Engleking, blond hair, light complexion, blue eyes, well built, about six feet tall. Made a considerable reputation for himself as a part-time boxer in the Twin Cities area as Red Engleking. Could be dangerous, though he is not believed to be carrying a weapon. The knife with which he repeatedly stabbed his wife was found beside her unconscious body. Meanwhile his wife, Jennie Engleking, is reported to be on the critical list at the South St. Paul city hospital. . . ."

Alan cried out. "Oh my God! My brother John . . . has gone and done it. I should have known he might've. He looked like he was ready to bust out at something that night at the WMSP transmitter. Go berserk."

Alan lay a moment longer in shock, then scrambled out of bed and grabbed for the phone. He called Burt Cowens at the *Chronicle*.

"Burt? I just now heard about Red Engleking."

"Yeh. Did you have any inkling he might do this?"

"Yes, but I didn't pay any attention to it. Too busy with my own silly private affairs."

"Ah."

"Burt, how about getting the paper to assign me to cover the stabbing? And find Red Engleking?"

There was a pause on Burt's end. "City desk, you know, usually handles murders."

"I know. But I know something about him. After all, I've been covering him all along. And he's told me about his people down there in Bonnie, Siouxland. I'll know where to go."

"All right, I'll see what I can do."

"Please, Burt."

A few minutes later Burt called back. "You got the job of tracking him down. But you're going to have to pinch some of it in between covering track and high school football."

"Thanks, Burt."

# Chapter 21

# RED

Around three o'clock, just before shutdown time, the shackles around the leg of a heavy sow let go and the sow fell from the moving chain and hit the cement floor with a fatty thud.

Red stepped back from where he'd been sticking pigs and looked down at the sow.

"Har!" Foreman Simes yelled. "Pig down!"

The sow lay square on its wide back, four feet in the air and stilled for the moment, eyes staring past its thick lashes. It was hard to tell if the sow lay still because it was stunned or because it had given up.

The moving chain rattled on.

"Har! Hey!" Simes bellowed. "Pete! Chuck! Grab that sow and get her hooked back on the wheel. Wake up."

Pete and Chuck ran up from the catching pen.

Simes yelled at Red, "And what the hell you looking at? Get back to work!"

Red didn't answer.

Simes gave Red a shove. "Get back to sticking!"

Red was numb from a long day's work. He hardly felt the shove.

Pete and Chuck each grabbed a leg of the sow and shagged her back to the shackling area and hooked her onto the revolving wheel. Up she went, and strangely mute slung into the sticking area again.

"Red!"

Red watched the sow come toward him. It hung head down with a helpless look. Red's knife hand hung slack at his side. Blood dripped off it down his leather apron.

Simes gave Red a kick in the rear. "Stick her!"

Red turned slowly on Simes, knife hand coming up a little.

Simes' head thickened back into his bristly neck. "Hey . . ." he whispered. Then Simes snapped around. "Bud! Grab a knife here and help Jack catch up."

Bud Netter dropped the chain he was holding and shuffled over. He took Red's place at the sticking trough.

Simes backed away from Red several steps. "Uhh . . . Red, maybe you better knock off for today. It's been a heller for all of us. The run is about done for the day anyway." Simes cursed. "That's what we get for it when they throw those blasted sows at us the last part of the run. After a sow's had her litter of pigs she's too heavy."

Still carrying his knife, Red walked past Simes, walked past his clothes locker, and, bloody apron and all, headed outside.

"Hey!" Simes yelled. "Ain't you gonna change into your street clothes?"

Red let the door close behind him.

Red headed for home. No one stopped him. People looked at him a little oddly, at his bloody knife and apron, but no one said anything. He climbed up the stiff bluff in the usual dirt path. He slipped through the chain-link fence into his backyard. He let himself into the back door of his house.

Red stopped in the kitchen. It was exactly four o'clock. The sun shone through Jen's neat white curtains, lighting up the kitchen with a pink light. He rubbed his eyes. The soft odd rosy light bobbled in front of him.

He shook his head. He couldn't shake himself out of that numb shell. On other days when he came home the shell fell the moment he stepped into his house. He could always manage a smile for Jen and begin to appreciate things around him. There were always the flowers in the window and the smell of bread baking or cooking in the oven. This time it was as though he'd been packed tight inside a small barrel. He rolled his big shoulders, trying to break out.

He pushed his feet forward, one at a time, into the living room, then around into the bedroom. The shades were drawn in the bedroom, down to the windowsill.

It took several moments for his hazed-over eyes to make things out. First the white bedspread, then the shiny bronze lamp on Jen's side of the bed, then the pillow with a dark head on it.

Jen's brown eyes opened. After a moment they narrowed into tight slits. Her lips widened in a loose grimace. Then, strangest of all, her arms and her legs came up, flipping the white bedspread to one side. Her crouched legs jiggled a little, then became still. From her tight lips came a strange name. "Uncle Red?"

Uncle Red? She'd never called him Red before. And Uncle? "Jen?" That strange loose mask on her face. That helpless look. "Peggie?"

Then another voice spoke up, clearly, in the bedroom. The voice was behind and above him on the right. "Grab that pig by the leg and, gott dammit, stick her!" The voice was like God talking. The sound of Dad was in it.

A strange swamp stink bloomed in his nose. "I can't."

"You're gonna stick that pig even if I have to take your hand and make you do it."

A grip fell on the back of his hand and caused it to raise the hand up and then caused it to drive the knife downward. The creature on the bed awoke and kicked its legs at him. But the knife found flesh. Blood spurted up.

The voice said, "You missed the throat, gott dammit!"

The grip on the back of his hand became very fierce. Again and again it caused him to strike downward.

At last the creature on the bed lay still.

The voice said, "Good. Now you better knock off for today, Red. It's been a heller."

Red tossed the knife on the bedstand. It clinked against the base of the bronze lamp. He turned and stepped through the living room and entered the kitchen again.

Drip. Drip.

The sound of the dripping broke into his shell.

The telephone rang in the living room, loud, jangling. It wouldn't give up. It rang a couple dozen times. Finally it quit.

Red could feel the shell fall away. On Dad's farm he'd often seen a chick peck its way out of a shell. That was the way it felt. He rolled his shoulders.

Drip. Drip.

He looked down at his bloody dripping work apron. God. He'd forgotten to change clothes before he left work. What a sight he must have been. It was hard to believe he'd become all that forgetful. Work had been getting him down, all right.

Jen was probably in the bedroom. He often found her taking a nap when he got home. She'd taken that last miscarriage pretty hard. Even acted a little nuts.

He stepped onto the back porch and removed the dirty apron and placed it carefully on a rubber mat. Later he'd wash and clean it.

He headed for the bedroom.

It was dusky in the bedroom. "Hey, why the shades down so far? Good gravy, girl, nobody's gonna peek in on you on that side of the house." He gave the first blind a little tug down and then let it almost all the way up.

He turned with a warm smile toward the bed. "Jen?"

Jen lay all bloody.

Then the rest of the shell sloughed off.

"My God." Jen, his sweet Jen, was dead.

He fell on her and shook her. "Jen!"

Her head rolled loosely on the pillow. There was an odd suppressed squeak in her belly.

"Holy smokes. I don't understand this at all. Something bad has happened here."

He got to his feet. And then he spotted it. His sticking knife from the plant lying on the bedstand. He'd killed her. He'd done it when he was inside that shell. When he didn't know any better.

"Man alive. I've got to get out of here. They'll arrest me and throw me in jail."

He hurried to the bathroom and washed the blood off his hands. Quickly he made moves to go. He made sure he had his handy scout jackknife in his pocket. Too bad his billfold was in his street clothes back at the plant. He needed money for the road. Looking around, his eye caught sight of their piggy bank. He opened it and picked out two five-dollar bills and a handful of loose change.

He ran out through the back porch, grabbing a blue denim jacket and a blue cap as he went. The blood on the pantlegs of his blue jeans would just have to dry somehow.

"Poor Jen."

# Chapter 22

# ALAN

Alan checked Red's house first. A cop stood guard on the front porch. Alan showed him his press card and was allowed to walk inside.

A fingerprint expert was busy dusting the surfaces of things and photographing them. "Don't you touch anything," he said.

"I won't." Alan walked into the bedroom. Drops of dried blood were still visible on the blue wall beside the bed.

Alan remembered the time he'd poked his head into the window of that very room, when he'd thought he needed his notes right away. Jen had been scared to death. Well, now someone had actually attacked her just as she'd feared. Except it'd turned out to be her husband. Alan wondered if deep down something in her hadn't already known it'd someday be her own husband who'd attack her.

Alan's eye fell on Jen's pocketbook. Alan pointed. "Has that been checked yet?"

The fingerprint man nodded. He had black hair and it hung about his eyes like a cap with the flaps down. "No prints there."

"Then Red didn't take any of her money."

"Not unless he wore gloves."

"Have you found any fingerprints?"

"He left prints everywhere. Like he didn't care."

"I heard they found his billfold down at the plant."

"Yeh."

"Wonder what he's using for money?"

"Piggy bank is covered with prints."

"Anybody look through his family album?"

"Not yet. Didn't figure he'd stop to bother to look at that."

"Mind if I have a look?"

"If you can find it. And if you do, handle it with your handkerchief."

Alan went to the living room. Right away he spotted what looked like an album on the radio. It was flanked by two pictures: one of Red and Jen just married, and one of a huge powerful man sitting quietly at rest on a settee in a studio. The big man had to be Red's father.

Alan studied the portrait of the big man. A lot of force there. Be hard to emulate him. Probably had a lot to do with Red's wanting to be a fighter.

Getting out a white handkerchief, Alan paged through the album. It was a big black scrapbook, with snapshots pasted in six to a page.

What a host of relatives. It appeared Red had at least a dozen uncles and aunts. Each of them seemed to have a raft of kids.

A packet of faded portraits fell out of the back of the album. Again with his handkerchief Alan drew out the portraits and paged through them. They appeared to be an older generation of Englekings. In one of the portraits Alan was sure he spotted Red's father Fat John when he was a boy. It was taken with an equally huge Engleking, except that this one had a vast beard. That had to be Red's grandfather. Looking further, Alan next made out a portrait of the bearded grandfather with yet another huge and older man, also bearded. That would have to be Red's great-grandfather. In that portrait there were also two boys and a girl and an older woman. Some names were written under the figures in the portrait in an old script. John Henry Engleking I, John Henry II, Alfred, Alberta, wife Adelheid.

The face of Alberta caught Alan's eye. He'd seen a face like that before. Jael's? But of course that was impossible. Alan stared. It looked familiar.

At last, not being able to fish it out of his memory, Alan gave up and closed the packet and replaced it in the back of the album.

It was curious, but there didn't seem to be any pictures of Jen and her relatives. Alan flipped through the entire album again. No Jen pictures. Hmm.

Alan placed the album back on the radio and pocketed his handkerchief.

Alan next called the city hospital.

Jen had regained consciousness. She was on the critical list but she had a chance to recover.

At least it isn't murder, Alan thought. Now the worst Red can get is assault and battery with intent to kill.

# Chapter 23

# RED

Red knew exactly where to go to catch a ride out of the Twin Cities. He clattered down the bluff behind his house and poked his nose into Nick's.

The place was full of diners. Another crowd of husky men were having a beer at the bar.

Red's eye fell on a trucker sitting by himself near the front window. The fellow was from Blue Wing. Yep. Aha. A ride. Blue Wing was about fifty miles from Bonnie.

The trucker had little to say as he drove through Savage and Shakopee and Belle Plaine. Red welcomed the silence.

It was seven o'clock when they hit Mankato. The sun was just setting over the deep Minnesota River Valley. The trees had turned red and yellow, and every one of them cast a purple shadow. The long slanting sunlight made the whole valley look like Judgment Day. It was beautiful.

He thought: "Poor Jen. I must've really been out of my head when I did that."

It was after ten when the trucker dropped him off where 60 crossed 16 just east of Blue Wing. "Hope you make it home all right, bud. If I had the time I'd take you there."

"I'll be all right," Red said.

The trucker nodded, then rolled west into town.

Standing alone on the road in the dark, Red for the first time began to have second thoughts about going home to Bonnie. Radio station WCCO in Minneapolis reached into northern Iowa. Everybody in that part of Siouxland would by now have heard of what he'd done to Jen.

He thought: "Maybe I ought to head for the Big Sioux River

breaks west of Bonnie instead. That outlaw country Dad was always talking about. Where all those whiskey makers live back in the hills."

When a fellow got into trouble with the law that was the place to hide. Even the sheriff didn't dare go in there. Moonshiners were dead shots.

Town lights glimmered west of him. Ahead about a quarter of a mile down 60 he could make out the red winking lights of a filling station.

He thought: "Better yet, if I must hide somewhere, why not that godforsaken Devil's Nest on the other side of Sioux City there."

Red had once heard an old-time trapper in Bonnie talking about Devil's Nest. It was located along the south bank of the Missouri River in Nebraska. It was good for nothing except grapes and rabbits and cattle rustlers. WCCO would hardly reach out there.

Devil's Nest it would be then. He hiked down the road toward the red light of the station.

An old codger with bloodshot eyes was sitting in a rickety swivel chair in the doorway. "Don't tell me you want gas?"

Red shot a look inside the station. Greasy benches, a tire lying loose just pulled off a wheel, a pile of rags. But no radio. Good. The old man hadn't heard about him yet. "No, no gas. But I could use a drink of water. And a couple of candy bars."

"So you're going to make me get up, are you?" The old geezer groaned and finally managed to stand up. "All right, two bars it is. Tap water is over there."

Red paid for the bars and ate them. It was the first food he'd had since noon. He drank from the tap. The water was hard but it had a sweetish smell.

The old fellow settled back in his chair. "Yep. Pretty lonely here nights. Still don't understand why Bart wants this joint kept open until midnight. No business to speak of after eight. But he owns it and so long as he's willing to pay me I'll do it."

"Think there'll be any trucks going down toward Sioux City yet tonight?" There was a bridge across the Missouri south of Sioux City into Nebraska. Once he was across the big river he would be home free.

"Sure. They'll come through here all night long."

"Can I ask them for a ride here?"

"No skin off my nose."

After a while Red had to visit the privy around in back. It was while he was buttoning up that he heard a truck pull in. He heard the old man mutter about having to move his bones, heard the trucker josh him back, then heard the clank of the hose into the truck's gas tank.

Red took just two steps around the corner of the station when he spotted who the trucker was. Hod Walling from Bonnie. The fellow who'd given him his first ride away from home to Sioux Falls. Hod's cap was still studded over with driving-permit buttons. Holy smokes. Red quickly backed around the corner out of sight. Hod Walling he didn't want to see just then. Red stood trembling. Suppose Hod got it into his head he had to visit the privy too? Be tough titty then.

Red hid behind the privy.

After a long wait, Red heard Hod start up his truck. Slowly the truck pulled out and, red taillights jiggling, vanished into the night toward the south.

The old codger had taken up his seat again in the rickety swivel chair. "Where was you? That fellow just in here had a ride for you."

Red tried to smile it off. "Man can't rush making a deposit on the First National."

"No, I guess not. Too bad."

Red nodded.

An hour later another truck pulled into the station. It was a cattle truck and filled with fat steers for the Sioux City market. The trucker was a stranger. Red caught a ride with him.

*Chapter 24*

# ALAN

---

The next Saturday, wearing a gray suit and gray suede oxfords, Alan drove down to Bonnie in his blue Dodge. He arrived in town around four, parked in front of Swaim's Cafe, and went in and had himself a cup of coffee and a doughnut. He was the only patron.

Alan sipped his coffee slowly. He read the various slogans tacked up on the wall above the counter. "We need to eat just like you. So we give no credit and we accept no checks from strangers." "Don't blame us for being hardhearted. Blame the other fellow who walked out of here without paying his bill."

"Where's everybody?" Alan asked the proprietor, Swaim.

Swaim was a lanky awkward fellow with a considerable Adam's apple. "Out cuttin' corn or pickin' corn."

After a second cup of coffee, Alan said, "I hear one of your Bonnie boys got into trouble in South St. Paul."

"Don't believe he did it."

Alan liked the smell of fresh doughnuts in the place. "Why not?"

"I know the family real well. It ain't in them. They're real peaceable people."

"They do butcher though, don't they?"

"What's that got to do with it?"

"From the point of view of the hog, it ain't peaceable."

Swaim picked up a rag and began wiping the counter around Alan's cup of coffee. "Another cup?"

"No, thanks. But you can tell me where Fat John lives."

"Mile and a half north of here. On the Canton road. Red barn and a cream-colored house on the right."

"Thanks."

Alan drove easy out of town, past a sandpit, past two farmsteads on the left, then a farmstead on the right, crossed an iron suspension bridge over the Big Rock River, finally spotted the farm on the right with the red barn. The barn was built into the side of a rise in the land.

A high-wheeled box wagon had just rolled onto Fat John's yard loaded with picked corn. The wagon was so heaping full the ears were about to spill off. A fat man got down off the wagon, and then, as Alan pulled into the yard, stopped in his tracks. The fat man was wearing paint-spattered overalls and a paint-spattered left shirt sleeve. A quaint little blue hat was perched on top of his big head of curly gold hair.

Alan stepped out of his car. "John Engleking?"

The big man looked at him, finally nodded reluctantly, chin sinking into a couple rolls of fat.

"I'm sorry to have to call on you like this. But I know your son Red."

A slow scowl thinned back Fat John's lips.

"He hasn't got in touch with you, has he?"

Fat John stared at Alan hard, hostile.

"Or shown up on your yard?"

A woman spoke up behind Alan. "What's it to you?"

Alan turned. "Hello."

The woman was every bit as fat as Fat John. She had to be Red John's mother. She was carrying a pail of cracked corn and oats. Feed dust lay over the broad toes of her shoes. Her red cheeks were mottled.

Fat John finally spoke up. "Etta, get in the house. I'll handle this."

"Red is my son too."

"In the house."

"I think I'll feed the chickens first."

"Either that or in the house."

Hunching herself around, Etta waddled off toward a small ramshackle building. Chickens spotted her and in a moment she was surrounded by a sudsing wash of white feathers.

Alan let his eyes wander over the yard. Fat John had machinery all over the place, rusting handles, singletrees dragging, parts missing. There were dead chickens, pieces of lumber, a couple piles of red cobs, scattered cornhusks. Alan wondered where Red's younger brother was. Probably out picking corn.

Fat John asked, "Where you from?"

Alan turned. "Minneapolis. I work for a newspaper. My name is Alan Ross. I've written stories about your boy as a boxer."

"Oh, so you're that bird. Red sent us some of your write-ups."

"Yes. I thought Red was a good joe. And I liked his wife Jen too."

Fat John said, "They didn't always get on too well. Her a city girl."

"You'd have preferred he married a local girl?"

"You bet."

"Jen has her points, though."

"Maybe so. But they ain't ourn."

Alan kicked at the ground. An old dead weed let go at the root and it popped up against his gray pantleg. "Well, I see you're terribly busy. I'm sorry to break in on you like this."

Fat John wiped his nose on the back of one of his fluffy husking mittens.

What a powerful-looking specimen Fat John was. Even slimming him down a hundred pounds Fat John would still have been a colossus. He was so thick through his thighs that he had to stand with his legs apart. No wonder the son was at odds with himself in trying to catch up with the father. Red could eat twenty meals a day enriched with butter and fat, plus honey and milk and sweet pastries, and he still wouldn't get to be half as big. His father was a weightlifter while Red was a boxer.

Alan noticed that Fat John had bags under his eyes like his own mother in Holabird had.

Alan said, "Thanks for your time. If I come across anything about Red I'll let you know."

"Yeh, I bet. I've heard of you snoopers. Making a living offa other people's hard luck."

"I'm sorry."

"Yeh. I bet."

A little sadly, Alan got into his old blue Dodge and drove off the yard.

# Chapter 25

# RED

The second trucker didn't ask Red what his name was. The trucker had a curved chin, and when he smiled the silhouette of his face resembled a grim quarter moon.

At Chokecherry Corner the trucker nodded at a filling station on the left and remarked that he usually stopped there for gas. A friend of his, Elof Lofblom, ran it, a real honest guy, and his wife Gertie made hamburgers like you wouldn't believe.

North of Sioux Center the trucker stopped once to check his load of steers. Every now and then the truck appeared to want to lean left, and that meant the steers were bunching up in one corner. It might also mean a steer was down. It was a strange sensation to feel the truck lean up under one's seat. But the trucker found nothing wrong. "They were gettin' a little lonesome, I guess. So they cozied up together."

It was three o'clock when the lights of Sioux City appeared on the brown horizon ahead. It was a clear night and the lights of the town and the low stars were all of a pattern.

The trucker took 75 all the way into the city and then took a right and within moments they were in the stockyards. Penned-up cattle bellowed lonesomely. The cattle in the rack behind the cab awoke and also let go with an occasional bellow.

The trucker pulled up behind a line of trucks waiting to be unloaded, motors running and kicking out little puffs of exhaust. The animals in the trucks jostled each other, making the trucks sway.

Red opened the door and stepped down. "Thanks for the ride."

"Glad to help out."

"Where's the bridge over the Missouri from here?"

The trucker pointed with his curved chin. "About a mile north of here."

"Thanks again."

The trucker raised his hand off the steering wheel as if to say that's the way things were.

Despite all the truck lights on and the stockyards lights glowing overhead, the place was full of shadows. Red welcomed the shadows.

He soon found the last street along the river and then headed north. Brush and tall weeds on his left hid the Missouri River. He walked past several warehouses on his right. Then came a railroad switching yard. Big steam engines in the yards rooted back and forth like oversized boars.

Soon he made out an arch of lights ahead on the left. That had to be the bridge. Just so there weren't any tollhouses on the bridge. The one place they were sure to watch out for him would be on the bridges.

Stumbling along over uneven ground, he finally reached the north end of the bridge. He looked out across the bridge. Yep. There was a tollhouse all right. Two of them, one on each side of the bridge, with lights on.

"How the heck am I going to get across without being seen?" he thought.

He lingered at the north end of the bridge.

No trucks came. No cars. No rides.

He waited until he began to see that dawn was about to break.

"Maybe I better try it now. Instead of in daylight. Those fellows in the tollhouses should be just a bit sleepy by now and not pay too much attention to me."

He started down the right lane, near the railing. Some forty feet below, moving water winked back reflections. He could hear the pushing flow of water gurgle against a bridge support.

He walked slowly. The Missouri was a tremendous river. It was like a wide lake flowing. He wondered how deep it was. It probably had big fish. And snapping turtles. It would be something if a man fell into it. The thought of it made him shiver.

He spotted a white board with some black lettering on it above the tollhouse in his lane:

20¢ FOR CAR AND DRIVER
5¢ FOR EACH ADDITIONAL PASSENGER

For the fun of it Red thought he'd offer the tollkeeper a nickel. It might make for a smile and so keep the fellow from looking at him too closely.

The tollkeeper hardly looked at Red as he approached. Red held out a nickel anyway.

The tollkeeper had the look of a student working his way through college. He was quite sleepy, as Red had guessed he might be. Eyes almost closed, he waved Red on. "We don't take money from people on foot."

Red gave his nickel a flip in the air, and with a nod dropped it in his pocket. "Okay." Then with yet another nod, he headed for the Nebraska side.

A half dozen steps down the bridge it hit Red that he hadn't been in the least nervous talking to the tollkeeper. Gone were the shakes he always had when he found himself in a pickle.

At the end of the bridge he took an old abandoned road heading north. He wanted to get out of South Sioux City as quick as possible. Dad often said it was one of the roughest towns in America. Sioux City was bad enough; but South Sioux City, that was the limit. There were many stories about a certain tough Covington Saloon built on the waterfront. It had a large chute in back pointed at the river. If somebody squawked about losing his money in a crooked game, the squawker was thrown down the chute into the Missouri.

The old road became a lane. It ran along the top of a very steep thickly wooded riverbank. To the right and below, dawn glowed across the yellow waters of the Missouri. The river looked like a great sheet of dirty gold pouring south across flat land.

He walked a good mile before the sun bobbed over the horizon behind him. His shadow reached out so far ahead it frittered off into light. There'd been a frost a few days before and it had changed the colors of the land, from a dark green to a light yellow-green. Bluejoint in the little runoff draws waved and undulated a mellow red-brown. A single cottonwood below the riverbank towered up into an immense explosion of shimmering gold.

He skirted the backyards of homes. Staying as close to the river as possible, he had to climb over fences, sometimes barbwire, sometimes board. Most homes were junky, worse even than the poorest parts of South St. Paul. Smoke rose over the chimneys of some of them.

An old highway with a graveled roadbed came curving toward the bank of the Missouri. He approached it carefully. No traffic. He spotted two signs ahead in the curve of the highway. One read: "State 12." The other, "Ponca, 8 Miles." He began to wonder a little if he was taking the right route to Devil's Nest.

Shading his eyes, he made out a red filling station ahead. State 12 wasn't one of the main highways. Perhaps the fellow running the station wouldn't be too suspicious of a guy drifting by. Red looked down at the blood spots on his pantlegs. They'd dried to a dark brown. They hardly looked like blood anymore. He decided to chance it.

The attendant in the station turned out to be a young punk scarred with acne, but otherwise well set up and handsome. He was having himself a cup of coffee and a hamburger. From the smell in the station he'd just made it on a hotplate.

Red asked, "This highway lead to Devil's Nest?"

"Yep. Seventy-five miles down the road."

"Good." The smell of hamburgers made Red hungry. He felt a drop of saliva on the edge of his lips. "You wouldn't have another one of those handy?"

"Take me just a half-jiffy to make one." The fellow set his half-eaten hamburger on a newspaper lying on a desk. "While you wait, how about a cup of coffee?"

"That'll suit me to a T."

"Coming up."

As Red sipped his coffee, he watched the young fellow slap up a patty of ground beef and then set it in a pan on a hotplate. No waste motion. The acne kid had brown hair, level dark-blue eyes, and long slim quick fingers.

The fellow flipped the patty over with a turner. "What the heck you going to Devil's Nest for?" The smell of seared fresh meat was sweet. "It's a helluva place, you know. Outlaws. Crazy Indians."

Red sipped his coffee. "There's a friend there I'm looking up." Again Red was pleased to note that, in a pinch, his fingers remained steady. The shakes really had left him. Meanwhile, Poor Jen was dead.

The fellow pressed down the patty with his turner, then used the edge of it to see if it was done. It was. He cut a bun in half, and with a dexterous motion made the bun pick up the patty as though the bun were a mouth. He set the hamburger out on a plate. "There you are, mister."

"What's the damages?"

"Two bits and a smile for a tip."

Red dug out a quarter. "I'll have the tip for you after I'm through."

"I'll ride with that."

A farmer drove up in a rattling Ford. Red listened to the fellow josh the old farmer. The fellow sure had a ready tongue.

The farmer fished a five-dollar bill out of his pocketbook. "Check the oil?"

"Yep, she's all good under."

"Okay if you say so." The farmer paid up and drove off.

The fellow came back in. He picked up his half-eaten hamburger and took a hearty bite.

Red finished his hamburger and licked his fingers. He was hungrier than ever. He sipped the last of his coffee.

"Want another cup of java?"

"Why not?"

Red savored the second cup, making it last.

The fellow got out a broom and swept up the place. "Some buddies of mine were in here last night chewing the fat and just generally futzing around."

The sun became brighter outdoors. Despite smoky windows even the filling station lit up brightly inside.

Finally Red got up from his stool. "I think I better be getting on."

"I was kinda hoping a rich friend of mine would come along. He sometimes drives up to Crofton to visit his mother. From there you could walk into Devil's Nest."

Red stretched. "Well, if he does show up, I'll be hiking down the road. Does State 12 go all the way to Crofton?"

"Yep. It wiggles back and forth a little, like animal tracks in snow, but it'll get you there."

Red started walking. The gravel road was well kept. No washboard rough spots. The road had been graded years before. Already wild flowers and wild grasses from the pastures to either side had repossessed the ditches.

The higher the sun climbed the more Red began to worry. For the next few days he'd better travel by night. He began to wonder if he shouldn't duck into some grove for the rest of the day. Later in the evening he could start walking west.

He'd walked some five miles, and was within sight of Ponca, when a sparkling green Packard pulled up beside him. "Want a ride?"

Red threw the driver a wary look. "How far you going?"

"Crofton."

"You're a friend of that filling-station fellow back there?"

"Well, I always have been. Get in." Red climbed in.

The Packard was as neat inside as an old maid's bedroom. The driver had light-gray eyes, very light straw hair combed straight back, a pugnose, and a well-set-out chin. He was in his middle twenties, well dressed in a light-gray suit and white shirt and red tie. He wore two-tone oxfords, white and black. He had an easy smile. "You gave me the once-over like you thought I might be a crook."

"I didn't mean to."

"Well, I'm kind of a fake at that. I inherited some money. From an uncle. And I just loaf the time away. Can't seem to stick to anything." The fellow laughed. "I'm mud rich, actually. I've got as much yellow mud in the bank as that old Missouri out there has yellow mud in its waters."

The motor purred underfoot. Red had never heard one run as smooth. "It's like riding in a sewing machine."

"That's a Packard for you. They run like silk. I'll take a Packard over a Rolls-Royce anytime." The fellow held out his right hand as he drove with his left. "Say, my name is Frank Stough."

Red took it after a moment, limply. Red quick thought of Jen's father's name. "George Haron."

"Well, George, and where are you from?"

Red couldn't look Stough in the eye. "Beloit."

"Wisconsin?"

"No, Iowa." Red worried that Stough would catch on. Beloit, some fifteen miles west of Bonnie, was a dead town. There weren't more than a dozen people left there, and it was no longer incorporated.

"What happened?"

"What do you mean what happened?"

"Fight with the wife or something?"

Red stared straight ahead.

"I guess I'm a little too nosy when it comes to family fights. You see, I run into all kinds of gals who want to marry me. And the more I hear about family fights, the better I feel about never having said yes."

A small sign with crude lettering came up. It pointed to the right. Ionia Volcano.

The sign startled Red. "A volcano down that road? I never heard of one in this part of the country."

"It isn't really a volcano. There's a kind of a steep cliff overlooking the Missouri there. Clays and shales full of iron sulfide. When it rains, the iron sulfide heats up and pretty soon it begins to smoke." Stough ran a hand through his straw hair. "But there's another story I like better. According to the old-timers, there were once some strange Indians living there. Fire-worshipers. They thought the smoking bluff was a sacred place. Nobody dared go near it except at certain times of the year. Then, under a full moon, they'd take their prisoners of war and torture them and then sacrifice them to their gods." Stough slowly shook his head. "I never seen the place myself, but they say there's a cavern under that smoking cliff where they did all that sacrificing. It's supposed to be full of bones."

Sacrifice. Red could see that fallen sow again, on its back, four legs tossed idly in the air, waiting, eyes knowing it was going to die.

Stough slowed down for Newcastle. The few houses and buildings in the dying downtown all needed paint.

On the other side of town the Packard picked up speed again. It's slow knitting hum became a high purring hum.

Stough pointed at some bluffs on their right, then at a long meadow on their left, all of it awash in high lemon light. "Look at that. What a day. Beautiful. I tell you, boy, there's nothing like living on a hill full of flying wild flowers."

They crossed a creek. Below lay a series of little dams. Red recognized them instantly as beaver dams. He and Dad had once watched a family of beavers build a dam on the Big Rock River in Dad's pasture. Dad had been happy to see the beavers. Their dam gave the fish a chance. The following year a big flood had ripped the dam out, and gone were the beavers.

The little town of Wynot showed up next.

Stough had a little story about Wynot. "There used to be an old German living here who was quite a character. Everybody loved him. And his favorite saying always was, 'Why not?' No matter what you happened to say, in favor or against, he still always said, 'Why not?' Like you and me might say, 'You betcha,' or, 'You tell 'em.' "

"We had a fellow at home once who always said, 'Ain't it?' Pretty soon he got the nickname of Ain't-it."

The road began to follow a snaking river, mostly cattle country, with only a little farming done in the bottoms. There were moving cattle on the hills and stiff haystacks in the valleys.

Red had the feeling he was only half there. He couldn't seem to catch up with what was going on. Here he was riding with a rich boy who had elegant clothes, while he himself had on a pair of blood-spotted jeans. While a part of him was scared to death, another part of him was heedless. Part of his brain had gone to sleep, as an arm on which one had slept too long might turn numb.

Stough asked, "Did you cut yourself?"

"What?"

"That blood there on your pantleg."

"Oh. That." Red struggled to make some kind of answer. "I was sharpening my knife and it slipped and I knicked myself in the belly."

Stough flicked a glance at Red's shirt. There was no slit in the shirt.

"I had my shirt open at the time."

"Yeh."

"Well, you don't have to believe me if you don't wanna."

Stough pursed his lips. Then Stough hit the steering wheel with the flat of his pale hand, stepped on the brakes and stopped the car.

Red stiffened over the top of his thighs.

Stough turned stiffly. "Get out."

"Why?"

"You smell like a liar. I might've known. Blood all over your clothes. Christ, you could be a murderer."

Red got out of the car and shut the door gently. "Thanks for the lift."

"Yeh." Stough's face slowly whitened when it came over him he really might have given a ride to a criminal. Then Stough put the Packard in gear and took off with a muted whoosh. Gravel spit back, spraying all over Red. A plume of yellow dust billowed up behind the green Packard.

Red decided he'd traveled long enough in daylight. He spotted a half dozen haystacks in a field on his right. He stepped down through the ditch, slipped between a barbwire fence, and hurried toward the haystacks.

He picked a haystack that had just been put up. A fresh haystack would show less sign it had just been disturbed. He chose the side away from the road, and working carefully, not liking all the stickle seeds in the hay, he managed to wedge himself into one of the layers of the stack. He worked himself deep into the stack, keeping his head near the edge. It took a while to arrange the outer strands of hay so that he could still breathe without being seen.

It was very comfortable inside the stack. Cozy. No hard spots. A little noisy when he moved. The fresh hay supported all parts of him equally: heels, buttocks, shoulders. It was a little like lying in a feather bed.

The smells were the best. He could make out dried wild roses, slough grass, bluejoint, sweet grass, daisies, and compass plant. The dried wild roses were like little pieces of colored paper onto which perfume had been spilled.

He could feel his whole body relax. He'd been as tight as a hay rope ever since he'd rushed out of his home in South St. Paul.

He wondered for a little while where Jen might be at that moment. Her body in a funeral parlor somewhere and her soul on the way to heaven?

He awoke once to hear the wind outside the stack. Good. The wind would whisk away all evidence that someone had crawled into the stack.

He slept.

An itching noise awoke him. At first he couldn't imagine what all that itching stuff was doing around his face. He lay utterly still for a moment. The little noises were all around him. Then one of the little noises landed on his eyelid. A bug. Beetle. Oh yes. He'd hidden himself in a haystack earlier during the day. A rich young fellow had kicked him out of his green Packard.

Red's hand found its way to his face and flicked the beetle off.

The little itching noises stilled.

A voice spoke up, almost right beside Red. It was outside the stack. "No sign of him here. By now he's long gone to Devil's Nest."

Another voice, Frank Stough's, said, "I was afraid of that. At first he looked like a dumbbell, you know. But after a while I caught on he was pretty sly."

"Well, thanks for warning us."

"It's okay," Stough said. "But are you sure he didn't crawl into one of these haystacks?"

"No sign of him in these stacks."

Footsteps died away.

Red lay as still as a post. He had caught his breath and had held it so long that to release it he had to first take in yet another little breath. He had to breathe hard for a while to catch up. Lying in the stuffy hay made it all the worse. It was like he was going to suffocate.

He heard a motor start up with a blast. That wasn't Stough's green Packard. That had to be the cop's car. The car roared off.

Red carefully parted the hay away from his eyes and looked out. Hey. The sun was just setting. Yellow evening light hung slanted through the tops of golden cottonwoods in the draw beyond the hayfield. In a half hour it would be dark enough for him to start walking again.

He felt awfully hungry. Somewhere along the line he was going to have to visit somebody's garden.

When he could no longer make out the golden cottonwoods he worked himself out of the stack and slid to the ground. He brushed himself off, remembering all the itching. He took off his cap and slapped it out, then ruffed out his hair. He next took off his denim jacket and shook that out. Itchy things gave him the goose bumps.

It was a clear night. The stars were out in nets of lights. He made out the North Star; and with the picture he had in his head of the land south of the Missouri River, he set a northwest course for Devil's Nest. There'd be no towns he'd have to pass through.

He hit Highway 81 an hour later. No cars coming either way. He leaped over a fence and hurried across the wide well-graveled road and then leaped over the fence on the other side. He was a good quarter of a mile into the field beyond before car lights showed coming down from the north.

Two hours later, brushing through cornfields, crossing hayfields, stumbling over freshly plowed fields, he made out a farmyard ahead. There was a light on in the house. He approached it carefully, alert for the dog.

He stepped across what appeared to be a garden. He scratched around with a hand to see if he couldn't find a row of carrots left over. The plot of ground felt like it had been uprooted. Aha. A potato digger had just gone through. But search as he might with his fingertips he couldn't find any loose potatoes.

He worked his way cautiously toward one of the little sheds near the house. Sometimes farmers had a smokehouse full of smoked beef near the house handy for the housewife.

Still no dog. Funny.

A hump of earth showed up between him and the light in the house. The light he'd seen was in the kitchen.

He couldn't make out what the hump might be. He bent down and with a hand felt his way around it. Coming around on the lighted side he spotted a slanting door. Ah. A storm cellar. Great. It would be full of canned goods. And have a root cellar.

He lifted the door slowly, hoping it wouldn't creak. It didn't. He opened it wide enough to slip down into it and then as he descended the steps he let the slanted door fall shut above him.

Lord, was it dark in the storm cellar. Blacker than black soot. The fine odor of fresh roots was strong in the air, potatoes, carrots.

He hit the earthen floor. He felt his way ahead, hands out and fingertips reaching, toes sliding lightly.

His fingers touched an upright, a four-by-six. He felt it up and down. Some ears of corn with the husks drawn back and tied in a knot hung from several nails. Seed sweet corn for next year.

He slid his toes forward and at last hit a pile of loose potatoes. He picked up several potatoes and stuffed them into his pockets. He moved to his right, hit another slanting pile. Carrots. He stuffed some of them into his pockets too.

He turned left and toed his way along bare earth. Finally he touched the edge of a cabinet. It had a pair of glass doors. He opened the doors and felt around inside. Canned goods. Hot diggity dog. He sniffed around the tops of the fruit jars to see if he could make out what was in them. Two of them smelled like they might be meat. A third one had to be canned pears, his favorite. Smelling yet another jar he thought he could make out crab apples. It puzzled him some that he could make out the various smells. Those jars had better not be spoiled.

Pockets bulging, arms full of glass jars, he toed his way back across the storm cellar, at last found the bottom step. He went up carefully until his hair touched the cellar door. He pushed the door open with his head, set the jars down in the grass, slid out sideways, and then with a guiding hand lowered the door without making a sound.

He'd just barely got clear of the mound of the storm cellar when a door slammed on the near side of the house. Someone was coming. He ducked and ran as lightly as possible behind the storm cellar. A light flicked on. Someone had come outside with a flashlight and was whipping it around. Had they heard him after all? Where was the dog? He waited in the dark.

The light flashed around the yard some more. Then the light stilled to one spot. In a moment Red heard water trickle. Ha. The old man had stepped outside a moment to relieve himself before going to bed. Thank God there'd been no dog. A dog would have smelled him.

When the light went out and the door slammed again, Red quickly slunk across the garden and headed for the open field. Then, safe, far enough away from the house, he sat down to eat. The ground was warm.

He'd been right about the meat jars. Cover off, he broke through the stiff suet on top and with two fingers pried out a nice long country sausage. Though cold, it tasted glorious. He finished off the jar by drinking the meat juice. Delicious. Hech. He wiped his mouth.

He next helped himself to a raw potato and several raw carrots. They too tasted great. Both were fresh and so crisp they cracked almost the moment his teeth touched them. He sucked bits of carrot from between his teeth.

He took the jar he thought was pears and gave its cover a good hard twist. It didn't budge. A tough one. One fist on the cover and the other around the jar, he gave it all he had, until his palms began to slide, even hurt. At last the cover gave way slowly and then opened easily. He'd been wrong it was pears. It turned out to be peaches. Well, peaches were good too. He fished out the top half slices with his fingers. He finished the rest by raising the jar to his lips and slugging down the juice and half slices. Delicious.

He carefully set the two empty fruit jars near a fence post. He dug out four quarters and dropped them in one of the jars to pay for the food. He hoped the farmer would find the jars. The good woman of the house couldn't afford to lose four perfectly good fruit jars plus the work of making the food.

Catching up the remaining two fruit jars, pockets still bulging, he headed northwest, keeping the north star on his right cheek. Looking back over his left shoulder he could make out the glow of the Crofton streetlights against a sky full of stars. Gradually as he walked and walked, crossed one field after another, the lights of Crofton faded away.

The country began to roll. He crossed a creek. He spotted starlight reflecting off some water on his right. He approached it carefully. By golly. A beaver dam. Water, all right. He had himself a good long drink. The water had an alkaline taste. There was a loud flap near him. He jumped. Cripes. A beaver had whacked its tail hard on the water.

He climbed a long incline. It was almost all wild pasture. It'd been some time since he'd come upon a fence. He could make out the crest of a height of land ahead. It was where the stars ended. The crest was ruffled. Presently he made out why. Trees.

He reached the top and entered the trees. He felt the trunks of several of them. Rough bark. Swirled-up branches and leaves, like a head of dark hair tossed about by a wind. Oaks. He pushed through the little grove and emerged on a high shoulder of a point. Despite the intense darkness he was instantly aware of a big drop in the land ahead. Far below, like a series of long curving bananas, lay a great wide river twinkling reflected starlight. The Missouri again. He'd arrived. Below down the long strange slopes was Devil's Nest. The slopes varied. Some of them were light in color, some dark. The light ones were probably grass, the others trees.

Off to the east, on his right, the horizon began to lighten. Dawn was on the way. Time to hole up again and get a good sleep.

He started walking down a slope. A dozen steps and it fell off rapidly. He had to stiffen himself against it to keep from running. He grabbed hold of the tops of the tall grasses to brake himself. He went down stepping sideways.

He kept to the lighter patches of ground. It was easier descending on the grass than down through the trees. Also it was cougar country, and cougars liked to pounce down out of trees.

As it lightened overhead, he could make out the outlines of trees and bushes. Birds awakened, first a couple of warm-up chirps, then a phrase or two tossed off, finally a hearty unraveling of pure early-morning joy.

Over on the right, on another falling shoulder of land, he spotted a thick patch of sumac. In the early dawn the sumac glowed a deep blood red. It would make a great place to hide in. Later on in the day, in sunshine, he'd figure out the lay of the land in more detail.

He sidestepped down through the slanting draw and then pushed his way up into the sumac. The sumac came to his waist. The growth was thick and made for hard going. When he got to the top of the shoulder of land he stopped for a last look around.

The great river far below shone like pink milk. It came from a long way off to the west, and it disappeared a long way off to the east. It was tremendous country. He'd never seen hills that high before. With a wry smile he remembered that an old-timer in Bonnie, a trapper named Willemstein, called the Devil's Nest hills the Almost Mountains. Devil's Nest was shaped like a triangular chute with the Missouri running along its bottom. All the land in the Nest fell in a series of shoulders and slopes, some covered with tan grass, some cropped out with groves of green trees. All the draws ran with a vague purple fog.

With a sigh, Red settled down in the sumac. He removed the carrots and the potatoes from his pockets and placed them in the grass. He put the two jars of food beside them. He found himself a comfortable little dip in the slanted land, just right for his length, and nuzzling his head into the thick grass, he let himself go.

He awoke scratching. Sunlight struck at him from the side. He sat up, head touching the scarlet leaves of a sumac bush. It was very silent out. A light breeze was blowing in from the north, coming off the water below and then up the irregular slopes to where he sat.

It itched something fierce under his belt. He couldn't figure out how mosquitoes could have bitten him under his belt.

He got up on his knees, head popping out above the tops of the sumac. The sun was still an hour high above the west horizon. The sky was clear all around. No sign of life, not even cattle or sheep. No barns or houses. Just wild falling land.

He settled back into the grass. He rubbed his face awake and ran a hand through his hair. Man, he'd slept hard. Sleeping on the ground out in the open turned out to be fine. There hadn't been any nightmares, either. What a mistake it had been for him to go to South St. Paul in the first place. Nothing had turned out right. Jen. God have mercy on her soul.

He licked his lips. He was hungry. He looked around for the food he'd placed in the grass. To his astonishment there were only one carrot and two potatoes left. What the devil. Mice. Mice had quietly run off with most of his raw vegetables. The sly little gray devils.

He ate the carrot and the two potatoes.

He checked the two fruit jars. Sure enough, one of them was canned crab apples, the other was canned sausage, as he'd guessed from the smell of the rubber rings. He was so hungry he devoured both jars. He set the empty jars neatly against the stalk of a sumac bush.

The itching under his belt got worse. Finally he loosened his belt and trousers and had a look. There was a row of pink bumps completely circling his waist. Mosquitoes couldn't have done it. They itched so ferociously it made him suck in funny little breaths each time he scratched them. Willing it, he gave himself one more scouring thorough scratch and then buttoned up his trousers and refastened his belt.

He got to his feet and had a careful look around. Still no sign of life anywhere. He studied the far bottoms along the riverbank. Nothing. And nobody fishing on the river. If there were outlaws in Devil's Nest they were well hidden.

He made out what looked like a sandy beach directly below. He decided to head for that first. He would wash up and then go look for trails.

Poor Jen. She was probably buried by now. Her father and mother would probably be sitting home again and crying quietly together. He wondered if his own father had been told she'd died. Most likely he had. Would Dad have gone up to the Twin Cities to the funeral? The thought of it all made Red shudder. God, what he'd done when he was out of his head.

He descended down through patches of purple leadplant and waving goldenrod. Clusters of sunflowers appeared to turn around and look at him. Wild clover stood mingled with old faded blazing star.

He spotted a huge spider, about the size of a mouse, clinging to the underside of a sumac twig. Its fat brown spotted body was almost perfectly camouflaged against a brown spotted scarlet leaf.

The trees thickened. Oaks first, then farther down ash and hackberry and elm. Here and there, towering over them all, stood a tremendous scraggly golden cottonwood. Only the cottonwoods had changed color; all the rest remained green.

An hour later he hit the bottoms. Ahead, through some thick brush, he made out the glitter of the river surface in the late-afternoon sunlight. The thick brush turned out to be mostly gooseberries and buffalo berries. To Red's delight and surprise, they were both heavy with ripe fruit. The gooseberries resembled round drops of dried blood and the buffalo berries pointed drops of fresh blood. He ate several handfuls of both. The gooseberries had a soft sweet taste and the buffalo berries a sharp puckery taste.

He pushed through to the sandy beach. The sand was curiously fine, spongy, here and there quaky. Better be careful. Some of it might be quicksand. He found a half-submerged cottonwood log and sat down.

What a river. The Missouri was so wide he could see the curve of the earth in its surface. The water at his feet was yellowish, while farther out in the slanting sun it was a rusty gold. All of it was pushing south, rippling, forming little whirlpools, rustling, making the farther shoreline appear to be moving north.

He took off his work shoes and socks and let his feet dangle in the lapping water. His socks stank. Stooping, he sloshed them back and forth in the water, wrung them out, then sloshed them some more, until satisfied the smell was gone. He wrung them out thoroughly and laid them over the rough bark of the cottonwood log. He washed his face, neck, then his arms. The water had an odd body to it, as though it might have been laced with lard.

"I maybe should wash my shorts too. They probably by now look like a mustard sack." He considered it; finally muttered, "No, I think I'll wait until tomorrow."

The sun sank. Blue shadows raced across the running gold-brown water. Herons along the farther shore began to fish in the shallows.

It was time to get moving and find shelter for the night. He put on his wet socks, then his shoes. Sighing, he headed down along the riverbank.

Sometimes the riverbank flattened into beaches, sometimes it rose as high as a barn. Once, right after he'd stepped on it, part of the bank collapsed under him and with a great sloshing sound fell into the river. He had to leap to save himself. He was careful from then on to stay well away from the edge of the bank.

A yellow coulee came down on his left, with a little trickling stream of water. Fresh water. He stepped down into the coulee, knelt, and cupping up the water by hand had himself a drink. Still that alkaline taste.

It came over him that someone was looking at him. Raising his eyes, he was astounded to see two men standing in the opening to a cave across the coulee. He'd been so intent on a good drink of water he hadn't noticed the dark opening of the cave. It was in shadow.

One of the men was Indian, the other white. The Indian was stubby, with rounded shoulders and short arms and short legs. He was dressed in faded jeans and faded denim jacket and a pair of laced boots. The white man was lanky, with long arms and legs. He too was dressed in faded jeans and a faded denim jacket. He had on a pair of ordinary work shoes.

Red slowly stood up, ready for anything. At least they weren't cops. Probably a couple of Devil's Nest outlaws. Red decided to make the best of it. "Hi. Hope I ain't buttin' in on your territory."

The Indian stared at him with old brown eyes. It was strange to see an old look on so young a bronze face.

The lanky one was a pouter. He pursed his lips in and out several times. Finally he grunted. "Hi."

Red advanced a step. "I'm George Haron."

"What you doin' here?"

Red shrugged. "Same thing you are."

"Yeh?"

"Like a hurt dog I decided to crawl off by myself awhile."

The lanky one looked Red up and down. Finally his eyes settled on the blood spots on Red's pants. The lanky one pushed his thick lips out until the upper lip touched his nose. It gave him a brutal look. "Well, okay. I'm Otis. And I ain't handing out my last name. And this is my buddy Dick His Many Mares."

Dick His Many Mares spoke up. "I'm Yankton Sioux." He said it proudly in a squeaky voice.

Otis said, "Well, Red, what are you on the lam for?"

"Nothing."

"You just said you was a hurt dog."

"Well, I was a pigsticker. Went berserk one day."

Otis lifted a shoulder and his eyes opened a wide very light gray. "You don't say." Otis looked at his buddy Dick. "By God, another one of those." Otis swung his deadly gray eyes at Red again. "Pretty funny, ain't it, that two guys from the kill should meet here in Devil's Nest."

"You a pigsticker too?"

"I was in beef kill." Otis made a pass at his own throat as if he was slitting it open with a knife.

Red felt sick.

Dick His Many Mares said, "Otis choked his boss."

Red turned to Dick. "And you?"

Dick only stared at him, brown eyes glittering.

Otis said, "Dick ain't sayin'. He ain't white like you and me."

Dick said, "Being a red man has nothing to do with me not telling."

Red studied Dick a moment. "You sound like my friend Alan Ross the newspaperman. Like you went to college."

Otis scoffed deep in his throat. "Yeh, that's the one bad thing agin him. I can take his being a damned redskin, but not that he reads books. Christ."

Red looked past the two at the opening of the cave. "You two holing up in there?"

"Yeh. That's home," Otis said. "C'mon in." Otis gestured with his thumb.

Red followed Otis with Dick coming after. Inside, the cave was dimly lit from the entrance. Seeping water over the years had slowly cut out a cavern in the hardened clay about the size of a granary. Water still dripped in the back part. There was an old table, with two boxes serving as chairs. A white iron bedstead covered with horse blankets stood in the darker part of the cave.

Otis picked up a third box from in back and set it near the table. "Have a chair."

Red sat down uneasily. There was a pitcher of water on the table with several glasses. The pitcher was a fancy one, as pure white as fresh snow with a red rose hand-painted on it. The glasses were special too, each with the image of a leaping deer cut into its side, making the glass sparkle like a diamond.

Otis and Dick sat down across from him. Otis carried a long knife in his belt. Otis picked up a bottle from the floor of the cave. "Dick and me went grapin' this fall over near Lindy. Care for some wine?"

"No."

Otis set the bottle back on the floor of the cave. "Fact is, we were looking for a third man."

Dick nodded agreement.

Otis said, "We need meat. Dick here has rigged us up a deer snare higher up the draw. We need two men to drive the deer and one to pull the string to the trap. You and me will beat up the deer and Dick'll pull the string. Okay?"

Red didn't like it that around Otis he felt a little like an underdog. Otis had the same jump on him that both Dad and his boss Simes had.

"What do you think?" Otis asked.

Red looked down at his hands. "So long as I don't have to do the sticking, okay."

Otis stared at him awhile. "Oh, one of those. You went berserk because you was a coward."

Red stared back at Otis. His lower lip trembled. He moved his hands ready on his lap. "Try me."

It was getting dark in the cave. Dick His Many Mares went to the mouth of the cave and looked out. He spoke over his shoulder. "Otis, it's time. Give me five minutes and then you start the drive." With a little wave of his small brown hand, Dick headed across the stream and vanished into the trees.

Otis waited for about five minutes, then with an abrupt motion and grunt he got to his feet. "Okay, let's go. I'll take the ridge across the draw and you take the one on this side. When we get near to where they're bedded down, I'll give you a hand signal to start hootin' and hollerin'. They ain't gonna jump unless they think you're about to step on them."

Red nodded.

"Well, let's go."

Red took the ridge on the right and Otis the ridge on the left. They went up slowly, hand on a knee at times when the going became steep. They moved through a patch of sumac, then a thin stand of scrub oak, then a patch of wolfberry. Red began to puff.

About halfway up the long slope Otis raised his hand, then pointed down at some gooseberries in the draw between them. It was immediately below where the stream had its start as a spring.

The sun was about to set far in the west over the winking Missouri, and its glow pinkened the tops of the highest bluffs. The air was crisp. There was a hint of frost in it. Breathing was sweet.

Otis began to wave both arms. "Hii! Yii! Hii! Yii! Shuch. Shuch." Red followed suit.

Both Otis and Red had to yell and kick their way deep into the lurking shadows of the gooseberries before the deer broke. But when the deer did break, they came up like tan paper airplanes launched by an invisible hand, a buck with a six-point rack, three does, white rumps flagging. They sailed like they were part of a dream. Neither Otis nor Red could possibly keep up, but their running on the ridge to either side gave the deer the hint they'd be better off sticking to the bottom of the draw.

Suddenly the front doe was jerked to a stop in midjump. She hung in the air for a second; then, dropping, she began to struggle and kick inside Dick's net.

The buck gave off an anguished sound and bounded sharply to his right, climbing the draw in front of Red. The other two does followed the buck bound for bound as though tied to him in tandem. In a moment the three vanished into a grove of ash.

Red stopped running. He gasped for air. He stared down at the struggling doe in the snare. "Poor deer."

Otis plunged down from his ridge, knife flashing. Dick popped out of some nearby bushes and joined Otis. Otis jumped for the doe, slipped an arm around her neck, and before she could get off another kick, slit her neck. Otis worked his knife delicately and deeply almost all the way around, finding the veins and the arteries. The doe's head flopped to one side. Blood gushed in a frothing rout on the deep grass.

Red couldn't stand to look at it, and he sank to the ground. He thought of Jen. Poor woman. He looked west. There the horizon had turned to a bloody red. He couldn't bear to look at that either. He turned farther and let his eyes come to rest on the long banana curve of the Missouri. The thought shot through him that it would be wonderful to dive into those rumpling tan dirty waters.

Otis and Dick stood back to let the doe bleed out.

Otis looked up to where Red sat on the ridge. "Hey, buddy, we got him. Come on down. Time to celebrate."

Dick said, "Come on join us and have a fresh hunk of raw liver. Mmm-mmm."

Red made a face.

"Suit yourself."

Otis and Dick were so happy about catching the doe they did a jig in the grass, first with hands clasping, then with arms around each other. They laughed and laughed, and finally fell in the grass. Otis began to goose Dick, and Dick laughed like a silly woman. They hugged each other.

Red shook his head. That a man might goose another, once, he could understand, but to keep on doing it, that had to be buggery. He'd heard the guys at the packinghouse talk about buggery, joshing about it, but he'd never believed such things happened.

Suddenly in the pink air, out of the corner of his eye, Red caught a flash of metal in the bushes on the other ridge above Otis and Dick.

Red flattened himself in the grass.

Then as if in a nightmare, three men rose slowly out of the bushes, first heads, then shoulders, then guns raised. All three took aim at the entwined Otis and Dick below, and at a little nod from one of them, fired. Three flashes, golden in the pink air, lashed down at the two below. "Bah-oom!" The three men lowered their guns.

Red recognized the one who'd given the little nod. Frank Stough. Hatless. With his light straw hair combed straight back and mocking light-gray eyes. The other two fellows wore tan hunting clothes, sportsmen with expensive shotguns.

Silence spread in the dusky draw. The doe dropped in her snare, her almost-decapitated head hanging off to one side. Nearby Otis and Dick lay in each other's arms, big holes blown into their sides, common blood gushing off into the grass, red vanishing in green.

Red watched through a fringe of grass, heart pounding violently into the ground under him.

Stough said, "Well, there's two more we don't have to worry about. Sure wish we could've found that George Haron though."

"Yeh," one of the tan men said.

The other tan man pushed out his upper lip.

The three men stepped carefully down toward Otis and Dick. With the ends of their shotguns they prodded the two prone figures.

"Dead all right."

"Yeh."

"Getting pretty dark out," Stough said. "No use looking for that killer Haron anymore tonight."

"No, I guess not."

After a while the three left.

Sure they were gone, Red rose out of the grass and, trembling, hurried down the hill to the cave.

# Chapter 26

# ALAN

Alan pulled up at the corner where the Canton road turned west. He didn't have a solitary lead as to where Red might have gone.

Across a fence, flights of geese were dropping down out of the north and landing in a long oval pond in a pasture. There was no wind out, yet the water was in a continual agitation from all the beating wings. The white geese resembled popcorn balls riding on a pan of bluing.

There was still the sheriff, of course. Alan gave it some further thought, then decided he should check with him too.

Alan turned the car around and headed north past Fat John's farm. The county seat, Rock Falls, lay off to the northeast some fifteen miles.

Sheriff Rexwinkel, big as a barrel of salt, with brown nervous eyes, didn't know where Red might be either. "Oh, we've been on the lookout for him," Sheriff Rexwinkel said. "But we ain't had one hint."

Alan nodded. The hard cement walls of the sheriff's office made him feel depressed. "Thanks."

"You're welcome. But I don't think he'll show."

"What makes you think that?"

"The boy comes from a good family. And if it's true he done what they say he done, he'll be too proud to show up around here. That family has got pride like you wouldn't believe."

"None of them ever had a police record?"

"Them? Nah."

Alan next went up to the clerk of courts. The clerk was a mild-mannered warm-hearted woman.

Alan said, "I wonder, I'm a reporter from the Minneapolis *Chronicle*, I'm curious to know if you have any record on any of the Englekings. You know, misdemeanors, divorces, lawsuits?"

The clerk shook her head slowly. "I don't recall any so long as I've been in office. And that's been twenty years."

"Nothing whatever then?"

"You're free to look at the records."

"Thanks."

Outside again, Alan walked toward his old blue Dodge. He hated going back to the Twin Cities without having found something. Somehow he had the feeling that Red would show up eventually at his father's farm, maybe at night if only for a glimpse of it. There were dark ties between Red and his father.

A siren wailed downtown behind Alan. For a second he wondered if it was some kind of alert. He checked his wristwatch. Six o'clock. Oh. Suppertime. He headed for the main street and found a cafe. He had himself a country steak, fried potatoes, cooked beans, a piece of apple pie with a dip of ice cream, and a cup of coffee. There were a dozen other customers in the cafe.

Alan ate slowly. He got the waitress to dig him up some of the area newspapers, Sioux City *Journal,* Sioux Falls *Leader,* Des Moines *Register,* and searched through them carefully while sipping his coffee. He couldn't find a single reference to Red. There probably hadn't been any new leads and the story had been dropped.

It was dark when Alan stepped outside again.

He sat awhile in his car. Thinking about one thing after another, he abruptly made up his mind. He'd go park his car near Fat John's farm and get as close to the yard as possible and watch. Red just might by now have arrived in the area and only be waiting for dark to sneak into his father's house.

Alan drove back to the Canton corner and parked his car a short ways into a cornfield out of sight. He got out and walked through to the end of the field, climbed a fence, then strolled up a pasture toward Fat John's yard. Once again Alan took pleasure in the fact that his peculiar near-albino eyes enabled him to see well in the dark. A cow trail was clearly defined in the grass.

He was within a dozen steps of the barn when a bristling form appeared on the high ground beside the barn. Fat John's dog. The dog cocked its head this way, that way. Then the dog got scent of him and began to bark, first challenging him, then yelping angrily when Alan kept on coming. At last the dog broke and came running toward him in a series of charges, barking louder and louder after each stop.

Alan hesitated; finally he decided he didn't want to get his pants ripped. He retreated down the pasture.

The dog kept barking until Alan was almost back to where he'd climbed over the fence.

His eyes picked out a tree stump, and, a little weary, he settled on it. It was a very still night. The last crickets of the year sawed their pretty songs in the grass. A fence post nearby made an odd rustling noise as if a mouse were digging a hole in it. There was a low whistling sound above him in the star-pricked sky, rising and falling, as though a multitude of birds were flying by.

He wondered how Jen was doing. What her thoughts were about her husband Red. Would she file a complaint against him?

Alan's thoughts next turned to Jael. She was probably in bed with Shelby right at that moment. He could just imagine her making her little squealing noises of joy. "Oh, Shelby, how I love the electricity of you!"

Yeh.

He checked his watch. Nine o'clock.

Finally, resigned he wouldn't find Red that night, Alan climbed the barbwire fence and got back in his car and started the motor. He let the motor run awhile, idling, while it warmed up. Soon hot air from the heater began to blast around his legs.

He was so goddam lonesome.

He drove into town. He pulled up at the Bonnie Hotel. The old hotel was a long rambling two-story building with a veranda running the length of it on the street side. The rocking chairs on the veranda were empty. A weak light burned in the lobby. Alan hit the bell on the desk lightly.

In a moment a sleepy old man came out. "Yes?"

"Do you have a room for me?"

The old man ran his finger along a row of keys, finally picked one. The old man had a badly bent forefinger. "Number 12. Down that hall on the right."

The room was adequate. It had an iron bedstead, a stiff chair, a commode, a rug, and a desk. The window looked out on an open lot beyond the alley.

The moment his head touched the thin white pillow, Alan felt sleep rush over him.

He dreamed he was running in a great cross-country race, from Holabird to Sioux Falls to Minneapolis to New York to London. The problem was the darn ocean. It was sticky to run across and he couldn't make any time.

The next morning Alan decided he should have a look at Red's church to get more of a feel of the man. The church was on the south end of town and services began at nine-thirty.

Alan was there early. He took a seat in back, in the far corner on the right, to have the whole church in view. People came in slowly, twos, threes, old maids, aged couples; then as time approached nine-thirty, in droves of four and five, whole families with father and mother and children.

Alan thought he spotted some of Red's relatives, same blond hair, same light-complected face with a tendency to be florid, same muscular walk.

Soon Fat John and his wife Fat Etta trundled into church, coming through the south door and turning and heading up the aisle halfway toward where Alan sat. They pushed into a pew and sat down. Fat John took up a seat against the wall. Both he and Fat Etta bowed their heads in a short prayer. As they prayed, every eye sitting behind them was on them. Prayer finished, Fat Etta looked up with a soft smile, while Fat John put an arm up on the bench and settled his head on his hand.

The sun was out in full power and it shone through the tall rippled glass windows along the south wall in slanting throws of gold. Dark hair became brown hair and blond hair became white hair. When the organist began to play preludes the hundred or so souls took on a holy radiance.

The sermon by a visiting minister turned out to be pretty flat.

After the service, Alan hung around in the churchyard for a while. There was talk about the fair corn crop coming up, and the nice warm weather, and the real good rain they'd had the week before. But nothing about Red or his crime. Alan couldn't even detect a strained air between Fat John's family and members of the church. People stopped to shake hands here and there, and talked a moment, and smiled at the antics of little children in a hurry to go home, and then quietly departed.

Alan was glad he'd gone to Red's church. He understood some things now. Red did come from good people like the sheriff said. Too good, perhaps. And therein lay the problem. When Red had suddenly been thrust into city life, into the organized killing side of it at the slaughterhouse, he'd been swamped by it. It was too much. The killing of animals on the farm once or twice a year, that was one thing; but the killing of animals day after day, month after month, that was another thing. To wade in blood, and to breathe air that sometimes was a fog of blood, hour after hour days on end was asking too much.

It came to Alan that now that he was so close to home he should go visit his father and mother. Holabird was only a few hours away. He hadn't seen them in several years. Dad was getting to be very old, and one of these days he'd be gone. They'd like it if he showed up on a Sunday afternoon.

Alan filled his car with gas and set off.

He pulled up at the house gate. He sat a moment to have a look around at the yard where he once had had so much fun. Not a loose piece of paper or tin can anywhere. The hip-roof barn needed paint but the doors hung tight and square in their frames. The same thing was true of the hog barn and the granary and the corncrib. The chicken house, which Ma took care of, had recently been painted a fresh white. And the two-story white house, built in the shape of an L with the point of the angle set into the prevailing northwest winds, was a handsome edifice. As usual Ma's curtains hung a neat sharp white and bunched together at the bottom in all the windows.

He spotted vague movement in the kitchen window, and then a face came up to a pane. It was Ma, with a wonderful pleased surprised look on her face. The face withdrew, and in a moment both Ma and Pa came bony-armed out of the kitchen door, hurrying, Ma with a hand to her forehead and Pa with a hand barely covering his slow wise old smile.

Alan got out of the car. "Hi."

"Son." Ma came down the stoop, then stopped and waited for him to come up. "Alan," Pa said quietly.

God but they'd aged since he'd last seen them. Ma's reddish-brown hair was almost completely white, with here and there only a hint of faded yellow in it. The bags under her eyes were more pronounced than ever. She looked older than Pa despite being thirty-six years younger. And Pa's red hair too had turned almost white. He showed his very old age in another way—his cheekbones seemed to show through a light blue, like frozen skim milk. At last both looked like they might be a touch albino.

Ma said, "Did you just drive in?"

Alan laughed, eyes wet. "No, I arrived yesterday and I've been waiting out here ever since for you two to come out of the house."

"Alan."

Alan said, "Well, Pa, and how are you?"

Pa said, "Oh, I'm able to sit up and take nourishment. Just peachy-dandy."

Alan went up and put his arms around his mother. The family had never been very demonstrative, and Ma almost broke down. She buckled a little in his arms. "Ma, now." He patted her over her back a couple of times, more out of not knowing what to do than to comfort. Lord, Ma really was skin and bones. He could feel each rib very plainly under his fingertips.

Alan next reached out a hand and shook Pa's hand. Pa's hand felt like a pair of old silver serving tongs. Pa showed no emotion except for the wise old smile.

Pa said, "What brings you here?"

Alan said, "I had to cover a story about a boy who came from this part of the country. He was a boxer who went berserk in the stockyards of South St. Paul. He's disappeared."

Ma said, "I'll bet you haven't had Sunday dinner yet, as you city people call it."

"No, I haven't."

"Good. Then I'll quick go make us a nice supper." Ma whirled around, old bones suddenly swift, and vanished into the house.

Pa stood silent a minute, a hand in his pocket, the other hand smoothing off his lips and chin. "I was about to go out and milk our only cow."

"Oh, then you're not milking many now?"

"No, I mostly let the calves run with their mothers. Then later on I fatten 'em up."

"How were the crops this year?"

"Better than last. Though there was some smut."

Alan swung his eyes around the yard. The corncrib was filled to the top. An occasional cornleaf stuck out between the cracks of the cribbing. "How about oats?"

"That was the best in years. We had so much we could sell some beyond what we needed for feed." Pa stepped onto the porch a second and came out with a glinting pail. "Coming with?"

"You bet, Pa."

They stepped across the yard and entered the cow barn. Cobwebs hung like old gray transparent rags from the stringers. A Shorthorn cow, spotted red, stood alone in the middle of a row of stanchions. She peered around at them with one brown eye and lowed.

Pa smiled, "Yes, yes, Betsie, I know I'm a little late. But special company dropped in on us." Pa picked up a one-legged stool and

settled himself beside Betsie. Soon he had the pail singing with spret-
tled milk. When he'd built up a little foam the sound of spurting milk
became muffled.

Alan found himself another stool and sat down across the gutter
from Pa. Alan was careful not to get dust on his new gray suit and
new gray suede oxfords. He picked up a straw and sailed it javelin-
style at the yellow cat. The cat began to play with the straw. After a
while, head buried in the cow's flank, Pa said, "Ma probably going to
ask you if you've found a girl yet. I think she'd like to see a grand-
child before she goes on."

"Oh."

Pa nodded against the cow. "Ma's got that twist in her bowel, you
know, and can't eat much sometimes."

Alan said, "I did have a girl but it didn't turn out good. She wasn't
the right one."

"What was the matter?"

"Her folks didn't like me, and they did everything they could to
break it up. Even throwing another man at her."

"Hmm. When you met her, did you notice if her eyes were split?"

"Eyes split? What's that got to do with it?"

"I always look to see if their eyes are split. That usually tells you if
their legs've been split."

"For godsakes, Pa, that's poppycock."

"It works, though. I looked at a lot of women before I met your
mother. All of 'em had split eyes. That's why I didn't marry 'em."

"And Ma didn't?"

"Why, son, surely your mother wouldn't have."

Alan picked up another straw and shot it at the cat. "Then you
were a virgin too when you got married?"

"I had nothing but pink skin for her, son."

Alan fell silent. Before he'd met Jael he'd had Irene Crist. Maybe
that was why his love affair with Jael hadn't been blessed. But then
that was country nonsense. Alan had a question to ask his father, yet
out of a fine delicacy didn't quite dare. Sex was like a muscle. If one
didn't exercise it, wouldn't it atrophy? The testicles, that is?

Pa finished milking Betsie. He tossed his stool one way and set the
pail to one side. "Alan, would you open the door? While I let Betsie
out?"

"Sure thing, Pa." Alan opened the door and stood to one side to let
Betsie pass outside. "Maybe I should've been a little more short with
this gal I knew."

Pa picked up the pail of milk again and headed for the house. "Maybe," he said over his shoulder. "But sometimes I've been a little sorry that I've been short with your mother. Lately I've got around to where I'd like to do something warm for her. Something real kind. But I wouldn't know what it would be."

Allan followed Pa. "Kiss her, Pa. You know, put your arms around her, play with her a little. Goose her up a little." Alan had to laugh as he spoke. The way Pa looked at him was wild.

Pa let his head sag a little to one side. It made his high forehead look even more noble. "That would be something, wouldn't it, after all these years of quiet living together. She'd pass out."

"She might not, Pa. She might suddenly turn young on you again."

They walked onto the enclosed front porch together.

Pa poured the nearly full pail of milk into the separator and started turning the crank. In a moment cream poured out of one spout into a stone crock and skim milk out of another into a pail. The high whine of the gears inside the separator had the sound of a modern symphony. Finished, Pa brought the crock of cream into the house, then filled two pitchers with skim milk.

The kitchen was filled with the sweet yeasty aroma of johnnycake baking in the oven.

Pa asked, "How long before supper?"

Ma peeked into the oven. "About twenty minutes."

"Good. Then I'll feed the calf first. Coming with, Alan?"

"Sure thing."

Pa fed the calf the rest of the skim milk.

On the way back to the house they stopped by the cattle tank a moment and had a look out over the night yard. The cattle, mostly Shorthorns, were feeding off the summer's new strawpile. A huge bull mused through the assembly of cows and heifers.

Pa leaned on a fence post. He humphed to himself. "That's funny."

Alan leaned an arm over a post too. "What is?"

"That tom bull of ours. That's the third time he's passed up Josie. Why, he hardly sniffed her."

Josie was the sprockled cow with lifted tail. Like the bull she was on the move through the herd too. Having been spurned by the bull, she tried to mount a nearby cow. The cow gave a shudder and shot out from under Josie. Alan said, "Yeh, she's bullin' all right."

"Horny as all get out," Pa said.

The bull mused farther through the browsing cattle. At last he found a charming heifer and proceeded to court her. He stood a half length behind her, his right side tight against her flank to let her know he was interested.

Pa said, "That bull knows something. Josie's no good."

"Oh, c'mon now, Pa."

"No, and by gum, I'm gonna get rid of her too as soon as that calf of hers is through with her. Weaned."

Alan smiled to himself. Pa had just expressed in country terms a theory he'd once overheard a professor of biology expound, that it was the olfactory organ that helped men and women select their mates. Eyes and touch had little to do with mating.

"You remember our neighbor down the road a ways, Bill Winters?" Pa coughed, almost as if he wished he hadn't brought up the subject, didn't want to say something raunchy in front of his son.

"Yeh?"

"Well, you know his reputation for trying to notch almost anything with a skirt on." Pa coughed again. "Well, he says he always knows when a woman's no good."

"When would that be?"

"When he don't get a rise in his pants for her."

Alan thought that over. "Well, it sure didn't help me any with Jael, Pa."

"Was that her name?"

"Yes."

"Did you ever look Jael up in the Bible?"

"No."

"Do that sometime."

The porch door behind them opened. "Yoo-hoo!"

"Well," Pa said, "grub's on. Let's tie on the feedbag."

Pa washed up first and combed his hair. Pa was still the gentleman when he got ready for meals. Pa went over and sat down in his swivel chair at the head of the table.

Alan freshened himself up next.

Ma said, "That's a nice suit you got on there, Alan. Good material. It looks real nice on you. And there's a little stripe running through it, I see."

"Yeh, that red stripe stands for the sin part of me."

Ma wasn't sure she liked that. "Don't blaspheme now, son."

"I'm just joking, Ma."

"Let's hope the Lord sees it that way."

Alan dried his hands and then went over and put his arm around his mother and gave her a little loving shake. "Oh, c'mon now, Ma, He will. The Lord must have had a sense of humor the way he made this earth and the inhabitants thereof."

"Amen," Pa said.

The johnnycake with country sausage and the carrots boiled in skim milk were delicious. Alan loaded his hot cornbread with butter and syrup until it was soaked a soft brown-gold. His mouth watered even before his fork got through cutting off a portion.

Ma watched Alan eat. It delighted her to see him eat like a hired hand. Slowly a pink flush pushed into her sallow cheeks.

Finished eating, Pa got out the Bible and read a chapter from the Second Book of Samuel. "And it came to pass in the eveningtide, that David arose from off his bed, and walked upon the roof of the king's house: and from the roof he saw a woman washing herself; and the woman was very beautiful to look upon."

Pa had a fine baritone voice, with now and then the lifting modulation of the orator in it. "And when the wife of Uriah heard that Uriah her husband was dead, she mourned for her husband. And when the mourning was past, David sent and fetched her to his house, and she became his wife, and bare him a son. But the thing that David had done displeased the Lord." Pa closed the Bible quietly.

Ma spoke up before Pa could begin to give thanks. She sometimes liked to discuss what had been read in the Scriptures. "There you go. Men. I've never been able to understand them."

Pa looked up mildly. "What's the matter with us now, wife?"

"The way that David treated Bathsheba." Ma tolled her head, looking down at her lap. "The Lord surely made a mistake when He made men like that. Like animals."

Pa smiled. "Part of God's divine purpose."

Ma shook her head. "No. No. That's where I think He made a mistake. He could have made you men like he made papa robins. The papa robin goes in unto the mama robin just once and then that's it. And they stick together for life."

Pa said, "You mean, mounts her."

Ma crooked her head against Pa. "What a pretty name that poor woman had. Bathsheba. I'll bet she was pretty."

Alan sat with widening eyes. Holy suffering peter. Pa, for all his age, thirty-six years older than Ma, Pa still thought vigorous while Ma thought dried-up. Pa and Ma, then, had had a lifelong difference about sex. It had been a sore point between them all their married lives. It was like discovering that behind the bedroom door where as a boy he could sometimes visit them there was yet another bedroom in which they really lived.

Ma said, "You men are like bulls. While we women think like dreamers."

Pa continued to smile at her in his warm sweet way. "Now how can you say that, Ma?"

Ma looked at him squarely. "I should have known what I got myself in for, when I had a peek in your green ledger and saw what you wrote down for the day we got married. Hmpf. 'Got married today. No wind to speak of. Rained in the evening.' That should've told me that all it was to you was thump-thump." Ma clapped her hands together, twice, like she might be slapping loose flour from them.

"We have a son present."

"I think it's about time our son learned how we women felt about things."

"Maybe he's learned it already."

Ma sat up straighter. Slowly she turned her water-blue eyes on Alan. "You've got a girlfriend?"

"I did have."

"Oh." Ma mused upon him a moment, thin cracked lips working. "What happened?"

The syrup-sweet johnnycake began to lie heavy on Alan's stomach. "She wasn't the right one, Ma."

"Did you love her?"

"Very much." Alan had to quick wipe an eye.

"What really happened?"

"Her parents didn't like me. And like I told Pa, they practically threw another fellow into her lap. A nice fellow, too."

"And she left you for him?"

"Yes. She's going to have his baby."

Ma's eyes turned up in their sockets. Then she said, almost under her breath, "She must've not been any good."

"She was only human, Ma."

Pa said, "Tell your mother what her name was, son."

"Jael Hemlickson," Alan said.

"Jael? Really?"

"Yes."

Ma's face became tortured. "Yes, there's been times when, like that

Jael in the Bible, I would have liked to have driven a nail into some-one's head too. Always driving a nail into me. Pinning me to earth so I couldn't break free."

Pa stared at Ma. Then after a second his eyes retreated into his head and a distant philosophic look spread over his face. Pa knew about the weathers.

Alan thought: "Well, at least Jael's last name, Hemlickson, didn't throw them. They maybe never heard about Socrates."

Pa said, "Nah, shall we give thanks?"

Ma threw him one more darning-needle look, then quietly sub-sided and closed her eyes and folded her hands in her lap.

"Heavenly Father, thank you for bringing home our son to us once more. He has been out into the world and has sampled the fleshpots of Egypt, yet he has returned whole in spirit and body. Heavenly Father, thank you for health, for peace of mind, for the good weather of the soul, for sweet and gentle companionship all these years. Heav-enly Father, thank you for the good food we have had again this day, for the increase of our flocks, for better crops. Forgive us our tres-passes as we forgive those who have trespassed against us. In Jesus' name we ask it. Amen."

All three sat a moment in silence. The clock on the stove ticked quietly.

Ma had one more question. The bags under her eyes were drawn up into hard little marbles. "Pa, come Judgment Day, which do you think the Lord is going to pay the most attention to, your prayer just now or your green diary?"

Pa turned in his highback swivel chair at the head of the table and looked out of the south window, far in the distance. It could be seen he had left them again, busy with his own thoughts, never shared with anyone.

It was while Ma was washing dishes that two memories snapped together in Alan's head. It was as though a bolt of lightning had crackled in his memory bank. Those bags under her eyes. "Say, Ma, where's our family album?"

"In the living room. On top of the phonograph. Why?"

"Just something." Alan hurried into the living room. He also re-membered the time, when his father and mother had let slip he'd had a twin brother at birth, he'd asked Ma, "What would you have named him?" and Ma had said, "We would have named him Alan like we did you, and then we would have named you John, after my wonderful grandfather, Grampa Great John. Grampa was my mother Alberta's father and she used to tell some great stories about him."

Alan further remembered the album he'd paged through in Red's house after the attempted murder where some names had been written under the portraits and one of them was Alberta.

Alan began flipping through the album. The album was an old one, with cotton-fat leather covers stained a deep purple and gold lettering. He turned one more page. There it was. "I knew it, I knew it! The same one. By God."

Ma came into the living room, fingertips dripping. "What are you talking about?"

"The same one. I'm related to him then. I'll be jiggered." He held the album out for Ma to look. "That's your mother, isn't it? Alberta Engleking?"

"Yes. It says there, doesn't it?"

Alan read the crabbed handwriting under the picture. "Alberta Engleking Tull." He stared at Ma. "I saw that same picture just a couple of days ago. In South St. Paul."

"Really? Why, I never."

"Yes, I did. I didn't connect the two before. But I'm related to Red John Engleking."

"That's the same name all right. Engleking. Is he the one who went berserk?"

"That's right."

"For heaven sakes."

Alan clapped a hand to his head. "So that was why I recognized him as the perfect dead ringer for my Haunt John. I wasn't so nuts after all."

Pa said, idly swinging back and forth a little in his swivel chair, "Was there ever any doubt in your mind?"

Alan's mind ran on. "Then your mother Alberta's brother was—"

"Big John."

"And Big John was the father of Fat John."

"Yes."

"Then you as Ada Tull are a full cousin of Fat John."

"I guess so."

"And I'm a full second cousin of young Red Engleking."

Ma nodded.

Alan stared at the picture of his grandmother Alberta. "She resembles Fat John all right. Same partly sad mocking expression around the lips and eyes. Same bags under the eyes." He looked at Ma, examining her face. "It's funny you didn't pick up that sardonic look. Though you did the bags."

"What's sardonic?"

"Well, kind of like they got a dark tongue."

Ma mused down at her drying fingertips. "There might be more of that in me than you might know. I can get pretty mad at your father sometimes."

"Well, Ma, if you ask me, if you're mad at him because he pesters you, you should be glad. Many a man of your own age has by now all dried up."

"Would that he would have dried up."

"C'mon, Ma, 'fess up now. Aren't you a little proud of him that he's still able to be a man? At his wonderful age?"

A little smile worked at the corners of her cracked lips. "Sometimes I guess I am at that. Especially when other women look at him and wish they had him."

"There you go."

Alan put the album back on top of the phonograph. He began to pace up and down. "I suppose it's too late to drive back to Bonnie yet tonight."

Ma wrung her hands. "Dear God, son, you only just got here. Stay awhile. It's so much fun to have you home. Breaks the monotony."

"I suppose it can wait a day or so."

Before they went to bed that night Ma made them chocolate milk. She first made a paste of chocolate and sugar and a couple drops of milk in each of their cups, then filled the cups with steaming milk. It made for a sweet sleepy drink.

Pa asked, "This boxer fellow you said went berserk, what did he do?"

"He stabbed his wife."

Ma whispered, "Poor woman. I can just see her."

Pa smiled his old wise smile. "Poor man. He must have been in real torment to have gone that far."

Alan nodded. "Yes, he was. And I think there was something going on in that Fat John family that didn't help any either."

Ma asked, eyes prying, "It had nothing to do with how he felt toward his wife?"

Alan said, "Well, I guess there was a little something between them too."

Pa looked in his cup to see if there still wasn't a drop of sweet chocolate left. There was. He held the cup to his lips and tipped his head back until the slack skin under his chin became tight. "Alan, there is no way anybody can ever unravel what happens between a man and his wife. Once that bedroom door closes, it's hard to find out what happens behind it." Pa pushed his cup away. "There are three important places on a farm. What happens in the barn when the men are alone. What happens in the kitchen. And what happens in the bedroom."

Ma said, "Making excuses for that killer, Pa?"

Alan said quickly, "But Jen isn't dead, Ma. She's going to be all right."

"But he stabbed her, didn't he?"

"Yes, but in such a way so as to be sure to miss her vital parts."

"Well I never."

Pa said, "The boy will be tried?"

"Yes."

"Will what you find help him?"

"I hope so. Though I'm here mostly to get the story for my paper."

Pa looked into the night-black window. "Newspapers are an awful nuisance, ain't they?"

"I guess they are. I'm not always sure I like what I'm doing."

"Quit it then."

Alan ran a finger across the checkerboard design in the blue-and-yellow tablecloth. "I may do just that."

Pa got up and wound the clock. "Time to look at the stars. And then to find that one right spot in the pillow."

Alan headed for the stair door. "See you in the morning."

"The Lord willing and the crick don't rise."

Alan had trouble finding sleep. In the dark of his old room he could make out the high school pennants still hanging on the wall. There was the smell of mothballs Ma'd put in the commode. He wished he could have back again those days when he'd been very happy going to high school, before he'd learned he had a twin brother at birth, before he'd met Jael Hemlickson.

The next morning he heard Pa getting up to make the coffee. Alan scrambled to get into his clothes. He wanted to do the chores one more time with Pa.

They sat together at the kitchen table. Ma was still asleep in her bedroom. The sun, just coming up, blazed with a dazzling light in the kitchen. It was a holy light, and it gave Pa the look of a saint. The sugar in the glass bowl became sands of gold.

Well into his second cup of coffee, Pa finally spoke up. "Why don't you buy out the local paper in Highmore? I can see you there. But not in the big city."

"Who would I talk to, Pa?"

"Oh, son, you don't want to live with skimmers all your life, do you? The Twin Cities is full of skimmers. They sit there in their fancy places and skim the cream off the farmers."

"Well, Pa, I tell you, if you can find me a young country woman who likes books as well as she likes the outdoors, I'll come home on the dead run."

Pa said nothing. He finished coffee.

They went outdoors together.

Alan had to relieve himself. As he stepped around the side of the house the sun came through the yellow-leaved ash trees like the sun of his boyhood. It was like music in his nose. Tears welled in his eyes, making the grass glisten with dew. The neighbor's roosters crowed. Then Ma's roosters in turn crowed.

Finished, Alan joined his father and helped him chase the red-and-white Betsie into the barn.

Pa settled beside Betsie and began pingpanging away into the pail. Alan settled on the other milk stool.

When his pail was about half full, Pa said, "You haven't got a girl now then?"

"No."

"Let me give you one piece of advice. Don't let it die out on you. Take like milking this cow now. If I didn't milk her every day"—Pa flexed his still-powerful forearms—"my arms would get to be as thin as an old maid's."

Alan had to laugh. What a father. One never knew what direction his inquiry would take. Pa had to have a good mind. Had he gone to college, God only knows what he might have become. Senator. Governor. Professor of philosophy even. "Pa, do you still keep a journal?"

"Yep."

"When you make out your will, how about leaving that journal to me?"

"What for?"

"I might want to edit it and publish it. As a record of one life lived out here in the Dakotas."

"That good it ain't, son."

"Some historical society might be interested in it."

Pa finished his cow and got up and threw his stool to one side. "I'll think about it. Now, open the door for the cow, will you?"

"Sure thing, Pa."

After Betsie had gone out to join her friends, Alan and Pa stood leaning over the lower half of the door for a moment. The sun was very wide and orange on the dry brown barnyard.

Alan noticed an odd arrangement of two-by-fours tacked onto the wooden fence by the cattleshed. "What's that?"

"Cowboy privy."

"What?"

"Yeh. I saw one of those down on a ranch near Lindy, Nebraska. You know, Lindy, where Lindbergh once landed on one of his barnstorming tours?"

Alan had to smile at its construction. It was easy to imagine a cowboy perched up on it, butt thrust out over the edge of a two-by-four, the heels of his cowboy boots hooked onto a two-by-four below. "What's wrong with your regular privy?"

"Well, that privy's more for Ma. She tacked up a little flowerpot in there. With fake flowers. And that was too much for me."

Alan burst out laughing. "You two are a case, all right."

" 'Course, I don't use my cowboy privy much winters."

"Where do you go then?"

"I don't."

"Oh, Pa."

"I chew tobacco all winter long, and that takes care of it." Then Pa added, soberly, "Actually, I don't chew anymore. Ma wouldn't let me get within a dozen feet of her. Though I miss it sorely."

After breakfast, Alan made moves to leave.

"Must you go?" Ma asked.

"Yes, Ma."

Both Ma and Pa got to their feet. Ma said, "Don't wait so long to come again, will you?"

"I won't."

Pa said, "I'll keep looking for you, son."

"Do that."

Ma said, "Look for what?"

"Oh, Pa mentioned I should buy out a local paper and do my newspapering here in the country."

Ma clasped her hands together over her flat chest. "Oh, Alan, that would be wonderful."

"I'll think about it, Ma."

Ma said, "I need more company of some kind. Because, after the meals are cooked, and the house is clean, all I got left to do is sit on my thumb and rotate."

Alan guessed it was Pa who'd actually said that first.

Ma spoke to the north window. "It's so lonesome out here sometimes that I think I can hear the angels sing, already welcoming me to my reward." The land outside the north window ran on forever, out through the thin row of ash trees and then out over the plowed fields and then on to where it curved away under a very light sky.

Alan suddenly felt all torn up. He couldn't leave them just like that, especially not Ma. "Aw, shucks, maybe I can stick around for a couple more days. I'll call my boss and make up some kind of an excuse." Alan knew he'd always regret it if either Pa or Ma should happen to drop dead before he could visit them again.

Alan spent part of those two days talking with Ma about her girlhood days. Ma also told him some more stories about her Grampa Great John. The more Alan heard about him the more he was reminded of what he'd seen of Fat John. Fat John had to be Grampa Great John's reincarnation.

By the time Alan got to Sioux Falls the air had become heavy and the sky misty. Soon clouds like mounds of fresh dough yeasted up just ahead of him, until at last the whole northeast horizon was full of risen thunderheads. If he kept on driving in that direction, toward the Twin Cities, he'd catch up with it. He didn't like driving in the rain, and after a little thought decided instead to drive down to Bonnie one more time. Now that he knew Fat John and all the other Englekings were relatives of his, he was eager to have another look at them.

A separate little thunderhead floated off to the right of the main mass of the storm. It had a very peculiar outline, elongated, human almost. It hung directly in front of him as he drove east on 38. Its outline kept changing from one thing to another, from a galloping horse to a cow jumping over the moon, then to a witch riding a broom. Fascinated, he leaned over his steering wheel to watch it. Then, just before he entered Rock Falls, the little storm cell changed shape again. And made him catch his breath. The whole thing had taken on the silhouette of Jael Hemlickson's head, the high noble forehead, the perfect nose, the impish smiling mouth, the well-set chin, the slender neck. He became so lost in watching it he unconsciously let up on the footfeed a little . . . until a trucker honked a horn behind him for going too slow down the main highway.

Alan pulled over to one side of the road to let the speeding trucker roar past.

When he looked up again, the little separate cloud had changed shape once more. It had become a pregnant woman, a woman who looked suspiciously like Irene Crist.

Irene Crist. He hadn't thought about her in a long time. She still worked at the *Chronicle*, but he rarely went down to the paper's library anymore. He wondered if she'd gone back to her English husband. Poor Irene.

In Rock Falls he took 75 south for Bonnie.

He drove along feeling a little shaken. To have first seen Jael in the sky and then Irene had to be an omen of some sort. Roman soothsayers read the entrails of animals for portents. Why should he have seen Jael in the sky just then? And then Irene. Auguries were in the air all right.

He headed for Fat John's yard first. It was late in the afternoon, about time to do chores.

The first thing to catch his eye was the half dozen cars parked by the house gate. Something was up. He parked behind the last car and got out. Just as he passed through the crooked house gate, Fat Etta emerged from the kitchen door with a dozen people following her. They were all crying. Fat Etta's face was red and mottled.

Alan hesitated. Were they all crying because the police had caught Red? He waited.

Fat Etta spotted him. Instantly her face turned even more red. "Yeh, and you're the cause of it too. You."

Alan said nothing.

"Coming here with your newspaper questions."

Alan caught on then it wasn't Red they were crying about. "What happened?"

"As if you didn't know."

"I don't know. What happened?"

Fat Etta sobbed. "That great man thrown flat on his back like that."

Alan turned to a young blond fellow who looked like he might be a younger brother of Red. "Something happen to your father?"

"He's had a stroke."

"Oh." Alan stood uncertainly a moment. "And here I came to visit him to tell him I'm a relative of his. I just found out. From my mother in South Dakota."

"Yeh?"

"Yes. My mother is a full cousin of your father." Alan sensed the young fellow didn't believe him. "Really. And I came to apologize for the other day." Alan's eyes began to flicker. He held out his hand. "I'm Alan Ross."

The young fellow put out his hand too. He shook hands without any pressure. "I'm Bert."

"Could I see your father?"

Fat Etta shook her head. "Doctor said not to bother him too much."

Alan drew back his head. "But I'm telling you, I'm a relative of his."

Bert turned reflective. "Ma, that must be that branch that moved to South Dakota."

Alan nodded. "That's right. That's where I just now came from. My mother now lives in Holabird."

Fat Etta said, "Is your mother the one who married that man was old enough to be her grampa?"

Alan bristled. "What's that got to do with it? If you've read your Bible you know that Mary, the mother of Jesus, was married to a man who was as old enough to be her grandfather."

"Yes, but that was in them times."

Bert said, "Ma, maybe Pa would like to know about that branch, what happened to them."

Fat Etta finally relented. "Well, all right. You take him in then, Bert." Then Fat Etta turned to her other crying relatives.

The bedroom in back reeked of sweated sheets. The tan shade was partly drawn. In the dim brown light Alan could barely make out a big bed. Fat John, what was left of him, lay on a red-and-gold checkered bedspread. He had on a new green Cambray shirt and a pair of new blue overalls. The clothes hung in folds on him. His once fat chubby face hung in loose falls of flesh, purplish in hue. Alan could just barely make out the old Fat John expression. Fat John looked like a man who was about to sink out of sight in a vat of sludge. The great chest was still there, rising and falling in shallow breath, but the girth of the belly had vanished. Alan was reminded of the time when an angel food cake collapsed in Ma's oven because he'd slammed the door too hard on coming home from school. Alan could hardly believe that a man could lose all that weight in so short a time.

Bert said, "He can't keep anything on his stomach. Doc said the stroke hit him in the middle of his brain. The part that runs his bowels."

Alan said, "How do you feel?"

"If I'd be any better," Fat John said in a hollow hoarse voice, "I'd be like you and then I'd be no good."

Alan smiled. Fat John's brain wasn't defeated by any means. "You'll be all right. Just give yourself some time."

"Yes," the ratchety voice said. "Doc won't let me have any meat.

And at this rate there won't be enough left of me for a dog to bark at. Sit down."

Bert found a chair for Alan.

Alan said, "I'm glad your wife let me see you a minute. I came back here to apologize for the other day. But mostly I came to tell you that on visiting my mother I discovered I'm related to you."

Fat John gave a wondering blue look.

Bert said, "Yeh, Dad. What do you know . . . this fellow's mother belongs to that branch of Englekings that moved to South Dakota."

Alan nodded. "My mother's name was Ada Tull and her mother was Alberta Engleking and Alberta was a sister of your father, John Henry."

"You don't say." The light-blue eyes stared until the lower eyelid fell open a little, showing red flesh.

Alan turned to Bert. "When did this happen to your dad?"

"We found him vomiting in the barn the very next morning after you was here."

"Oh," Alan said. "I'm terribly sorry."

The hoarse voice said, "Well, we Englekings always had bad throats. Chokers."

Bert smoothed back his blond hair. "Of course it don't help any either we still ain't heard from my brother."

"Red, you mean."

"Yeh." Bert rubbed his flat chickentail nose. "That's where Dad went wrong. Trying to make a butcher out of him."

Fat John said, "I admit it. But it's too late now."

Alan said, "Too late? I wouldn't say that. If his wife Jen doesn't prefer charges against him, there isn't much the law can do to him."

Fat John's eyes lighted up. "Then it's true she's still alive?"

"Yes."

A flush moved up into Fat John's slack cheeks. "Then maybe there's hope yet everything will be all right."

"I'm sure of it," Alan said.

"Well," the great man breathed from his bed.

Alan felt miserable about the story he'd soon have to write about Fat John's family. Once a reporter knew something he could hardly back away from it.

Fat John said, "Maybe it all goes back to the mistake my pa made. Back when we lived in Sioux County, Bonnie had a tough reputation. It was the outermost edge. Yet he had to move down here."

Bert said, "It wasn't really the Bonnie people themselves who were tough, Dad. It was all them roughnecks who came up from Sioux City on the train with their annual river picnics. It was outsiders who gave our town a bad reputation. They thought they could get away with things out here in the sticks."

Fat John said, "That's not the way I heard it. The local people did a lot of drinking and fighting too. Why, once our two doctors got into a terrible fight on Main Street and one had to patch the other one up. And I remember the time one Saturday night the firemen had to be called out to hose down all the hotheads." Fat John shook his head. "I don't think it did our John any good to grow up in a place like this."

"But Dad," Bert said, "our John never hung around with that tough bunch much."

Fat John looked at Alan with steady eyes. "Now that I see you again I can see you are an Engleking all right. All that light skin."

Alan smiled inwardly.

Fat John raised himself up a little in his pillow. There was a ruckling noise in his throat and he had to cough several times to clear it. Bert went to help him, but Fat John pushed him off. "Tell me, do you like that newspaper work you're doing up there in the Cities?"

"Pretty much so."

"Do you meet a lot of important people?"

"Sometimes. One of them is your son Red. He's a heckuva boxer. When he wants to be."

"Yeh?"

"I don't think it's in him to be a heavyweight champion, though. He just isn't the killer type." That was the wrong thing to say. "He's too gentle."

Fat John mused to himself. "Do you get to go to a lot of parties?"

"A few."

"At these parties, I suppose you run into a lot of really smart people? Famous scientists?"

"I've met some bright professors."

"Any millionaires? Like Jim Hill and Weyerhaeuser and Winton?"

"I think maybe there was a millionaire or two at some of the parties I went to."

Fat John ran the huge chub of his hand through his gold hair. "Yeh, ha? I suppose you ran into a lot of pretty dames there?"

"Some."

"Really pretty?"

"Yes."

"Nothing like you see around here?"

Alan cocked his head to one side. "I wouldn't say that. Beauty queens often come from the country."

Fat John surged up in his bed and sat upright. "Then you never really was at any wild orgies?"

"Not really."

"As a reporter, do you have to check out all those rapes and murders?"

"I'm over in sports and I mostly handle track and boxing."

"Ever meet Jack Dempsey?"

"Once. I met him in a depot between trains. He was on his way to a resort in northern Minnesota. On vacation."

Fat John's eyes became shrewd for a moment. "I suppose you make a lot of money? Got it rich?"

"No. In fact, I was only making sixty dollars a month until the Newspaper Guild came in."

"That's a union, sort of, ain't it?"

"Yes."

"Unions are of the devil. Did you join?"

"Yes. For the very practical reason that my salary doubled when the Guild came in. And all I had to pay was two dollars a month in dues. A sixty for two is a pretty good trade-off."

"I suppose you have some great talks with your friends there."

"Wonderful talks."

"That's the one thing we don't have out here."

Bert had been listening with mounting astonishment. "But Dad, we've got our minister to talk to."

Fat John shrugged inside his slack clothes. "He don't dare say what he really thinks about eternity."

Bert said, "But Dad, what about me? I've been trying to talk to you about Eugene V. Debs. But you won't listen."

"That socialist!"

"Well, we could have at least talked about it." Bert resettled his belt over the flab around his waist. "Debs was a lot like Jesus, Dad."

"Bert, you were always my favorite. Until you started sticking your nose into that socialist shit."

Alan leaned back. It was good to see the shrunken great man up in his blood again. Afraid that the dialogue might prove to be too lively for a man who'd just had an accident upstairs, Alan changed the subject. "I think I better go now. I've got a long ways to drive yet tonight. But I tell you, if I hear anything about your John, I'll call you. You've got a telephone, haven't you?"

"Sure. That'd be nice of you."

"Don't mention it."

Fat John held out a hand. "Come again. Now that we know we're related, maybe the two of us can have some good talks together."

"I'm sure we can."

"This ain't loose talk now. Polite."

"Not at all. I'll try and come."

"If you should happen to run into my son before I do, tell him not to worry anymore about helping me pay off the mortgage on this farm."

"I'll do that."

# Chapter 27

# RED

Red stood very still in the center of the cave. He was in the grip of that numbing shell again.

A voice spoke behind him up on the right. "Swim."

"What?" He turned around. Narrowing his eyes, he tried to pierce the darkness in the cave. "What?"

Silence.

He could feel his ears opening. Had Frank Stough and his two killer friends somehow got down into the cave ahead of him?

Again the voice spoke. "Swim."

He whirled around this time, looking behind him up on the right. "Swim where?"

"Swim the river. Get out of here."

"The big Missouri? Don't be crazy. That's not like swimming the Big Rock at home."

"Swim."

He hugged himself. He thought: "Gosh, I feel funny. It's like I'm not my own boss anymore. What's happening to me? I don't like it that I'm hearing voices again."

Crickets whirred in the cave. There were echoes upon echoes of whirrs. Outside the stream trickled quietly over rocks. Farther off the great river ruffled along heavy and dark.

"Come to think of it, though, getting across that river is going to be the only way out of here." He looked back over his right shoulder. "Only, swimming in the dark I'm going to be awful scairt."

Silence.

"But I suppose if I wait until daylight they'll find me."

A frog croaked in the back of the cave.

"But I guess I better do it."

He stepped outside. It was almost dark. The great brown river ran touched here and there by silver starlight. He took off his work shoes and tied them together in a pair. He stuffed his socks inside his shoes. He next removed his overalls and rolled his shoes up in them. Taking one of the suspenders, he tied the packet over his back behind his neck. He stepped tender-footed on the coarse gravel and entered the Missouri where the little stream ran into it. For a little way the sand under the water felt solid. The water was cold where it lapped over his ankle. He carefully followed the ridge of sand the little stream had carried into the river, feeling with his toes a sloping off on the right and then on the left. He waded in until the water rimmed up over his knees. The deeper he went in the colder it was. The water reached his shorts, then his groin. Ooo. He considered going back to the cave. Perhaps there was some way to hide in the far back part of it.

"Swim."

"All right."

Very reluctant, with an awful groan, he leaned forward and slid into the water, gasping as the cold took hold of his chest. His head went under, then bobbed to the surface. Bbbt. The water tasted like stale beer. His swimming in the Big Rock River back home had mostly been dogpaddle-style. He breasted along. In a few minutes he felt the big stream catch him and carry him downriver. Between dips he could make out a light quite a way down on the far shore. If he swam hard maybe he could make that. It appeared to be high up on a bank.

Something bumped him from underneath. It had the smoothness and the slickness of an enormous fish. A whale? It found him again and touched his left hand. Ah. A tree trunk. A submerged sawyer. A huge one. Bark off and as slick as a skinned weasel.

He pumped along. The work warmed him. The water didn't feel as cold. There was one comfort. The water was moving too fast for a crab to latch onto his toe. Nor for that matter a snapping turtle.

His right hand hit sand and the next instant his knee hit it and then the water shoved him to a kneeling position on a sandbar. Godsakes. The water was only a few inches deep. The river made a lively rippling noise as it swilled over the sandbar. He could feel, in the dark, the sandbar increase as the river brought ever more sand to it.

He rested on his knees awhile catching his breath. Well, swimming across the Big Muddy wasn't so bad after all if a fellow could rest on a sandbar every once in a while. He looked for the light on the opposite shore. It was there all right. Still downstream. Except that now there seemed to be a half dozen lights and rather high up on a little hill. He couldn't recall having seen any buildings there the day before. Perhaps trees had hidden them. He worried it was a town. If it did turn out to be a little burg he'd skirt past it.

Breath caught, he slid off the sandbar and into the deeper water again, heading for the lights. The great river seemed not to move for a little way. Some sort of backwater. He paddled through it. He felt better about swimming across the wide river. The chilly water made him work to stay warm and helped his swimming.

He hit one more low sandbar, slithered over it, and then found himself in the mainstream. It carried him along with a rush. It actually seemed to push him up out of the water a little. Bits of flotsam, bark, sticks, dead bodies of odd-shaped critters touched him. His hands kept whacking into odd sudsy mosslike things. And stink? It was like riding a cultivator behind a farting horse. Peeuu.

He decided not to fight the powerful current, not to force himself directly across it. It helped. The stream seemed to work with him. He dogpaddled slowly. He was careful to keep spitting out the water that leaked into his mouth. His skin itched. Probably from all the poison he was swimming in. He wondered what had happened to all those itching bites he'd gotten the night he'd slept on the hill. Dad had once talked of chigger bites in the woods. Hey. That's what they were.

The lights across on the other shore appeared to be higher. He was making headway all right. They'd been quite a way downstream but now they were almost directly across from him. The Big Muddy was sure carrying him down in a hurry.

He finally worked his way into calmer waters. It became heavier going. He had to supply his own power. He was awfully tired. He wondered what awful critters there might be down in the depths below him. There was supposed to be some kind of monster fish in the Missouri, with a mouth like a huge scissors.

"Swim."

"You know, I'm not my own boss any more. That shell has taken over."

He looked up out of the water. The lights were gone. He'd sailed past them. Or they were up behind a very high bank.

He flailed with open hands in the water. He began to gasp for breath. Backwater was hard to swim in. It was heavy water.

His nose hit something. With a swipe of his hand, quick, he brushed it away. It was a decaying animal floating in the water.

Terrible rotting stink. The animal came at him again as though alive. He put a couple of fingers against it and gave it a push past him. It was a dead calf. The flesh under the sopped pelt gave way like a mushy apple.

Something reached down from above. Twigs. Looking up, he saw against the stars that he'd swum under some overhanging brush from the bank. He'd made it across.

He dogpaddled down along the shore, brushing the bushes away, letting his feet sink in the water to feel for the bottom and not finding any, paddling. At last his foot hit sludge, then soft dirt, then harder bottom. He scrabbled up the steep underwater slope and emerged on a crumbling dirt bank.

He looked up. Against the stars he could make out a considerable cliff. It was at least as high as a three-story building. Scratching, feeling his way, toes sometimes catching on the roots of trees, he climbed all the way up the sloping cliff. At the very top his hand came upon a woven-wire fence. He grabbed hold of it. With his free hand he felt through it and was astonished to touch the wiggling snout of a hog. He couldn't believe it. Everything had become so unreal. He'd heard a voice, he'd stabbed his wife Jen, he'd seen two men shot, he'd swum the widest river in the world . . . and here was a hog. It was all crazy. He was breaking off from the rest of the world.

There was an oink and a wild snort on the other side of the fence. And almost immediately after a dog began to bark wildly not a dozen yards away.

Red held himself stiff. The dog had better be quieted somehow or it'd rouse everybody up. With hogs and a dog it had to be a farm of some kind.

Red began to suckwhistle at the dog in a winning way. He made a guess as to the dog's name. "Here, Shep," he called softly. "Here, Shep." He suckwhistled again, began to pat his wet knee with his hand, making the sound of a brood mother dog flopping its tail as it lay on the floor. It was the one happy sound all dogs remembered from puppyhood.

The dog fell silent.

Staring hard in the dark through the fence, Red made out the lighter silhouette of the dog.

"Yuh, Shep. Good dog. Here. Here." With a slow gesture Red reached over the fence and let the dog smell his fingertips. With his other hand he continued to pattycake his own knee.

The dog smelled Red's fingertips and its tail came up. The dog began to lick Red's hand and wriggle its gray body back and forth like a fish swimming.

Red climbed the fence and with a jump landed in the pigpen. Petting the dog at his side, he made his way across the pen. Ahead he made out the darker outlines of a low building. Hog house. Better not go in there. Rouse up all the hogs. They'd snort like elephants and really wake up the farmer.

He stopped, the dog holding at his side. He swung his eyes around, trying to make out other buildings. On his right was something resembling a huge sleeping dog. Ah, a haystack. Or straw stack. Perfect place to get a good sleep after his long cold swim. That last sleep he'd had in that farmer's haystack had been wonderful. Barefoot he walked carefully across the pen. Several times he stepped on a fresh hog turd and in disgust shook and wriggled his foot free of it. Finally he hit a chest-high woven-wire fence. He felt behind his neck to make sure of his rolled-up overalls with the shoes in them, and then, with a hunching motion, vaulted over the fence. He landed on a layer of soft straw. It had spilled off the side of the stack. Good. Straw was better than hay.

The dog whined on the other side of the fence. It wanted to come with him.

"Shh. You go home now. G'wan. Home."

The dog whined some more.

"G'wan."

Reluctantly the dog backed off and then, slinking, vanished in the dark.

Red unhooked the rolled-up overalls from around his neck and placed them on the ground. He took off his shirt and underwear and wrung them out, tight, until the last drops squeaked. He shook out the wrinkles and slipped into them again. That felt better. He next slipped into his overalls. Surprisingly they'd kept pretty dry. He made sure what little money he had was secure in his overalls pocket. He slipped on his socks and his shoes. Then, feeling his way around the straw stack, he found a corner where the farmer had hacked out some of the straw. It made for steps, and Red clambered to the top of the stack. He crept along the top until he came to a level spot. He lay down and scratched out some of the straw from around him and spread it over his body. Right away he felt warmer. His clothes felt somewhat squishy and clung plakked to his skin, but it was all right. Looking up, he saw millions of stars. For the first time his limbs began to ache with fatigue, with cold.

He wondered if that voice would talk to him again. When it didn't, he decided he was too tired to hear it. Tomorrow he'd work out what was wrong with him.

He fell asleep.

"Hey, you."

Red opened his eyes. Through the loose webbing of straw he saw a young man looking down at him.

The young man had a fork in his hands, about to pitch some straw off the stack. He was wearing black denim trousers, black shirt, and a rope for a belt. He had a young man's beard, black and fuzzy, and his hair was cropped off crudely about his ears. His cheeks were apple red in the morning sun, and his blue eyes were quirked in surprise. "Whatcha doin' here?"

Red sat up, wisps of straw falling off to either side. "I needed a place to sleep."

"You look like you fell in the cattle tank."

"I swam across the river last night."

The young man wondered down at him. "I think maybe we better go see Elder Waldner. C'mon."

Blinking his eyes in the slanting morning sun, Red looked around. It stunned him to see a whole flock of buildings, most of them made of blocks of hard-cut clay the color of caraway cheese. It made him think of a fairy tale about a mouse who'd gone to heaven where all the houses were made of cheese. Looming over the buildings were the umbrella tops of massive river cottonwoods. The cottonwoods were so tremendous they made him feel small. He had to work to keep seeing what he saw in front of him. "Where am I?"

"The Bon Homme Colony. We're a colony of Hutterites. A brotherhood."

Hutterites. The minister back home had once talked about them, saying that if the truth were known the Hutterites were perhaps the true Christians. The Hutterites believed in owning all things in common. Also they were willing to die for their beliefs. Red looked from building to building. "It's like a little city here."

The young man kept staring at Red. "We got houses and barns and shops and granaries, sure. Ovens and communal kitchens and dining rooms. A schoolhouse even. And a brand-new steam-powered flour mill."

Red noted that besides all the hogs, there were sheep and cattle and horses. And chickens and geese.

"Ya, we're like in Noah's ark here. Come, like I say, I better take you to our elder. Michael Waldner. He'll know what to do with you. I'm just the hog boss."

Red made a face.

"I won't hurt you. Come. Pretty soon it'll be time for breakfast. You're bound to be hungry after what you went through." The young man stuck his fork into the straw and slid down the side of the stack.

Red followed him. His legs stung when he hit the ground.

"So you swum across the big sewer there. I've always wanted to try it once. Just to see if I could do it."

"Why didn't you?"

"I was afraid they might think I was running away and then they'd hold a meeting over me, and that I didn't want. Because I like it here. We got a great life in Christ here. We are the chosen and the elect. We are fighters for and witnesses of God."

The hogs heard them talking and came out of the hog house with a great chousing of hunkering grunts.

Red asked, "What's your name?"

The young man weaved a path through the hogs. He held out a huge red hand. "Ted Glanzer. And yours?"

"George Haron."

"Haron. Sounds good to me. You could be a Mennonite."

"What's the difference?"

"They ain't as strick as we are. They go out in the world more."

The hogs ruckled up close around them. Some like dogs almost nipped them in the heels.

Glanzer vaulted over a wooden fence, and Red did the same.

The hogs charged against the fence behind them and then stuck their round pink working snouts through the cracks in the board fence to get a scent of where the two men were going.

Other men were just then emerging from what looked like a barracks. Sleepily they combed hair out of their eyes. When they spotted Glanzer leading a stranger across the yard, they stopped to stare. They hadn't often seen strangers either. Then, giving Red a quiet nod of hospitality, they went about their chores.

Glanzer headed straight for the side door of the newest barracks. He walked in without knocking. "Mike, look what I found this morning." Glanzer held the door open for Red to follow him inside. "George, this is our elder, Michael Waldner."

An old man was sitting at a table reading in a very thick old book. "What, Ted?"

"I found this fellow sleeping on the straw stack by the hog pen."

Michael Waldner stood up. Waldner's black denim pants were baggy at the knee. But his black shirt had just been ironed. He had on an old brown vest. His face looked very much like the aged parchment pages of the book he'd been reading. Yet his light-gray eyes were as sharp as a hawk's, wary, flickering. His balding dome head gave him the look of a man with a huge brain. At last old Waldner said in a clear young voice, "You're not of our kind."

Red didn't know what to say. He had difficulty remembering what he and Glanzer had talked about just a few moments before.

"Well, stranger, what do you have to say for yourself?"

"I swam the Missouri last night, Mr. Waldner."

Waldner's eyes settled on Red's blue overalls. "Someone improperly dressed is sent away, you know."

"Oh, I mean to be on my way. I just slept on your straw pile overnight, that's all. I meant no harm."

Waldner nodded. "Where are you going?"

"I don't know."

"Do you belong to a church? There is no hope of heaven if one dies outside the church."

"That's what Dad believed too."

"You were raised a Christian then?"

"Yes."

"What faith?"

"Christian Church. In my hometown, Bonnie, we sometimes called it the Little Church."

"Oh. We know of them." Waldner studied him kindly. "They may well be saved too. Are you still a good Christian?"

"Not after what I've done."

Waldner studied him some more. "We do not require of anyone that he confess his sins. This is a place without walls, without police. When you are ready we will listen. When there has been an inner awakening in your soul we will listen."

Red continued to have trouble believing that what was happening to him was happening exactly the way it was. Truly he'd fallen back in time with these Hutterites. Their black clothes, their old-country speech, their separatist beliefs, all of it had to be part of a book, not real life. Red stared at the old tome lying on the table. Maybe Ted Glanzer and the old man had emerged out of that old book as ghosts.

Waldner saw where he was looking. He placed his old hand on the open pages. "Yes. This is our history. It tells where we came from and what we believe in. It is our sacred book. It was written with a feather and homemade ink."

Red nodded.

"Are you looking for a home?"

"I guess so. Someplace where I can figure out what to do next."

"What kind of work can you do?"

"I was a farm boy."

Glanzer spoke up. "Mike, maybe he can help me with the hogs. I can use a man there."

Red shuddered. "Oh God, not that."

Waldner mused upon Red awhile. "Where would you like to work?"

"Out in the field."

"That's about over now." Waldner mused to himself. "We still have some garden work to do, though. Dig up the potatoes. Would you like that?"

"Anything outdoors."

"Well, we have room for those that have been cast out." Waldner looked at Red's blue overalls again. "Meanwhile, we better get you some decent clothes. Ted, why don't you tell one of the women to get this man a complete outfit? About your size, I'd guess. And bring them here."

"Then you're not going to turn me in?" Red asked.

"We never turn anybody in. Though we sometimes ask people to leave. Nah, Ted, to, get one of the women to bring him some new clothes."

Glanzer nodded and was gone.

Waldner sat down. "Just place your old clothes outside the shower room and the women folks will clean them up for you. We'll keep them for you until the day."

"Thanks. I can hardly believe this is happening to me."

Waldner stroked his long beard. There was a snow-white spot the size of a silver dollar in the center of his chin whiskers. "We are all servants and apostles of Jesus Christ. To get where we did, our forefathers had to suffer much poverty and tribulation, much torture and suffering, even death itself. This was the will of our Lord so that we might show fellowship and love and faithfulness to our fellow man. Yes, thousands were executed in the old country by fire and sword. We are the fortunate few who survived. That is why we are pleased to help the unfortunate in this new country. *In Gottes Segen ist alles gelegen.* You are ready to work then?"

"Yes."

"Because we are all together like a big clockwork here where one wheel drives the other and so makes the whole thing tick."

Red nodded.

"After you've had breakfast the council will have a meeting and they'll decide where you will work."

A woman of about thirty entered, carrying an armful of clothes. She had on a long black dress with a cowl. Thick black hair bushed out from under the cowl. Her eyes were light-gray, almost the color of hail. "Where do you want these, Mike?"

Waldner nodded toward Red. "They're for him, Magdalena. Show him where the shower is." Then Waldner, eyes half closing in inner reverie, returned to his old book and with a finger began tracing out the lines of a strange script on the parchment page.

Magdalena walked ahead of Red down a beaten path. She headed for a small wooden shed standing next to a long clay-block building. At every step the heels of her work shoes just barely showed under her long black dress. She walked as though she might be a runner, striding off her hips rather than swinging them.

Red wondered if she was married and had kids.

Magdalena handed him the black clothes at the door of the wooden shed. She gave him a brief measuring look, her light-gray eyes turning luminous for a moment, and then walked away.

"Thanks." Red stepped inside. The shower had a clean soapy smell. He found the hot-water faucet and took off his dried-stiff clothes and gave himself a thorough scrubbing. The bar of soap was homemade, with grit in it, and soon his skin turned red. But scrub as he might he still felt dirty. He covered himself from head to foot with running soapsuds.

He dried himself off harshly. His skin still didn't feel right. He dressed in a pair of fresh longjohns and gray socks and then slipped into the black shirt and black denim pants. Michael Waldner had made a good guess as to his size. The clothes didn't feel too funny on him. He put on his own shoes again.

A bell rang on the yard outside.

In a moment there was a rap on the door. It was Glanzer. "We're gonna have breakfast now. Better come along."

Red removed his money from his stiff dirty clothes and then placed the dirty clothes in a pile on a bench outside the shower room. He followed Glanzer across the yard. Men from all parts of the colony came heading for the same building, the dining hall. Ted and the rest washed up in a row of basins just inside the hall and then took seats on benches on both sides of a long bare polished wooden table. Because he was a guest Red sat next to Glanzer. Otherwise the oldest man sat nearest the stoves and the youngest fartherest away. None of the young men wore a beard.

Glanzer explained, "We don't wear beards until we get married. That way the young girls can tell who's single."

Red looked around for Michael Waldner.

Glanzer said, "The elder, the pastor, eats by himself."

There was a murmur of soft talk along the table. All the men gave Red a brief but searching look, then looked down at their bowls. The oldest man bowed his head and they all prayed silently.

The morning sun, striking underneath the great cottonwoods outside, turned the white-plastered walls into pink candy. The smells were wonderful: fresh-baked bread, perking strong coffee, steaming porridge. The womenfolk, hovering over the stoves along the wall on the left, soon began to bring food to the men: each a bowl of swollen oatmeal, thick slices of bread on a breadboard, several little dishes piled high with yellow homemade butter. No sugar. But there were several jars of honey.

The men ate with a hearty appetite yet in a controlled thoughtful manner. No one said a word. The women brought seconds of everything, and then, satisfied enough had been set out for the men, retired to another table across the dining hall and had their own breakfast. Two old women continued to minister at the stoves. Some of the women, as they ate, pushed back their black cowls and black shawls. They talked subdued as they ate, like the murmur of doves settling down in a cote. Magdalena was among them.

Red asked, "Where are the little children?"

Glanzer said, "They eat by themselves."

Red helped himself to a third slice of the soft fresh bread and loaded it with butter and honey.

After the meal a portion of the Scripture was read. Again there was prayer.

Glanzer told Red he should go sit under the trees for a while. The council was now going to meet to decide what to do with him.

Red found a wooden bench under the largest cottonwood on the yard. There were chickens and children everywhere, scratching and playing in the grass. The air was filled with their sharp cackles and their sweet cries of joy. Looking up at the golden leaves of the tremendous tree, Red wondered again if he hadn't somehow, by some kind of awful magic, stumbled back into another life he might have lived before this life. The unreal golden air touched everything, the children's laughing faces, the white feathers of the chickens, the light-yellow clay walls of the buildings, the deep-blue grass underfoot.

A half dozen little children, three or four years old, began to play a game with Red. The girls were dressed in long gray dresses and the boys in hand-me-down black overalls and shirts. The girls wore scarves and the boys were bareheaded. Most of them were blond. They'd whisper together in a cluster, then run toward Red daringly, calling him a name in German, and then at the last moment, not quite daring to face him, shrieking in pretended fear, would shy off and run back to their former safe spot.

Red smiled at them. They reminded him of calves back home on Dad's farm, who'd come up to the fence, noses out, tails up, and then at the last moment, when one looked at them, they'd beller and dash off to their mother cows.

Michael Waldner was suddenly behind him. He sighed. Then the old man took a seat beside Red. "You like the little children?"

"Yes."

"Good."

"I always wanted at least one. But my wife kept losing them."

"You are married then?"

"Yes."

"Well, we don't mean to pry. If you want to stay you can. It was decided that you can help Timothy Hofer get in the rest of the potatoes. Timothy's young helper said he'd switch to hogs."

Tears welled in Red's eyes.

Waldner had huge smithy hands. He roughed them together as though he were glad that a good piece of work had been done. "We don't chastise the little children here. We try to win them over with love. You catch more flies with honey than you do with vinegar."

"Then you don't make anybody stick a hog at butchering time if he doesn't want to?"

Waldner's old eyes opened in shrewd surprise. "Who would do such a thing?"

Red said, "My father would."

The little cluster of children dared to make one more sortie. They fluttered up and called out the German name, and again shied off, laughing, almost shrieking hysterically.

Waldner called out to them mildly, "Children, now now, Jesus was nice to strangers."

The children threw Red another kind of look, and then smiled a foolish smile to themselves.

The Hutterites were a happy people. They didn't have to worry about private debts or mortgages on farms, or do work they hated. They had to work but each man did what he liked doing best. Some men liked to make meat. Well, they could do the slaughtering. There were also some who liked to till the fields and to lie down in green pastures and to live beside still waters.

"Here's Timothy," Michael Waldner said.

"Oh." Red jumped to his feet.

Timothy Hofer gave Red a powerful handshake. "Well, ready for a little work?"

"You betcha."

"Good. I can use you."

Timothy was even more powerfully built than Glanzer. He had a bushy red-brown beard, dark hair, and a pair of steady brown eyes. His black shirt was already spotted with sweat. "You know horses?"

"Dad had horses."

"Let's go, then."

Michael Waldner got to his feet too. A kindly smile worked in his gray whiskers. "Besides your clothes, did you have anything else on you when you came this morning?"

"Nothing besides a little money."

"How much?"

Red dug into his pocket and brought up all his current wealth, two five-dollar bills and a nickel and two pennies.

Waldner said, "As long as you stay with us I think you'd better leave those two bills with me. You see, the most we ever give anybody is a dollar a week for spending money. Board and room and clothes and salvation are free. It wouldn't look good for others to know you have ten dollars in your pockets. The loose change is all right."

"But . . ."

"You'll get them back when and if you leave."

Timothy said, "That's right, George, it's the rule. But we're honest here and you'll get them back."

Red handed over the two bills reluctantly.

Timothy led the way to a low wagon. Together they climbed the front wheel onto a spring seat. Timothy loosened the lines and handed them over to Red. "You drive."

They took a beaten road out through a grove of lofty cottonwoods. They rolled through speckled shadows. Great tree trunks, some of them a dozen feet thick, reared up clay-colored on both sides of the road. High overhead floated clouds of yellow leathery leaves, sometimes coarse gold where the breeze stirred them. The road opened out onto a field of some twenty acres on a flat of land beside the river.

Another man was already ahead of them driving a pair of horses down a row. The horses were hitched to a rhythmically shaking potato digger. Potatoes spilled out onto the loosened dirt behind the digger, big ones, little ones, most of them of the pale-tan variety. Sometimes the potatoes came jostling out of the earth so lively they resembled nests of gophers being uprooted.

Each taking a pail, Red and Timothy got down from their wagon and started picking up the potatoes. At first it wasn't very hard work and the pails filled fast. Even the pile in the wagon grew fast as they followed the potato digger around the field.

By the second time around Red's back began to ache. Bending over to pick potatoes awakened muscles he'd never known he had. Sticking a hog was a lot different.

Around ten o'clock Magdalena and two young boys came to help them. Timothy referred to the two boys as in-betweeners. They were between the age of fifteen and marriage. Magdalena gave Red a wondering look, her eyes blazing up a luminous gray for a fleeting second.

After another hour Red was surprised to see that Magdalena worked faster and harder than both Timothy and himself. Her nimble fingers picked up potatoes by threes and fours, heaping them in a pail, her body rising and falling effortlessly.

Just a few rods to the south and below them, the vast Missouri flowed and winked and dappled in the sun. Looking at the river, Red had the sensation that the bluffs on the far side were slowly marching to the northwest.

Red wondered when someone would come across the river with a boat to ask the Hutterites if they had seen anyone who might have swum across.

Magdalena found a potato that made her stop and laugh. She held it up to Timothy. "Look at this." She threw a quick dazzling side glance for Red to see too. The potato had four knobs, one on top, two on the bottom, and one ludicrously in the middle like it might be coming out of its belly button.

Timothy wasn't amused. "I've seen worse."

"Worse?" Magdalena cried with another laugh, her belly rolling out in an undulant motion. "Don't you mean better? This is the closest one I've ever seen yet to look like a human being."

Timothy eyed the knob on the potato's belly. "Just break off those knobs and throw 'em into your pail. They'll break off anyway."

Magdalena threw Timothy an arched look. With a laugh she broke off the head knob first and then the two leg knobs. "A perfect basket case but still able to be a father of potatoes."

Timothy stared at the obscene potato and then brusquely took it from her. He broke off the offending knob in the middle, tossed both it and what was left of the potato into his own pail. "What's the matter with you? Every time a stranger shows up you like to show off a little, don't you?"

"Sure. I'm still looking for a man," she said.

Red was amazed. The other women in the colony went about like sick chickens, but she acted bold.

Timothy said, "Trouble with you is, Magdalena, you're too choosy. You had your chance."

They went back to work.

Later on, after Magdalena with her swift fingers had worked herself some distance in advance of them, Red asked, "How old is she?"

"About thirty."

"What's wrong with her?"

"She says the men here are all too dumb. And that includes me."

Red's pail was full, and he emptied it into the wagon. "Otherwise she's all right?"

"Best worker we got. She often works with the men. She also knows her Bible better than most."

Sweat dripped off Red's chin. It made his whiskers itch. He hadn't shaved since he'd left South St. Paul. He looked at Timothy's bush. "You people probably won't mind if I let my beard grow?"

"You're married, ain't you?"

"Yes."

"We quit shaving when we get married. The Lord Jesus didn't shave."

"But the Lord Jesus never married."

Timothy said quietly, "The Church is the bride of Christ."

"That's right. My church teaches that too."

Timothy's pail was full, and he stumped over to the wagon to empty it. "One thing about Magdalena. Sex is okay in marriage. But in her case watch out for the heat in the eye."

By noon they'd got up three wagons full of potatoes. Red helped Timothy shovel them into the root cellar next to the kitchen.

The dinner bell rang. In a few moments the bearded menfolk began to drift in from all parts of the colony, walking slowly under the trees. The little children, fed ahead of time, full of pep, played running games across the grass.

The men sat at the same long hand-polished wooden table. The women brought the men huge bowls of steaming potatoes, boiled beef, mounds of yellow squash, string beans, three big dishes of colony-made golden butter, and a half dozen big round breads. The oldest man at the head of the table cut the bread. He cut liberal slices, at least an inch thick, and he wielded his big glittering knife with the flourish of a master. He liked to watch where each slice went, who got the end crust, who got the widest middle cut, and who got the in-betweens.

Red ate until he could hardly see. His cheeks stung with surfeit with all the well-buttered bites.

After a short rest on the benches under the trees, he and Timothy and Magdalena went at the potatoes again.

Some clouds moved in over the Missouri in the afternoon and it became cool out.

Magdalena said, "We better try and finish today. Spuds don't like frost."

Timothy surveyed the incoming line of clouds. "It won't freeze under that."

When the bell rang at five they weren't quite finished. There were still a dozen rows to go.

Timothy shrugged. "Well, that's it. We work here because we like to work, not because there's a slavedriver whipping us along."

They brought the potatoes to the yard. Red thought they might be able to shovel them off before dinner.

Timothy shook his head. "We'll let them stand till morning. We got to wash up now for church."

"Church? But this is a weekday."

A little red smile parted Timothy's brown bush of a beard. "We have church every night at five-thirty. And twice on Sunday."

They washed up. When Red looked in the mirror to comb his hair he didn't recognize the face he saw. It wasn't just the thickening reddish bristles over his chin and cheeks that threw him off; it was more that the person he now felt himself to be and the body he walked around in had separated. Wearing black clothes made Red feel he was an actor in a church play.

Timothy found a black Sunday jacket for Red. "The Lord loves a well-kept man," he said. The jacket was tight across Red's shoulders. Timothy smiled. "Too small, eh? Well, it'll have to do until the womenfolk can make you one to fit."

They walked across the yard toward a one-story wooden building marked "School House." They filed in behind other solemn men. The men all took seats on the left, the women on the right. All sat according to age, the youngest in the front seats, the oldest on the back benches. The council sat up front facing the congregation, the two preachers sitting behind the wide teacher's desk. The walls were bare and white, without a single decoration. There were no curtains.

After all were seated, a period of silence was observed. In the soft hush, heads were bowed in silent prayer.

Presently Michael Waldner, the preacher, nodded to the other old whiskered man sitting next to him, the assistant preacher.

The assistant preacher got to his feet and announced the hymn and read the first line. It was in strange German. Red understood only parts of it. Then the whole congregation took up the hymn, singing in slow majestic rhythms. Red was surprised to hear how lustily the women sang, almost drowning out the men's voices. Also they were a little in the lead of the men as if they wanted to speed up the tempo. The women might act pretty cowed on the yard and in the dining hall, but in church they really let go.

The hymn singing finished, the assistant preacher sat down and Michael Waldner got up. He stood quietly a moment behind the desk, sharp gray eyes roving over his people. Then in a low even voice he invited everyone to hear the word of God. He too spoke in that strange German tongue. Red managed to make out a little of what the preacher was saying. The world was merely a place of passage. Our true home was in heaven. Preacher Waldner also talked about the persecution in the old country. He told of a man who'd been so beaten up he had to be picked up and carried off in a linen cloth.

As he listened, Red had the strange feeling his real self was trying to reenter his new body.

Preacher Waldner read a little out of a flat leather tome. He read in a style from an old time. He instructed them not to walk after the flesh but to seek after the spirit. To be carnally minded was death. To be spiritually minded was life and peace.

Preacher Waldner next spoke in American. "You have noticed that we have a stranger in our midst. He needed refuge. We will not judge him. Jesus taught us that members of the brotherhood may show love for those that have been cast out. Our brethren often had to live in holes in the earth. And this man, who swam across a great river so that he might no longer live in such a hole, shall be given every chance to live inside the church. Because there is no hope of heaven if one dies outside the church. Therefore, be loving and kind to him."

Red almost cried.

"Christ is coming soon, very soon. Therefore, personal suffering is necessary so that we may be ready for him. Therefore, let us share our goods and be kind unto the old and the little ones and let us make a home for the penitent stranger. Amen."

Preacher Waldner slowly bowed his head, and everyone got down on his knees, faces lifted up, hands folded to chin. Preacher Waldner recited a long prayer softly in falling accents.

Then everyone stood up and headed for the dining hall.

Supper was simple: bread, cheese, fried potatoes, butter, and honey.

After supper, the children ran through the halls of the barracks playing games, running in and out of the rooms without fear of scolding, having a happy time. Some of the men put on topcoats and sat under the cottonwoods in the falling sunlight.

Red was shown a bare room with just a bed, a chair, a desk, and a pot under the bed. There were no pictures on the thick block walls. He found his old clothes cleaned and pressed and laid out on a shelf.

Tired, Red took off his black clothes and slipped under the blankets. The single window faced the great river. Spangles of light bounced off the river's surface where the sun still struck it and moved over the ceiling in his room.

Soon he heard singing. The womenfolk in the kitchen, where they were washing dishes, repeated the hymn sung in church. They sang for a long time. Then in the various rooms in the barracks there was more singing, mostly hymns. The Hutterites had good voices and they sang joyfully. They lost themselves in it as though it were a sweet confession ever pleasant to make. A few male voices rose high over it all in a strange eerie otherworldly falsetto.

# Chapter 28

# ALAN

A few days later Alan reported back for work.

Burt looked up from his corner, where he was slowly crafting out another one of his meticulous columns. "Well, look who's here. Our rambling tumbleweed is back."

"Hi, guys."

Quinsey and Hank looked up smiling from their typewriters, where they too were pecking out stories for the day. Mark, sitting in the slot, stuck another story in a brass capsule and shot it up the pneumatic tube. "Hi."

Alan sat down facing Burt. "My boxer friend has just totally vanished. I checked everywhere down there. And unless they're the coolest liars in the world, his relatives don't know where he is either."

"The cops are still looking?"

"Everywhere. He's left no clue."

"What did the city desk say?" Burt asked.

"For now they're dropping it."

"What about you?"

"In my spare time I'm gonna keep after it."

"Good."

"Specially since I found out that I'm related to him."

"What?"

"Yep. He's my full second cousin. I've got a stake in it now."

Mark in the slot piped up, "Relative, eh? Think you can be objective about it then?"

"No. But it will make me hot to find out."

Burt pursed his lips, working them in and out. "Alan, relative or not, stay on the story as you can. When you find something, bring it to me."

"Okay."

Later in the morning Alan couldn't get a copy boy to get him a cut from the library for a story he was writing. The city desk was on to something important and all the boys were busy scurrying around up there answering roars for a "Boy!" here and a "Boy!" there. Alan finally went down himself to get the cut.

He found Irene Crist at Roberta's desk. He hadn't seen Irene in a while. "Well. Hi."

"Hi yourself."

He told her what he needed.

Irene looked in the files and found the cut for him. A part-mischievous, part-strained expression worked in her thin lips. Her eyes looked unnaturally large behind her thick glasses. "I hear you've been away."

"Yes. Down in Siouxland covering a story."

"Hope you had fun."

"I did. And you? What have you been doing? Back with your husband?"

"Yes and no."

Alan couldn't resist being blunt. "I take it that means you're living with him but not sleeping with him."

"Something like that."

"What a waste."

Her mannish lips thinned and her heavy jaw came out. "That's what I think too."

"Maybe we ought to do something about that."

"Maybe we should."

Alan checked around in the dimly lighted library. "Where's Roberta?"

"She's home with a headache."

"You're doing double duty then."

"Yes. Until ten tonight."

"Got a ride home?"

She began to smile to herself. "Streetcar."

"Listen. I got some catching up to do upstairs and I'm staying on until about then. I'll take you home."

She spoke softly, so softly he almost didn't hear her. "All right."

Alan worked right through dinnertime until nine o'clock. Then he went down and had himself a T-bone steak at Kirk's cafe-and-poolhall.

Alan propped a fresh newspaper against the catsup bottle and the sugar jar. All the while that he read the news and absentmindedly cut up his steak, his mind was also busy with something else. He really shouldn't be seeing Irene Crist. For one thing it was wrong so long as she was married. For another he really didn't like her all that well so as to jeopardize her marriage. But he was so lonesome for affection that he was ready to reach out for almost anything. Having lost Jael to Shelby made it all the worse.

He finished his late dinner at ten. He strolled over to the *Chronicle* entrance and was pleased to see Irene waiting for him. Smiling, he took her arm and led her across the street, jaywalking, and then helped her into his old blue Dodge.

He started down Hiawatha.

"Where are you going?" she asked, smiling covertly out of her coat collar. "I don't live with my mother anymore."

"That's right. Where do you live now?"

"Highland Park. Over in St. Paul."

He nodded. A better class of people lived there. He headed the car in that direction, taking the West River Road along the Mississippi River gorge.

"Though there is no rush to go home."

"There isn't?"

"Not really. He goes his way and I go mine."

Alan quirked an eyebrow at her. "I've heard that some of the English gentlemen prefer blonds . . . if the blonds are little boys."

Irene lowered her head. "There are some American gentlemen who have the same preferences."

"I suppose there are." He circled the next island in the road and headed back up the river. "What really is the trouble between you two?"

"He despises America. And wants me to live in England. Well, I hate to leave my mother alone here. I wouldn't be able to visit her much."

Alan mused over the steering wheel. "I wouldn't mind a trip to England."

"A trip, yes. But to live there?"

They rolled across the Franklin Avenue bridge. The Mississippi moved under them like a vast sheet of black tar speckled with dancing yellow dots. They cruised up the East River Road, going up past the back side of the University Hospitals. About a third of the windows were lit up. They crossed the University of Minnesota campus, going past the law school, the library, Northrop Auditorium, and finally the Mall. And soon they pulled up at Alan's house.

"I'm going to leave it up to you, Irene. We can talk here. Or we can go up to my rooms."

She rustled about inside her coat. She crossed her legs, her stockings whistling in the dark of the car. She appeared to swell up with indecision.

He leaned toward her. "At least let's have a kiss."

She first held her face away from him. But when he gently but firmly took her strong chin in hand and turned her head, she finally let go and kissed him.

Some students walking by spotted Alan and Irene in the car and began laughing about them.

"Frat boys," Alan said. "Let's go upstairs."

"All right."

"No regrets now?"

"No regrets. I can't go on living like this with no touchings."

As he opened the front door, he said, "My landlady doesn't like it if I have a girl up in my rooms. Here, let me pick you up and I'll carry you. Then all she'll hear is one set of feet walking up."

She put her arms around his neck and he lifted her and took her upstairs.

Just as they were to enter his rooms, she put a hand to his ear. "Don't put any lights on."

His heart began to beat very fast. He carried her over the threshold. He slid his feet along the floor until his knees struck the bed. Then he lowered her gently. He sat down beside her.

He turned to kiss her. He could barely make out her face in the vague light coming from the streetlamp outside.

She ducked away and instead stood up and dropped her coat off her shoulders. She stood wavering a moment.

"Irene."

"Oh, what the heck," she said, and catching up the hem of her dress and flipping it upward as she crossed her arms she removed her dress.

He kicked off his shoes and slipped out of his jacket and loosened his tie.

They sat on the edge of the bed awhile, kissing, and finally together fell back on the bed.

"Be rough with me." She laughed a bit wild in the dark. "To make up for all those times when he didn't."

"Shh, not so loud," he whispered.

"Can she hear us up here?"

"No. But I got two new neighbors upstairs here. A couple of puritans from Pella, Iowa. They keep looking at me as though I'm the devil incarnate."

"God, I hope you can be a devil tonight."

They became warm together in the dimly lit room. It was winter outside but they still heard an oriole sing twice.

After a lovely wondering silence, eyes stirring idly under closed lids, they sat up together.

"What time is it?" Irene asked.

"I'll have to put on a light. This wristwatch isn't much help in the dark."

"Skip it. He won't be home yet anyway."

He drove her once more down the West River Road and then across the Mississippi into Highland Park.

Irene picked her nose in the dark, thinking he wouldn't see her do it.

When they came to within a block of her apartment she asked him to stop. "I think I better walk in alone from here. Play it safe."

"As you wish."

She gave him a quick kiss and left in a rush of whistling stockings.

He watched her until she'd safely disappeared through the front door of her apartment house.

Two weeks later, as Alan stepped into the elevator in the *Chronicle* building, he ran into Roberta. With Roberta was Jerre Thornton, Jael's friend.

Roberta arched her back becomingly. "I suppose you heard about Irene."

"No. What's happened?"

"She finally did it. Cut the umbilical cord."

"You mean, she went to England with her husband?"

"Yes. She quit her job a week ago. By now she's somewhere far out on the Atlantic."

Alan fell into a reverie. Never dip your pen in the company ink.

The elevator creaked slowly upward.

Roberta said, "Alan, have you met Irene's replacement?"

Alan smiled. "Oh yes. Jerre and I once had an occasion to meet." He liked Jerre's brownish blond hair and thoughtful blue eyes.

Jerre asked, "Have you heard from Jael lately?"

"Not a word."

The elevator stopped for the library floor. As Jerre followed Roberta out, she said, "I haven't either. And I'm a little worried. She and Shelby ran off to Milwaukee and got married, you know. They're going to have a baby."

"Yes, I know." Alan let the grating close. "Glad to see you again, Jerre."

"Glad to see you again too, Alan."

As the elevator continued on up to the next floor, Alan thought: "Jerre's blue eyes really look at you. Level and steady. And she's going to grow into her beauty; not have it fade on her."

It hurt to think about Jael again. "Let's hope she knows whose baby it is," he thought.

# Chapter 29

# RED

Four months later, in February, Red was named temporary hay boss. His job was to keep a good supply of hay in the mow in the horse barn. Every day when the weather was good he went out with a team of horses and a rack and brought in hay from the stacks in the wild sloughs. It was hard work. Some of the haystacks had been rained on just before last fall's first frost, and he had to chop his way down through the top layers with a hay knife.

There never was any rush. They were feeding only six horses for use on the yard and to go to town with during the winter, while the rest of the herd ran wild in the draws of the pastures north of the buildings. Horses wintered well. They were good at digging grass out of deep snow.

One afternoon, after Red had finished unloading another jag of hay into the mow, he decided he could use a rest. His shoulders and back ached. He set the fork into a crevice in the floor of the rack, made sure the team of grays was securely tied to a post near the corner of the barn, and then, climbing through the door, stepped down to the floor of the mow. Most of the mow was stacked high with hay, but the pile sloped off near the door. He opened his dark mackinaw and dropped onto the hay. There was no wind outside, and it was warm in the mow. A good smell of dried daisies rose from the hay. He napped.

He was awakened by crackling hay. Opening his eyes, he was surprised to see Magdalena standing at his feet. She'd climbed up the ladder into the mow and was carrying an egg pail.

She smiled down at him with glowing eyes. "Lazy."

"Well, I worked hard. Besides, it's not like we have to hurry to get a crop in."

"Pretty nice. With the mow door facing away from the yard where nobody can see what you're doing, you thought you could get away with it."

He stretched until every muscle in his body felt better. He didn't like being awakened. Though if somebody had to awaken him, better that it was Magdalena. He'd come to like her. During the winter they'd become good friends, though at no time did either one make it appear he was courting her. They often stopped to chat after worship or after an evening meal, and sometimes when they ran into each other while visiting a neighbor in the barracks. The brotherhood continued to be all one family for them both, and they behaved very much as though they were brother and sister.

Magdalena said, "Well, George, can't say as I blame you much. Winter always gets me down. Around about now in February I get the darks. Especially living single like this."

Red nodded. He too had begun to miss sleeping with Jen very much. Jen had never been too eager for sex, but every now and then she would pleasure him, and it had always been a soothing thing. The last several weeks he'd awakened nights full of desire and hadn't known what to do except pray for strength to combat it. Preacher Mike Waldner had preached a special sermon on the subject for the in-betweens and other single men.

Magdalena set the egg pail down and settled beside him on the sloping slough hay. "Ever get lonesome for your wife?"

Red started. What did she know? He countered, "Don't you ever get lonesome for your man?"

"Yes, I do. I'm sorry I didn't marry him."

"Then you had relations with him?"

"I sure did. And it was a lot of fun too."

Magdalena was someone to dream about. Red still loved Jen, but Jen was gone now and here was this fine-looking woman to hand and it was easy to see she liked him, and so why not, what the heck, pretty soon the law would catch up with him and then all relations with a woman would be forbidden him forever.

Magdalena slowly smiled at him. Her gray eyes turned into a racing silver. "When are you gonna ever kiss me?"

Red blushed. Then two things began to happen to him. Desire stirred in his thighs until it hurt. And that clamping motion of a shell slowly compressing his brain took over again.

"It's hard for me to believe that a man of your age can be so shy."

"But it's a sin, Magdalena, so long as we live here with these wonderful religious people."

"Well, some of them do have children, don't they?"

Red could hardly stand it. He had to shift in the hay to ease the tightness in his thigh. "They're married."

"Well?"

Red shook his head. His hands felt warm, sweaty, and he took off his mittens.

"Why not? What have you done, George?"

He clammed up.

Magdalena took off her mittens too and stuffed them in the pockets of her heavy black velvet coat. Then she reached up and cupped his chin in her hand. "Kiss me."

"No."

"Then I will." She leaned toward him and kissed him full on the lips. Her lips opened a little and were moist.

Red shuddered he was so thick with it. Jen had never given him wet kisses. Jen's had always been dry.

Magdalena opened her coat and draped part of it over him. "Come. Kiss me. It has been so long. Believe me, it is well worth condemnation." Her leg moved under her voluminous black dress and lay over his thighs where he was thickest.

Desire won out. It pushed the shell to one side. He grabbed her and hugged her and rolled her over on her back. He pulled up her dress. He became abrupt and rough.

"Just a minute here, mister. Not like that."

Rebuffed, Red slackened off.

"We're not animals of the field, you know. Like you're a bull that just humps himself up on a cow and then kebang is done."

"Well then, how must I . . . ?"

"Play a little first. I want some hugging and kissing first. A lot of it. I want it to last a long time. Otherwise it'll just be a chore for me."

"Oh."

She rose a little under him. "You don't know that a woman can enjoy it like a man?"

"Well, she has her fun, I suppose. Having him in her."

"That's all for a woman? Ohh. I can see already that you are a real greenhorn. Thank God, my first man was wonderful in bed at least. He taught me to enjoy it like he did. Not that he knew that from the beginning. He'd read it in a book written by a woman."

Red was astounded. "You mean, a woman actually wrote a book about a man and a woman doing it?"

"That's right. She was a brave woman. I read it then too."

"How in the world did you land in a place like this after that?"

"Hey, hey, why shouldn't these women here know about that too?"

Magdalena laughed out loud. "Judging by the looks of some of the couples, they've learned about it too. You can always spot such a woman. She smiles easier and walks around like she's got a secret she's glad she found out about."

"Well, how does this work then for the woman?"

Magdalena laughed some more. "This sure is a funny way for us to be talking up in a hay mow. And like you say, in a brotherhood yet."

"How does it, though?"

"When a man spills his seed, he faints a little, doesn't he?"

"Yes, I guess he does."

"A woman can faint like that too. And can have just as much fun in it."

"What happens if she don't?"

"She can get crabby. Or sickly. Or unhappy with her life. She can even have miscarriages. But the worst is, she misses a chance to like her husband as much as he likes her."

Miscarriages. For godsakes. So maybe that was the trouble with Jen. Poor woman. "According to this woman writer, would it help such a wife to go see a doctor?"

Magdalena almost hooted. "This woman writer said that most doctors are ignoramuses when it comes to sex. They're almost worse than ministers. And it's mostly because talking about sex is dangerous for doctors. Some husband might come shooting for them."

"But there are some doctors who might know?"

Magdalena smiled at him with a gleam in her eye. She had caught on he was thinking of his woman somewhere. "Yes, but you have to hope you land in the hands of the right one."

Red thought to himself. Jen never did get out of it what he did. She often lay there like a trapped mouse. But the worst was, she kept losing all them babies. Too bad she was gone. It would have been wonderful for her to have had that.

"Come," Magdalena said, drawing him close again. "Come, I'll teach you how. But go slow now. There's no hurry. We're not hurrying to get a crop in."

Red filled with hunger for her again. He discovered that Magdalena was not wearing underwear.

Magdalena teased him. "Wow, what a gopher you got there. He sure likes to sit up and take notice of things."

Two months later, in early April, it was time to work in the gardens again.

Timothy and Magdalena and Red planted onion sets in long rows across freshly plowed black earth. Each one followed a string stretched taut between two stakes to make the rows straight. Timothy's method was to make a hole in the ground with a pointed stob, then drop in a little brown onion, and close the hole with a stomp of his foot, leaving a wispy tail sticking out. Magdalena preferred to plant while down on her knees, making the little hole with a forefinger and then dropping the tiny onion in. Red liked Magdalena's method best, except that he used his thumb for a digger.

It was warm out. The buds on the cottonwood trees had thickened, resembling squirrel fists. Birds had come north, their beaks open and singing all morning long.

Red slowly fell behind Timothy and Magdalena. Soon by the time he reached one end of the field they were at the other end. He tried to plant faster but somehow couldn't gain on them.

He was nearing the end of the field again when a gopher popped up out of its hole a dozen feet away. It sat on its tail and looked at him, nose twitching, head swiveling this way and that.

Red reached for a clod and threw it at the gopher. The gopher let go with a tiny animal shriek and ducked down its hole.

Presently the same gopher popped out of a hole farther along. Its lips worked in an odd way as though it were trying to dislodge something caught between its teeth with its tongue.

Red made a lunging motion with his head. The gopher ducked out of sight again.

A dozen onion sets later, the gopher reappeared from yet a farther hole, sitting on its tail. The gopher cocked its head this way and that, seemingly looking around to see where Magdalena and Timothy were, then worked its lips a couple of more times. "Quit looking at Magdalena. You haven't paid for Jen yet."

Red quick looked around to see where Magdalena and Timothy were. They were too far away to have heard.

The gopher crooked its head around at Red in a critical manner. It was a handsome gopher with black stripes running down its back and with a gleaming yellow belly.

Red had second thoughts. Maybe he'd only imagined the voice coming from the gopher. The other times he'd heard the voice speaking behind him and slightly up on the right.

"You haven't paid for Jen yet," the voice repeated.

"I know that."

Magdalena had moved up closer. She heard Red. "What?"

"Nothing," Red said quickly. To disarm her he smiled at her. "I was only talking to myself. You know."

Magdalena nodded. "I do it myself sometimes. Especially when I hear voices."

"You . . . hear . . . voices?"

"Yes. If it isn't God talking to me."

"You mean, you sometimes hear a voice talking from behind you?"

"Yes."

"Oh."

"That's not so strange. A lot of Christians hear them."

"Oh."

Red went back to planting onion sets, jabbing his thumb into the earth and then dropping in a spindling onion. When he looked up moments later the gopher had disappeared.

His head really began to feel compressed and the hant voice spoke up again. "It's time for you to leave the colony."

"Why?" Red whispered, low.

"Because it's time to pay your debts. All those of the Little Church faith pay their debts."

"But I was beginning to enjoy this brotherhood."

"Yes, so I see. She's pretty nice, ain't she?"

"Don't be nuts!" Red exploded.

"What?" Magdalena said, pausing in her planting.

"Nothing," Red said quickly. "Nothing." He laughed a light laugh. "I guess I was talking to myself again."

"Better watch that," Magdalena said with a smile, "or people'll begin to talk. Like they do about me sometimes. You know." And she pointed a finger at her temple and whirled it around several times.

Red planted some more. Wet dirt had begun to plak up on his knees and he brushed it off with the side of his hand. He began to plant his onions erratically. He jabbed them into the earth instead of planting them with a loving touch. Onions would not thrive unless planted tenderly. "I'm not my own boss anymore," he murmured.

Magdalena had caught up even with him in the next row. "What?"

"Was I talking to myself again?"

Magdalena looked at him gravely. "Are you all right?"

"Sure."

She shook her head a little and went on planting.

Red became quite upset and fumbled with his onions. He had to reset some of them a couple of times.

He planted slower. He wanted Magdalena to gain on him, get her out of earshot. He looked back to see where Timothy was. Timothy was about the same distance behind him.

The hant voice behind him spoke once more. "So you've fallen in love with Magdalena, eh? What about Jen?"

"Jen's dead. You know that."

"Just as sure as God's in His heaven, word is going to trickle back to even this place what you done to her."

Red jabbed more onion sets into the black earth.

"Repentance is good for the soul, my friend."

Red rammed one more little onion into the earth—and then gave up. He stood up, closed his little sack of onion sets, and headed back toward Timothy.

Magdalena called after him, "Where you going?"

Red ignored her. A couple of steps more and he stopped in front of Timothy. "Boss?"

Timothy looked up.

"Boss, I've got to go in and see the preacher about something."

"Is it important?"

"I have something to confess to him."

"That's different. Go, brother, and God be with you."

"Thanks. What shall I do with what's left of these onion sets?"

"Give them to me. I'll plant them."

Red placed the little sack of onion sets on the ground near Timothy, then headed for the yard.

He could sense as he walked away that Magdalena was feeling sorry for him.

When he arrived on the yard, it was just recess time and the children were playing under the cottonwoods, David, Tim, Eddie, Gary, Ellis. It made him weep inside when he saw those little boys. He didn't have a boy of his own. He and Jen had tried so hard, and all they'd got for their efforts was a bunch of miscarriages. His whole life was a case of miscarriages.

He walked swiftly through the sparse shadows and headed directly for Michael Waldner's room. Several of the young women, washing the milk pails, stopped to watch him go. They looked at him wonderingly.

He rapped on Waldner's door.

"Come in."

Red stepped in. He found Waldner sitting at his table reading in the old leather-bound book, the one written with a feather. Waldner had on a new set of blue suspenders and they matched his blue socks exactly. Waldner's black denim pants were baggier than usual.

"You don't need to knock on my door, son. Most people just walk in. We have no secrets from each other here. Sit down."

Red settled in a chair across the table from Waldner. "But I have a secret."

Waldner's wise old gray eyes waited. His parchment face remained relaxed.

"My name is not George Haron. It's John Engleking. And they usually call me Red."

Waldner's hands closed the old leather-bound book. "So."

"And I think I killed my wife in South St. Paul. In fact, I know I killed her."

Waldner spoke in a clear easy voice. "How did it happen?"

"I was working in the Steele Packinghouse hog kill. I hated that place. That was why when I first got here I didn't want to work with Ted Glanzer and his hogs. And I guess the hog kill finally got to me. I went berserk one day and the next thing I knew I found myself standing in our bedroom. There on the bed lay my wife Jen, stabbed to death. There was blood all over my hands. And it came to me that I'd done it when I was out of my head. And then I ran."

"Didn't you notice you had the knife with you when you walked home?"

"No."

"I see." Waldner slowly folded his arms.

"She's dead all right, Mr. Waldner."

"George . . . John . . . what is the state of your soul today?"

"That I'm terribly sorry about it. So sorry I don't know how to begin to tell you. That I'm beginning to hear voices. I heard one just a few minutes ago."

"Ah."

"It's time I went back to South St. Paul to pay for what I did to Jen."

"Ah."

"When a fellow begins to hear voices, he's reached the end of his rope. If he ain't already gone crazy."

"Christ will help you through."

"Yes, I guess I know that now."

"You are sure?"

"Yes. You sometimes hear voices, don't you?"

"Yes. I hear God talking to me. He speaks through my conscience."

Red fingered the corner of the yellow tablecloth where it hung over the edge of the table. "Doesn't it say somewhere in the Bible that God sometimes talks to one out of the middle of a cloud?"

Waldner's old veined nostrils moved. "Yes, God sometimes reveals Himself in strange ways."

Red stood up. "Can I have my money back? I'll need it to travel with."

Waldner fell into deep thought. He stroked his gray beard. He lifted a suspender and let it snap. "Son, sit down a minute. I have a suggestion to make."

Red sat down.

"Son, I think I'll go with you to the Twin Cities."

Red's eyes opened. "To make sure I do report to the police there?"

"No. No. What I had in mind was to go with you to a pastor of your own church and tell him what a good worker you've been here at our colony. That we respect you. That you are not a criminal. A troubled man, yes; a criminal, no."

"Oh."

"Does your church have a congregation there?"

Red looked down. "Yes. In Minneapolis."

"Then you didn't attend church while in the Cities?"

"No. Jen didn't care for my church."

Waldner crooked his head to one side, sharp eyes gradually becoming kindly. "Well, you've attended religious service faithfully while here. All this I want to point out to your pastor." Waldner ran the backs of his fingernails up and down his brown vest. The shirt collar of his black shirt showed dandruff. "What is your pastor's name there?"

"Reverend Gabrielson. He came from Edgerton. Not too far from where Pa lives. They used to call him Pinky before he became a minister."

"Well, I'm going to bring you to Reverend Gabrielson. And then you and he can decide what to do next. Go to the police or not. But first you must report to your own church, before you report to the civil authorities. God is above the law."

"Mr. Waldner, you don't have to go along with me, because you don't really have to worry about me not doing the right thing."

"Son, it just happens that we've decided that I should go to the Twin Cities on business. We have two tons of honey we don't know what to do with. The little towns around here are already oversupplied." As Waldner played with his beard the round white spot in it took on different shapes. "So we thought we could maybe trade the honey for some farm equipment. We've been in contact with an Arthur Porter of the Porter Electric Company who is interested in such a deal."

"Oh. That's different."

"I think maybe you should go to your room now and change into your old clothes. And I'll see to it that you get your ten dollars back. And then early tomorrow morning we'll have one of the boys drive us to Sioux Falls, where we'll catch a train for Minneapolis."

"All right, Mr. Waldner."

Red went to his room and changed into his old clothes, blue jeans, blue workshirt, blue denim jacket. He set out his blue denim cap on the table ready to go. Very neatly he folded up his colony black clothes and placed them on a chair.

Later that night, Red said goodbye to everybody, Ted Glanzer, Timothy Hofer, and all the little children.

Magdalena took it in stride. "I always knew that I'd never get you. Well, I'll just chalk it up to experience. Besides, I think it's time I leave here myself. I don't deserve to live with these people. I've sinned too much against their precepts. Also, like you, I have a few debts to pay."

The next day, late in the afternoon, they arrived at the Great Northern depot in Minneapolis. The high dome of the depot echoed with the clangor of switching engines and the orotund calls of the dispatcher. Passengers hurried through wisps of sweet steam.

Waldner, for all his old-country black clothes and his round black hat, was city-wise. He led Red out to the front of the depot and hailed a taxi. When Red fumbled out his two five-dollar bills to have the fare ready, Waldner gently pushed his money away.

"But it's my turn now," Red protested. "You paid for my train ticket."

"No, the colony paid for the ticket, just as it will pay for this. After all, haven't you been a good worker for us all these months?"

The taxi took them swiftly and easily south to the parsonage of the Christian Church on Twenty-eighth Street. There was the smell of a woman's lingering perfume in the yellow taxi.

Waldner paid the driver as they got out. "Now," Waldner said, setting his round black hat firmly on his bald head, "let us see what sort of pastor Reverend Gabrielson is. We want a forgiving man for what lies ahead."

Waldner rang the bell. The parsonage was a green-and-white bungalow. To the right of it stood the church, a modest structure with a square tower and square windows.

Presently the door opened. A plump woman with brown eyes, brown hair, and a naturally good smile greeted them. "Hello."

Waldner removed his hat and held it against his chest. "Is the reverend in?"

"Yes, he is. Step in, won't you?"

They were ushered into a dusky living room. The curtains were partially drawn. A brown mohair davenport and two mohair chairs stood squared around a large glass-topped coffee table. The wall-to-wall beige carpet was thick. Someone had just baked some coconut cookies.

"Please sit down. I'll go get him."

Red sat down on the edge of an easy chair and hooked his blue cap over his kneee. Waldner sat with his round black hat in his lap. He propped his elbows up on the wide mohair arms of his chair and with his fingers formed a steeple over his mouth. The white spot in his beard under the shadow of the steeple resembled a second mouth.

Reverend Gabrielson came in briskly. He had a round pink face with a high forehead and upshooting curly brown hair. His thick red lips formed a natural smile. He couldn't have frowned if he tried. "Well, well, I am Reverend Gabrielson."

Both Waldner and Red got to their feet.

"Sit down, sit down."

Waldner introduced himself, then introduced Red. "We've come to you first before we go to the police."

"Oh?" Reverend Gabrielson took a hardback chair and drew it up to the coffee table.

"Yes. We are Hutterites and we live in the Bon Homme Colony on the Missouri River west of Yankton, South Dakota. We are pacifists. We are a community ruled by love. In the past we have taken in persecuted refugees. This man suddenly appeared at our door one morning, cold, wet, miserable. He'd swum the Missouri. He has been with us at the colony for some months now."

Reverend Gabrielson flicked a wondering look at Red.

"He has been a good man with us. He has worked hard. He has attended our services. He has been kind to the little children. He is a gentle man."

Reverend Gabrielson cracked his fingers by pressing one fist inside the other. "Excuse me, but what is all this leading up to?"

Waldner slowly stroked his beard. He was not going to be rushed. "We are very much like the Dakota Sioux. It is not for nothing that we have settled in their land, land that was taken away from them by other whites. Like the Sioux, we strive not for self-expression or self-interest, but strive to understand how we are related to all beings and all things. All is one and one is all."

Red blinked back tears. Red wished his father could have been like Waldner.

"That is why we didn't ask this man any questions. We felt that, given time, he would tell us what was wrong."

Reverend Gabrielson kept flicking looks at Red.

"Yesterday, this man came to me and confessed. He told me that he thinks he killed his wife in South St. Paul."

"So that's it!" Reverend Gabrielson exclaimed, brown eyes flashing. "I remember reading about you last fall. Red Engleking. The boxer. I spotted the name at the time and then I knew I'd met you somewhere."

Red began to sweat. "Yes, in Edgerton. With my father."

"Fat John. That's right." Reverend Gabrielson cracked his knuckles some more. "Hmm." Then he gave Red a level look. "So you've been with Hutterites all this time. When the whole world has been looking for you. I'll bet you don't know what really happened, do you?"

Red and Waldner looked at each other. Both sat up.

"You didn't know that your wife is alive and well."

Red sank back in his chair. "She . . . is?"

A wonderful smile moved in Waldner's beard.

Reverend Gabrielson went on. "Yes. You missed her vital parts."

Red's eyes almost popped out. "Man, I'll bet she hates me after what I did to her."

"No, that's the interesting thing. She doesn't. The law wanted her to make a complaint against you. To prosecute you. But she refused."

"My Jen refused?"

"Yes."

Waldner said, "Then the law isn't looking for him anymore?"

Reverend Gabrielson said, "No. With no complaint the law doesn't know anything."

Red said, "But wasn't the papers full of it? Och, I just squirm inside when I think of it."

"Yes, the papers were full of it. But what does that prove? Nothing. That's only hearsay. No, the law has to have a fact before it can act, and in this instance the only fact it can act on was if the wife had filed a complaint. She didn't, and you are free."

Red sat stunned. He looked warily around in Reverend Gabrielson's living room. There was bound to be some kind of catch somewhere.

Reverend Gabrielson had a question. "What I am curious about, though, is why you two came to me."

Waldner stroked his beard. "This man told me he was raised in the faith of the Christian Church in Bonnie. He did say he didn't go to your church here. But I felt that I should still turn him over to a preacher of his faith near the scene of the crime. God comes first and then comes man's law."

Reverend Gabrielson nodded. "Now I get it. Soo." He turned to Red. "Well, son, you're free to go. That is, if your conscience says you're free."

Waldner raised a hand. "Maybe he should go to his wife now to see what she has to say about it all. If she bears him no grudge, and has truly forgiven him, then all he has left to worry about is, why did he attack her in the first place? And fail?"

"True," Reverend Gabrielson said.

Waldner stood up. "Well, John Engleking, I've brought you safely to harbor and now I can go. I have much work yet to do before I leave the Twin Cities tomorrow."

Reverend Gabrielson stood up too. "Won't you stay for dinner?"

"No, I must get on with my errands." Waldner held out a hand to Red. "May God smile kindly on you from now on forever more."

Red stood up and grabbed Waldner's hand in both of his. "I can't thank you enough for what you did for me. Giving me a home until I could get my head screwed on straight again. The colony was a good place to heal up in."

Waldner said, "If you ever get in that part of the country again, please drop by. We shall always be glad to see you."

"I will." The tears rolled down Red's cheeks. "I will."

Reverend Waldner left.

Red headed for the door too.

Reverend Gabrielson gently took Red by the arm. "How about you staying for dinner though?"

"No, I better go see Jen."

"Are you sure you're ready to see her?"

"I think so."

"Come, sit down with me a moment. Like Mr. Waldner says,

maybe you should give thought as to why you tried to hurt her in the first place. And deliberately missed her."

Red let himself be led back to his chair.

Reverend Gabrielson looked around in the living room. "Heh, it's so dark in here. My wife always has it so dusky. She's got it in her head that light fades things." He went over and raised the blinds along the south side. Light bloomed into the living room. "Now, that's better. It's always good to shed a little light on things." He took the chair Waldner had sat in. "Now, is there anything you'd like to tell me? To make sure that your heart is clean? Pure? Because surely a part of you must have had some reason for wanting to strike her."

Red looked down at where his fingers were twirling his blue denim cap around and around.

Reverend Gabrielson gave him a warm smile. "Look, I mean you no harm. I don't even ask that after this you come to my church here on Twenty-eighth. But naturally I am concerned about you. You. What turmoil there must have been in you before you went . . . berserk."

A shaft of afternoon light fell across Red's neck and back. Red thought to himself: "This is something I should talk to my wife about. Not him."

"Red?"

Red stood up. "No, I think I better first go see Jen."

"How about a cup of coffee first?"

Red looked Reverend Gabrielson in the eye. "I get it. You're worried that I may go hurt Jen some more."

"In part, yes. And also I have concern for the state of your soul."

Red thought: "Bid him a polite goodbye and go. He wants to find out about your hearing voices and then you'll really be in trouble. Because those voices are the state of your soul." Red said, "I gotta go. I'm sorry."

Reverend Gabrielson said, "Well, wouldn't you at least want me to offer a prayer to God in your behalf?"

"Well . . ."

"Come, let us pray. There's nothing so comforting and as blessed as two people praying together."

Reluctantly Red sat down again. He didn't fold his hands; just balled them up tight inside his blue cap.

Reverend Gabrielson folded his hands and lifted his pink face to the ceiling. "Heavenly Father, we come to Thee in the late afternoon of this day to plead for mercy and forgiveness for this once lost soul. We thank Thee for bringing him back. We thank the Holy Ghost for having entered his heart and for having persuaded him to return home to pay his just debt to society. He is now going back to his wife. May the two of them at last find peace with each other. May her heart be filled with forgiveness; may his heart be filled with forgiveness in turn for whatever it was in her that made him think of hurting her in the first place. Let the rivers of their lives flow smoothly and silently together as one stream again. In Jesus' name we ask it. Amen."

Red stood up. "Now I've really got to go."

"Of course." Reverend Gabrielson stood up too. "Just a minute while I get my hat. I'm going to take you home."

"Oh, but I can take a streetcar."

"I won't hear of it. I'm taking you home."

Red didn't like it. He was anxious to get away from the minister. He wanted to be with his own thoughts, alone, before walking into his own house.

Reverend Gabrielson got his hat, a rakish brown model. "Come."

"All right. I'll let you take me to the stockyards. But from there I want to walk. Alone."

They stepped out of the house and got into a green Chevy standing in the driveway.

Reverend Gabrielson started up the motor and then once more, as if he weren't very happy that Red was getting away without really having confessed what happened, cracked his knuckles together. With a sigh, he shifted into reverse and backed out onto the street.

Red got off at Steele Avenue.

He didn't move until he was sure Reverend Gabrielson had disappeared around a corner. Then he decided to retrace what must have been his steps that last time he'd come home from the Steele Packinghouse.

He walked all the way down to the main gate. He stood staring at it awhile. It was by now very late in the afternoon. The workers had all gone home, the gate was closed, and the guards had left.

He tried to imagine what he must have looked like that day, bloody sticking knife still in hand. Funny that nobody had stopped him.

For the life of him he couldn't remember a thing from the time when Simes kicked him in the rear and yelled at him to stick her, until he woke up standing over his wife Jen lying in their bed and wondering who had killed her.

Red turned and headed back up Steele Avenue toward Nick's

Cafe. A truck pulled out of an alley ahead of him, also headed toward Nick's. The driver waved at him as if he knew him.

A steamboat whistled long and lonesome on the Mississippi River behind the packing plant. It meant the ice had gone out of the river and spring had at last come to the far north country.

He stopped a moment to peek through the plate-glass windows of Nick's Cafe to see who might be around. Suppertime there usually weren't many customers, mostly just beer sots who had nothing to go home to. He thought he recognized a foreman from another department in Steele. He made out Nick talking to the cook in back.

Slowly he turned up the path past Nick's and began to climb the stiff bluff. There were no fresh tracks. Apparently no one had used the path since he'd climbed it last fall. He stepped through the hole in the chain-link fence and crossed the backyard. No one was about. All the backyards up and down the line were empty.

He stood a moment at the foot of the back steps. He was pleased to see that he wasn't trembling. In the old days his nerves would have been in a swivet. Ever since he'd hurt Jen he'd pretty well licked those bad nerves.

Red went up the steps and opened the door onto the back porch.

Everything was spick-and-span. His freshly washed work clothes hung on their usual hooks behind the door. The garbage can had the cover on tight and didn't smell. There was no dust on the little work table under the north window. His rubbers and galoshes stood in a neat row under the table. The smell was sweet and clean. His glance went to the work clothes behind the door. For goodness sakes. Even his bloody leather apron had been scrubbed and cleaned. He hoped that was a good sign for what was to come.

Easy, he turned the knob of the door to the kitchen and stepped inside. He closed the door behind him softly. He took off his cap and combed back his hair with his fingers.

Jen was working over the stove. An overhead light gave her face and hair the look of a cameo. There was no sign of a scar on her face. She was turning over the fried potatoes with a turner.

Red spoke softly, remembering how Jen always jumped when he didn't call out her name first to let her know he was coming. One had to approach her as one approached a horse from the rear, first letting it know you were standing behind it. "Jen? Hi."

Jen surprised him. She turned slowly, calmly, and looked him directly in the eye, brown eyes deep pools of inner thought. "Well. Look what the cat dragged in."

"Yes, Jen." His glance almost shied off.

"So you found your way home."

"Yes."

She looked right through him.

"I'm sorry, Jen. I guess I was out of my head that day."

"That's what I figured."

"I'm really sorry."

"I guess it's all right. You're finally back again."

"Jen?"

"Yes?"

"I'd like to give you a hug."

"Well, what's holding you back?"

"You mean, I can?"

"If you wanna."

Red began to puff. "Oh, Jen."

A tiny smile edged into her lips.

He tossed his cap onto a stool and took a step toward her.

She helped him the last step by setting aside the turner and lifting her arms toward him.

He hugged her until both had trouble breathing.

After a while she leaned back inside his embrace and said, "I've made supper only for one."

"It's all right. I'm not hungry."

"But I'm willing to share it with you."

"Whatever you say, Jen." He took a deep breath inside her tumbled hair. "My, you smell good. Just like always. Kind of like a chocolate cake."

She smelled his shirt. "And you smell like a bachelor."

He clung to her, swaying, sometimes almost toppling. "Oh, Jen."

Jen broke free of his arms. "We're going to burn the potatoes in a minute."

"Yes, I'm beginning to smell 'em."

She turned the potatoes and then put her arms around him again.

He lifted her chin and kissed her. They kissed dry-lipped. "Really, I must've been out of my head that day. 'Cause you know, I really like you. I always did. You're the only one I ever got even a little close to."

"Well, there was some things wrong with me too, husband."

"I don't believe it."

"But there was. And I want to tell you about them."

"Let's do that later. Maybe when we're in bed and can talk in the dark. For now I just want to hold you and hug you and smell you and just generally be happy I'm back here."

"All right."

"I suppose you were a little hard up while I was gone."

"I sure was."

"What did you do? How did you pay for the groceries?"

"I went to work at Nick's."

Red shook his head. "Well, tomorrow I'll look for a job again."

Jen said, "Got any ideas?"

"No."

"Wanna know something? I heard one of the men from the Steele employment office say they should have given you the job you wanted in the first place. Outdoors in the yards. He was telling Nick."

"Hey. Maybe I better look into that."

Jen set the table for two, opening up an extra can of beans and dropping a country sausage in some boiling water. She put out some napkins. "It's all right if we eat here in the kitchen like always, isn't it? It's cozier here."

"Of course." Red washed up, almost harshly, and combed his hair. He winced when he looked in the mirror and saw how long his beard was. "Have I got time to shave?"

"That'd be a good idea. You scratched me all up."

By the time he finished shaving she had the sausage steaming on the table.

They ate with relish, not saying much, every now and then breaking out with wide smiles.

They washed dishes together.

She went into the living room and pulled on several lamps. "Shall I turn on the radio?"

"That'd be a good thing. It's been a long time since I've heard the news and music."

They sat on the davenport together, holding hands, not saying much, listening.

When the mantel clock struck nine, she looked up brightly. "Well, time for all good people to go to bed."

"Yes, I guess it is." He wondered how he was going to handle going into the bedroom where he'd hurt her. He wondered too how she'd take it. He locked both the front and the back doors, turned down the heat.

"Coming?" she called from the bedroom.

"Coming."

She was already in bed, lying on her own side like always, the reading light on above her head.

"Wow," he said, "you still know how to get in bed quick, don't you? Quick as a whip."

"Last one in is a cookie thief."

He laughed. He sat down on the edge of the bed and slowly began to undress. He felt very tight in his belly, all drawn up from below. There'd be no thought of being a man with her tonight. It was best they first got acquainted all over again. Especially now that he knew what Magdalena had told him.

She reached under his pillow for his nightshirt and with a laugh flung it over his eyes.

He couldn't remember that she'd ever been that playful. She'd really missed him. Unless she was up to something.

"Peuu," she said. "When's the last time you took a bath?"

"That's right. I got pretty nervous and sweaty on the way up here. I better shower first."

"Do that."

He covered his shame by pulling the nightshirt around his hips and went to the bathroom. Again he scrubbed himself harshly with soap. Under the hot spraying water he could feel the drek running off. He toweled himself harshly too, until his pink skin was almost red. He slipped into his nightshirt and headed for the bedroom again. He crawled in beside her.

"That's much better," she said. "I'd rather have you smelling like a bar of soap than a sweaty bachelor."

He stretched out, happy to be in his old place again.

She reached up and turned off the light.

They lay in silence for a while. Neither moved to touch the other.

A car with the cutout open roared by outside. Some young punk was showing off with his girl.

Next the refrigerator clicked on in the kitchen and slowly revved up into a low even humming noise.

She turned on her side facing him and drew her knees up and put her arms around them. "I did something bad—"

"You don't need to tell me anything, Jen. I'm long past jealousy."

"Oh ho, what makes you think jealousy is in it?"

"Well, I don't know. I just said that."

She took several deep breaths. "Well, I still better tell you."

"Oh, Jen, you don't have to tell me anything. What I did there . . .

well, there ain't nothing you could have done that can compare to that."

"You might be surprised. Have you ever wondered why I never called you . . . Red? When everybody else did?"

"Well, yeh, but I didn't pay it no particular mind."

"John, the truth is, my uncle Red, my father's brother, he raped me."

Red shot up in bed. He was so startled by what she'd said that for a moment he could see in the dark. "So that accounts for why you was always so skittish. Afraid to be home alone."

"Yes."

"Why! The son of a bitch." Red balled his fists and shadow-boxed in bed a couple of times. "Good thing he's dead or I'd tear him asshole from appetite. Even if he was your uncle."

Jen made a noise in the dark as if she had to squelch a laugh. She went on bravely, "I was only a young girl then. I'd just started having my periods. If I'd been more grown up it wouldn't have happened. I would have pushed him off. But I was afraid my folks would quit liking him if I told on him. I wanted them to like him because I loved him so then. But pretty soon, of course, I just had to speak up."

"What happened then?"

"Pa and Ma were shocked. And Uncle Red pretty much quit coming."

"Well, I should think they would've been!"

Another young punk went roaring by with his cutout open.

"The son of a bitch."

Jen said, "Now that you know, I suppose you won't want to have anything more to do with me. That I'm ruined in your eyes."

Red fell back in bed. "Oh, Jen, after what I did? My dear woman, of course I still like you." He groaned and turned on his side toward her and reached out and put a hand on her shoulder. "What counts is what we are for each other now."

"And if you hadn't pulled off that nutsy stunt with that knife on me, would you still say that?"

Red groaned again.

"Because while Uncle Red stuck his business into me, you stuck a knife into me. And more than once too."

"Jen." She'd jumped the track a little in her argument but it was all right.

"Well, what he done was worse," Jen said. "He knew what he was doing and you didn't."

They lay silent for a long while, lying on their sides facing each other. Their breaths touched each other's faces.

Jen said, "That's why I didn't sign a complaint against you, my husband."

"Yes, Jen."

"Husband, I notice you don't have the shakes anymore."

"That's right." He turned it over in his mind; finally decided not to tell her that he hadn't had them really since he'd attacked her. "Having the shakes kinda runs in our family, but I guess I'm gonna be the lucky one and get over it."

After another silence, Jen said, "Then tomorrow you're going down to the plant to see if they've got a job for you in the yards?"

"Yes."

Jen went on, almost whispering, "Good! Then I'll quit that job at Nick's. I'm so sick and tired of all that talk about killing down there."

"All right, Jen."

Jen sighed a couple of times. Then, slowly, she dropped off to sleep.

Red thought: "There's one thing for sure, though. I'm not going to tell her I sometimes hear voices. It's a burden I'll have to bear alone. She'd sure think I was crazy and would be scared all the more of me. Besides, she's probably not telling me everything either."

He drew up his knees, almost to his chin. Already he could feel sleep creeping up from his toes. He thought again of Magdalena and what she'd taught him. "Some things are best left unsaid." The clamping sensation that the shell had had on his head slowly began to let up a little.

# Chapter 30

# ALAN

───────────◆•◆───────────

A Friday morning in early May.

Driving to work under the just-budding greening trees, Alan wondered why he bothered to live. All that morning beauty would be lost to him while he was inside. Worse yet, he had to be a reporter. Reporters at best were only voyeurs. Peeping toms. A newspaperman could stick his nose into anything on the grounds that he was helping to keep the republic an open and free society. It was all right to steal a picture from a suspect's family because that was a way of serving truth.

Alan parked his car in the lot across from the *Chronicle* and jaywalked across the street. He took a final whiff of the sweet morning air, then ducked into the shadows of the building.

He found Quinsey Quinn in an even more foul mood. The rest of the boys, Burt, Mark, and Hank, were leaning back and laughing at Quinsey's angry sallies. It appeared that Quinsey had hit a deep chuckhole on the way to work that morning and had broken an axle.

"No matter what route I take to work," Quinsey raged, "Hennepin Avenue, Nicollet Avenue, Third Avenue, every one of them looks like a blasted-out no-man's-land. What in God's name is that mayor of ours doing there all day long in the City Hall—picking cheese out of his belly button?"

Alan took the cover off his typewriter and slipped some paper into it.

"And then when you do finally get here at work, what do you see as you traipse your way through the city room?" Quinsey went on, "Why, over in the women's-page department you see a gaggle of neurotic chicks already having a coffee party this early in the morning. With gingersnaps yet!"

Burt said from his corner, "Quinsey."

"And when you go to the composing room, what's the first thing you run into up there?" Quinsey flung up a gartered arm. "Why, no one else but a seventy-year-old woman named Betsey Balch who lifts up a haunch and blasts away as casually as though she was burping."

Mark said, "The worst is that awful smell."

Quinsey said, "By God, if it wasn't for the Christmas whiskey we get free here from all those rich sports nuts in town, I'd quit. For a fact I would."

"Aren't you happy here, Quinse?" Burt teased.

Quinsey stopped to light what was left of his stub of a cigar. "Usually when I'm asked that question the boss is standing beside me."

"Harley Smathers isn't here now."

"After what Harley ran into this morning, he's probably got the place full of stoolies."

Burt's brows went up. "What'd he run into?"

"During the night somebody chalked horse hooves on the floor running from the elevator door to Harley's desk. Somebody's gonna catch hell today."

"I didn't notice any when I came in."

"By that time they'd swabbed them off. I just now heard about it in the men's can. Minus McNab was telling me about it."

The phone rang on Alan's desk. Alan picked up the receiver. "Alan Ross here."

"Say, this is Nick. You know, Nick's Cafe?"

"Yes?"

"Customer just now told me that he saw Red Engleking peeking in through the window here the other night."

"What?" Alan stared at the black mouthpiece of the phone. "Are you sure you heard that?"

"That's what the man says."

"That means he's back in town."

"Yeh. I thought you'd like to know."

"You bet. Thanks." Alan hung up.

Burt threw Alan a sharp gray look. "What was that all about?"

"A guy claims he saw Red Engleking back in town." Alan stood up. "I better go check that."

"Right now. Before the other papers hear about it."

Alan took the back stairs in a series of flying jumps, shot out the side door, and dashed across the street to his car in the *Chronicle* parking lot.

Alan took all the shortcuts on the way over, eyes peeled for cops, both ahead and in the rearview mirror. It took him only thirty-five minutes.

He pulled up in front of 324 First Avenue South just as Red and Jen were coming out of their front door.

Alan jumped out of his car. "Hey, wait. I'd like to talk to you people a minute first."

Red scowled at him.

Alan said, "I only just now heard you were back in town."

Red said, "I was afraid this would happen."

"Listen," Alan said, "I won't take much of your time." He looked around, worried that people might already be staring at them out of the windows along the street. "Can't we go inside a minute?" Alan took them both by the arm and turned them around toward their front door. "Just for a minute."

They went inside with him reluctantly, especially Red.

Red and Alan settled on the davenport while Jen sat in an armchair.

"My God, man," Alan said, "where have you been all this time? I looked everywhere for you. I even went down to your dad's home near Bonnie looking for you."

"You did?"

"By the way, if you've just come home, I suppose you don't know what's happened down there then, do you?"

Red's blue eyes opened, waiting.

"That your father had a stroke?"

"What?"

"Yes. The first time I visited him, he was all right. But the second time he was in bed."

"Gollies! Dad in bed!"

"He's all right. He looks like he's gonna make it. He's just weak."

Red stared.

"I talked to him. He was alert. Real sharp, in fact."

"Well, at least that's a relief to hear."

Alan said, "That reminds me, Red. The last thing your father said to me was, 'Tell him not to worry anymore about helping me pay off the mortgage on this farm.' "

Red brightened up. "Did he say that?"

"That's right."

"He really did, huh. Wow." Red reached over and picked up Jen's hand. "Did you hear that? Maybe the old man's had a couple of good years I didn't know about. That's sure gonna help us get a fresh start."

Jen nodded. "It sure is."

Alan pinned Jen with a look. "Then it's true that you're not going to file a complaint against your husband."

"Well! I wouldn't be sitting here holding hands with him if I was, would I?"

Alan didn't dare get out pencil and scratch paper to take notes for fear the two would clam up. "You're probably aware, though, that people are going to be terribly curious to know why you aren't."

"Well, the reason I ain't," Jen started to say, "is because—"

Red interrupted her. "What you mean, Alan, is your newspaper is being nosy."

"Red, most wives wouldn't let their husbands get off that easy."

Red pursed his lips. "No, I suppose not."

Jen said, "John, what's wrong with telling him? He been a good friend of ours, hasn't he? He hasn't wrote any bad things about you so far."

"No, that he hasn't."

Jen swung her brown eyes to Alan. "It's true that what my husband did to me was awful. But then you see, I did an awful thing once too. So I really can't point the finger."

Alan waited.

Jen went on. "There was what my Uncle Red—"

Red broke in again. "Hyar! You don't need to hang all our dirty linen out on the line."

Jen flashed a look at Red. She had to go on. "Besides, there was other bad things I done too, John. There was what I done every time I had a mis—"

Red's voice crackled. "Dammit, I don't want to hear any more, Jen. Telling all them things just won't do anybody any good. Excepting maybe yourself."

"They're pretty bad, John."

Red said, "All the more reason then."

"John, ain't this a free country? Can't a person say what's on their mind?"

Red shook his head. "If you want to blurt everything out, I guess I can't stop you. But, really, wife, I don't want to hear any more. We got this far now in the forgiving business and let's not ruin it with any more things to forgive."

Alan began to feel sorry for them. He decided to change the subject. "I'm still puzzled where you hid all this time, Red. Like I said, I looked everywhere for you."

"I stayed in a Hutterite colony. In South Dakota. I happened to land on their yard after swimming across the Missouri."

"For godsakes."

Red nodded, smiling. "Yeh, that was quite a thing."

Jen said, with a wily smile, "Tell us what happened at the colony. If it ain't bad."

Red held his head to one side. "Naw, it wasn't bad. I learned a lot of things there." Red seemed to sweat over how to say it. "Something happened to me there. And it helped me come back here to face the music."

Jen said, "You didn't run into some nice little old maid there, did you?"

"Naw! Not that. It was something else."

Jen pushed some more. "Tell us about it."

"They were very nice to me. Gave me food and clothes."

"Oh," Jen said, "that accounts for why you returned with your clothes hardly wore. And smelling old."

"They never bothered me. Never asked me any questions. They just took me in like true Christians."

Alan said, "You didn't tell them anything?"

"No. Not at first. They left me alone. And then one day, this thing happened, and I went in and told the preacher there, Michael Waldner, what I'd done, that I wanted to go back and do the right thing about what I did to my wife."

Alan said, "What'd he say? Didn't he get excited?"

"No, he didn't. In fact, it was him who took me back to the Twin Cities. And, instead of turning me over to the police, he turned me over to a minister from my own denomination."

Alan's brows went up. That was pretty steep.

Red shook his head as if he himself still had trouble believing it. "And that's when I learned Jen was alive and wasn't going to file a complaint against me. So that let Waldner off the hook and I came home here."

Alan had to wink moisture out of his eyes. "Say, there's something else I've got to tell you. You won't believe this . . . but you and I are related."

"We are?" Red said.

"We're full second cousins."

"Not really."

"When you'd run off after hurting Jen, and she was in the hospital,

I was in this house to ask the cops what happened. I spotted that album over there on the radio, and just out of curiosity, I paged through it. One picture caught my eye. It's the one with 'Alberta' written under it. It seemed to me I'd seen that face before. But at the time I couldn't quite place it. Shortly after, I was home with my folks in South Dakota, and spotting my mother's album, it hit me that I should take a gander at that. And sure enough, there was the same picture. And then from my mother I learned that this Alberta was her mother, and also that this Alberta was a sister of your grampa, John Henry Engleking."

Red stared, mouth open. Then his mouth snapped to. "What a ko-hinky-dinky."

"It sure is. And that explained something to me. Why I once thought you were a dead ringer for a brother I'd whomped up for myself." Alan explained that he'd had a twin brother at birth who'd died, and that for a long time he used to wonder what this dead brother might have looked like had he lived.

The startled look in Red's eyes deepened, and then subtly changed to something else, as if he'd suddenly come to an understanding about something. "Then you wasn't interested in me so much as you was in this . . . hant brother of yours?"

"Well, yes, in the beginning I was. But when I got to know you that changed."

Red dropped his eyes and picked at a callus in his big hand. "Oh." He fell into deep thought.

"Anything wrong?" Alan asked. Alan had the distinct feeling that Red was one up on him in understanding something.

"No. But I do think Jen and me better get going." Red stood up. "You see, Jen and me was on our way to see the doctor when you dropped by."

Alan got to his feet too. "Anything wrong?"

"Not really."

Jen said, "This crazy nut of a husband of mine thinks I'm not good enough in—"

"Shh!" Red lovingly reached down and clapped a hand over her mouth.

Jen pushed the hand away. "When I'm perfectly willing to go along like always."

Red said, "It's not good enough for you, Jen. And now you keep quiet."

Alan asked, "Do you need a ride?"

"Well, yeh, I guess we could use one. We was gonna walk."

"Come, I'll take you over."

When Alan got back to the paper he told Burt he couldn't write the story.

"Why not?"

"I think we should just leave them alone."

"Is there a story there?"

"There's a story there all right. A big deep one. But I'm not going to write it. Somebody else can do it." Alan gave Burt a sad smile. "I guess I don't have the killer instinct in me. I just don't have it in me to pounce on people like a good newspaperman should."

Burt gave him a long stare. There was no criticism in it; just puzzlement.

Quinsey looked around from where he was writing down some notes. "That's quite an indictment of our profession, Alan."

"I'm sorry," Alan said. "I was only describing it."

Burt said, "But in so doing you're showing pounce now."

"No," Alan said, "I'm only saying it for the sake of knowledge, not gain. I'm sorry."

"It's all right, my boy," Quinsey said. "This is a free country." Then Quinsey added, "Excuse me while I get back to my speech. I've got to talk to a bunch of babbitts tomorrow at a luncheon and I'm trying to find the right story to lead it off with." Quinsey carried around with him a little red-edged black book in which he'd jotted down stories he heard, clean or dirty.

Burt finally said, "Well, I guess it's all right, Alan, so long as the city side don't hear about it. Did you see Red? Talk to him?"

"Yes, I did."

Mark spoke up. "I told you, Alan, I didn't think you could be objective about it."

Later in the afternoon Alan had to get a cut from the library. He found Jerre Thornton working alone. Roberta had gone home.

Jerre gave him a quiet smile. "So. You finally decided we here in the library could be of some use to you after all."

"Just the way it worked out."

Jerre's smile widened and became warm. "So what have you been doing for it lately?"

Alan was shocked. Genteel Jerre ask such a question? Alan swallowed. Jerre probably didn't realize what she was saying, was only innocently repeating a flip remark she'd heard somewhere.

Jerre saw the expression on his face, and she blushed. "I'm sorry, but that slipped out. I didn't mean for it to sound like it did."

It was an interesting slip. It meant she'd been thinking about him. Maybe even of dating him. "I'm sorry if I've seemed offish to you. But I've got a rule about dating girls from the same place of business. As Quinsey put it so aptly once, 'Never dip your pen in the company ink.'"

It took her a moment to get the full savor of Quinsey's remark. Then she laughed. It was a wonderful, free, even naive, laugh. "That Quinsey. My father thinks he's a god."

Alan smiled. "Well, some of us in sports think the same thing." He cocked his head to one side. "I'm sorry, but I think that's a good rule though."

"Maybe somebody should think about quitting here so we can date."

"Jerre, don't quit a job over me. Not just yet anyway."

"It still hurts a little, doesn't it?"

"When I go to sleep I sometimes think about her."

Jerre's face clouded over. She had a very pink complexion, but when something troubled her it made her face turn a touch purplish. "Jael doesn't really deserve all that devotion from you."

The next morning, around nine, the phone rang on Burt's desk. Alan was deep in a story about spring training for the track team. Quinsey, Mark, and Hank were busy with their stories.

Burt hung up. He did it slowly. Finally he spoke up. "Alan?"

"Yes?"

"Harley Smathers wants to see you."

Alan was startled. "Wonder what he wants?"

Quinsey stilled at his typewriter. Mark and Hank also stopped work.

Something was about to happen. Alan got to his feet. "Well, I guess I better go face the firing squad."

Quinsey snorted. "Let's hope that's only a pun, my boy."

Alan gave Burt a look, found nothing of comfort in Burt's expression, and then went out in the hallway and took the half flight up into the newsroom. He skirted the water cooler and kicked through a layer of discarded copy on the floor. He knocked on Smathers' door.

Smathers' secretary, a tall handsome woman, opened the door. She had a sad look in her gray eyes for him. She went on through the door and settled in her perch just outside it.

Alan stepped in. He stood hesitantly on the thick blue carpet leading from the door to where Smathers sat behind a wide shiny walnut desk.

"Sit down," Smathers said, tipping back in his swivel chair.

Alan took a nearby chair.

Smathers tried to relight a half-smoked cigar with a match. It took some hard sucking to get it going.

Alan watched him with a weak smile.

Smathers blew out a wavering smoke ring. "Alan, I'm afraid I've got to tell you that we no longer have any need for your services."

Alan tried to center his eyes on the glowing end of Smathers' cigar but instead found them blinking back and forth. "What's wrong with my work?"

"The management has decided it isn't satisfactory."

"You mean, Burt has complained about my work?"

Smathers frowned. He hadn't expected to be questioned. "It's the management. But I don't care to go into particulars."

Alan remembered something. It had to do with the Jeffry family who owned the *Chronicle*. When old man Thomas Jeffry died, he'd failed to make out a will and specify which of his four sons, Lloyd, Jack, Philip, and Bose, should run the paper. The result was a family fight, which was only resolved when the family lawyer suggested that an outsider be hired to run the paper for the four brothers. The four brothers had reluctantly agreed, and Harley Smathers was hired. Everyone who knew the boys felt that the oldest son, Lloyd, should have been named publisher by their father. Lloyd was the only one who really cared about the paper. Lloyd still put in eight hours a day in the accounting division and never once let out a peep that a stranger was running what rightfully should have been his to manage.

Smathers blew another smoke ring. "I'm sorry, Alan, but I'm only following orders."

Alan said nothing. Alan was sure Lloyd Jeffry had nothing to do with the firing. Alan was even more sure the other three playboy brothers had nothing to do with it either. It was Smathers. Smathers had never liked him, and had often shown it when he came down to the sports department by the elegant way he always lifted his leg and planted his expensive shoe on Alan's desk while Alan was typing out a story. "Maybe I better go down and see Lloyd Jeffry. Talk to the horse's mouth himself."

Smathers' face darkened. "Won't do you any good. You're fired, as of now. Clean out your desk and leave the place."

All of a sudden Alan had an impulse to cry. He had all he could do to keep tears from flooding his eyes. He'd loved working for Burt Cowens and being a colleague of Quinsey Quinn's. Alan covered his eyes with his hands. He could feel his eyes working back and forth under his eyelids. Well, he sure didn't have much pounce, did he, sitting there bawling like a baby, with his eyes not being able to fix on a point.

Smathers got to his feet. He towered over Alan. "You can go now. My secretary will mail your final check out to you in a day or two." Smathers came around the side of his desk and went over to open the door. "Now, please leave, will you? I have a paper to get out yet today."

Alan left.

The secretary sitting outside Smathers' door gave Alan a commiserating smile. She knew. And no doubt by now the whole damn paper knew.

Alan wanted a moment to compose himself. He had himself a drink at the water cooler.

When Alan finished drinking, there was Smathers standing behind him. Alan had the feeling that Smathers had contemplated giving him a kick in the butt. He smiled at Smathers, this time naturally. "You know, Harley," he said familiarly, and inside himself he was a little aghast at his own sudden guts, "you're going to be sorry for this someday. Because I'm going to be a famous man before I'm through. And when my biographer lights on your having fired me, he's not going to say very many nice things about you. Because he'll be writing it from my point of view."

Smathers' hard black eyes lighted up. A flicker of admiration for the way Alan had spoken up sparked in them. "Well, Alan, if that happens, I'll be the first to congratulate you. Because then I can always claim that you learned your trade under me."

Alan wiped his mouth with his handkerchief, and nodded. Smathers had a touch of class after all.

Alan's hard-won smile lasted all the way into the sports department. He walked over to Burt's desk. "Guess what. Old Smithereens fired me."

Burt leaned back. His old swivel chair made a loud creaking sound. Quinsey, Mark, and Hank looked up from their typewriters. Burt looked sorry. "So he indicated to me over the phone."

Alan said, "You didn't tell him about what happened yesterday in South St. Paul, did you?"

Burt got a little angry. "Of course not."

"I didn't think so." Alan scratched his head. "Well, there must have been some other reason then. Maybe it's because the paper's cutting back. Then it's always a case of last hired, first fired."

Burt shook his head. "That's not the reason."

"No. What then?"

"Smathers hates unions. And what you did on that picket line out by the WMSP transmitter didn't exactly make you a favorite son of his. Nor O'Brian. I hear he's going to get the axe next."

Alan clapped a hand to his brow. "So that's it! For godsakes, after so long a time."

Burt said, "Well, Alan, I told you at the time you shouldn't let those radicals from New York tell you how you should get along with your bosses."

"I'll be a son of a bitch," Alan continued.

Quinsey said, "Alan, maybe it's for the best. Because the real truth is, you probably weren't meant to be a sportswriter. You're a writer all right, but not in sports."

"Thanks."

"No, really, my boy. Every now and then I catch a hint in your stories that you're too good for us. And then there's the kind of books you read."

Alan fell silent. What was there to say to such a remark?

Alan shook hands with Burt and with the others. Mark and Hank also showed sympathy. Alan cleaned out his desk, and with a final wave of the hand, left.

He was about to take the elevator down when he remembered something. He took the stairs down to the next floor instead. He headed for the paper's library. He set his bag of things outside the door and walked in.

"Jerre Thornton, how would you like to go to Europe with me?"

"Fine. When do we leave?"

"When my ship comes in."

Jerre saw then something was wrong. "What's up?"

"I just now got fired."

Her eyes opened. "That's too bad."

"Yeh, I really liked it here."

"What will you do?"

Alan could feel his eyes trying to center on her lips. "For one thing, take you out to dinner. Now I can, you know."

A big smile opened her face. "Oh, Alan, that would be just wonderful."

"As for a job, I'll find something."

# Chapter 31

# RED

Just before they stepped into the doctor's office, Red took Jen by the arm and turned her so he could look her in the eye. "Now remember. We're not going to this doctor because there's something wrong with us. But because we're not doing something right. And we want to find out what it is."

Jen flashed him a sharp brown look. "Who did you talk to about us?"

Red brushed her question aside. "Don't you want babies?"

"What do you think?"

Red knew what he wanted for them both. They still got along only so-so in the bedroom. She allowed him his husband's rights twice a week when she wasn't in her period. She was no longer skittish, no longer sucked in breaths of fear. But she remained shy and would never undress in front of him. Before she wouldn't take off her clothes because she didn't want to arouse him; now she didn't because she didn't think it was good for him to see those knife scars. She really didn't care all that much for it. And he loved her so much. Here she stood before him in a soft green dress, a dress the color of spring grass, and her arms were tanned a light brown from working in her little garden behind the house. She was wearing a wide floppy straw hat whose edges rose and fell with each step she took. Except for one thing, Magdalena couldn't compare with her. Red shook his head slowly, thinking, If this woman pretty soon don't get something more out of it, she's gonna be back where she was before, laying there like a trapped mouse.

Jen murmured, "You crazy nut you. Sometimes I just don't understand you at all."

"Come," he said. "Let's go in."

Inside the clinic, they were ushered into a little room. They took white chairs across from each other. Between them stood a padded white examining table. A diploma from a medical school hung on one wall, a painting of a doctor sitting patiently beside a boy in a bed on the other wall. Off to one side was a small table with glass tubes and palate sticks and thermometers on it.

They waited and waited. Red became restless and wanted to get out and take a walk. Jen sat subdued with her knees together. Every now and then she drew her green dress farther over her knees.

Presently a doctor came in. He was as bald as a peeled egg. The top of his head actually shone as if he'd had it shellacked. He had thick heavy brown eyebrows. He sat down on a low white stool facing them. "Well well. I'm Dr. Donaldson." His intent brown eyes flicked back and forth over them. He was lean, with hollow cheeks and hollows between the tendons over the backs of his hands. He was about fifty.

Red shifted nervously on his chair. Jen didn't move. She continued to look down at where her knees were pressed together.

Dr. Donaldson spotted who they were. A warm smile curled back his lips. His lips were large and had a curious way of not working as a pair. "What seems to be the trouble here?"

Red hitched himself forward to the edge of his chair. He threw a swift look at Jen, then plunged into it. Somebody had better hear it sometime. "Well, my wife here ain't gettin' out of it what I am. 'Course I try to pleasure her. But at the same time, at the end there, I get a big kick out of it, and she don't. And it may be, it just may be, that that's why she has all them miscarriages. She's all bound up because she's never had a chance to relax after coming."

"Red!" Jen said, embarrassed, giving him a hurt look. It was one of the few times she'd called him by his nickname.

"It's true though, wife."

"Soo." Dr. Donaldson threw a look over his shoulder as if at the other doctors somewhere in the clinic. He worked his liberal lips. "You may be right, Mr. Engleking. Sex may be only a very small part of marriage, like a key is only a small part of a door, but if you don't have the key you don't have a door. But before we go into that, we probably should give you both an examination. Mr. Engleking, why don't you step out first and I'll examine your wife. And then later she can step out."

About twenty minutes later, Red and Jen were sitting in the same chairs again with Dr. Donaldson sitting on his low white stool. Jen smiled a funny crimped smile, and Red was flushed.

Dr. Donaldson held a thick black book in his hands. "Now," he said, "you both appear to be in excellent health. Both of you are perfectly normal. There is no reason why you shouldn't have babies in the normal way. Your wife appears to have had several unfortunate . . ."

Jen threw the doctor a sharp appealing look.

Red caught the look. What had she told him?

Dr. Donaldson went on unperturbed, ". . . little accidents. Nothing really unusual in that either." He looked at each in turn. "Now, I've shown you both pictures in this book giving the human genitalia in detail. As a doctor sees it. And you now both know that, generally speaking, a woman does have in her the potential to have orgasm. Mr. Engleking, let me tell you again, your wife is perfectly normal in that respect." He opened the book to where he'd been using a finger as a marker. "I'll show it to you both again. To make sure you both retain a clear picture of it. Here is where the clitoris is located. It is a little penis, really, of about the size of a slippery bean. You stroke that gently, and long enough, just like you might stroke a male penis, and something is going to happen. All men know what that something is. And there is no reason in the world why a woman can't have that same pleasure." He closed the book with a snap. A warm, even endearing, smile moved his thick uneven lips. "Now. Let me counsel you both to have patience."

Red and Jen looked at Dr. Donaldson with intent eyes as long as they could, then looked down at their hands.

"Missus, you with your husband. You sir, with your wife. Take your time. Don't strain for it. Just ride easy. Play. Have fun. Tickle each other. Jolly each other up before you become serious about doing it. And keep doing this so that you both become completely relaxed. Like a couple of happy monkeys hanging by their tails from a branch. Swing easy. And then one day, when you least expect it, hey! wow! there it is." He looked Red hard in the eye. "So, sir. Learn to pace yourself. You don't have to come to orgasm right away. Like a bull with a cow. Let me say it again: take your time. Do you hear?" Then Dr. Donaldson turned to Jen, an even warmer smile softening his face. "And you, missus, you've got to understand that your man has his problems too. Okay?"

Jen nodded. Red already knew from Magdalena what the doctor was talking about.

"I might tell you that you're lucky you landed with me. Most doctors would say I shouldn't be telling you these things. Their argument would be that it wrecked Eden when Eve learned there was one apple tree she couldn't eat from."

Both Red and Jen looked at the doctor, bewildered at his confession.

"All right. You can go now. And you don't have to report back to me unless it doesn't work. If it doesn't work out, say, in six months, then you can make another appointment. Good luck!"

On the way home, Jen finally said, "He was a nice doctor, but I didn't like it that he compared me to a cow."

"I take it then that I should be mad too because he compared me to a bull."

Jen broke into a big smile. She dug her elbow into his ribs. "You!"


A couple of weeks later, Red woke up to the sound of rain gently trickling against their bedroom window. His first thought was that, shucks, now he'd get soaking wet working down in the yards. He slowly nubbed the back of his head into his pillow. His hair squinched. He was just barely up out of sleep and it would be easy to slip down into it again.

Then he remembered it was his day off. Doggone it. He'd have to sit in the house all day instead, twiddling his thumbs.

Of course he could always tease the good wife.

Tease the wife. Come to think of it, that might not be such a bad idea.

He rolled his head slowly back and forth in his pillow some more. The rain continued to fall against the window.

The only trouble was, he still hadn't been able to give her pleasure. In an easy-does-it way, they had tried a lot of things. They'd even tried it once taking a walk along the Mississippi River. But nothing had worked.

Still another thought came to him. "You know, I haven't heard much from my hant lately. I sure hope he don't leave me altogether. The time may come when I may need him. Some things are just too big to handle alone."

He listened to Jen breathing beside him. What a sweet gal she was. He loved her.

He thought: "Wonder what I can do to get her to relax more, take it easy. Every time I put my hand on her she still tightens up a little. I surely wisht I could get her to ride the same horse with me."

Jen stirred next to him. She began to murmur. In a moment she broke out into speech, sharp, scared. "What do you want? Get out of here!"

He felt so very sorry for her. She was like a little girl who had been beaten up so bad she needed a lot of comforting and warm love before she'd feel whole again.

Comforting. That gave him an idea. Why not make her a queen for a day? Make her stay in bed all day long and do everything for her.

Jen took a couple of irregular breaths, and then sat up. "It's raining."

"Yes, hon."

"Shucks. And I was gonna do the wash today. Can't hang it out in the rain." Jen sighed and lay back in her pillow. "Wonder what I can do instead."

Red leaned up on an elbow over her. "I know what let's do. How would you like it if all day long you could just lay in bed and listen to the rain patter on the window? Huh? Be a queen for the day. Have somebody else make the meals and clean up the dishes and sweep up."

"Who's gonna do that for me?"

"Me. This is my day off. So why don't I be your servant for the day, hand and foot? What do you say? Would you like that?"

"You must be crazy."

Red took her by the shoulders and gave her a loving shake. "No, I'm not crazy. I'd like to do that for you once. It'd be fun."

"What will the neighbors say?"

"For godsakes, Jen, you don't think for a minute that I'm gonna call 'em up and tell them?"

Jen began to smile. "Well, I've never had anybody do that for me before. I guess it would be kind of fun at that." Her smile became impish. "What if I have to go potty?"

"By golly, Jen, I'll even hold the pot steady for you."

"Och! That I'd like to see. Hah."

Red bent over her, serious. "Look, what's the first thing you do in the morning?"

She thought a moment. "Brush my teeth."

He bounded out of bed, white nightshirt wrinkling down his legs. "One toothbrush coming up." He hurried to the kitchen sink and came back with her toothbrush, toothpaste, and a glass of water. He got in bed with her and straddled himself over her. "Okay, open your mouth."

"Hey! You really are crazy. I can brush my own teeth in bed if it comes to that."

"No no. Open up now. We're doing this now just to have a little fun. Just think, you actually have a husband who wants to brush your teeth."

And just for the heck of it she did open her mouth.

He brushed her teeth gently, thoroughly. "Here, spit in this. That's it. Ah. Now those back teeth and we're done."

Finished, she spat some more in the glass. "I've never had that done to me before. Goodness." Then she began to laugh and giggle. "What next?"

"Potty?"

"You're not really gonna—"

"Come come, if you gotta go you gotta go."

"No," she said, "that I do by myself."

"All right. Then while you go potty I'll bring this back to the sink." Jen slowly emerged from the sheets and went to the bathroom.

Red was back the moment she was finished. "What do you do next?"

"Wash my face and arms and hands."

"Oh yes. Coming up." He got a basin of warm water. Soon he was washing her gently under the ears and around over the nose and into the roots of her brown hair.

"You crazy nut you."

"What next?"

"Make breakfast."

"Okay, coming up." He dressed himself in clean overalls, shirt, and socks. Presently he carried in a tray of bacon and eggs, toast, peeled orange, and coffee. He next got himself a tray of food and sat in a chair at the foot of her bed. "Everything okay?"

"Perfect."

And so it went through the whole day. When she dreamily mentioned something about a backrub, he gave her one. The backrub turned out to make her mighty tempting, but he bit his teeth together to keep from becoming aroused. This was one time he was going to do something for her that would be pure giving. He wanted her to know that he could be nice to her without having sex in mind all the time.

He washed the dishes and swept out the kitchen. She napped. He dusted the living room. She napped some more. He made dinner for them, peeling potatoes, and frying them each a small steak, and cutting up lettuce for salad. Just as for breakfast, he washed her face and then served her in bed while he himself ate at the foot of the bed. After dinner he napped, like she did, though he was careful to take his nap on the couch in the living room. Later in the afternoon he brought the mail to her. Finally in the evening he made supper.

When he went to bed that night, and lay back in his pillow, he smiled to himself in the dark. "Well, hon, how did you like being a queen for the day?"

She reached a hand across to him and slipped it up around his face. "It was wonderful."

"You liked that, eh?"

"It was wonderful." She pulled his face around and gave him a warm wet kiss. "And now, how would you like to be a king for the night?"

He sat up slowly. "Oh no. Not that. I didn't have that in mind at all. I was just doing it for the fun of doing it. To pleasure you. With nothing else in mind."

She fell silent. She breathed in his face. "You really mean that, don't you?"

"I sure do."

She laughed, and fell back on her pillow. "Why, you wonderful crazy nut you."

A month later, coming home from the stockyards, he found Jen working at the stove. She was cutting up the boiled potatoes left over from noon hour into a frying pan. Some canned baloney was bubbling in a pan on the far side of the black-and-nickel range. Coffee was about ready to perk. He sat down in his armchair in his corner by the table.

"Have a hard day?" she asked.

"Yeh. It was terrible in all that rain. Stink? God."

She sliced up the last potato and set the frying pan on the hottest stovelid. She next set the table—plates, forks, knives.

As she brushed past him, Red slipped an arm around her and drew her down on his lap. The smell of the ready woman was in her clothes. He gently took hold of her breasts and gave them a close warm shake. "Mmm. You're so delicious I could easy eat you."

"That's the baloney you must be smelling."

He began to tickle her. He rubbed his bristles against her cheek.

"Cut it out," she said, relaxing into him.

He felt himself becoming aroused, and he lifted her up and set her on himself so that she could feel him. He continued to tickle her, making her wiggle harder to get away from his fingers.

"Husband, you know tickling ain't good for me. It'll give me the needles. Eee! Cut it out."

"I'm not tickling you that way. I'm tickling you in a friendly way. Mmm? Mmm?"

"Cut it out."

He laughed. It thrilled him to think she liked what he was doing. And he really wasn't tickling her to drive her into hysterics. Only to jollify her. He became very thick under her. Just for the fun of it he pulled up her dress past her bottom and then drew down her silk pants.

"Hey, you. The potatoes are burning."

"I like burnt potatoes once in a while."

"Oh you nut you!" The craziness of her sitting on him that way excited her.

He next bared himself.

"For godsakes, what are you doing under there, sitting here in our kitchen like this, you horse you? Eeek!"

"Mmm. Mmm." He tickled her in her sides again. Then he lifted her up and set her on himself.

"Oooee, you're big today, Red." Her half-closed eyes glittered.

He smiled until it hurt.

"The potatoes!" Her voice became catchy with sweet lust.

He tickled her lightly some more, wrestling her up a little, jollifying her.

"The potatoes," she whispered, thickly, "they're burning up."

"Hon."

"But in a chair, dear."

They wrestled a little, she backing into him and then sometimes starting up.

He ground his teeth to keep control of himself. What counted now was her pleasure, not his.

Of a sudden she seemed to bunch up, then more, and more, and then she fainted. She almost fell to the floor. "Red!" she whispered.

"It happened!" he whispered in turn, as he held her to keep from falling. He thought: "That Magdalena was right."


A couple of nights later when they tried it in bed it didn't work. Jen seemed to have slipped back to where she was before. There was something about a bedroom that was a stumbling block for her.

Still Jen and Red schemed and plotted to outwit their hants. Red even suggested with a laugh that she take a spatula to bed with them.

"What? Not on your life," Jen cried. "You nut you."

Laughing, experimenting, they finally got things in hand in the boudoir too.

As the days went by, Red became less and less happy with his work. He was thankful he no longer had to stick pigs inside the plant, that he was working outdoors in the yards, but pushing cattle from one pen to another, and cleaning up after them, whether it was sunny or rainy, gradually got him down. It was not the kind of life he'd once dreamed of having.

For some time Red managed not to let Jen see his disappointment. They were having such a good time, coming home always brightened him up.

One evening Jen caught him sitting alone on the davenport in the living room with a sad face. He had not even bothered to turn on the radio for the evening news. She'd been shopping for groceries and came home late.

After she'd put away the groceries and had started the potatoes, she came quietly into the living room. "What's wrong, my husband?"

"Nothing." Right away he had a smile for her. "Not with you anyway."

She sat down beside him and picked up his hand. "Tell me."

"I changed clothes, but you can still smell me, can't you?"

"Yes, but it's not that bad."

"That means it's really bad. And I just hate that stink."

"I bet you miss the farm. Back home."

"No, not my dad's."

"What then?"

"I miss the brotherhood. I was happy there."

"Well, if you miss it so much, and since it's done you so much good, maybe that's where we ought to go."

Red pinched her hard. "You'd be willing to go with me?"

"Of course. Maybe it would be good for me. I have my past, you know. Things to forget. And I'd like to be doing something too I thought was a good thing. Instead of cooking just to cook." Quickly she added, "Not that I'm unhappy with my husband."

"Oh."

She waited a few moments and then said, "Well?"

"You won't get lonesome for the city?"

"You forget I was raised in a small town. And that brotherhood of yours sounds like a little town sort of. Besides, what's to get lonesome for here? I'll be glad to get shed of this place."

"Okay. Then let's go. But how should we go about it?"

"Maybe you should write a letter to Preacher Waldner. And if he agrees, we'll sell all our goods, pay our debts, everywhere, and take the bus down."

After dinner they sat down together at the oak table in the dining room and wrote the letter. Red wanted her to write it because her penmanship was better, but Jen said it should be in his hand, the man's. Wetting the pencil point again and again, Red finally got the letter done.

A week later, on a Saturday afternoon, there was a knock on the door. It was Michael Waldner.

Red was happy to see him. He almost embraced him. Red introduced him to Jen.

They talked a long time, through supper, and well into the evening. It could be seen after a while that Preacher Waldner liked Jen. Satisfied with what he saw, he took out Red's folded letter from his shirt pocket. "About this now. Are you both serious about coming to the brotherhood?"

Red looked at Jen. It was for her to speak.

Jen nodded. "I go where my husband goes. I want him to be happy. You don't know what a difference it's made since he no longer has to go to that awful kill. Though I can see that working out in the yards is not the right thing for him either. So I say, let's go."

"No regrets?"

"No."

"And you, John?"

"No."

Preacher Waldner leaned forward. The little round white dot in his beard appeared to smile. "We had a very good year. The extra money we got for our cattle at the yards here was more than we expected. It was decided that we should buy a pickup. It takes too long for us to drive to the nearest town in a horse and buggy or the wagon. Also, the merchants in the little towns around aren't above gouging us a little. We'd like to be able to go to Sioux Falls once in a while and shop there for better bargains."

Red knew what was coming.

"So, we need a driver. You drive a car, don't you, John?"

"Sure. I often drove Dad's."

"So. Well. We decided that if you will come, you can do all the driving for us. Betweentimes you can be our fence boss. There usually isn't much fencing to do, but at the same time we don't want any trouble with our neighbors because of our bull. That sound all right to you?"

Jen asked, "Can I go along with my husband sometimes?"

Michael Waldner nodded. "Whenever it's been decided that some of our ladies should go to town and buy some cloth goods, you go along."

Red and Jen looked at each other. Everything would be taken care of. Food. Clothes. Heart. And now and then a little trip to the outside world.

Michael Waldner had a final question to ask. "You'll be wanting to see your father, no doubt, John?"

"We'll see him on the way down."

"He probably won't like it."

Red nodded. But what Dad had once done to him still festered. Michael Waldner had been much more of a father to him.

"You've forgiven him, John?"

"You aren't required to live with someone you've forgiven, are you?"

Michael Waldner's eyes opened. "That's a fine point." He smiled. "No, you're not."

Jen got up. "Now that that's settled, I think I'll go wash the dishes."

While she was in the kitchen, Red said, "There was one thing I didn't want to talk about in front of her."

"I know. And you needn't worry. Magdalena left us long ago. She found a job in Sioux Falls for a while, and the last I heard she got married."

"Oh." From the way Preacher Waldner looked at him, Red knew he had caught on about him and Magdalena. Red said, "At the time I thought Jen was dead."

"I know, son. We always had more hope for you than for Magdalena."

Jen poked her head around the corner of the door. "What are you two talking about? I don't want to miss a thing."

Red had to quick think. "We were talking about the good old days when I lived at the brotherhood."

# Chapter 32

# ALAN

---

Alan was dreaming.

Jael Hemlickson had come to see him. She was weeping bitterly as she came to the side of his bed. She had eyes of hate for the woman sleeping beside him. Her long fingernails were as sharp as the claws of a cat. She wept. Her eyes began to melt out of their sockets. She pulled a shawl over her face, shrouding her eyes. Her nails came thrusting out of the open sleeves of her black coat. She whispered hoarsely, "Oh, Alan, the electricity of you. Oh, Alan, it was such a mistake for me to have a baby with Shelby Hines. Shelby has no power, so my baby is a simpleton. Oh, Alan, that woman is not worthy of you. I know her. She was once my dearest friend and now my bitterest enemy. Come, get out of that bed of lust and follow me. We'll live in the castle I inherited from my royal ancestor. True love at last in the right surroundings."

Alan lay transfixed. He strove to say something, but his tongue lay inert in the hollow of his cavernous mouth. Jael reached down and took hold of his root and gave it a yank. He tried to yell but he couldn't get his throat to work.

"Where's your scissors and I'll snip it off and take it with me," Jael said. "At least she won't have that." Magically she found a shears in the voluminous pocket of her black coat and opened the shears and worked it.

Hey! this was getting serious.

He rose partway up out of darkness. He was still mostly asleep but he could also hear the refrigerator running and rain falling against the window. He looked around in himself for some way to give himself another push up into light. His hands wouldn't move.

Still mostly asleep, he heard Jerre beside him murmuring. She too was having a dream. Then she spoke out loud, quite sharply: "Don't you dare! That's mine now." Jerre twitched some more. "Jael, you had your chance once and now it's my turn. Besides, you're married to another man and have his baby."

Alan tried to understand what was going on. Was it possible that he and Jerre were having the same dream at the same time? Or was he just dreaming that they were having it together?

He tried to sit up. Couldn't.

Well, that proved he was dreaming the whole thing.

He lay hanging between being half asleep and half awake.

Of course it would be lovely if he could have Jael now and then in dream. And maybe in dream he could satisfy her. He'd taught Jerre how to. She'd been just as green as Jael. Except that Jerre didn't have the least hint of the flirt in her. Jerre was all for him from the very beginning. While Jael had always withheld part of herself, a piece of her he could never win over.

It was lovely to lie halfway between sleep and wakefulness.

Too bad he'd never be able to love Jerre with the same enchantment he felt for Jael. He and Jerre had everything except for a certain heady thrilling magic. Maybe it had been a mistake to marry Jerre. She'd been Jael's friend once.

A wave of sleep came along, and he sank in it.

There Jael was again. This time she'd come naked into their apartment. She was smiling. It was a smile she knew could get him to do anything. She knew how to wind him around her little finger. She walked up to his bed and lifted up his legs and swung them out of bed and made him sit up. Then she pushed forward and straddled his knees. His eyes were exactly level with her pudendum. The two little curves of flesh half hidden in the hair were still as pure as the day she was born. She stood very still waiting for the magic to work again. She whispered down at him, "Come, my golden cock, the golden hen awaits you."

He hung in the wave.

"I know Jerre has you now. But there is no reason why we can't have each other in dream now and then. There is no love as sweet as the love you have in dreams. It is always perfect."

He made a little swimming motion with his back and he began to rise toward her.

"You use your dreams to help you decide what you want to do in real life, so why not use it to have ecstasy with me now and then?"

"I love you, Alan."

He rose very rapidly. That wasn't Jael talking. That was Jerre.

Jerre said, "Don't listen to her, Alan. She betrayed you once before."

Alan could hardly believe it. He and Jerre actually were in the same dream. My God. Then they truly were one.

A ringing noise sounded somewhere.

He floated to the surface and pop! was awake. He sat up.

Somebody was ringing their bell downstairs.

He glanced around at where Jerre was sleeping. She was lying on her side away from him. She was twitching. Her left hand lay over her bare hip. The wedding ring on her finger gleamed in the morning light. He looked at the clock on the chair. It was eleven! Thank God it was Saturday, his day off, or he'd really be late for work.

He scrambled out of bed and stepped into a pair of blue trousers. He ran his hand through his hair and then hustled downstairs. He opened the door. There was instantly a wonderful smell of fresh rain having just fallen.

It was the postman in blue, carrying a leather bag full of stacked mail. There were wet splotches on his shoulders from the rain. He held out a package to Alan. "Special delivery, sir. Insured. Will you sign here?"

Numbly Alan took the man's pencil and signed a yellow slip of paper.

"Thank you." The mailman gave him a nod, and then turned and stepped across the lawn to the next house.

Alan took the mail and the package upstairs. The package wasn't very big, about the size of a shoebox. Probably another wedding gift. He and Jerre had been married only two weeks and were still getting gifts from friends. It was addressed to both of them: "Mr. and Mrs. Alan Ross." There was no return address.

The sun suddenly popped from behind the clouds and was so bright in their apartment he had to narrow his eyes against it. He looked for his dark glasses and put them on.

Jerre sat up in bed, blond hair falling away from her cheeks, blue eyes low under their lids. "What is it?"

"Mailman. There was a special delivery for us."

Jerre swung her legs over the edge of the bed. She moved a little stiffly. She would never have Jael's exquisite way of getting out of bed.

He sat down beside Jerre and gave her the package.

She opened it, first breaking the string, then unrolling the paper and lifting the shoebox out of it. "Shoes?" she said, shaking it and listening to it.

"Open it."

She removed the cover.

They looked in the shoebox a moment or two; looked at each other in astonishment; looked in the box again.

Set in some soft white paper was a mousetrap with a wiener caught in it.

Alan said, "That darn Bill O'Brian and his practical jokes."

"How do you know it's Bill?"

Alan said, "It's just like him." Bill didn't think much of people who thought they were in love. Also Bill was a little jealous of Alan that he'd got a good job writing abstracts for a doctor's magazine, *Medicine Man*.

Jerre held her head to one side, a frown between her eyes. "I know he's kind of a pest. But I didn't think he'd stoop to this."

Alan began to smile. "At least he had the grace to buy a new mousetrap and a fresh wienie."

"Yes. We can use the mousetrap and the wienie we can eat." Jerre began to smile too.

"Ha! I don't think Bill ever planned we should put it to practical use."

"What we ought to do is actually catch a mouse in this trap and then wrap it up in that shoebox and send it to him with a note to say, 'Apparently there's been some mistake in this merchandise and we're returning it herewith.' "

"Hey. To suggest that he himself is a mouse caught in a trap at work."

"This is so silly it's funny."

They fell back in bed laughing about it.

The wiener gave Alan an idea. "Why don't we have a picnic together? It's such a lovely day. It's always lovely after a rain. It's a shame to waste it inside."

"Let's."

"I've always wanted to take a girl out in a canoe on the Lake of the Isles."

"And I've always wanted to be seduced in a canoe, and especially on the Lake of the Isles."

"All right, we'll do it. Pack a picnic dinner and just float the afternoon away on water."

"Wonderful."

Within the hour they were driving across town. They drove in happy silence along the Mississippi River and through downtown Minneapolis.

Alan was always touched by the sights of Minneapolis. He loved the city. On some afternoons, when the air was fresh and misty after a rain, Minneapolis became a soft-edged holy citadel, full of mellow sunlight, set off by citron shadows under the trees. The beauty of the blond women coming down Nicollet Avenue was like the bold slash of an axe down the side of a red pine.

He thought: "Living here, it's hardly a wonder I fell in love with two blond women. First Jael, then Jerre. Seeing all those blond bombshells during noon lunch hour was bound to have worked on me. No wonder the Indians worshiped the albino animals. They thought them *wakan.*"

He adjusted his dark glasses as they headed into the sun down Hennepin Avenue.

He thought: "Looking back, it was probably a good thing I first met Jael, then met Jerre. Having had Jael, I was ready for something deeper in a woman, someone serious and true-telling and at the same time full of winning humor. Jerre."

He turned right on Lake Street and headed for the boathouse on Lake Calhoun. As he pulled up and parked the car, he remembered the first time he and Jerre had made love.


. . . . All unexpectedly, on the Saturday after their first date, Jerre came to visit him. The doorbell rang, and when he went down to answer it, there was Jerre with her shy little smile but her blue eyes bold. She was a strange combination, a woman who could be very modest but who at the same time knew what she wanted. Without a word he'd led her upstairs to his apartment. She stood shyly in the door, looking around slowly, taking everything in, and in a moment deciding she liked what she saw.

"Have you had lunch?" he asked.

She gave him a soft smile and shook her head.

"How about a headcheese sandwich and some milk?"

"I'd like that." She looked out of the windows at the trees outside. Her blue eyes smiled.

Soon he had the sandwiches ready and they ate.

He felt the warmth of Jerre and wanted to touch her. They hadn't touched the night he took her out to dinner. He reached over and placed a hand on her wrist.

She looked down at his hand. After a moment her little smile widened.

"Some more milk?"

"Please."

He poured her some out of the milk bottle. He put the bottle back in the refrigerator, and then as he came past her he leaned down and touched his cheek against hers. He held his cheek there for a moment.

Slowly she pressed her cheek against his, and then, turning toward him, at the same time turning his head toward her, she kissed him. It was a child's warm puckered kiss. He felt even warmer toward her.

When they finished their sandwiches, he got up and took her by the hand and led her to his bed. "I want to hold you," he said.

They sat together. They kissed again. And again. The third time she opened her lips a little. Soon they lay back on the bed. They breathed with open lips.

He felt constricted the way he lay and he moved to ease it.

She quick moved. "Do you want to make love?"

"Well, no, I was just . . ."

She made a motion then to show him she was willing.

He couldn't hold himself back. He loved her warmth, her strange withdrawn air at the same time that she could be refreshingly bold. She pumped hard under him. She had two go-ups for his one go-down. And then, all too soon, it was over for him. "I'm sorry," he said. "I tried to hold back for you."

"It's all right," she whispered. "I'm so happy."

It was later that he taught her how to be satisfied. Or rather she taught herself. She wanted him more than he wanted her and so was ahead of him. . . .


They got a canoe at the Calhoun boathouse, and to the sound of her little cries as they stepped into the dipping bark, they were soon paddling out through the lagoon under the bridges, and then into the Lake of the Isles.

The water was as smooth as the opal eye of a dove.

They paddled until they came to the first island and then they let the canoe drift. They watched the fish below in the water. They looked up at the trees on the island. They dreamed the afternoon away.

When Alan heard the six-o'clock whistles blowing in the far distance, he picked up his paddle and worked their canoe around between two islands in the lake. He aimed the canoe for a sandy beach and gave it a good run up it.

They stepped out. He made a little tepee-shaped stick fire and she spread out a tablecloth and got out the food. They ate in lazy fashion.

When the evening shadows from the north island reached where they were sitting, they picked up their things and loaded them back into the canoe.

"When must we bring the canoe back?" she asked.

"We have until midnight," he said.

"Good. That'll give us time."

"Then you still want to be seduced in a canoe?"

"I surely do." She got into the canoe up front.

Something in him turned over. It almost made him dizzy.

He spotted a late-fall daisy at the edge of the trees. He went over and pulled it out by the root. "This one won't come to seed anymore this year, so I guess it will be all right to pick it." He took his seat in the canoe, at the back. Gently he pulled off the petals, one by one, letting them fall in his lap. "She loves me, she loves me not." The last one turned out to be "She loves me."

She smiled from her seat. "You see."

He looked down at the fallen petals in his lap. "Wonder if petals are good for you. To eat, I mean."

She said, "They almost have to be. Nature went out of her way to make them beautiful."

"That's right," he said. He picked up several of the delicate white petals and caught them on his lips. He nibbled on them. "Mmm. They're good. Mmm. Kind of like the peeling of a grape."

"Give me a couple." She reached out a hand across the canoe.

He handed her several, and then helped himself to a few more.

She lipped and nibbled on them too. "Yes. Like the peeling of those little sweet green grapes." She tasted some more. "Wonder why it hasn't become a fad in America to eat flowers."

"I don't know."

"Let's you and me start the fad then."

"Okay, let's. Jerre, from now on you and I shall live on flowers and water forever."

# Epilogue

# RED & JEN

---

The next year, in the warm sweet month of May, Jen came to full term and had her first baby. It was a boy. At Red's suggestion they named him John to keep up the Engleking line.

# ALAN & JERRE

---

The same year, in the mellow month of September, Jerre came to full term and had her first baby. It was a boy. Jerre, knowing everything, suggested they name him John.